John Varley

KT-562-602

The Barbie Murders

Futura

An Orbit Book

First published in Great Britain in 1983
by Futura Publications, a Division of
Macdonald & Co (Publishers) Ltd
London & Sydney
Reprinted 1986

ISBN 0 7088 8097 5

Printed and bound in Great Britain by
Hazell Watson & Viney Limited,
Member of the BPCC Group,
Aylesbury, Bucks

Futura Publications
A Division of
Macdonald & Co (Publishers) Ltd
Greater London House
Hampstead Road
London NW1 7QX
A BPCC plc Company

THE BARBIE MURDERS

Also by John Varley

ACKNOWLEDGMENTS

"Bagatelle," copyright © 1976 by Universal Publications and Distributing Corporation for *Galaxy Magazine*, August 1974.

"The Funhouse Effect," copyright © 1976 by Mercury Press Inc. for *The Magazine of Fantasy and Science Fiction*, December 1976.

"The Barbie Murders," copyright © 1978 by Davis Publications for *Isaac Asimov's Science Fiction Magazine*, February 1978.

"Equinoctial," copyright © 1977 by David Gerrold from *Ascents of Wonder*, published by Popular Library.

"Manikins," copyright © 1976 by Ultimate Publishing Company for *Amazing Science Fiction Story Magazine*, January 1976.

"Beatnik Bayou," copyright © 1980 by John Varley from NEW VOICES III, published by Berkley Publishing Corporation, April 1980.

"Good-bye, Robinson Crusoe," copyright © 1977 by Davis Publications for *Isaac Asimov's Science Fiction Magazine*, Spring 1977.

"Lollipop and the Tar Baby," copyright © 1977 by Damon Knight from ORBIT 19, published by Harper & Row, Inc.

"Picnic on Nearside," copyright © 1974 by Mercury Press Inc. for *The Magazine of Fantasy and Science Fiction*, August 1974.

CONTENTS

THE
BARBIE MURDERS

Bagatelle

THERE WAS A BOMB on the Leystrasse, level forty-five, right out-side the Bagatelle Flower and Gift Shoppe, about a hundred meters down the promenade from Prosperity Plaza.

"I am a bomb," the bomb said to passersby. "I will explode in four hours, five minutes, and seventeen seconds. I have a force equal to fifty thousand English tons of trinitrololuene."

A small knot of people gathered to look at it.

"I will go off in four hours, four minutes, and thirty-seven seconds."

A few people became worried as the bomb talked on. They remembered business elsewhere and hurried away, often toward the tube trains to King City. Eventually, the trains became over-crowded and there was some pushing and shoving.

The bomb was a metal cylinder, a meter high, two meters long, mounted on four steerable wheels. There was an array of four television cameras mounted on top of the cylinder, slowly scan-ning through ninety degrees. No one could recall how it came to be there. It looked a little like the municipal street-cleaning ma-chines; perhaps no one had noticed it because of that.

"I am rated at fifty kilotons," the bomb said, with a trace of pride.

The police were called.

"A *nuclear* bomb, you say?" Municipal Police Chief Anna-Louise Bach felt sourness in the pit of her stomach and reached

1

for a box of medicated candy. She was overdue for a new stomach, but the rate she went through them on her job coupled with the size of her paycheck had caused her to rely more and more on these stopgap measures. And the cost of cloned transplants was going up.

"It says fifty kilotons," said the man on the screen. "I don't see what else it could be. Unless it's just faking, of course. We're moving in radiation detectors."

"You said 'it says.' Are you speaking of a note, or phone call, or what?"

"No. It's talking to us. Seems friendly enough, too, but we haven't gotten around to asking it to disarm itself. It could be that its friendliness won't extend that far."

"No doubt." She ate another candy. "Call in the bomb squad, of course. Then tell them to do nothing until I arrive, other than look the situation over. I'm going to make a few calls, then I'll be there. No more than thirty minutes."

"All right. Will do."

There was nothing for it but to look for help. No nuclear bomb had ever been used on Luna. Bach had no experience with them, nor did her bomb crew. She brought her computer on line.

Roger Birkson liked his job. It wasn't so much the working conditions—which were appalling—but the fringe benefits. He was on call for thirty days, twenty-four hours a day, at a salary that was nearly astronomical. Then he got eleven months paid vacation. He was paid for the entire year whether or not he ever had to exercise his special talents during his thirty days duty. In that way, he was like a firefighter. In a way, he *was* a firefighter.

He spent his long vacations in Luna. No one had ever asked Birkson why he did so; had they asked, he would not have known. But the reason was a subconscious conviction that one day the entire planet Earth would blow up in one glorious fireball. He didn't want to be there when it happened.

Birkson's job was bomb disarming for the geopolitical administrative unit called CommEcon Europe. On a busy shift he might save the lives of twenty million CE Europeans.

Of the thirty-five Terran bomb experts vacationing on Luna at the time of the Leystrasse bomb scare, Birkson happened to be closest to the projected epicenter of the blast. The Central Computer found him twenty-five seconds after Chief Bach rang off from her initial report. He was lining up a putt on the seventeenth green of the Burning Tree underground golf course, a half kilometer from Prosperity Plaza, when his bag of clubs began to ring.

Birkson was wealthy. He employed a human caddy instead of the mechanical sort. The caddy dropped the flag he had been holding and went to answer it. Birkson took a few practice swings, but found that his concentration had been broken. He relaxed, and took the call.

"I need your advice," Bach said, without preamble. "I'm the Chief of Municipal Police for New Dresden, Anna-Louise Bach. I've had a report on a nuclear bomb on the Leystrasse, and I don't have anyone with your experience in these matters. Could you meet me at the tube station in ten minutes?"

"Are you crazy? I'm shooting for a seventy-five with two holes to go, an easy three-footer on seventeen and facing a par five on the last hole, and you expect me to go chasing after a hoax?"

"Do you know it to be a hoax?" Bach asked, wishing he would say yes.

"Well, no, I just now heard about it, myself. But ninety percent of them are, you know."

"Fine. I suggest you continue your game. And since you're so sure, I'm going to have Burning Tree sealed off for the duration of the emergency. I want you right there."

Birkson considered this.

"About how far away is this 'Leystrasse'?"

"About six hundred meters. Five levels up from you, and one sector over. Don't worry. There must be dozens of steel plates between you and the hoax. You just sit tight, all right?"

Birkson said nothing.

"I'll be at the tube station in ten minutes," Bach said. "I'll be in a special capsule. It'll be the last one for five hours." She hung up.

Birkson contemplated the wall of the underground enclosure. Then he knelt on the green and lined up his putt. He addressed the ball, tapped it, and heard the satisfying rattle as it sank into the cup.

He looked longingly at the eighteenth tee, then jogged off to the clubhouse.

"I'll be right back," he called over his shoulder.

Bach's capsule was two minutes late, but she had to wait another minute for Birkson to show up. She fumed, trying not to glance at the timepiece embedded in her wrist.

He got in, still carrying his putter, and their heads were jerked back as the capsule was launched. They moved for only a short distance, then came to a halt. The door didn't open.

"The system's probably tied up," Bach said, squirming. She didn't like to see the municipal services fail in the company of this Terran.

"Ah," Birkson said, flashing a grin with an impossible number of square teeth. "A panic evacuation, no doubt. You didn't have the tube system closed down, I suppose?"

"No," she said. "I . . . well, I thought there might be a chance to get a large number of people away from the area in case this thing does go off."

He shook his head, and grinned again. He put this grin after every sentence he spoke, like punctuation.

"You'd better seal off the city. If it's a hoax, you're going to have hundreds of dead and injured from the panic. It's a lost cause trying to evacuate. At most, you might save a few thousand."

"But . . ."

"Keep them stationary. If it goes off, it's no use anyway. You'll lose the whole city. And no one's going to question your judgment because you'll be dead. If it doesn't go off, you'll be sitting pretty for having prevented a panic. Do it. I *know*."

Bach began to really dislike this man right then, but decided to follow his advice. And his thinking did have a certain cold logic. She phoned the station and had the lid clamped on the city. Now the cars in the cross-tube ahead would be cleared, leaving only her priority capsule moving.

They used the few minutes delay while the order was implemented to size each other up. Bach saw a blonde, square-jawed young man in a checkered sweater and gold knickers. He had a friendly face, and that was what puzzled her. There was no trace of worry on his smooth features. His hands were steady, clasped calmly around the steel shaft of his putter. She wouldn't have called his manner cocky or assured, but he did manage to look cheerful.

She had just realized that he was looking her over, and was wondering what he saw, when he put his hand on her knee. He might as well have slapped her. She was stunned.

"What are you...get your hand off me you...you groundhog."

Birkson's hand had been moving upward. He was apparently unfazed by the insult. He turned in his seat and reached for her hand. His smile was dazzling.

"I just thought that since we're stalled here with nothing else to do, we might start getting to know each other. No harm in that, is there? I just hate to waste any time, that's all."

She wrenched free of his grasp and assumed a defensive posture, feeling trapped in a nightmare. But he relented, having no interest in pursuing the matter when he had been rebuffed.

"All right. We'll wait. But I'd like to have a drink with you, or maybe dinner. After this thing's wrapped up, of course."

"'This thing...' How can you think of something like that...?"

"At a time like this. I know. I've heard it. Bombs get me horny, is all. So okay, so I'll leave you alone." He grinned again. "But maybe you'll feel different when this is over."

For a moment she thought she was going to throw up from a combination of revulsion and fear. Fear of the bomb, not this awful man. Her stomach was twisted into a pretzel, and here he sat, thinking of sex. What was he, anyway?

The capsule lurched again, and they were on their way.

The deserted Leystrasse made a gleaming frame of stainless steel storefronts and fluorescent ceiling for the improbable pair hurrying from the tube station in the Plaza: Birkson in his anachronistic golf togs, cleats rasping on the polished rock floor, and Bach, half a meter taller than him, thin like a Lunarian. She wore the regulation uniform of the Municipal Police, which was a blue armband and cap with her rank of chief emblazoned on them, a shoulder holster, an equipment belt around her waist from which dangled the shining and lethal-looking tools of her trade, cloth slippers, and a few scraps of clothing in arbitrary places. In the benign environment of Lunar corridors, modesty had died out ages ago.

They reached the cordon which had been established around the bomb, and Bach conferred with the officer in charge. The hall was echoing with off-key music.

"What's that?" Birkson asked.

Officer Walters, the man to whom Bach had been speaking, looked Birkson over, weighing just how far he had to go in deference to this grinning weirdo. He was obviously the bomb expert Bach had referred to in an earlier call, but he was a Terran, and not a member of the force. Should he be addressed as 'sir'? He couldn't decide.

"It's the bomb. It's been singing to us for the last five minutes. Ran out of things to say, I guess."

"Interesting." Swinging the putter lazily from side to side, he walked to the barrier of painted steel crowd-control sections. He started sliding one of them to the side.

"Hold it . . . ah, sir," Walters said.

"Wait a minute, Birkson," Bach confirmed, running to the man and almost grabbing his sleeve. She backed away at the last moment.

"It said no one's to cross that barrier," Walters supplied to Bach's questioning glance. "Says it'll blow us all to the Farside."

"What is that damn thing, anyway?" Bach asked, plaintively.

Birkson withdrew from the barrier and took Bach aside with a tactful touch on the arm. He spoke to her with his voice just low enough for Walters to hear.

"It's a cyborged human connected to a bomb, probably a uranium device," he said. "I've seen the design. It's just like one that went off in Johannesburg three years ago. I didn't know they were still making them."

"I heard about it," Bach said, feeling cold and alone. "Then you think it's really a bomb? How do you know it's a cyborg? Couldn't it be tape recordings, or a computer?"

Birkson rolled his eyes slightly, and Bach reddened. Damn it, they were reasonable questions. And to her surprise, he could not defend his opinion logically. She wondered what she was stuck with. Was this man really the expert she took him to be, or a plaid-sweatered imposter?

"You can call it a hunch. I'm going to talk to this fellow, and I want you to roll up an industrial X-ray unit on the level below this while I'm doing it. On the level above, photographic film. You get the idea?"

"You want to take a picture of the inside of this thing. Won't that be dangerous?"

"Yeah. Are your insurance premiums paid up?"

Bach said nothing, but gave the orders. A million questions were spinning through her head, but she didn't want to make a fool of herself by asking a stupid one. Such as: how much radiation did a big industrial X-ray machine produce when beamed through a rock and steel floor? She had a feeling she wouldn't like the answer. She sighed, and decided to let Birkson have his head until she felt he couldn't handle it. He was about the only hope she had.

And he was strolling casually around the perimeter, swinging his goddamn putter behind him, whistling bad harmony with the tune coming from the bomb. What was a career police officer to do? Back him up on the harmonica?

The scanning cameras atop the bomb stopped their back and forth motion. One of them began to track Birkson. He grinned his flashiest, and waved to it. The music stopped.

"I am a fifty kiloton nuclear bomb of the uranium-235 type," it said. "You must stay behind the perimeter I have caused to be erected here. You must not disobey this order."

Birkson held up his hands, still grinning, and splayed out his fingers.

"You got me, bud. I won't bother you. I was just admiring your casing. Pretty nice job, there. It seems a shame to blow it up."

"Thank you," the bomb said, cordially. "But that is my purpose. You cannot divert me from it."

"Never entered my mind. Promise."

"Very well. You may continue to admire me, if you wish, but from a safe distance. Do not attempt to rush me. All my vital wiring is safely protected, and I have a response time of three milliseconds. I can ignite long before you can reach me, but I do not wish to do so until the alloted time has come."

Birkson whistled. "That's pretty fast, brother. Much faster than me, I'm sure. It must be nice, being able to move like that after blundering along all your life with neural speeds."

"Yes, I find it very gratifying. It was a quite unexpected benefit of becoming a bomb."

This was more like it, Bach thought. Her dislike of Birkson had not blinded her to the fact that he had been checking out his hunch. And her questions had been answered: no tape array could answer questions like that, and the machine had as much as admitted that it had been a human being at one time.

Birkson completed a circuit, back to where Bach and Walters were standing. He paused, and said in a low voice, "Check out that time."

"What time?"

"What time did you say you were going to explode?" he yelled.

"In three hours, twenty-one minutes, and eighteen seconds," the bomb supplied.

"That time," he whispered. "Get your computers to work on it. See if it's the anniversary of any political group, or the time something happened that someone might have a grudge about." He started to turn away, then thought of something. "But most important, check the birth records."

"May I ask why?"

He seemed to be dreaming, but came back to them. "I'm just feeling this character out. I've got a feeling this might be his birthday. Find out who was born at that time—it can't be too many, down to the second—and try to locate them all. The one you can't find will be our guy. I'm betting on it."

"What are you betting? And how do you know for sure it's a man?"

That look again, and again she blushed. But, damn it, she had to ask questions. Why should he make her feel defensive about it?

"Because he's chosen a male voice to put over his speakers. I know that's not conclusive, but you get hunches after a while. As to what I'm betting . . . no, it's not my life. I'm sure I can get this one. How about dinner tonight if I'm right?" The smile was ingenuous, without the trace of lechery she thought she had seen before. But her stomach was still crawling. She turned away without answering.

For the next twenty minutes, nothing much happened. Birkson continued his slow stroll around the machine, stopping from time to time to shake his head in admiration. The thirty men and women of Chief Bach's police detail stood around nervously with nothing to do, as far away from the machine as pride would allow. There was no sense in taking cover.

Bach herself was kept busy coordinating the behind-the-scenes maneuvering from a command post that had been set up around the corner, in the Elysian Travel Agency. It had phones and a computer output printer. She sensed the dropping morale among her officers, who could see nothing going on. Had they known that surveying lasers were poking their noses around trees in the Plaza, taking bearings to within a thousandth of a millimeter, they might have felt a little better. And on the floor below, the X-ray had arrived.

Ten minutes later, the output began to chatter. Bach could hear it in the silent, echoing corridor from her position halfway between the travel agency and the bomb. She turned, and met a young officer with the green armband of a rookie. The woman's hand was ice-cold as she handed Bach the sheet of yellow printout paper. There were three names printed on it, and below that, some dates and events listed.

"This bottom information was from the fourth expansion of the problem," the officer explained. "Very low probability stuff. The three people were all born either on the second or within a three-second margin of error, in three different years. Everyone else has been contacted."

"Keep looking for these three, too," Bach said. As she turned away, she noticed that the young officer was pregnant, about in her fifth month. She thought briefly of sending her away from the scene, but what was the use?

Birkson saw her coming, and broke off his slow circuits of the bomb. He took the paper from her and scanned it. He tore off the bottom part without being told it was low probability, crumpled it, and let it drop to the floor. Scratching his head, he walked slowly back to the bomb.

"Hans?" he called out.

"How did you know my name?" the bomb asked.

"Ah, Hans, my boy, credit us with some sense. You can't have got into this without knowing that the MuniPol can do very fast investigations. Unless I've been underestimating you. Have I?"

"No," the bomb conceded. "I knew you would find out who I was. But it doesn't alter the situation."

"Of course not. But it makes for easier conversation. How has life been treating you, my friend?"

"Terrible," mourned the man who had become a fifty kiloton nuclear weapon.

Every morning Hans Leiter rolled out of bed and padded into his cozy water closet. It was not the standard model for residential apartment modules, but a special one he had installed after he moved in. Hans lived alone, and it was the one luxury he allowed himself. In his little palace, he sat in a chair that massaged him into wakefulness, washed him, shaved him, powdered him, cleaned his nails, splashed him with scent, them made love to him with a rubber imitation that was a good facsimile of the real thing. Hans was awkward with women.

He would dress, walk down three hundred meters of corridor, and surrender himself to a pedestrian slideway which took him as far as the Cross-Crisium Tube. There, he allowed himself to be fired like a projectile through a tunnel below the Lunar surface.

Hans worked in the Crisium Heavy Machinery Foundry. His job there was repairing almost anything that broke down. He was good at it; he was much more comfortable with machines than with people.

One day he made a slip and got his leg caught in a massive roller. It was not a serious accident, because the failsafe systems turned off the machine before his body or head could be damaged, but it hurt terribly and completed ruined the leg. It had to be taken off. While he was waiting for the cloned replacement limb to be grown, Hans had been fitted with a prosthetic.

It had been a revelation to him. It worked like a dream, as good as his old leg and perhaps better. It was connected to his severed leg nerve, but was equipped with a threshold cut-off circuit, and one day when he barked his artificial shin he saw that it had caused him no pain. He recalled the way that same injury had felt with his flesh and blood leg, and again he was impressed. He thought, too, of the agony when his leg had been caught in the machine.

When the new leg was ready for transplanting, Hans had elected to retain the prosthetic. It was unusual, but not unprecedented.

From that time on, Hans, who had never been known to his co-workers as talkative or social, withdrew even more from his fellow humans. He would speak only when spoken to. But people had observed him talking to the stamping press, and the water cooler, and the robot sweeper.

At night, it was Hans' habit to sit on his vibrating bed and watch the holovision until one o'clock. At that time, his kitchen would prepare him a late snack, roll it to him in his bed, and he would retire for the night.

For the last three years Hans had been neglecting to turn the set on before getting into bed. Nevertheless, he continued to sit quietly on the bed staring at the empty screen.

When she finished reading the personal data printout, Bach was struck once more at the efficiency of the machines in her control. This man was almost a cipher, yet there were nine thousand words in storage concerning his uneventful life, ready to be called up and printed into an excruciatingly boring biography.

"... so you came to feel that you were being controlled at every step in your life by machines," Birkson was saying. He was sitting on one of the barriers, swinging his legs back and forth. Bach joined him and offered the long sheet of printout. He waved it away. She could hardly blame him.

"But it's true!" the bomb said. "We all are, you know. We're part of this huge machine that's called New Dresden. It moves us around like parts on an assembly line, washes us, feeds us, puts us to bed and sings us to sleep."

"Ah," Birkson said, agreeably. "Are you a Luddite, Hans?"

"No!" the bomb said in a shocked voice. "Roger, you've missed the whole point. I don't want to destroy the machines. I want to serve them better. I wanted to become a machine, like my new leg. Don't you see? We're part of the machine, but we're the most inefficient part."

The two talked on, and Bach wiped the sweat from her palms. She couldn't see where all this was going, unless Birkson seriously hoped to talk Hans Leiter out of what he was going to do in—she glanced at the clock—two hours and forty-three minutes. It was maddening. On the one hand, she recognized the skill he was using in establishing a rapport with the cyborg. They were on a first-name basis, and at least the damn machine cared enough to argue its position. On the other hand, so what? What good was it doing?

Walters approached and whispered into her ear. She nodded, and tapped Birkson on the shoulder.

"They're ready to take the picture whenever you are," she said. He waved her off.

"Don't bother me," he said, loudly. "This is getting interesting. So if what you say is true," he went on to Hans, getting up and pacing intently back and forth, this time inside the line of barriers, "maybe I ought to look into this myself. You really like being cyborged better than being human?"

"Infinitely so," the bomb said. He sounded enthusiastic. "I need no sleep now, and I no longer have to bother with elimination or eating. I have a tank for nutrients, which are fed into the housing where my brain and central nervous system are located." He paused. "I tried to eliminate the ups and downs of hormone flow and the emotional reactions that followed," he confided.

"No dice, huh?"

"No. Something always distracted me. So when I heard of this place where they would cyborg me and get rid of all that, I jumped at the chance."

Inactivity was making Bach impulsive. She *had* to say or do something.

"Where did you get the work done, Hans?" she ventured.

The bomb started to say something, but Birkson laughed loudly and slapped Bach hard on the back. "Oh, no, Chief. That's pretty tricky, right Hans? She's trying to get you to rat. That's not done, Chief. There's a point of honor involved."

"Who is that?" the bomb asked, suspiciously.

"Let me introduce Chief Anna-Louise Bach, of the New Dresden Police. Ann, meet Hans."

"Police?" Hans asked, and Bach felt goose-pimples when she

detected a note of fright in the voice. What was this maniac trying to do, frightening the guy like that? She was close to pulling Birkson off the case. She held off because she thought she could see a familiar pattern in it, something she could use as a way to participate, even if ignominiously. It was the good guy-bad guy routine, one of the oldest police maneuvers in the book.

"Aw, don't be like that," Birkson said to Hans. "Not all cops are brutes. Ann here, she's a nice person. Give her a chance. She's only doing her job."

"Oh, I have no objection to police," the bomb said. "They are necessary to keep the social machine functioning. Law and order is a basic precept of the coming new Mechanical Society. I'm pleased to meet you, Chief Bach. I wish the circumstances didn't make us enemies."

"Pleased to meet you, Hans." She thought carefully before she phrased her next question. She wouldn't have to take the hard-line approach to contrast herself with affable, buddy-buddy Birkson. She needn't be an antagonist, but it wouldn't hurt if she asked questions that probed at his motives.

"Tell me, Hans. You say you're not a Luddite. You say you like machines. Do you know how many machines you'll destroy if you set yourself off? And even more important, what you'll do to this social machine you've been talking about? You'll wipe out the whole city."

The bomb seemed to be groping for words. He hesitated, and Bach felt the first glimmer of hope since this insanity began.

"You don't understand. You're speaking from an organic view-point. Life is important to you. A machine is not concerned with life. Damage to a machine, even the social machine, is simply something to be repaired. In a way, I hope to set an example. I wanted to become a machine—"

"And the best, the very ultimate machine," Birkson put in, "is the atomic bomb. It's the end point of all mechanical thinking."

"Exactly," said the bomb, sounding very pleased. It was nice to be understood. "I wanted to be the very best machine I could possibly be, and it had to be this."

"Beautiful, Hans," Birkson breathed. "I see what you're talking about. So if we go on with that line of thought we logically come to the conclusion..." and he was off into an exploration of the fine points of the new Mechanistic world view.

Bach was trying to decide which was the crazier of the two, when she was handed another message. She read it, then tried to find a place to break into the conversation. But there was no convenient place. Birkson was more and more animated, almost frothing at the mouth as he discovered points of agreement between the two of them. Bach noticed her officers standing around nervously, following the conversation. It was clear from their expressions that they feared they were being sold out, that when zero hour arrived they would still be here watching intellectual ping-pong. But long before that, she could have a mutiny on her hands. Several of them were fingering their weapons, probably without even knowing it.

She touched Birkson on the sleeve, but he waved her away. Damn it, this was too much. She grabbed him and nearly pulled him from his feet, swung him around until her mouth was close to his ear and growled.

"Listen to me, you idiot. they're going to take the picture. You'll have to stand back some. It's better if we're all shielded."

"Leave me *alone*," he shot back, and pulled from her grasp. But he was still smiling. "This is just getting interesting," he said, in a normal tone of voice.

Birkson came near to dying in that moment. Three guns were trained on him from the circle of officers, awaiting only the order to fire. They didn't like seeing their Chief treated that way.

Bach herself was damn near to giving the order. The only thing that stayed her hand was the knowledge that with Birkson dead, the machine might go off ahead of schedule. The only thing to do now was to get him out of the way and go on as best she could, knowing that she was doomed to failure. No one could say she hadn't given the expert a chance.

"But what I was wondering about," Birkson was saying, "was why today? What happened today? Is this the day Cyrus Mc-Cormick invented the combine harvester, or something?"

"It's my birthday," Hans said, somewhat shyly.

"Your *birthday*?" Birkson managed to look totally amazed to learn what he already knew. "Your birthday. That's *great*, Hans. Many happy returns of the day, my friend." He turned and took in all of the officers with an expansive sweep of his hands. "Let's sing, people. Come on, it's his birthday, for heaven's sake. *Happy birthday to you, happy birthday to you, happy birthday dear Hans...*"

He bellowed, he was off-key, he swept his hands in grand circles with no sense of rhythm. But so infectious was his mania that several of the officers found themselves joining in. He ran around the circle, pulling the words out of them with great scooping motions of his hands.

Bach bit down hard on the inside of her cheek to keep herself steady. *She had been singing, too.* The scene was so ridiculous, so blackly improbable...

She was not the only one who was struck the same way. One of her officers, a brave man who she knew personally to have shown courage under fire, fell on his face in a dead faint. A woman officer covered her face with her hands and fled down the corridor, making helpless coughing sounds. She found an alcove and vomited.

And still Birkson capered. Bach had her gun halfway out of the shoulder holster, when he shouted.

"What's a birthday without a party?" he asked. "Let's have a big party." He looked around, fixed on the flower shop. He started for it, and as he passed Bach he whispered, "Take the picture *now.*"

It galvanized her. She desperately wanted to believe he knew what he was doing, and just at the moment when his madness seemed total he had shown her the method. *A distraction.* Please, let it be a distraction. She turned and gave the prearranged signal to the officer standing at the edge of Prosperity Plaza.

She turned back in time to see Birkson smash in the window of the flower shop with his putter. It made a deafening crash.

"Goodness," said Hans, who sounded truly shocked. "Did you have to do that? That's private property."

"What does it matter?" Birkson yelled. "Hell, man, you're going to do much worse real soon. I'm just getting things started." He reached in and pulled out an armload of flowers, signaling to others to give him a hand. The police didn't like it, but soon were looting the shop and building a huge wreath just outside the line of barriers.

"I guess you're right," said Hans, a little breathlessly. A taste of violence had excited him, whetted his appetite for more to come. "But you startled me. I felt a real thrill, like I haven't felt since I was human."

"Then let's do it some more." And Birkson ran up and down one side of the street, breaking out every window he could reach. He picked up small articles he found inside the shops and threw them. Some of them shattered when they hit.

He finally stopped. Leystrasse had been transformed. No longer the scrubbed and air-conditioned Lunar environment, it had become as shattered, as chaotic and uncertain as the tension-filled emotional atmosphere it contained. Bach shuddered and swallowed the rising taste of bile. It was a precursor of things to come, she was sure. It hit her deeply to see the staid and respectable Leystrasse ravaged.

"A cake," Birkson said. "We have to have a cake. Hold on a minute, I'll be right back." He strode quickly toward Bach, took her elbow and turned her, pulled her insistently away with him.

"You have to get those officers away from here," he said, conversationally. "They're tense. They could explode at any minute. In fact," and he favored her with his imbecile grin, "they're probably more dangerous right now than the bomb."

"You mean you think it's a fake?"

"No. It's for real. I know the psychological pattern. After this much trouble, he won't want to be a dud. Other types, they're in it for the attention and they'd just as soon fake it. Not Hans. But what I mean is, I have him. I can get him. But I can't count on your officers. Pull them back and leave only two or three of your most trusted people."

"All right." She had decided again, more from a sense of helpless futility than anything else, to trust him. He *had* pulled a neat diversion with the flower shop and the X-ray.

"We may have him already," he went on, as they reached the end of the street and turned the corner. "Often, the X-ray is enough. It cooks some of the circuitry and makes it unreliable. I'd hope to kill him outright, but he's shielded. Oh, he's probably got a lethal dosage, but it'd take him days to die. That doesn't do us any good. And if his circuitry *is* knocked out, the only way to find out is to wait. We have to do better than that. Here's what I want you to do."

He stopped abruptly and relaxed, leaning against the wall and gazing out over the trees and artificial sunlight of the Plaza. Bach could hear songbirds. They had always made her feel good before. Now all she could think of was incinerated corpses. Birkson ticked off points on his fingers.

She listened to him carefully. Some of it was strange, but no worse than she had already witnessed. And he really did have a plan. He really did. The sense of relief was so tremendous that it threatened to create a mood of euphoria in her, one not yet justified by the circumstances. She nodded curtly to each of his suggestions, then again to the officer who stood beside her, confirming what Birkson had said and turning it into orders. The young man rushed off to carry them out and Birkson started to return to the bomb. Bach grabbed him.

"Why wouldn't you let Hans answer my question about who did the surgical work on him? Was that part of your plan?" The question was half belligerent.

"Oh. Yeah, it was, in a way. I just grabbed the opportunity to make him feel closer to me. But it wouldn't have done you any good. He'll have a block against telling that, for sure. It could even be set to explode the bomb if he tries to answer that question. Hans is a maniac, but don't underestimate the people who helped him get where he is now. They'll be protected."

"Who are they?"

Birkson shrugged. It was such a casual, uncaring gesture that Bach was annoyed again.

"I have no idea. I'm not political, Ann. I don't know the Antiabortion Movement from the Freedom for Mauretania League. They build 'em, I take 'em apart. It's as simple as that. *Your* job is to find out how it happened. I guess you ought to get started on that."

"We already have," she conceded. "I just thought that . . . well, coming from Earth, where this sort of thing happens all the time, that you might know . . . damn it, Birkson. *Why*? Why is this happening?"

He laughed, while Bach turned red and went into a slow boil. Any of her officers, seeing her expression, would have headed for the nearest blast shelter. But Birkson laughed on. Didn't he give a damn about anything?

"Sorry," he forced out. "I've heard that question before, from other police chiefs. It's a good question." He waited, a half-smile on his face. When she didn't say anything, he went on.

"You don't have the right perspective on this, Ann."

"That's Chief Bach to you, damn you."

"Okay," he said, easily. "What you don't see is that this thing is no different from a hand grenade tossed into a crowd, or a bomb sent through the mail. It's a form of communication. It's just that today, with so many people, you have to shout a little louder to get any attention."

"But . . . who? They haven't even identified themselves. You're saying that Hans is a tool of these people. He's been wired into the bomb, with his own motives for exploding. Obviously he didn't have the resources to do this himself, I can see that."

"Oh, you'll hear from them. I don't think they expect him to be successful. He's a warning. If they were *really* serious they could find the sort of person they want, one who's politically committed and will die for the cause. Of course, they don't *care* if the bomb goes off; they'll be pleasantly surprised if it does. Then they can stand up and pound their chests for a while. They'll be famous."

"But where did they get the uranium? The security is . . ."

For the first time, Birkson showed a trace of annoyance.

"Don't be silly. The path leading to today was irrevocably set in 1945. There was never any way to avoid it. The presence of a tool implies that it will be used. You can try your best to keep it in the hands of what you think of as responsible people, but it'll never work. And it's *no different*, that's what I'm saying. This bomb is just another weapon. It's a cherry bomb in an anthill. It's gonna cause one hill of ants a hell of a lot of trouble, but it's no threat to the race of ants."

Bach could not see it that way. She tried, but it was still a nightmare of entirely new proportions to her. How could he equate the killing of millions of people with a random act of violence where three or four might be hurt? She was familiar with that. Bombs went off every day in her city, as in every human city. People were always dissatisfied.

"I could walk down...no, it's up here, isn't it?" Birkson mused for a moment on cultural differences. "Anyway, give me enough money and I'll bet I could go up to your slum neighbor-hoods right this minute and buy you as many kilos of uranium or plutonium as you want. Which is something you ought to be doing, by the way. Anything can be bought. *Anything.* For the right price, you could have bought weapons-grade material on the black market as early as 1960 or so. It would have been very expensive; there wasn't much of it. You'd have had to buy a *lot* of people. But now...well, you think it out." He stopped, and seemed em-barrassed by his outburst.

"I've read a little about this," he apologized.

She did think it out as she followed him back to the cordon. What he said was true. When controlled fusion proved too costly for wide-scale use, humanity had opted for fast breeder reactors. There had been no other choice. And from that moment, nuclear bombs in the hands of terrorists had been the price humanity accepted. And the price they would continue to pay.

"I wanted to ask you one more question," she said. He stopped and turned to face her. His smile was dazzling.

"Ask away. But are you going to take me up on that bet?"

She was momentarily unsure of what he meant.

"Oh. Are you saying you'd help us locate the underground uranium ring? I'd be grateful..."

"No, no. Oh, I'll help you. I'm sure I can make a contact. I used to do that before I got into this game. What I meant was, are you going to bet I can't find some? We could bet...say, a dinner together as soon as I've found it. Time limit of seven days. How about it?"

She thought she had only two alternatives: walk away from him, or kill him. But she found a third.

"You're a betting man. I guess I can see why. But that's what I wanted to ask you. How can you stay so calm? Why doesn't this get to you like it does to me and my people? You can't tell me it's simply that you're used to it."

He thought about it. "And why not? You can get used to anything, you know. Now what about that bet?"

"If you don't stop talking about that," she said, quietly, "I'm going to break your arm."

"All right." He said nothing further, and she asked no further questions.

The fireball grew in milliseconds into an inferno that could scarcely be described in terms comprehensible to humans. Everything in a half-kilometer radius simply vanished into super-heated gases and plasma: buttresses, plate-glass windows, floors and ceilings, pipes, wires, tanks, machines, gewgaws and trinkets by the million, books, tapes, apartments, furniture, household pets, men, women, and children. They were the lucky ones. The force of the expanding blast compressed two hundred levels below it like a giant sitting on a Dagwood sandwich, making holes through plate steel turned to putty by the heat as easily as a punch press through tinfoil. Upwards, the surface bulged into the soundless Lunar night and split to reveal a white hell beneath. Chunks flew away, chunks as large as city sectors, before the center collapsed back on itself to leave a crater whose walls were a maze of compartments and ant-tunnels that dripped and flowed like warm gelatin. No trace was left of human bodies within two kilometers of the explosion. They had died after only the shortest period of suffering, their bodies consumed or spread into an invisible layer of organic film by the combination of heat and pressure that passed through walls, entered rooms where the doors were firmly shut. Further away, the sound was enough to congeal the bodies of a million people before the heat roasted them, the blast stripped flesh from bones to leave shrunken stick figures. Still the effects attenuated as the blast was channeled into corridors that were structurally strong enough to remain intact, and that very strength was the downfall of the inhabitants of the maze. Twenty kilometers from the epicenter, pressure doors popped through steel flanges like squeezed watermelon seeds.

What was left was five million burnt, blasted corpses, and ten million injured so hideously that they would die in hours or days. But Bach had been miraculously thrown clear by some freak of the explosion. She hurtled through the void with fifteen million ghosts following her, and each carried a birthday cake. They were singing. She joined in.

"Happy birthday to you, happy birthday . . ."

"Chief Bach."

"Huh?" She felt a cold chill pass over her body. For a moment she could only stare down into the face of Roger Birkson.

"You all right now?" he asked. He looked concerned.

"I'm . . . what happened?"

He patted her on both arms, then shook her heartily.

"Nothing. You drifted off for a moment." He narrowed his eyes. "I think you were daydreaming. I want to be diplomatic about this . . . ah, what I mean . . . I've seen it happen before. I think you were trying to get away from us."

She rubbed her hands over her face.

"I think I was. But I sure went in the wrong direction. I'm all right now." She could remember it now, and knew she had not passed out or become totally detached from what was going on. She had watched it all. Her memories of the explosion, so raw and real a moment before, were already the stuff of nightmares.

Too bad she hadn't come awake into a better world. It was so damn unfair. That was the reward at the end of a nightmare, wasn't it? You woke up to find everything was all right.

Instead, here was a long line of uniformed officers, bearing birthday cakes to a fifty kiloton atomic bomb.

Birkson had ordered the lights turned off in the Leystrasse. When his order had not been carried out, he broke out the lights with his putter. Soon, he had some of the officers helping him.

Now the beautiful Leystrasse, the pride of New Dresden, was a flickering tunnel through hell. The light of a thousand tiny birthday candles on five hundred cakes turned everything red-orange and made people into shadowed demons. Officers kept arriving with hastily wrapped presents, flowers, balloons. Hans, the little man who was now nothing but a brain and nerve network floating in a lead container; Hans, the cause of all this, the birthday boy himself, watched it all in unconcealed delight from his battery of roving television cameras. He sang loudly.

"I am a bomb! I am a bomb!" he yelled. He had never had so much fun.

Bach and Birkson retreated from the scene into the darkened recess of the Bagatelle Flower Shoppe. There, a stereo viewing tank had been set up.

The X-ray picture had been taken with a moving plate technique that allowed a computer to generate a three dimensional model. They leaned over the tank now and studied it. They had been joined by Sergeant McCoy, Bach's resident bomb expert, and another man from the Lunar Radiation Laboratory.

"This is Hans," said Birkson, moving a red dot in the tank by means of a dial on the side. It flicked over and around a vague gray shape that trailed dozens of wires. Bach wondered again at the pressures that would allow a man to like having his body stripped from him. There was nothing in that lead flask but the core of the man, the brain and central nervous system.

"Here's the body of the bomb. The two sub-critical masses. The H.E. charge, the timer, the arming barrier, which is now withdrawn. It's an old design, ladies and gentlemen. Old, but reliable. As basic as the bow and arrow. It's very much like the first one dropped on the Nippon Empire at Hiroshima."

"You're sure it'll go off, then?" Bach put in.

"Sure as taxes. Hell, a kid could build one of these in the bathroom, given only the uranium and some shielding equipment. Now let me see." He pored over the phantom in the tank, tracing out wiring paths with the experts. They debated possibilities, lines of attack, drawbacks. At last they seemed to reach a consensus.

"As I see it, we have only one option," Birkson said. "We have to go for his volitional control over the bomb. I'm pretty sure we've isolated the main cable that goes from him to the detonator. Knock that out, and he can't do a thing. We can pry that tin can open by conventional means and disarm that way. McCoy?"

"I agree," said McCoy. "We'd have a full hour, and I'm sure we can get in there with no trouble. When they cyborged this one, they put all their cards on the human operator. They didn't bother with entry blocks, since Hans could presumably blow it up before we could get close enough to do anything. With his control out, we only have to open it up with a torch and drop the damper into place.

The LRL man nodded his agreement. "Though I'm not quite as convinced as Mr. Birkson that he's got the right cable in mind for what he wants to do. If we had more time . . ."

"We've wasted enough time already," Bach said, decisively.

She had swung rapidly from near terror of Roger Birkson to total trust. It was her only defense. She knew she could do nothing at all about the bomb, and had to trust someone.

"Then we go for it. Is your crew in place? Do they know what to do? And above all, are they *good*? Really good? There won't be a second chance."

"Yes, yes, and yes," Bach said. "They'll do it. We know how to cut rock on Luna."

"Then give them the coordinates, and go." Birkson seemed to relax a bit. Bach saw that he had been under some form of tension, even if it was only excitement at the challenge. He had just given his last order. It was no longer in his hands. His fatalistic gambler's instinct came into play and the restless, churning energy he had brought to the enterprise vanished. There was nothing to do about it but wait. Birkson was good at waiting. He had lived through twenty-one of these final countdowns.

He faced Bach and started to say something to her, then thought better of it. She saw doubt in his face for the first time, and it made her skin crawl. Damn it, she had thought he was *sure*.

"Chief," he said, quietly, "I want to apologize for the way I treated you these last few hours. It's not something I can control when I'm on the job. I . . ."

This time it was Bach's turn to laugh, and the release of tension it brought with it was almost orgasmic. She felt like she hadn't laughed for a million years.

"Forgive me," she said. "I saw you were worried, and thought it was about the bomb. It was just such a relief."

"Oh, yeah," he said, dismissing it. "No point in worrying now. Either your people hit it or they don't. We won't know if they don't. What I was saying, it just sort of comes over me. Honestly. I get horny, I get manic, I totally forget about other people except as objects to be manipulated. So I just wanted to say I like you. I'm glad you put up with me. And I won't pester you anymore."

She came over and put her hand on his shoulder.

"Can I call you Roger? Thanks. Listen, if this thing works, I'll have dinner with you. I'll give you the key to the city, a ticker tape parade, and a huge bonus for a consultant fee . . . and my eternal friendship. We've been tense, okay? Let's forget about these last few hours."

"All right." His smile was quite different this time.

Outside, it happened very quickly. The crew on the laser drill were positioned beneath the bomb, working from ranging reports and calculations to aim their brute at precisely the right spot.

The beam took less than a tenth of a second to eat through the layer of rock in the ceiling and emerge in the air above the Ley-strasse. It ate through the metal sheath of the bomb's underside, the critical wire, the other side of the bomb, and part of the ceiling like they weren't even there. It had penetrated into the level above before it could be shut off.

There was a shower of sparks, a quick sliding sound, then a muffled thud. The whole structure of the bomb trembled, and smoke screeched from the two drilled holes in the top and bottom. Bach didn't understand it, but could see that she was alive and assumed it was over. She turned to Birkson, and the shock of seeing him nearly stopped her heart.

His face was a gray mask, drained of blood. His mouth hung open. He swayed, and almost fell over. Bach caught him and eased him to the floor.

"Roger . . . what is it? Is it still . . . will it go off? Answer me, *answer me*. What should I so?"

He waved weakly, pawed at her hands. She realized he was trying to give her a reassuring pat. It was feeble indeed.

"No danger," he wheezed, trying to get his breath back. "No danger. The wrong wire. We hit the wrong wire. Just luck, is all, nothing but luck."

She remembered. They had been trying to remove Hans' control over the bomb. Was he still in control? Birkson answered before she could speak.

"He's dead. That explosion. That was the detonator going off. He reacted just too late. We hit the disarming switch. The shield dropped into place so the masses couldn't come together even if the bomb was set off. Which he did. He set it off. That sound, that *mmmmmmwoooooph!*" He was not with her. His eyes stared back into a time and place that held horror for him.

"I heard that sound—the detonator—once before, over the telephone. I was coaching this woman, no more than twenty-five, because I couldn't get there in time. She had only three more minutes. I heard that sound, then nothing, nothing."

She sat near him on the floor as her crew began to sort out the mess, haul the bomb away for disposal, laugh and joke in hysterical relief. At last Birkson regained control of himself. There was no trace of the bomb except a distant hollowness in his eyes.

"Come on," he said, getting to his feet with a little help from her. "You're going on twenty-four-hour leave. You've earned it. We're going back to Burning Tree and you're going to watch me make a par five on the eighteenth. Then we've got a date for dinner. What place is nice?"

The Funhouse Effect

"DID YOU SEE WHAT'S playing at the theater tonight, Mr. Quester?" The stewardess was holding a printed program in her hand.

"No, and I haven't the time now. Where's the captain? There are some things he should—"

"Two old flat movies," she went on, oblivious to his protests. "Have you ever seen one? They're very interesting and entertaining. *A Night to Remember* and *The Poseidon Adventure*. I'll make a reservation for you."

Quester called out to her as she was leaving.

"I'm trying to tell you, there's something badly wrong on this ship. Won't anybody listen?"

But she was gone, vanished into the crowd of merrymakers. She was busy enough without taking time to listen to the wild tales of a nervous passenger.

Quester was not quite right in thinking of *Hell's Snowball* as a ship. The official welcoming pamphlet referred to it as an asterite, but that was advertising jargon. Anyone else would have called it a comet.

Icarus Lines, Inc., the owners, had found it drifting along at a distance of 500 AU. It had been sixty kilometers in diameter, weighing in at about one hundred trillion tons.

Fortunately, it was made up of frozen liquids rich in hydrogen. Moving it was only a matter of installing a very large fusion motor, then sitting back for five years until it was time to slow it down for orbit in the umbra of Mercury.

The company knew they would not get many passengers on a bare snowball. They tunneled into the comet, digging out state-rooms and pantries and crew's quarters as they went. The ship-fitters went in and paneled the bare ice walls in metal and plastic, then filled the rooms with furniture. There was room to spare, power to spare. They worked on a grand scale, and they had a grand vision. They intended to use the captive comet for sight-seeing excursions to the sun.

Things went well for fifty years. The engine would shove the *Snowball* out of the protective shadow and, with the expenditure of ten million tons of ice and ammonia for reaction mass, inject it into a hyperbolic orbit that would actually brush the fringes of the solar corona. Business was good. *Hell's Snowball* became the vacation bonanza of the system, more popular than Saturn's Rings.

But it had to end. This was to be the last trip. Huge as it is, there comes a time when a comet has boiled off too much of its mass to remain stable in a close approach to the sun. *Hell's Snowball* was robbed of a hundred million tons with each trip. The engineers had calculated it was good for only one more pass before it cracked apart from internal heating.

But Quester was beginning to wonder.

There was the matter of the engines. Early on the fourth day of the excursion, Quester had gone on a guided tour of the farside of the comet to see the fusion engines. The guide had quoted statistics all the way through the tunnel, priming the tourists for the mind-wrenching sight of them. They were the largest rocket engines ever constructed. Quester and everyone else had been prepared to be impressed.

He *had* been impressed; first at the size of the pits that showed where the engines had been, then at the look of utter amazement on the face of the tour guide. Also impressive had been the speed with which the expression had been masked. The guide sputtered for only a moment, then quickly filled in with a story that almost sounded logical.

"I wish they'd tell me these things," he laughed. Did the laugh sound hollow? Quester couldn't tell for sure. "The engines weren't due for removal until tomorrow. It's part of our accelerated salvage program, you see, whereby we remove everything that can be of use in fitting-out the *Icarus*, which you all saw near Mercury when you boarded. It's been decided not to slow *Hell's Snowball* when we complete this pass, but to let it coast on out where it came from. Naturally, we need to strip it as fast as possible. So equipment not actually needed for this trip has been removed already. The rest of it will be taken off on the other side of the sun, along with the passengers. I'm not a physicist, but evidently there is a saving in fuel. No need to worry about it; our course is set and we'll have no further need of the engines." He quickly shepherded the buzzing group of passengers back into the tunnel.

Quester was no physicist, either, but he could work simple equations. He was unable to find a way whereby Icarus Lines would save anything by removing the engines. The fuel was free; by their own admission whatever was left on the comet was to be discarded anyway. So why did it matter if they burned some more? Further, ships removing passengers and furnishings from the *Snowball* on the other side would have to match with its considerably velocity, then expend even more to slow down to solar system speeds. It sounded wasteful.

He managed to put this out of his mind. He was along for the ride, to have fun, and he wasn't a worrier. He had probably dropped a decimal point somewhere in his calculations, or was forgetting a little-known fact of ballistics. Certainly no one else seemed worried.

When he discovered that the lifeboats were missing, he was more angry than frightened.

"What are they doing to us?" he asked the steward who had come when he pressed the service bell. "Just because this is the last trip, does that mean we're not entitled to full protection? I'd like to know what's going on."

The steward, who was an affable man, scratched his head in bewilderment as he once more examined the empty lifeboat cradle.

"Beats me," he said, with a friendly grin. "Part of the salvage operation, I guess. But we've never had a spot of trouble in over fifty years. I hear the *Icarus* won't even carry lifeboats."

Quester fumed. If, sometime in the past, an engineer had decided *Hell's Snowball* needed lifeboats, he'd have felt a damn sight better if the ship still *had* lifeboats.

"I'd like to talk to someone who knows something about it."

"You might try the purser," the steward ventured, then quickly shook his head. "No, I forgot. The purser didn't make this trip. The first mate . . . no, she's . . . I guess that leaves the captain. You might talk to him."

Quester grumbled as he swam down the corridor toward the bridge. The company had no right to strip the ship before its final cruise. On the way there, he heard an announcement over the public address system.

"Attention. All passengers are to report to A Deck at 1300 hours for lifeboat drill. The purser . . . correction, the second officer will call the roll. Attendance is required of all passengers. That is all."

The announcement failed to mollify him, though he was puzzled.

The door to the bridge was ajar. There was a string spanning the open doorway with a hand-lettered sign hanging from it.

"The captain can be found at the temporary bridge," it read, "located on F Deck aft of the dispensary." Inside the room, a work crew was removing the last of the electronic equipment. There was the smell of ozone and oil, and the purple crackle of sparks. The room was little more than an ice-walled shell.

"What . . . ?" Quester began.

"See the captain," the boss said tiredly, pulling out one of the last memory banks in a shower of shorting wires. "I just work here. Salvage crew."

Quester was reminded more of a wrecking crew. He started back toward F Deck.

"Correction on that last announcement," the PA said. "Lifeboat drill has been cancelled. The social director wishes to announce that he is no longer taking reservations for tours of the engine room. The second officer . . . correction, the third officer has requested all personnel to stay clear of the reactor room. There has been a slight spillage during the salvage program. Passengers are not to worry; this incident presents no danger to them. The power requirements of the ship are being taken over by the auxiliary reactor. The social director wishes to announce that tours of the auxiliary reactor are suspended. That is all."

"Is it just me?" Quester asked himself as he drifted by the groups of other passengers, none of whom seemed upset by any of this.

He located the temporary bridge, at the end of a little-used corridor that was stacked high with plastic crates marked "Immediate Removal—Rush, Urgent, Highest Priority." He insinuated his way past them with difficulty and was about to knock on the door when he was stopped by the sound of voices on the other side. The voices were angry.

"I tell you, we should abort this trip at once. I've lost the capability to maneuver the ship in the event of an emergency. I told you I wanted the attitude thrusters to remain in place until after perihelenion."

"Captain, there is no use protesting now," said another voice. "Maybe I agree with you; maybe I don't. In any case. the engines are gone now, and there's no chance of installing them again. There is to be no argument with these orders. The company's in bad shape, what with outfitting the new asterite. Can you picture what it would cost to abort this trip and refund the fares to seven thousand passengers?"

"Hang the company!" the captain exploded. "This ship is *unsafe!* What about those new calculations I gave you—the ones from Lewiston? Have you looked them over?"

The other voice was conciliatory. "Captain, Captain, you're wasting energy worrying about that crackpot. He's been laughed out of the Lunar Academy; his equations simply do not work."

"They look sound enough to me."

"Take it from me, Captain, the best minds in the system have assured us that the *Snowball* will hold together. Why, this old hunk of junk is good for a dozen more trips, and you know it. We've erred, if at all, on the conservative side."

"Well, maybe," the captain grumbled. "I still don't like that lifeboat situation, though. How many did you say we had left?"

"Twenty-eight," the other soothed.

Quester felt the hair stand up on the back of his neck.

He peeked into the room, not knowing what he would say. But there was no one there. The voices were coming from a speaker on the wall. Evidently the captain was in another part of the ship.

He considered going to his cabin and getting drunk, then decided it was a bad idea. He would go to the casino and get drunk.

On the way he passed a lifeboat cradle that was not empty. It was the site of bustling activity, with crews hurrying up and down ramps into the ship. He stuck his head in, saw that the seats had been stripped and the interior was piled high with plastic crates. More were being added every minute.

He stopped one of the workers and asked her what was going on.

"Ask the captain," she shrugged. "They told me to stack these boxes in here, that's all I know."

He stood back and watched until the loading was complete, then was told to stand clear as the nullfield was turned off to allow the boat to drift clear of the *Snowball*. At a distance of two kilometers, the engines fired and the boat was away, blasting back toward the inner planets.

"Twenty-seven," Quester mumbled to himself and headed for the casino.

"Twenty-seven?" the woman asked.

"Probably less by now," Quester said with a broad shrug. "And they only hold fifty people."

They were sitting together at the roulette table, pressed into close company by the random currents of humanity that ebbed and flowed through the room. Quester was not gambling; his legs had just happened to give out, and the nearest place to collapse had been the chair he was sitting in. The woman had materialized out of his alcoholic mist.

It was nice to get back to gravity after the weightless levels of the *Snowball*. But, he discovered, getting drunk in a weightless state was less hazardous. One needn't worry about one's balance. Here in the casino there was the problem of standing. It was too much of a problem for Quester.

The casino was located at one end of a slowly rotating arm, which was mounted horizontally on a pivoted mast that extended straight up from *Hell's Snowball*. On the other end of the arm were the restaurants that served the passengers. Both modules were spherical; the structure resembled an anemometer with silver balls instead of cups on the ends. The view was tremendous. Overhead was the silver sphere that contained the restaurants. To one side was the slowly moving surface of the comet, a dirty gray even in the searing sunlight. To the other side were the stars and the main attraction: Sol itself, blemished with a choice collection of spots. The viewing was going to be good this trip. If anyone was alive to view it, Quester added to himself.

"Twenty-seven, you say?" the woman asked again.

"That's right, twenty-seven."

"One hundred Marks on number twenty-seven," she said and placed her bet. Quester looked up, wondering how many times he would have to repeat himself before she understood him.

The ball clattered to a stop, on number twenty-seven, and the croupier shoveled a tottering stack of chips to the woman. Quester looked around him again at the huge edifice he was sitting in, the incalculable tonnage of the spinning structure, and laughed.

"I wondered why they built this place," he said. "Who needs gravity?"

"Why did they build it?" she asked him, picking up the chips.

"For him," he said, pointing to the croupier. "That little ball would just hang there on the rim without gravity." He felt himself being lifted to his feet, and stood in precarious balance. He threw his arms wide.

"For that matter, that's what all the gravity in the system's for. To bring those little balls down to the number, the old wheel of fortune; and when they've got your number, there's nothing you can do because your number's up, that's all there is, twenty-seven, that's all . . ."

He was sobbing and mumbling philosophical truths as she led him from the room.

The ride in the elevator to the hub of the rotating structure sobered Quester considerably. The gradually decreasing weight combined with the Coriolis effect that tended to push him against one wall was more than an abused stomach could take. The management knew that and had provided facilities for it. Quester vomited until his legs were shaky. Luckily, by then he was weightless and didn't need them.

The woman towed him down the passageway like a toy balloon. They ended up in the grand ballroom.

The ballroom was a hemisphere of nullfield sitting on the surface of the *Snowball*. From inside it was invisible. The dance area was crowded with couples trying out free-fall dances. Most of them had the easy grace of a somersaulting giraffe.

Quester sobered a bit in the near-zero gee. Part of it was the effect of the antinausea drugs he had taken for free-fall; they also tended to reduce the effects of alcohol.

"What's your name?" he asked the woman.

"Solace. You?"

"I'm Quester. From Tharsis, Mars. I'm . . . I'm confused about a lot of things."

She floated over to a table, still towing Quester, and fastened him to one of the chairs. He turned his attention from the twisting bodies in the dance area to his companion.

Solace was tall, much taller than a man or a woman would naturally grow. He estimated she was two and a half meters from head to toe, though she had no toes. Her feet had been replaced with peds, oversized hands popular with spacers. They were useful in free-fall, and for other things, as he discovered when she reached across the table with one slender leg and cupped his cheek with her ped. Her legs were as limber and flexible as her arms.

"Thanks," she said, with a smile. "For the luck, I mean."

"Hmmm? Oh, you mean the bet." Quester had to drag his attention back from the delightful sensation on his cheek. She was beautiful. "But I wasn't advising you on a bet. I was trying to tell you . . ."

"I know. You were saying something about the lifeboats."

"Yes. It's astounding, I . . ." He stopped, realizing that he couldn't remember what was astounding. He was having trouble focusing on her. She was wearing a kaleidoholo suit, which meant she was naked but for a constantly shifting pattern of projections. There seemed to be fifty or sixty different suits contained in it, none persisting for longer than a few seconds. It would melt smoothly from a silver sheath dress to an almost military uniform with gold braid and buttons to a garland of flowers to Lady Godiva. He rubbed his eyes and went on.

"They're salvaging the ship," he said. "The last I heard there were only twenty-seven lifeboats left. And more are leaving every hour. They're taking the electronic equipment with them. And the furnishings and the machinery and who knows what else. I overheard the captain talking to a company representative. *He's* worried, the *captain!* But no one else seems to be. Am I worrying over nothing, or what?"

Solace looked down at her folded hands for a moment, then brought her eyes back up to his.

"I've been uneasy, too," she said in a low voice. She leaned closer to him. "I've shared my apprehensions with a group of friends. We . . . get together and share what we have learned. Our friends laugh at us when we tell them of our suspicions, but . . ." She paused and looked suspiciously around her. Even in his befuddled state Quester had to smile.

"Go on," he said.

She seemed to make up her mind about him and leaned even closer.

"We'll be meeting again soon. Several of us have been scouting around—I was covering the casino when we met—and we'll share our findings and try to come to a consensus on what to do. Are you with us?"

Quester fought off the feeling, quite strong since his suspicions began to haunt him, that he was somehow trapped in an adventure movie. But if he was, he was just getting to the good part.

"You can count me in."

With no further ado, she grabbed his arm in one of her peds and began towing him along, using her hands to grab onto whatever was handy. He thought of objecting, but she was much better than he at weightless maneuvering.

"May I have your attention, please?"

Quester looked around and spotted the captain standing in the center of the stage, in front of the band. He was not alone. On each side of him were women dressed in black jumpsuits, their eyes alertly scanning the audience. They were armed.

"Please, please." The captain held up his arms for quiet and eventually got it. He wiped his brow with a handkerchief.

"There is no cause for alarm. No matter what you may have been hearing, the ship is in no danger. The stories about the main engines having been removed are lies, pure and simple. We are looking for the people who planted these rumors and will soon have all of them in custody. The chief engineer wishes to announce that tours of the engine room will be resumed—"

One of the women shot the captain a glance. He mopped his brow again and consulted a slip of paper in his hand. The hand was shaking.

"Ah, a correction. The engineer announces that tours will *not* be resumed. There is, ah ... that is, they are being overhauled, or ... or something." The woman relaxed slightly.

"The rumor that the main reactor has been shut down is unfounded. The surgeon has told me that there has been no spillage of radioactive material, and even if there had been, the amount was insignificant and would only have been a danger to those passengers with high cumulative exposures. The surgeon will be collecting dosimeters at 1400 hours tomorrow.

"Let me repeat: there is no cause for alarm. As captain of this ship, I take a very dim view of rumormongering. Anyone caught disseminating stories about the unspaceworthiness of this vessel in the future will be dealt with sternly."

"Lifeboat drill will be held tomorrow on A Deck, as scheduled. Anyone who has not as yet been checked out on his life jacket will do so by noon tomorrow, ship's time. That is ... is that all?" This last was addressed to the woman to his left, in a whisper. She nodded curtly, and the three of them walked off the stage, their magnetized shoes sticking to the deck like flypaper.

Solace nudged Quester in the ribs.

"Are those women bodyguards?" she whispered. "Do you think his life is in danger?"

Quester looked at the way the women gripped the captain's elbows. Not bodyguards, but guards, certainly ...

"Say, I just remembered I still have some unpacking to do," he said. "Maybe I can join you and your friends later on. I'll just nose around, see what I can pick up, you know, and—"

But he couldn't squirm free of her grip. Those peds were *strong*.

"May I have your attention, please? Lifeboat drill for tomorrow has been canceled. Repeat, canceled. Passengers showing up at the cradles for lifeboat drill will be interrogated, by order of the captain. That is all."

On the way to Solace's room, the two were shoved out of the way by a group of people in uniform. Their faces were determined, and some of them carried clubs.

"Where does that corridor lead?" he asked.

"To the bridge. But they won't find anything there, it's been—"

"I know."

"I think we're being followed."

"Wha'?" He looked behind him as he bounced along in her wake. There was someone back there, all right. They turned a corner and Solace hauled Quester into a dimly lit alcove, bumping his head roughly against the wall. He was getting fed up with this business of being dragged. If this was an adventure, he was Winnie-the-Pooh following Christopher Robin up the stairs. He started to object, but she clapped a hand around his mouth, holding him close.

"Shhh," she hissed.

A fine thing, Quester grumbled to himself. Can't even speak my mind. He thought he was better off before, alone and puzzled, then he was with this mysterious giantess towing him around.

Of course, things could have been worse, he reflected. She was warm and naked to the touch no matter what his eyes told him. And *tall*. Floating there in the hall, she extended above and below him by a third of a meter.

"How can I think of something like that at a time like this?" he began, but she hushed him again and her arms tightened around him. He realized she was really scared, and he began to be so himself. The liquor and the sheer unlikelihood of recent events had detached him; he was drifting along, rudderless. Nothing in his life had prepared him to cope with things like the black-suited man who now eased slowly around the corner in shadowy pursuit of them.

They watched him from the concealment of the alcove. Many of the lights in the corridor were not working or were mere empty sockets. Earlier, Quester had been alarmed at this, adding it to his list of ways not to run a spaceship. Now, he was grateful.

"He doesn't look much like a man at all," Solace whispered. And sure enough, he didn't. Nor a woman. He didn't look too human.

"Humanoid, I'd say," Quester whispered back. "Pity no one told us. Obviously the system's been invaded by the first intelligent race of humanoids."

"Don't talk nonsense. And be quiet." The man, or whatever it was, was very close now. They could see the ill-fitting pink mask, the lumps and nodules in odd places under his sweater and pants. He passed them by, leaving a pungent odor of hydrogen sulfide.

Quester found himself laughing. To his surprise, Solace laughed along with him. The situation was so grotesque that he had to either laugh or scream.

"Listen," he said, "I don't *believe* in sinister humanoid invaders."

"No? But you believe in superhuman heavy-planet Invaders like the ones that have occupied the Earth, don't you? And you haven't even *seen* them."

"Are you telling me you do believe that thing was an . . . an alien?"

"I'm not saying anything. But I'm wondering what those people were doing, earlier, armed with clubs. Do you believe in mutiny?"

"Solace, I'd *welcome* a mutiny, I'd throw a party, give away all my worldly wealth to charity if only such a normal, everyday thing would happen. But I don't think it will. I think we've fallen through the looking glass."

"You think you're crazy?" She looked at him skeptically.

"Yep. I'm going to turn myself in right now. You're obviously not even here. Maybe this ship isn't even here."

She twisted slightly in the air, bringing her legs up close to his chest.

"I'll prove to you I'm here," she said, working with all four hands and peds at unbuttoning him.

"Hold it. What are you . . . how can you think of that at a time like . . ." It sounded familiar. She laughed, holding his wrists with her hands as her peds quickly stripped him.

"You've never been in danger before," she said. "I have. It's a common reaction to get aroused in a tight spot, especially when the danger's not immediate. And you are, and so am I."

It was true. He was, but didn't like doing it in the hallway.

"There's not room here," he protested. "Another of those critters could come along."

"Yes, isn't it exciting?" Her eyes were alight by now, and her breath was fast and shallow. "And if you think there isn't room, you haven't done it in free-fall yet. Ever tried the Hermesian Hyperbola?"

Quester sighed, and submitted. Soon he was doing more than

submitting. He decided she was as crazy as everyone else, or, alternatively, he was crazy and she was as sane as everybody else. But she was right about the free-fall. There was plenty of room.

They were interrupted by a crackle of static from the public address. They paused to listen to it.

"Attention, your attention please. This is the provisional captain speaking. The traitor running-dog lackey ex-captain is now in chains. Long Live the Revolutionary Committee, who will now lead us on the true path of Procreative Anti-Abortionism."

"Free-Birthers!" Quester yelped. "We've been hijacked by Free-Birthers!"

The new captain, who sounded like a woman, started to go on, but her voice was cut short in a hideous gurgle.

"Long Live the Loyalist Faction of the Glorious Siblings of the—" a new voice began, but it, too, was cut short. Voices shouted in rapid succession.

"The counterrevolution has been suppressed," shouted yet another captain. "Liberate our wombs! Our gonads—our Freedom! Attention, attention! All female persons aboard this ship are ordered to report at once to the infirmary for artificial insemination. Shirkers will be obliterated. That is all."

Neither of them said anything for a long time. At last Solace eased herself away a bit and let him slip out of her. She let out a deep breath.

"I wonder if I could plead double jeopardy?"

"Insanity four, reality nothing," Quester giggled. He was in high spirits as they skulked their way down the dim corridors.

"Are you still on that?" Solace shot back. She sounded a bit tired of him. She kept having to hang back as he struggled to keep up with her supple quadridexterous pace. "Listen, if you want to get fitted for a straitjacket, the tailor's in the other direction. Me, I don't care how ridiculous the situation gets. I'll keep coping."

"I can't help it," he admitted. "I keep feeling that I *wrote* this story several years ago. Maybe in another life. I dunno."

She peered around another corner. They were on their way to the temporary bridge. They had stopped three times already to watch black-suited figures drift by. Everyone else they had seen—those dressed in holiday clothes—had ducked into doorways as quickly as they themselves. At least it seemed that the passengers were no longer in the holiday mood, were aware that there was something wrong.

"You a writer?" she asked.

"Yes. I write scientifiction. Maybe you've heard of it. There's a cult following, but we don't reach the general public."

"What's it about?"

"Scientifiction deals with life on Earth. It's set in the future—each of us creates our own hypothetical future with our own ground rules and set of assumptions. The basic assumption is that we figure out a way to fight the Invaders and reclaim the Earth, or at least a beachhead. In my stories we've managed to rout the Invaders, but the dolphins and whales are still around, and they want their allies back, so humans fight them. It's adventure stuff, purely for thrills. I have a hero called the Panama Kid."

She glanced back at him, and he couldn't read the expression. He was used to taking the defensive about his vocation.

"Is there a living in that?"

"I managed to get aboard the *Snowball* for the final trip, didn't I? That wasn't cheap, but then you know that. Say, what do you do for a living?"

"Nothing. My mother was a holehunter. She made a strike in '45 and got rich. She went out again and left the money to me. She's due back in about fifty years, unless she gets swallowed by a hole."

"So you were born on Pluto?"

"No. I was born in free-fall, about one hundred AU from the sun. I think that's a record so far." She grinned back at him, looking pleased with herself. "You made up your mind yet?"

"Huh?"

"Have you decided if you're the author or a character? If you really think you're crazy, you can shove off. What can you do but accept the reality of your senses?"

He paused and really thought about it for the first time since he met her.

"I do," he said firmly. "It's all happening. Holy Cetacean, *it really is happening.*"

"Glad to have you with us. I *told* you you couldn't experience the Hermesian Hyperbola and still doubt your senses.

It hadn't been the love-making, Quester knew. That could be

as illusory as anything else; he had the stained sheets to prove it. But he believed in *her*, even if there was something decidedly illogical about the goings-on around her.

"Attention, attention."

"Oh, shit. What now?" They slowed near a speaker so they could listen without distortion.

"Glad tidings! This is the provisional captain, speaking for the ad hoc steering committee. We have decided to steer this comet into a new, closer approach to the sun, thus gaining speed for a faster departure from solar space. It has been decided to convert this vessel hereafter to be referred to as the *Spermatozoa*, into an interstellar colony ship to spread the seed of humanity to the stars. All passengers are hereby inducted into the Proletarian Echelon of the Church of Unlimited Population. Conversion of all resources into a closed-ecology system will begin at once. Save your feces! Breathe shallowly until this crisis is past. Correction, correction, there is no crisis. Do not panic. Anyone found panicking will be shot. The steering committee has determined that there is no crisis. All surviving officers with knowledge of how to work these little gadgets on the bridge are ordered to report immediately."

Quester looked narrowly at Solace.

"Do you know anything about them?"

"I can pilot a ship, if that's what you mean. I've never flown anything quite this...*enormous*...but the principles are the same. You aren't suggesting that we help them, are you?"

"I don't know," he admitted. "I didn't really think in terms of plans until a few minutes ago. What was *your* plan? Why are we headed for the bridge?"

She shrugged. "Just to see what the hell's going on, I guess. But maybe we ought to make some preparations. Let's get some life jackets."

They found a locker in the hall containing emergency equipment. Inside were twenty of the nullfield devices called life jackets. More accurately, they were emergency spacesuit generators, with attached water recyclers and oxygen supply. Each of them was a red cylinder about thirty centimeters long and fifteen in diameter with shoulder straps and a single flexible tube with a metal connector on the end. They were worn strapped to the back with the tube reaching over the shoulder.

In operation, the life jackets generated a nullfield that con-
formed closely to the contours of the wearer's body. The field
oscillated between one and one and a half millimeters from the
skin, and the resulting bellows action forced waste air through the
exhaust nozzle. The device attached itself to a tiny metal valve
that was surgically implanted in all the passengers. The valve's
external connection was located under Quester's left collarbone.
He had almost forgotten it was there. It was just a brass-colored
flower that might be mistaken for jewelry but was actually part
of a plumbing system that could route venous blood from his
pulmonary artery to the oxygenator on his back. It then returned
through a parallel pipe to his left auricle and on to his body.

Solace helped him get into it and showed him the few manual
controls. Most of it was automatic. It would switch on the field
around him if the temperature or pressure changed suddenly.

Then they were off again through the silent corridors to confront
the hijackers.

At the last turn in the corridor before reaching the temporary
bridge, they stopped to manually switch on their suit fields. Solace
instantly became a mirror in the shape of a woman. The field
reflected all electromagnetic radiation except through pupil-sized
discontinuities over her eyes which let in controlled quanta of
visible light. It was disquieting. The funhouse effect, it was called,
and it looked as if her body had been twisted through another
spatial dimension. She almost disappeared, except for a pattern
of distortions that hurt Quester's eyes when he looked at it.

They reached the door leading to the bridge and stopped for
a moment. It was a perfectly ordinary door. Quester wondered
why he was here with this impulsive woman.

"Do we knock first, or what?" she mused. "What do you think,
Quester? What would the Panama Kid do?"

"He'd knock it down," Quester said without hesitation. "But
he wouldn't have gotten here without his trusty laser. Say, do you
think we ought to go back and . . ."

"No. We'd better do it now before we think about it too hard.
These suits are protections against any weapon I know of. The
most they can do is capture us."

"Then what?"

"Then you can talk us out of it. You're the one who's fast with words, aren't you?"

Quester remained silent as she backed up and planted herself against the opposite wall, coiled and ready to hit the door with her shoulder. He didn't want to point out that skill with a typer and skill at oratory are not necessarily related. Besides, if she wanted to risk forcible insemination, it was her business.

Just on the off chance, he touched the door plate with his palm. It clicked, and the door opened. It was too late. Solace howled and barreled end-over-end into the room, reaching out with all four limbs like a huge silver starfish to grab onto something. Quester rushed after her, then stopped short as soon as he was into the room. There was no one in it.

"Talk about your anticlimax," Solace breathed, getting herself sorted out from a pile of crates at the far end of the room. "I . . . never mind. It was my fault. Who'd have thought it'd be unlocked?"

"*I* did," Quester pointed out. "Hold it a minute. We're sort of, well, we're being pretty hasty, aren't we? I haven't really had time to stop and think since we got going, but I think we're going at this the wrong way, I really do. Damn it, this isn't an adventure, where everything goes according to a set pattern. I've written enough of them, I ought to know. This is life, and that means there's got to be a rational explanation."

"So what is it?"

"I don't know. But I don't think we'll find it this way. Things have been happening . . . well, think about the announcements over the PA, for instance. They are *crazy!* No one's that crazy, not even Free-Birthers."

Quester's chain of thought was interrupted by the noisy entrance of four people in life jackets. He and Solace jumped up, banged their heads on the ceiling, and were quickly captured.

"All right, which one of you is the provisional captain?"

There was a short silence, then Solace broke it with a laugh.

"Lincoln?" she asked.

"Solace?"

The four were part of Solace's short-lived cabal. It seemed the ship was crawling with people who were concerned enough about the situation to try and do something about it. Before Quester caught all the names, they were surprised by another group of four, with three more close on their heels. The situation threatened to degenerate into a pitched battle of confused identities until someone had a suggestion.

"Why don't we hang a sign on the door? Anybody who comes in here thinks we're the hijackers." They did, and the sign said the provisional captain was dead. While new arrivals were pondering that and wondering what to do next, someone had time to explain the situation.

Someone arrived with a tray of drinks, and soon the would-be liberators were releasing their tensions in liquor and argument. There were fifteen pet theories expounded in as many minutes.

Now that he felt he had his feet under him, Quester adopted a wait-and-see attitude. The data was still insufficient.

"'When you have eliminated the impossible,'" he quoted, "'whatever is left, however improbable, must be the truth.'"

"So what does that gain us?" Solace asked.

"Only a viewpoint. Me, I think we'll have to wait until we get back to Mercury to find out what's been happening. Unless you bring me a live alien, or Free-Birther, or . . . some physical evidence."

"Then let's go look for it," Solace said.

"Attention, attention. This is the ship's computer speaking. I have grave news for all passengers. The entire crew has been assassinated. Until now, I have been blocked by a rogue program inserted by the revolutionaries which has prevented me from regaining control of operations. Luckily, this situation has been remedied. Unluckily, the bridge is still in the hands of the pirates! They have access to all my manual controls from their position, and I'm afraid there is but one course open to those of you who wish to avoid a catastrophe. We are on a trajectory that will soon intersect with the solar chromosphere, and I am powerless to correct it until the bridge is regained. Rally to me! Rise in righteous fury and repulse the evil usurpers! Storm the bridge! Long live the counterrevolution!"

There was a short silence as the implications sank in, then a babble of near panic. Several people headed for the door, only to come back and bolt it. There was an ominous roar from outside.

". . . chromosphere? Where the hell *are* we? Has anyone been out on the surface lately?"

". . . some pleasure cruise. I haven't even *seen* the sun and now they say we're about to . . ."

". . . pirates, revolutions, counterrevolutions, Free-Birthers, *aliens*, for heaven's sake . . ."

Solace looked helplessly around her, listened to the pounding on the door. She located Quester hunkered down beside an instrument console and crouched beside him.

"Talk your way out of *this* one, Panama Kid," she yelled in his ear.

"My dear, I'm much too busy to talk. If I can get the back off this thing . . ." He worked at it and finally pulled off a metal cover. "There was a click from here when the computer came on the line."

There was a recorder inside, with a long reel of tape strung between playback heads. He punched a button that said rewind, watched the tape cycle briefly through, and hit the play button.

"Attention, attention. This is the ship's computer speaking. I have grave news for all passengers."

"We've *heard* that one already," someone shouted. Quester held his head in his hands for a moment, then looked up at Solace. She opened her mouth to say something, then bit her lip, her eyebrows almost touched in a look of puzzlement so funny that Quester would have laughed out loud. But the roof of the bridge evaporated.

It took only a few seconds. There was a blinding white light and a terrible roaring sound; then he was whisked into the air and pulled toward the outside. In an instant, everyone was covered in a nullfield and milling around the hole in the roof like a school of silverfish. In two's and three's they were sucked through. Then the room was empty and Quester was still in it. He looked down and saw Solace's hand around his ankle. She was grasping the firmly anchored computer console with one ped. She hauled him down to her and held him close as he found handholds. His teeth were chattering.

The door burst open, and there was another flurry of astonished passengers sucked through the roof. It didn't take as long this time; the hole in the roof was much larger. Beyond the hole was blackness.

Quester was surprised to see how calm he was once his initial shock had dissipated. He thanked Solace for saving him, then went on with what he had been about to say before the blowout.

"Did you talk to anyone who actually saw a mutineer, or a Free-Birther, or whatever?"

"Huh? Is this the time to . . . ? No, I guess I didn't. But we saw those aliens, or whatever they—"

"Exactly. Whatever they were. They could have been anything. Someone is playing an awfully complicated trick on us. Something's happening, but it isn't what we've been led to believe."

"We've been led to believe something?"

"We've been given clues. Sometimes contradictory, sometimes absolutely insane, and encouraged to think a mutiny is going on; and this recorder proves it isn't happening. Listen." And he played back the recordings of various announcements they had heard earlier. It sounded tinny in their middle-ear receivers.

"But what does that prove?" Solace wanted to know. "Maybe this thing just taped them as they happened."

Quester was dumfounded for a moment. The theory of a vast conspiracy had appealed to him, even if he didn't know the reason for it.

He played past the point of the computer's announcement and sighed with relief when he heard that there was more. They let it natter on to no one about crises in the engine room, spillage in the second auxiliary reactor, and so on. It was obvious that it was playing a scenario that could no longer happen. Because the ship had already broken down completely and they were headed directly for . . .

They seemed to reach that thought simultaneously and scrambled up toward a hole in the ceiling to see what was going on. Quester forgot, as usual, to hang onto something and would have drifted straight up at near-escape velocity but for Solace's grasping hands.

The sun had eaten up the sky. It was huge, *huge*.

"That's what we paid to see," Solace said, weakly.

"Yeah. But I thought we'd see it from the ballroom. It's sort of . . . *big*, isn't it?"

"Do you think we're . . . ?"

"I don't know. I never thought we'd get this close. Something the captain said—no, wait, it wasn't the captain, was it? But one of the recordings said something about . . ."

The ground heaved under them.

Quester saw the revolving casino complex off to his right. It swayed, danced, and came apart. The twin balls broke open, still rotating, and spilled tables and roulette wheels and playing cards and dishes and walls and carpets to the waiting stars. The debris formed a glittering double spiral of ejecta, like droplets of water spraying from the tips of a lawn sprinkler. Bits of it twisted in the sunlight, cartwheeling, caroming, semaphoring, kicking.

"Those are people."

"Are they . . . ?" Quester couldn't ask it.

"No," Solace answered. "Those suits will protect them. Maybe they can be picked up later. You see, when you hit something wearing one of these suits, you—"

She didn't have time to finish, but Quester soon had a demonstration of what she was talking about. The ground opened a few meters from them. They were swept off their feet and tumbled helplessly across the dirty white surface until they hung suspended over the pit.

Quester hit the far side of the rift and bounced. He felt little of the impact, though he hit quite hard, because the suit field automatically stiffened when struck by a fast-moving object. He had cause to be thankful for that fact, because the rift began to close. He clawed his way along the surface toward the sunlight, but the walls of ice closed on him like a book snapped shut.

For a brief moment he was frozen while the ice and rock around him shook and vaporized under the incredible pressures of shearing force. He saw nothing but white heat as frozen methane and water became gas in an instant without an intermediate liquid stage. Then he was shot free as the masses came apart again.

He was still frozen into a climbing position, but now he could see. He was surrounded by chunks of debris, ranging from fist-sized rocks glowing bright red to giant icebergs that sublimated and disappeared before his eyes. Each time the suit began to lose its rigidity he was hit by another object and frozen into a new position as the suit soaked up the kinetic energy.

In a surprisingly short time, everything had vanished. Every particle of the explosion was impelled away from every other particle by the pressures of expanding superheated steam.

But Solace was still clinging to his ankle. She was the only thing left in his universe apart from a few tiny flashing stars of debris far in the distance, tumbling, tumbling.

And the sun.

He could look directly at it as it swung past his field of vision once every ten seconds. It could barely be seen as a sphere; each second it looked more like a flat, boiling plane. The majestic, crushing presence of it flattened his ego with a weight he could barely tolerate. He found Solace in his arms. He looked at her face, which was endless mirrors showing a vanishing series of suns rebounding from his face to hers and back to infinity. The funhouse effect, so disconcerting only an hour ago, seemed familiar and reassuring now in comparison to the chaos below him. He hugged her and closed his eyes.

"Are we going to hit it?" he asked.

"I can't tell. If we do, it'll be the hardest test these suits have ever had. I don't know if they have limits."

He was astounded. "You mean we might actually . . . ?"

"I tell you, I don't know. Theoretically, yes, we could graze the chromosphere and not feel a thing, not from the heat, anyway. But it would be bound to slow us down pretty quickly. The deceleration could kill us. The suits protect us from outside forces almost completely, but internal accelerations can break bones and rupture organs. This suit doesn't stop gravity or inertia from working."

There was no use thinking too long on that possibility.

They were hurtling through the corona now, building up a wake of ionized particles that trailed after them like the tail of a tiny comet. They looked around them for other survivors but could find nothing. Soon, they could see little but a flickering haze as the electrical potential they had built up began discharging in furry feathers of hot plasma. It couldn't have lasted longer than a few minutes; then it began to fade slowly away.

There came a time when the sun could be seen to have shrunk slightly. They didn't speak of it, just held onto each other.

"What are our chances of pickup?" Quester wanted to know.

The sun was now much smaller, receding almost visibly behind them. They were concerned only for the next twenty hours, which was the length of their oxygen reserves.

"How should I know? Someone must know by now that something's happened, but I don't know if any ships can get to us in time. It would depend on where they were at the time of the disaster."

Quester scanned the stars as they swept past his field of vision. They had no way to slow their rotation; so the stars still went around them every ten seconds.

He didn't expect to see anything but was not surprised when he did. It was the next-to-last in a long series of incongruities. There was a ship closing in on them. A voice over the radio told them to stand by to come aboard and asked them how they enjoyed the trip.

Quester was winding up for a reply, but the speaker said one word, slowly and clearly:

"Frightfulness."

And everything changed.

I woke up and found out it had all been a dream.

The very first story I wrote, back when I was five years old, ended with words very much like that last sentence. I'm not ashamed of it. The thought was not new, but it was original with me. It was only later that I learned it's not a fair way to end a story, that the reader deserves more than that.

So here's more.

I woke up and found out it had *almost* all been a dream. The word, "frightfulness," was a posthypnotic trigger that caused me to remember all the things which had been blocked from me by earlier suggestion.

I don't know why I'm bothering to explain all this. I guess old writing habits die hard. No matter that this is being written for a board of psychists, mediartists, and flacks; I have to preserve the narrative thread. I've broken the rules by changing to first person at the end, but I found I could not write the account Icarus Lines requested of me unless I did it in the third person.

"I" am Quester, though that's not my real name. I am a scientifiction writer, but I have no character named the Panama Kid. Solace's name is something else. It was suggested that I change the names.

I signed aboard *Hell's Snowball* knowing that it was going to break apart along the way. That's why so much of it had been stripped. They retained only enough to preserve a tenuous illusion that the trip was a normal one, then threw in everything they could think of to scare the daylights out of us.

We knew they would. We agreed to and submitted to a hypnotic treatment that would fool us into thinking we were on a normal trip and were released into the crazy world they cooked up for us. It's the first time they had ever tried it, and so they threw in everything in the book: aliens, accidents, mutiny, confusion, crackpots, and I didn't even see it all. The experience is different for each passenger, but the basic theme is to put us into a scary situation with evident peril of life and limb; shake well, and then let us come through the experience safe and sound.

There was no danger, not from the first to the last. We were on a stable, carefully calculated orbit. The life jackets were enough to keep us absolutely safe against anything we would encounter, and we were conditioned to have them on at the right time. As proof of this, not a single passenger was injured.

We were *all* nearly scared to death.

It says here you want to know the motive. I remember it clearly now, though I remembered an entirely different one at the time. I went on the Disaster Express because I had just sold a novel and wanted to do something wild, out of character. That was the wildest thing I could think of, and I could wish I had gone to a museum instead. Because the next question you want me to answer is how I feel about it now that it's over, and you won't like it. I hope I'm in the majority and you people at Icarus will give this thing up and never run another like it.

There used to be something called a "haunted house." One was led blindfolded through it and encountered various horrors, the effect being heightened by the unknown nature of the things one touched and was touched by. People have done things like that for as long as we have history. We go to movies to be scared, ride on roller coasters, read books, go to funhouses. Thrills are never cheap, no matter what they say. It takes skill to produce them, and art, and a knowledge of what will be genuinely thrilling and what will be only amusing.

You people had mixed success. Part of it was the kitchen-sink approach you took on this first trip. If you unified your theme the next time, stuck to a mutiny or an invasion, for instance, instead of mucking it up with all the other insanity you put in . . . but what am I saying? I don't want you to improve it. It's true that I was a little bemused by the unreality of the opener, but it was stark terror all the way when we approached the sun. My stomach still tightens just to think about it.

But—and I must cry it from the rooftops—you have gone too far. I'm basically conservative, as are all scientifiction writers, being concerned as we are with the past on Earth rather than the future in the stars. But I can't avoid thinking how frivolous it all was. Have we come to this? While our precious home planet remains under the three-hundred-year Occupation, do we devote ourselves to more and more elaborate ways of finding thrills?

I hope not.

There is a second consideration, one that I find it difficult to put into words. You hear of the "shipboard romance," when passengers become involved with each other only to part forever at their destination. Something of the sort happened to me and to Solace. We grew close on that loop through the corona. I didn't write about it. It's still painful. We clung to each other for two days. We made love with the stars at our feet.

We might even have remained involved, if our minds had been our own. But upon the utterance of that magic word we suddenly found that we were not the people we had been presenting ourselves as being. It's difficult enough to find out that one you care for is not the person she seemed to be; how much harder when it is *you* who are not what you thought you were?

It is a tremendous identity crisis, one that I am only now getting over. I, Quester, would not have behaved as I did aboard the *Snowball* if I had been in possession of all my faculties. We were tested, destructively tested in a way, to see if the injunction against discovering the underlying facts was strong enough to hold. It was, though I was beginning to see through the veils at the end. With a more consistent emergency I'm sure I would have had no inkling that it was anything but real. And that would be *much* worse. As it was, I was able to retain a degree of detachment, to entertain the notion that I might be insane. I was *right*.

The trip to the sun is thrill enough. Leave it at that, please, so that we may be sure of our loves and fears and not come to think that all might be illusion. I'll always have the memory of the way Solace looked when she woke from the dream she shared with me. The dream was gone; Solace was not the person I thought she might be. I'll have to look for solace elsewhere.

The Barbie Murders

THE BODY CAME TO the morgue at 2246 hours. No one paid much attention to it. It was a Saturday night, and the bodies were piling up like logs in a millpond. A harried attendant working her way down the row of stainless steel tables picked up the sheaf of papers that came with the body, peeling back the sheet over the face. She took a card from her pocket and scrawled on it, copying from the reports filed by the investigating officer and the hospital staff:

Ingraham, Leah Petrie. Female. Age: 35. Length: 2.1 meters. Mass: 59 kilograms. Dead on arrival, Crisium Emergency Terminal. Cause of death: homicide. Next of kin: unknown.

She wrapped the wire attached to the card around the left big toe, slid the dead weight from the table and onto the wheeled carrier, took it to cubicle 659A, and rolled out the long tray.

The door slammed shut, and the attendant placed the paperwork in the out tray, never noticing that, in his report, the investigating officer had not specified the sex of the corpse.

Lieutenant Anna-Louise Bach had moved into her new office three days ago and already the paper on her desk was threatening to avalanche onto the floor.

To call it an office was almost a perversion of the term. It had a file cabinet for pending cases; she could open it only at severe risk to life and limb. The drawers had a tendency to spring out at her, pinning her in her chair in the corner. To reach "A" she had to stand on her chair; "Z" required her either to sit on her desk or to straddle the bottom drawer with one foot in the legwell and the other against the wall.

But the office had a door. True, it could only be opened if no one was occupying the single chair in front of the desk.

Bach was in no mood to gripe. She loved the place. It was ten times better than the squadroom, where she had spent ten years elbow-to-elbow with the other sergeants and corporals.

Jorge Weil stuck his head in the door.

"Hi. We're taking bids on a new case. What am I offered?"

"Put me down for half a Mark," Bach said, without looking up from the report she was writing. "Can't you see I'm busy?"

"Not as busy as you're going to be." Weil came in without an invitation and settled himself in the chair. Bach looked up, opened her mouth, then said nothing. She had the authority to order him to get his big feet out of her "cases completed" tray, but not the experience in exercising it. And she and Jorge had worked together for three years. Why should a stripe of gold paint on her shoulder change their relationship? She supposed the informality was Weil's way of saying he wouldn't let her promotion bother him as long as she didn't get snotty about it.

Weil deposited a folder on top of the teetering pile marked "For Immediate Action," then leaned back again. Bach eyed the stack of paper—and the circular file mounted in the wall not half a meter from it, leading to the incinerator—and thought about having an accident. Just a careless nudge with an elbow . . .

"Aren't you even going to open it?" Weil asked, sounding disappointed. "It's not every day I'm going to hand-deliver a case."

"You tell me about it, since you want to so badly."

"All right. We've got a body, which is cut up pretty bad. We've got the murder weapon, which is a knife. We've got thirteen eyewitnesses who can describe the killer, but we don't really need them since the murder was committed in front of a television camera. We've got the tape."

"You're talking about a case which has to have been solved ten minutes after the first report, untouched by human hands. Give it to the computer, idiot." But she looked up. She didn't like the smell of it. "Why give it to me?"

"Because of the other thing we know. The scene of the crime. The murder was committed at the barbie colony."

"Oh, sweet Jesus."

The Temple of the Standardized Church in Luna was in the center of the Standardist Commune, Anytown, North Crisium. The best way to reach it, they found, was a local tube line which paralleled the Cross-Crisium Express Tube.

She and Weil checked out a blue-and-white police capsule with a priority sorting code and surrendered themselves to the New Dresden municipal transport system—the pill sorter, as the New Dresdenites called it. They were whisked through the precinct chute to the main nexus, where thousands of capsules were stacked awaiting a routing order to clear the computer. On the big conveyer which should have taken them to a holding cubby, they were snatched by a grapple—the cops called it the long arm of the law—and moved ahead to the multiple maws of the Cross-Crisium while people in other capsules glared at them. The capsule was inserted, and Bach and Weil were pressed hard into the backs of their seats.

In seconds they emerged from the tube and out onto the plain of Crisium, speeding along through the vacuum, magnetically suspended a few millimeters above the induction rail. Bach glanced up at the Earth, then stared out the window at the featureless landscape rushing by. She brooded.

It had taken a look at the map to convince her that the barbie colony was indeed in the New Dresden jurisdiction—a case of blatant gerrymandering if ever there was one. Anytown was fifty kilometers from what she thought of as the boundaries of New Dresden, but was joined to the city by a dotted line that represented a strip of land one meter wide.

A roar built up as they entered a tunnel and air was injected into the tube ahead of them. The car shook briefly as the shock wave built up, then they popped through pressure doors into the tube station of Anytown. The capsule doors hissed and they climbed out onto the platform.

The tube station at Anytown was primarily a loading dock and warehouse. It was a large space with plastic crates stacked against all the walls, and about fifty people working to load them into freight capsules.

Bach and Weil stood on the platform for a moment, uncertain where to go. The murder had happened at a spot not twenty meters in front of them, right here in the tube station.

"This place gives me the creeps," Weil volunteered.

"Me, too."

Every one of the fifty people Bach could see was identical to every other. All appeared to be female, though only faces, feet, and hands were visible, everything else concealed by loose white pajamas belted at the waist. They were all blonde; all had hair cut off at the shoulder and parted in the middle, blue eyes, high foreheads, short noses, and small mouths.

The work slowly stopped as the barbies became aware of them. They eyed Bach and Weil suspiciously. Bach picked one at random and approached her.

"Who's in charge here?" she asked.

"We are," the barbie said. Bach took it to mean the woman herself, recalling something about barbies never using the singular pronoun.

"We're supposed to meet someone at the temple," she said. "How do we get there?"

"Through that doorway," the woman said. "It leads to Main Street. Follow the street to the temple. But you really should cover yourselves."

"Huh? What do you mean?" Bach was not aware of anything wrong with the way she and Weil were dressed. True, neither of them wore as much as the barbies did. Bach wore her usual blue nylon briefs in addition to a regulation uniform cap, arm and thigh bands, and cloth-soled slippers. Her weapon, communicator, and handcuffs were fastened to a leather equipment belt.

"Cover yourself," the barbie said, with a pained look. "You're flaunting your differentness. And you, with all that hair . . ." There were giggles and a few shouts from the other barbies.

"Police business," Weil snapped.

"Uh, yes," Bach said, feeling annoyed that the barbie had put her on the defensive. After all, this was New Dresden, it was a public thoroughfare—even though by tradition and usage a Standardist enclave—and they were entitled to dress as they wished.

Main Street was a narrow, mean little place. Bach had expected a promenade like those in the shopping districts of New Dresden; what she found was indistinguishable from a residential corridor. They drew curious stares and quite a few frowns from the identical people they met.

There was a modest plaza at the end of the street. It had a low roof of bare metal, a few trees, and a blocky stone building in the center of a radiating network of walks.

A barbie who looked just like all the others met them at the entrance. Bach asked if she was the one Weil had spoken to on the phone, and she said she was. Bach wanted to know if they could go inside to talk. The barbie said the temple was off limits to outsiders and suggested they sit on a bench outside the building.

When they were settled, Bach started her questioning. "First, I need to know your name, and your title. I assume that you are . . . what was it?" She consulted her notes, taken hastily from a display she had called up on the computer terminal in her office. "I don't seem to have found a title for you."

"We have none," the barbie said. "If you must think of a title, consider us as the keeper of records."

"All right. And your name?"

"We have no name."

Bach sighed. "Yes, I understand that you forsake names when you come here. But you had one before. You were given one at birth. I'm going to have to have it for my investigation."

The woman looked pained. "No, you don't understand. It is true that this body had a name at one time. But it has been wiped from this one's mind. It would cause this one a great deal of pain to be reminded of it." She stumbled verbally every time she said "this one." Evidently even a polite circumlocution of the personal pronoun was distressing.

"I'll try to get it from another angle, then." This was already getting hard to deal with, Bach saw, and knew it could only get tougher. "You say you are the keeper of records."

"We are. We keep records because the law says we must. Each citizen must be recorded, or so we have been told."

"For a very good reason," Bach said. "We're going to need

access to those records. For the investigation. You understand? I assume an officer has already been through them, or the deceased couldn't have been identified as Leah P. Ingraham."

"That's true. But it won't be necessary for you to go through the records again. We are here to confess. We murdered L. P. Ingraham, serial number 11005. We are surrendering peacefully. You may take us to your prison." She held out her hands, wrists close together, ready to be shackled.

Weil was startled, reached tentatively for his handcuffs, then looked to Bach for guidance.

"Let me get this straight. You're saying you're the one who did it? You, personally."

"That's correct. We did it. We have never defied temporal authority, and we are willing to pay the penalty."

"Once more." Bach reached out and grasped the barbie's wrist, forced the hand open, palm up. "*This* is the person, this is the body that committed the murder? This hand, this one right here, held the knife and killed Ingraham? This hand, as opposed to 'your' thousands of other hands?"

The barbie frowned.

"Put that way, no. *This* hand did not grasp the murder weapon. But *our* hand did. What's the difference?"

"Quite a bit, in the eyes of the law." Bach sighed, and let go of the woman's hand. Woman? She wondered if the term applied. She realized she needed to know more about Standardists. But it was convenient to think of them as such, since their faces were feminine.

"Let's try again. I'll need you—and the eyewitnesses to the crime—to study the tape of the murder. *I* can't tell the difference between the murderer, the victim, or any of the bystanders. But surely you must be able to. I assume that . . . well, like the old saying went, 'all Chinamen look alike.' That was to Caucasian races, of course. Orientals had no trouble telling each other apart. So I thought that you . . . that you people would . . ." She trailed off at the look of blank incomprehension on the barbie's face.

"We don't know what you're talking about."

Bach's shoulders slumped.

"You mean you can't ... not even if you saw her again ... ?"
The woman shrugged. "We all look the same to this one."

Anna-Louise Bach sprawled out on her flotation bed later that
night, surrounded by scraps of paper. Untidy as it was, her thought
processes were helped by actually scribbling facts on paper rather
than filing them in her datalink. And she did her best work late
at night, at home, in bed, after taking a bath or making love.
Tonight she had done both and found she needed every bit of the
invigorating clarity it gave her.

Standardists.

They were an off-beat religious sect founded ninety years earlier by someone whose name had not survived. That was not
surprising, since Standardists gave up their names when they
joined the order, made every effort consistent with the laws of the
land to obliterate the name and person as if he or she had never
existed. The epithet "barbie" had quickly been attached to them
by the press. The origin of the word was a popular children's toy
of the twentieth and early twenty-first centuries, a plastic, sexless,
mass-produced "girl" doll with an elaborate wardrobe.

The barbies had done surprisingly well for a group which did
not reproduce, which relied entirely on new members from the
outside world to replenish their numbers. They had grown for
twenty years, then reached a population stability where deaths
equalled new members—which they call "components." They had
suffered moderately from religious intolerance, moving from
country to country until the majority had come to Luna sixty years
ago.

They drew new components from the walking wounded of
society, the people who had not done well in a world which
preached conformity, passivity, and tolerance of your billions of
neighbors, yet rewarded only those who were individualist and
aggressive enough to stand apart from the herd. The barbies had
opted out of a system where one had to be at once a face in the
crowd and a proud individual with hopes and dreams and desires.
They were the inheritors of a long tradition of ascetic withdrawal,
surrendering their names, their bodies, and their temporal aspi-
rations to a life that was ordered and easy to understand.

Bach realized she might be doing some of them a disservice

in that evaluation. They were not necessarily all losers. There must be those among them who were attracted simply by the religious ideas of the sect, though Bach felt there was little in the teachings that made sense.

She skimmed through the dogma, taking notes. The Standardists preached the commonality of humanity, denigrated free will, and elevated the group and the consensus to demi-god status. Nothing too unusual in the theory; it was the practice of it that made people queasy.

There was a creation theory and a godhead, who was not worshipped but contemplated. Creation happened when the Goddess—a prototypical earth-mother who had no name—gave birth to the universe. She put people in it, all alike, stamped from the same universal mold.

Sin entered the picture. One of the people began to wonder. This person had a name, given to him or her *after* the original sin as part of the punishment, but Bach could not find it written down anywhere. She decided that it was a dirty word which Standardists never told an outsider.

This person asked Goddess what it was all for. What had been wrong with the void, that Goddess had seen fit to fill it with people who didn't seem to have a reason for existing?

That was too much. For reasons unexplained—and impolite to even ask about—Goddess had punished humans by introducing differentness into the world. Warts, big noses, kinky hair, white skin, tall people and fat people and deformed people, blue eyes, body hair, freckles, testicles, and labia. A billion faces and fingerprints, each soul trapped in a body distinct from all others, with the heavy burden of trying to establish an identity in a perpetual shouting match.

But the faith held that peace was achieved in striving to regain that lost Eden. When all humans were again the same person, Goddess would welcome them back. Life was a testing, a trial.

Bach certainly agreed with that. She gathered her notes and shuffled them together, then picked up the book she had brought back from Anytown. The barbie had given it to her when Bach asked for a picture of the murdered woman.

It was a blueprint for a human being.

The title was *The Book of Specifications. The Specs,* for short.

Each barbie carried one, tied to her waist with a tape measure. It gave tolerances in engineering terms, defining what a barbie could look like. It was profusely illustrated with drawings of parts of the body in minute detail, giving measurements in millimeters.

She closed the book and sat up, propping her head on a pillow. She reached for her viewpad and propped it on her knees, punched the retrieval code for the murder tape. For the twentieth time that night, she watched a figure spring forward from a crowd of identical figures in the tube station, slash at Leah Ingraham, and melt back into the crowd as her victim lay bleeding and eviscerated on the floor.

She slowed it down, concentrating on the killer, trying to spot something different about her. Anything at all would do. The knife struck. Blood spurted. Barbies milled about in consternation. A few belatedly ran after the killer, not reacting fast enough. People seldom reacted quickly enough. But the killer had blood on her hand. Make a note to ask about that.

Bach viewed the film once more, saw nothing useful, and decided to call it a night.

The room was long and tall, brightly lit from strips high above. Bach followed the attendant down the rows of square locker doors which lined one wall. The air was cool and humid, the floor wet from a recent hosing.

The man consulted the card in his hand and pulled the metal handle on locker 659A, making a noise that echoed through the bare room. He slid the drawer out and lifted the sheet from the corpse.

It was not the first mutilated corpse Bach had seen, but it was the first nude barbie. She immediately noted the lack of nipples on the two hills of flesh that pretended to be breasts, and the smooth, unmarked skin in the crotch. The attendant was frowning, consulting the card on the corpse's foot.

"Some mistake here," he muttered. "Geez, the headaches. What do you do with a thing like that?" He scratched his head, then scribbled through the large letter "F" on the card, replacing it with a neat "N." He looked at Bach and grinned sheepishly. "What do you do?" he repeated.

Bach didn't much care what he did. She studied L. P. Ingraham's remains, hoping that something on the body would show her why a barbie had decided she must die.

There was little difficulty seeing *how* she had died. The knife had entered her abdomen, going deep, and the wound extended upward from there in a slash that ended beneath the breastbone. Part of the bone was cut through. The knife had been sharp, but it would have taken a powerful arm to slice through that much meat.

The attendant watched curiously as Bach pulled the dead woman's legs apart and studied what she saw there. She found the tiny slit of the urethra set back around the curve, just anterior to the anus.

Bach opened her copy of *The Specs*, took out a tape measure, and started to work.

"Mr. Atlas, I got your name from the Morphology Guide's files as a practitioner who's had a lot of dealings with the Standardist Church."

The man frowned, then shrugged. "So? You may not approve of them, but they're legal. And my records are in order. I don't do any work on anybody until the police have checked for a criminal record." He sat on the edge of the desk in the spacious consulting room, facing Bach. Mr. Rock Atlas—surely a *nom de métier*—had shoulders carved from granite, teeth like flashing pearls, and the face of a young god. He was a walking, flexing advertisement for his profession. Bach crossed her legs nervously. She had always had a taste for beef.

"I'm not investigating you, Mr. Atlas. This is a murder case, and I'd appreciate your cooperation."

"Call me Rock," he said, with a winning smile.

"Must I? Very well. I came to ask you what you would do, how long the work would take, if I asked to be converted to a barbie."

His face fell. "Oh, no, what a tragedy! I can't allow it. My dear, it would be a crime." He reached over to her and touched her chin lightly, turning her head. "No, Lieutenant, for you I'd build up the hollows in the cheeks just the slightest bit—maybe tighten up the muscles behind them—then drift the orbital bones out a little bit farther from the nose to set your eyes wider. More attention-getting, you understand. That touch of mystery. Then of course there's your nose."

She pushed his hand away and shook her head. "No, I'm not coming to you for the operation. I just want to know. How much work would it entail, and how close can you come to the specs of the church?" Then she frowned and looked at him suspiciously. "What's wrong with my nose?"

"Well, my dear, I didn't mean to imply there was anything *wrong;* in fact, it has a certain overbearing power that must be useful to you once in a while, in the circles you move in. Even the lean to the left could be justified, aesthetically—"

"Never mind," she said, angry at herself for having fallen into his sales pitch. "Just answer my question."

He studied her carefully, asked her to stand up and turn around. She was about to object that she had not necessarily meant herself personally as the surgical candidate, just a woman in general, when he seemed to lose interest in her.

"It wouldn't be much of a job," he said. "Your height is just slightly over the parameters; I could take that out of your thighs and lower legs, maybe shave some vertebrae. Take out some fat here and put it back there. Take off those nipples and dig out your uterus and ovaries, sew up your crotch. With a man, chop off the penis. I'd have to break up your skull a little and shift the bones around, then build up the face from there. Say two days work, one overnight and one outpatient."

"And when you were through, what would be left to identify me?"

"Say that again?"

Bach briefly explained her situation, and Atlas pondered it.

"You've got a problem. I take off the fingerprints and foot-prints. I don't leave any external scars, not even microscopic ones. No moles, freckles, warts or birthmarks; they all have to go. A blood test would work, and so would a retinal print. An X-ray of the skull. A voiceprint would be questionable. I even that out as much as possible. I can't think of anything else."

"Nothing that could be seen from a purely visual exam?"

"That's the whole point of the operation, isn't it?"

"I know. I was just hoping you might know something even the barbies were not aware of. Thank you, anyway."

He got up, took her hand, and kissed it. "No trouble. And if you ever decide to get that nose taken care of..."

She met Jorge Weil at the temple gate in the middle of Anytown. He had spent his morning there, going through the records, and she could see the work didn't agree with him. He took her back to the small office where the records were kept in battered file cabinets. There was a barbie waiting for them there. She spoke without preamble.

"We decided at equalization last night to help you as much as possible."

"Oh, yeah? Thanks. I wondered if you would, considering what happened fifty years ago."

Weil looked puzzled. "What was that?"

Bach waited for the barbie to speak, but she evidently wasn't going to.

"All right. I found it last night. The Standardists were involved in murder once before, not long after they came to Luna. You notice you never see one of them in New Dresden?"

Weil shrugged. "So what? They keep to themselves."

"They were *ordered* to keep to themselves. At first, they could move freely like any other citizens. Then one of them killed somebody—not a Standardist this time. It was known the murderer was a barbie; there were witnesses. The police started looking for the killer. You guess what happened."

"They ran into the problems we're having." Weil grimaced. "It doesn't look so good, does it?"

"It's hard to be optimistic," Bach conceded. "The killer was never found. The barbies offered to surrender one of their number at random, thinking the law would be satisfied with that. But of course it wouldn't do. There was a public outcry, and a lot of pressure to force them to adopt some kind of distinguishing characteristic, like a number tattooed on their foreheads. I don't think that would have worked, either. It could have been covered.

"The fact is that the barbies were seen as a menace to society. They could kill at will and blend back into their community like grains of sand on a beach. We would be powerless to punish a guilty party. There was no provision in the law for dealing with them."

"So what happened?"

"The case is marked closed, but there's no arrest, no conviction, and no suspect. A deal was made whereby the Standardists could practice their religion as long as they never mixed with other citizens. They had to stay in Anytown. Am I right?" She looked at the barbie.

"Yes. We've adhered to the agreement."

"I don't doubt it. Most people are barely aware you exist out here. But now we've got this. One barbie kills another barbie, and under a television camera..." Bach stopped, and looked thoughtful. "Say, it occurs to me... wait a minute. *Wait a minute*." She didn't like the look of it.

"I wonder. This murder took place in the tube station. It's the only place in Anytown that's scanned by the municipal security system. And fifty years is a long time between murders, even in a town as small as... how many people did you say live here, Jorge?"

"About seven thousand. I feel I know them all intimately." Weil had spent the day sorting barbies. According to measurements made from the tape, the killer was at the top end of permissible height.

"How about it?" Bach said to the barbie. "Is there anything I ought to know?"

The woman bit her lip, looked uncertain.

"Come on, you said you were going to help me."

"Very well. There have been three other killings in the last month. You would not have heard of this one except it took place with outsiders present. Purchasing agents were there on the loading platform. They made the initial report. There was nothing we could do to hush it up."

"But why would you want to?"

"Isn't it obvious? We exist with the possibility of persecution always with us. We don't wish to appear a threat to others. We wish to appear peaceful—which we *are*—and prefer to handle the problems of the group within the group itself. By divine consensus."

Bach knew she would get nowhere pursuing that line of reasoning. She decided to take the conversation back to the previous murders.

"Tell me what you know. Who was killed, and do you have any idea why? Or should I be talking to someone else?" Something occurred to her then, and she wondered why she hadn't asked it before. "You *are* the person I was speaking to yesterday, aren't you? Let me rephrase that. You're the body . . . that is, this body before me . . ."

"We know what you're talking about," the barbie said. "Uh, yes, you are correct. We are . . . *I* am the one you spoke to." She had to choke the word out, blushing furiously. "We have been . . . *I* have been selected as the component to deal with you, since it was perceived at equalization that this matter must be dealt with. This one was chosen as . . . *I* was chosen as punishment."

"You don't have to say 'I' if you don't want to."

"Oh, thank you."

"Punishment for what?"

"For . . . for individualistic tendencies. We spoke up too personally at equalization, in favor of cooperation with you. As a political necessity. The conservatives wish to stick to our sacred principles no matter what the cost. We are divided; this makes for bad feelings within the organism, for sickness. This one spoke out, and was punished by having her own way, by being appointed . . . *individually* . . . to deal with you." The woman could not meet Bach's eyes. Her face burned with shame.

"This one has been instructed to reveal her serial number to you. In the future, when you come here you are to ask for 23900."

Bach made a note of it.

"All right. What can you tell me about a possible motive? Do you think all the killings were done by the same . . . component?"

"We do not know. We are no more equipped to select an . . . individual from the group than you are. But there is great consternation. We are fearful."

"I would think so. Do you have reason to believe that the victims were . . . does this make sense? . . . *known* to the killer? Or were they random killings?" Bach hoped not. Random killers were the hardest to catch; without motive, it was hard to tie killer to victim, or to sift one person out of thousands with the opportunity. With the barbies, the problem would be squared and cubed.

"Again, we don't know."

Bach sighed. "I want to see the witnesses to the crime. I might as well start interviewing them."

In short order, thirteen barbies were brought. Bach intended to question them thoroughly to see if their stories were consistent, and if they had changed.

She sat them down and took them one at a time, and almost immediately ran into a stone wall. It took her several minutes to see the problem, frustrating minutes spent trying to establish which of the barbies had spoken to the officer first, which second, and so forth.

"Hold it. Listen carefully. Was this body physically present at the time of the crime? Did these eyes see it happen?"

The barbie's brow furrowed. "Why, no. But does it matter?"

"It does to me, babe. *Hey, twenty-three thousand*!"

The barbie stuck her head in the door. Bach looked pained.

"I need the actual people who were *there*. Not thirteen picked at random."

"The story is known to all."

Bach spent five minutes explaining that it made a difference to her, then waited an hour as 23900 located the people who were actual witnesses.

And again she hit a stone wall. The stories were absolutely identical, which she knew to be impossible. Observers *always* report events differently. They make themselves the hero, invent things before and after they first began observing, rearrange and edit and interpret. But not the barbies. Bach struggled for an hour, trying to shake one of them, and got nowhere. She was facing a consensus, something that had been discussed among the barbies until an account of the event had emerged and then been accepted as truth. It was probably a close approximation, but it did Bach no good. She needed discrepancies to gnaw at, and there were none.

Worst of all, she was convinced no one was lying to her. Had she questioned the thirteen random choices she would have gotten the same answers. They would have thought of themselves as having been there, since some of them had been and they had been told about it. What happened to one, happened to all.

Her options were evaporating fast. She dismissed the witnesses, called 23900 back in, and sat her down. Bach ticked off points on her fingers.

"One. Do you have the personal effects of the deceased?"

"We have no private property."

Bach nodded. "Two. Can you take me to her room?"

"We each sleep in any room we find available at night. There is no—"

"Right. Three. Any friends or co-workers I might..." Bach rubbed her forehead with one hand. "Right. Skip it. Four. What was her job? Where did she work?"

"All jobs are interchangeable here. We work at what needs—"

"*Right!*" Bach exploded. She got up and paced the floor. "What the hell do you expect me to *do* with a situation like this? I don't have *anything* to work with, not one snuffin' *thing*. No way of telling *why* she was killed, no way to pick out the *killer*, no way... ah, *shit*. What do you expect me to *do*?"

"We don't expect you to do anything," the barbie said, quietly. "We didn't ask you to come here. We'd like it very much if you just went away."

In her anger Bach had forgotten that. She was stopped, unable to move in any direction. Finally, she caught Weil's eye and jerked her head toward the door.

"Let's get out of here." Weil said nothing. He followed Bach out the door and hurried to catch up.

They reached the tube station, and Bach stopped outside their waiting capsule. She sat down heavily on a bench, put her chin on her palm, and watched the ant-like mass of barbies working at the loading dock.

"Any ideas?"

Weil shook his head, sitting beside her and removing his cap to wipe sweat from his forehead.

"They keep it too hot in here," he said. Bach nodded, not really hearing him. She watched the group of barbies as two separated themselves from the crowd and came a few steps in her direction. Both were laughing, as if at some private joke, looking right at Bach. One of them reached under her blouse and withdrew a long, gleaming steel knife. In one smooth motion she plunged it into the other barbie's stomach and lifted, bringing her up on the balls of her feet. The one who had been stabbed looked surprised for a moment, staring down at herself, her mouth open as the knife gutted her like a fish. Then her eyes widened and she stared horror-stricken at her companion, and slowly went to her knees, holding the knife to her as blood gushed out and soaked her white uniform.

"*Stop her!*" Bach shouted. She was on her feet and running, after a moment of horrified paralysis. It had looked *so* much like the tape.

She was about forty meters from the killer, who moved with deliberate speed, jogging rather than running. She passed the barbie who had been attacked—and who was now on her side, still holding the knife hilt almost tenderly to herself, wrapping her body around the pain. Bach thumbed the panic button on her communicator, glanced over her shoulder to see Weil kneeling beside the stricken barbie, then looked back—

—to a confusion of running figures. Which one was it? *Which one?*

She grabbed the one that seemed to be in the same place and moving in the same direction as the killer had been before she looked away. She swung the barbie around and hit her hard on the side of the neck with the edge of her palm, watched her fall while trying to look at all the other barbies at the same time. They were running in both directions, some trying to get away, others entering the loading dock to see what was going on. It was a madhouse scene with shrieks and shouts and baffling movement.

Bach spotted something bloody lying on the floor, then knelt by the inert figure and clapped the handcuffs on her.

She looked up into a sea of faces, all alike.

The commissioner dimmed the lights, and he, Bach, and Weil faced the big screen at the end of the room. Beside the screen was a department photoanalyst with a pointer in her hand. The tape began to run.

"Here they are," the woman said, indicating two barbies with the tip of the long stick. They were just faces on the edge of the crowd, beginning to move. "Victim right here, the suspect to her right." Everyone watched as the stabbing was re-created. Bach winced when she saw how long she had taken to react. In her favor, it had taken Weil a fraction of a second longer.

"Lieutenent Bach begins to move here. The suspect moves back toward the crowd. If you'll notice, she is watching Bach over her shoulder. Now. Here." She froze a frame. "Bach loses eye contact. The suspect peels off the plastic glove which prevented blood from staining her hand. She drops it, moves laterally. By the time Bach looks back, we can see she is after the wrong suspect."

Bach watched in sick fascination as her image assaulted the wrong barbie, the actual killer only a meter to her left. The tape resumed normal speed, and Bach watched the killer until her eyes began to hurt from not blinking. She would not lose her this time.

"She's incredibly brazen. She does not leave the room for another twenty minutes." Bach saw herself kneel and help the medical team load the wounded barbie into the capsule. The killer had been at her elbow, almost touching her. She felt her arm break out in goose pimples.

She remembered the sick fear that had come over her as she knelt by the injured woman. *It could be any of them. The one behind me, for instance . . .*

She had drawn her weapon then, backed against the wall, and not moved until the reinforcements arrived a few minutes later.

At a motion from the commissioner, the lights came back on.

"Let's hear what you have," he said.

Bach glanced at Weil, then read from her notebook.

"'Sergeant Weil was able to communicate with the victim shortly before medical help arrived. He asked her if she knew anything pertinent as to the identity of her assailant. She answered no, saying only that it was "the wrath." She could not elaborate.' I quote now from the account Sergeant Weil wrote down immediately after the interview. '"It hurts, it hurts." "I'm dying, I'm dying." I told her help was on the way. She responded: "I'm dying." Victim became incoherent, and I attempted to get a shirt from the onlookers to stop the flow of blood. No cooperation was forthcoming.'"

"It was the word 'I'," Weil supplied. "When she said that, they all started to drift away."

"'She became rational once more,'" Bach resumed, "'long enough to whisper a number to me. The number was twelve-fifteen, which I wrote down as one-two-one-five. She roused herself once more, said "I'm dying." '" Bach closed the notebook and looked up. "Of course, she was right." She coughed nervously.

"We invoked section 35b of the New Dresden Unified Code, 'Hot Pursuit,' suspending civil liberties locally for the duration of the search. We located component 1215 by the simple expedient of lining up all the barbies and having them pull their pants down. Each has a serial number in the small of her back. Component 1215, one Sylvester J. Cronhausen, is in custody at this moment.

"While the search was going on, we went to sleeping cubicle 1215 with a team of criminologists. In a concealed compartment beneath the bunk we found these items." Bach got up, opened the evidence bag, and spread the items on the table.

There was a carved wooden mask. It had a huge nose with a hooked end, a mustache, and a fringe of black hair around it. Beside the mask were several jars of powders and creams, grease-paint and cologne. One black nylon sweater, one pair black trousers, one pair black sneakers. A stack of pictures clipped from magazines, showing ordinary people, many of them wearing more clothes than was normal in Luna. There was a black wig and a merkin of the same color.

"What was that last?" the commissioner asked.

"A merkin, sir," Bach supplied. "A pubic wig."

"Ah." He contemplated the assortment, leaned back in his chair. "Somebody liked to dress up."

"Evidently, sir." Bach stood at ease with her hands clasped behind her back, her face passive. She felt an acute sense of failure, and a cold determination to get the woman with the gall to stand at her elbow after committing murder before her eyes. She was sure the time and place had been chosen deliberately, that the barbie had been executed for Bach's benefit.

"Do you think these items belonged to the deceased?"

"We have no reason to state that, sir," Bach said. "However, the circumstances are suggestive."

"Of what?"

"I can't be sure. These things *might* have belonged to the victim. A random search of other cubicles turned up nothing like this. We showed the items to component 23900, our liaison. She professed not to know their purpose." She stopped, then added, "I believe she was lying. She looked quite disgusted."

"Did you arrest her?"

"No, sir. I didn't think it wise. She's the only connection we have, such as she is."

The commissioner frowned, and laced his fingers together. "I'll leave it up to you, Lieutenant Bach. Frankly, we'd like to be shut of this mess as soon as possible."

"I couldn't agree with you more, sir."

"Perhaps you don't understand me. We have to have a warm body to indict. We have to have one soon."

"Sir, I'm doing the best I can. Candidly, I'm beginning to wonder if there's anything I *can* do."

"You still don't understand me." He looked around the office. The stenographer and photoanalyst had left. He was alone with Bach and Weil. He flipped a switch on his desk, turning a recorder *off*, Bach realized.

"The news is picking up on this story. We're beginning to get some heat. On the one hand, people are afraid of these barbies. They're hearing about the murder fifty years ago, and the informal agreement. They don't like it much. On the other hand, there's the civil libertarians. They'll fight hard to prevent anything happening to the barbies, on principle. The government doesn't want to get into a mess like that. I can hardly blame them."

Bach said nothing, and the commissioner looked pained.

"I see I have to spell it out. We have a suspect in custody," he said.

"Are you referring to component 1215, Sylvester Cronhausen?"

"No. I'm speaking of the one you captured."

"Sir, the tape clearly shows she is not the guilty party. She was an innocent bystander." She felt her face heat up as she said it. Damn it; she had tried her best.

"Take a look at this." He pressed a button and the tape began to play again. But the quality was much impaired. There were bursts of snow, moments when the picture faded out entirely. It was a very good imitation of a camera failing. Bach watched herself running through the crowd—there was a flash of white— and she had hit the woman. The lights came back on in the room.

"I've checked with the analyst. She'll go along. There's a bonus in this, for both of you." He looked from Weil to Bach.

"I don't think I can go through with that, sir."

He looked like he'd tasted a lemon. "I didn't say we were doing this today. It's an option. But I ask you to look at it this way, just look at it, and I'll say no more. This is the way *they themselves* want it. They offered you the same deal the first time you were there. Close the case with a confession, no mess. We've already got this prisoner. She just says she killed her, she killed all of them. I want you to ask yourself, is she wrong? By her own lights and moral values? She believes she shares responsibility for the murders, and society demands a culprit. What's wrong with accepting their compromise and letting this all blow over?"

"Sir, it doesn't feel right to me. This is not in the oath I took. I'm supposed to protect the innocent, and she's innocent. She's the *only* barbie I *know* to be innocent."

The commissioner sighed. "Bach, you've got four days. You give me an alternative by then."

"Yes, sir. If I can't, I'll tell you now that I won't interfere with what you plan. But you'll have to accept my resignation."

Anna-Louise Bach reclined in the bathtub with her head pillowed on a folded towel. Only her neck, nipples, and knees stuck out above the placid surface of the water, tinted purple with a generous helping of bath salts. She clenched a thin cheroot in her teeth. A ribbon of lavender smoke curled from the end of it, rising to join the cloud near the ceiling.

She reached up with one foot and turned on the taps, letting out cooled water and refilling with hot until the sweat broke out on her brow. She had been in the tub for several hours. The tips of her fingers were like washboards.

There seemed to be few alternatives. The barbies were foreign to her, and to anyone she could assign to interview them. They didn't want her help in solving the crimes. All the old rules and procedures were useless. Witnesses meant nothing; one could not tell one from the next, nor separate their stories. Opportunity? Several thousand individuals had it. Motive was a blank. She had a physical description in minute detail, even tapes of the actual murders. Both were useless.

There was one course of action that might show results. She had been soaking for hours in the hope of determining just how important her job was to her.

Hell, what else did she want to do?

She got out of the tub quickly, bringing a lot of water with her to drip onto the floor. She hurried into her bedroom, pulled the sheets off the bed and slapped the nude male figure on the buttocks.

"Come on, Svengali," she said. "Here's your chance to do something about my nose."

She used every minute while her eyes were functioning to read all she could find about Standardists. When Atlas worked on her eyes, the computer droned into an earphone. She memorized most of the *Book of Standards*.

Ten hours of surgery, followed by eight hours flat on her back, paralyzed, her body undergoing forced regeneration, her eyes scanning the words that flew by on an overhead screen.

Three hours of practice, getting used to shorter legs and arms. Another hour to assemble her equipment.

When she left the Atlas clinic, she felt she would pass for a barbie as long as she kept her clothes on. She hadn't gone *that* far.

People tended to forget about access locks that led to the surface. Bach had used the fact more than once to show up in places where no one expected her.

She parked her rented crawler by the lock and left it there. Moving awkwardly in her pressure suit, she entered and started it cycling, then stepped through the inner door into an equipment room in Anytown. She stowed the suit, checked herself quickly in a washroom mirror, straightened the tape measure that belted her loose white jumpsuit, and entered the darkened corridors.

What she was doing was not illegal in any sense, but she was on edge. She didn't expect the barbies to take kindly to her masquerade if they discovered it, and she knew how easy it was for a barbie to vanish forever. Three had done so before Bach ever got the case.

The place seemed deserted. It was late evening by the arbitrary day cycle of New Dresden. Time for the nightly equalization. Bach hurried down the silent hallways to the main meeting room in the temple.

It was full of barbies and a vast roar of conversation. Bach had no trouble slipping in, and in a few minutes she knew her facial work was as good as Atlas had promised.

Equalization was the barbie's way of standardizing experience. They had been unable to simplify their lives to the point where each member of the community experienced the same things every day; the *Book of Standards* said it was a goal to be aimed for, but probably unattainable this side of Holy Reassimilation with Goddess. They tried to keep the available jobs easy enough that each member could do them all. The commune did not seek to make a profit; but air, water, and food had to be purchased, along with replacement parts and services to keep things running. The community had to produce things to trade with the outside.

They sold luxury items: hand-carved religious statues, illuminated holy books, painted crockery, and embroidered tapestries. None of the items were Standardist. The barbies had no religious symbols except their uniformity and the tape measure, but nothing in their dogma prevented them from selling objects of reverence to people of other faiths.

Bach had seen the products for sale in the better shops. They were meticulously produced, but suffered from the fact that each item looked too much like every other. People buying hand-produced luxuries in a technological age tend to want the differences that non-machine production entails, whereas the barbies wanted everything to look exactly alike. It was an ironic situation, but the barbies willingly sacrificed value by adhering to their standards.

Each barbie did things during the day that were as close as possible to what everyone else had done. But someone had to cook meals, tend the air machines, load the freight. Each component had a different job each day. At equalization, they got together and tried to even that out.

It was boring. Everyone talked at once, to anyone that happened to be around. Each woman told what she had done that day. Bach heard the same group of stories a hundred times before the night was over, and repeated them to anyone who would listen.

Anything unusual was related over a loudspeaker so everyone could be aware of it and thus spread out the intolerable burden of anomaly. No barbie wanted to keep a unique experience to herself; it made her soiled, unclean, until it was shared by all.

Bach was getting very tired of it—she was short on sleep—when the lights went out. The buzz of conversation shut off as if a tape had broken.

"All cats are alike in the dark," someone muttered, quite near Bach. Then a single voice was raised. It was solemn; almost a chant.

"We are the wrath. There is blood on our hands, but it is the holy blood of cleansing. We have told you of the cancer eating at the heart of the body, and yet still you cower away from what must be done. *The filth must be removed from us*!"

Bach was trying to tell which direction the words were coming from in the total darkness. Then she became aware of movement, people brushing against her, all going in the same direction. She began to buck the tide when she realized everyone was moving away from the voice.

"You think you can use our holy uniformity to hide among us, but the vengeful hand of Goddess will not be stayed. The mark is upon you, our one-time sisters. Your sins have set you apart, and retribution will strike swiftly.

"There are five of you left. Goddess knows who you are, and will not tolerate your perversion of her holy truth. Death will strike you when you least expect it. Goddess sees the differentness within you, the differentness you seek but hope to hide from your upright sisters."

People were moving more swiftly now, and a scuffle had developed ahead of her. She struggled free of people who were breathing panic from every pore, until she stood in a clear space. The speaker was shouting to be heard over the sound of whimpering and the shuffling of bare feet. Bach moved foward, swinging her outstretched hands. But another hand brushed her first.

The punch was not centered on her stomach, but it drove the air from her lungs and sent her sprawling. Someone tripped over her, and she realized things would get pretty bad if she didn't get to her feet. She was struggling up when the lights came back on.

There was a mass sigh of relief as each barbie examined her neighbor. Bach half expected another body to be found, but that didn't seem to be the case. The killer had vanished again.

She slipped away from the equalization before it began to break up, and hurried down the deserted corridors to room 1215.

She sat in the room—little more than a cell, with a bunk, a chair, and a light on a table—for more than two hours before the door opened, as she had hoped it would. A barbie stepped inside, breathing hard, closed the door, and leaned against it.

"We wondered if you would come," Bach said, tentatively.

The woman ran to Bach and collapsed at her knees, sobbing.

"Forgive us, please forgive us, our darling. We didn't dare come last night. We were afraid that...that if...that it might have been you who was murdered, and that the wrath would be waiting for us here. Forgive us, forgive us."

"It's all right," Bach said, for lack of anything better. Suddenly, the barbie was on top of her, kissing her with a desperate passion. Bach was startled, though she had expected something of the sort. She responded as best she could. The barbie finally began to talk again.

"We must stop this, we just have to stop. We're so frightened of the wrath, but...but the *longing!* We can't stop ourselves. We need to see you so badly that we can hardly get through the day, not knowing if you are across town or working at our elbow. It builds all day, and at night, we cannot stop ourselves from sinning yet again." She was crying, more softly this time, not from happiness at seeing the woman she took Bach to be, but from a depth of desperation. "What's going to become of us?" she asked, helplessly.

"Shhh," Bach soothed. "It's going to be all right."

She comforted the barbie for a while, then saw her lift her head. Her eyes seemed to glow with a strange light.

"I can't wait any longer," she said. She stood up, and began taking off her clothes. Bach could see her hands shaking.

Beneath her clothing the barbie had concealed a few things that looked familiar. Bach could see that the merkin was already in place between her legs. There was a wooden mask much like the one that had been found in the secret panel, and a jar. The barbie unscrewed the top of it and used her middle finger to smear dabs of brown onto her breasts, making stylized nipples.

"Look what *I* got," she said, coming down hard on the pronoun, her voice trembling. She pulled a flimsy yellow blouse from the pile of clothing on the floor, and slipped it over her shoulders. She struck a pose, then strutted up and down the tiny room.

"Come on, darling," she said. "Tell me how beautiful I am. Tell me I'm lovely. Tell me I'm the only one for you. The only one. What's the *matter*? Are you still frightened? I'm not. I'll dare anything for you, my one and only love." But now she stopped walking and looked suspiciously at Bach. "Why aren't you getting dressed?"

"We . . . uh, I can't," Bach said, extemporizing. "They, uh, someone found the things. They're all gone." She didn't dare remove her clothes because her nipples and pubic hair would look too real, even in the dim light.

The barbie was backing away. She picked up her mask and held it protectively to her. "What do you mean? Was she here? The wrath? Are they after us? It's true, isn't it? They can see us." She was on the edge of crying again, near panic.

"No, no, I think it was the police—" But it was doing no good. The barbie was at the door now, and had it half open.

"You're her! What have you done to . . . no, no, you stay away." She reached into the clothing that she now held in her hand, and Bach hesitated for a moment, expecting a knife. It was enough time for the barbie to dart quickly through the door, slamming it behind her.

When Bach reached the door, the woman was gone.

Bach kept reminding herself that she was not here to find the other potential victims—of whom her visitor was certainly one—but to catch the killer. The fact remained that she wished she could have detained her, to question her further.

The woman was a pervert, by the only definition that made any sense among the Standardists. She, and presumably the other dead barbies, had an individuality fetish. When Bach had realized that, her first thought had been to wonder why they didn't simply leave the colony and become whatever they wished. But then why did a Christian seek out prostitutes? For the taste of sin. In the larger world, what these barbies did would have had little meaning. Here, it was sin of the worst and tastiest kind.

And somebody didn't like it at all.

The door opened again, and the woman stood there facing Bach, her hair disheveled, breathing hard.

"We had to come back," she said. "We're so sorry that we

panicked like that. Can you forgive us?" She was coming toward Bach now, her arms out. She looked so vulnerable and contrite that Bach was astonished when the fist connected with her cheek.

Bach thudded against the wall, then found herself pinned under the woman's knees, with something sharp and cool against her throat. She swallowed very carefully, and said nothing. Her throat itched unbearably.

"She's dead," the barbie said. "And you're next." But there was something in her face that Bach didn't understand. The barbie brushed at her eyes a few times, and squinted down at her.

"Listen, I'm not who you think I am. If you kill me, you'll be bringing more trouble on your sisters than you can imagine."

The barbie hesitated, then roughly thrust her hand down into Bach's pants. Her eyes widened when she felt the genitals, but the knife didn't move. Bach knew she had to talk fast, and say all the right things.

"You understand what I'm talking about, don't you?" She looked for a response, but saw none. "You're aware of the political pressures that are coming down. You know this whole colony could be wiped out if you look like a threat to the outside. You don't want that."

"If it must be, it will be," the barbie said. "The purity is the important thing. If we die, we shall die pure. The blasphemers must be killed."

"I don't care about that anymore," Bach said, and finally got a ripple of interest from the barbie. "I have my principles, too. Maybe I'm not as fanatical about them as you are about yours. But they're important to me. One is that the guilty be brought to justice."

"You have the guilty party. Try her. Execute her. She will not protest."

"*You* are the guilty party."

The woman smiled. "So arrest us."

"All right, all right. I can't, obviously. Even if you don't kill me, you'll walk out that door and I'll never be able to find you. I've given up on that. I just don't have the time. This was my last chance, and it looks like it didn't work."

"We didn't think you could do it, even with more time. But why should we let you live?"

"Because we can help each other." She felt the pressure ease up a little, and managed to swallow again. "You don't want to kill me, because it could destroy your community. Myself . . . I need to be able to salvage some self-respect out of this mess. I'm willing to accept your definition of morality and let you be the law in your own community. Maybe you're even right. Maybe you *are* one being. But I can't let that woman be convicted, when I *know* she didn't kill anyone."

The knife was not touching her neck now, but it was still being held so that the barbie could plunge it into her throat at the slightest movement.

"And if we let you live? What do you get out of it? How do you free your 'innocent' prisoner?"

"Tell me where to find the body of the woman you just killed. I'll take care of the rest."

The pathology team had gone and Anytown was settling down once again. Bach sat on the edge of the bed with Jorge Weil. She was as tired as she ever remembered being. How long had it been since she slept?

"I'll tell you," Weil said, "I honestly didn't think this thing would work. I guess I was wrong."

Bach sighed. "I wanted to take her alive, Jorge. I thought I could. But when she came at me with the knife . . ." She let him finish the thought, not caring to lie to him. She'd already done that to the interviewer. In her story, she had taken the knife from her assailant and tried to disable her, but was forced in the end to kill her. Luckily, she had the bump on the back of her head from being thrown against the wall. It made a blackout period plausible. Otherwise, someone would have wondered why she waited so long to call for police and an ambulance. The barbie had been dead for an hour when they arrived.

"Well, I'll hand it to you. You sure pulled this out. I'll admit it, I was having a hard time deciding if I'd do as you were going to do and resign, or if I could have stayed on. Now I'll never know."

"Maybe it's best that way. I don't really know, either."

Jorge grinned at her. "I can't get used to thinking of *you* being behind that godawful face."

"Neither can I, and I don't want to see any mirrors. I'm going straight to Atlas and get it changed back." She got wearily to her feet and walked toward the tube station with Weil.

She had not quite told him the truth. She did intend to get her own face back as soon as possible—nose and all—but there was one thing left to do.

From the first, a problem that had bothered her had been the question of how the killer identified her victims.

Presumably the perverts had arranged times and places to meet for their strange rites. That would have been easy enough. Any one barbie could easily shirk her duties. She could say she was sick, and no one would know it was the same barbie who had been sick yesterday, and for a week or month before. She need not work; she could wander the halls acting as if she was on her way from one job to another. No one could challenge her. Likewise, while 23900 had said no barbie spent consecutive nights in the same room, there was no way for her to know that. Evidently room 1215 had been taken over permanently by the perverts.

And the perverts would have no scruples about identifying each other by serial number at their clandestine meetings, though they could do it in the streets. The killer didn't even have that.

But someone had known how to identify them, to pick them out of a crowd. Bach thought she must have infiltrated meetings, marked the participants in some way. One could lead her to another, until she knew them all and was ready to strike.

She kept recalling the strange way the killer had looked at her, the way she had squinted. The mere fact that she had not killed Bach instantly in a case of mistaken identity meant she had been expecting to see something that had not been there.

And she had an idea about that.

She meant to go to the morgue first, and to examine the corpses under different wavelengths of lights, with various filters. She was betting some kind of mark would become visible on the faces, a mark the killer had been looking for with her contact lenses.

It had to be something that was visible only with the right kind of equipment, or under the right circumstances. If she kept at it long enough, she would find it.

If it was an invisible ink, it brought up another interesting question. How had it been applied? With a brush or spray gun?

Unlikely. But such an ink on the killer's hands might look and feel like water.

Once she had marked her victims, the killer would have to be confident the mark would stay in place for a reasonable time. The murders had stretched over a month. So she was looking for an indelible, invisible ink, one that soaked into pores.

And if it was indelible...

There was no use thinking further about it. She was right, or she was wrong. When she struck the bargain with the killer she had faced up to the possibility that she might have to live with it. Certainly she could not now bring a killer into court, not after what she had just said.

No, if she came back to Anytown and found a barbie whose hands were stained with guilt, she would have to do the job herself.

Equinoctial

PARAMETER KNEW SHE WAS being followed. They had been behind her for days, always far enough behind that they couldn't get a permanent fix on her, but never so far that she could lose them. She was in danger, but now was not the time to worry about it.

Now was one of the big moments in her life. She proposed to savor it to the full and refused to be distracted by the hunters. She was giving birth to quintuplets.

Uni, Duo, Tri, Quad . . . Hopelessly trite. *Doc, Happy, Sneezy, Grumpy*—no, there were seven of those. *Army, Navy, Marine, Airforce, Coastguard?* That was a pentagon, for an interesting pun. But who wanted to be called Coastguard? What *was* a Coastguard, anyway?

She put the naming ordeal out of her mind. It wasn't important; they would pick their own names when the time came. She just thought it might be nice with *five* to have something to tag them with, if only for bookkeeping purposes.

"They just got another sighting," she thought, but it wasn't her own thought. It was the voice of Equinox. Equinox was Parameter's companion, her environment, her space suit, her alter ego; her Symb. She looked in the direction she had come from.

She looked back on the most spectacular scene in the solar system. She was 230,000 kilometers from the center of Saturn, according to the figures floating in the upper left corner of her field of vision. To one side of her was the yellow bulk of the giant planet, and all around her was a golden line that bisected the universe. She was inside the second and brightest of the Rings.

But Saturn and the Rings was not all she saw. About ten degrees away from Saturn and in the plane of the Rings was a hazy thing like the bell of a trumpet. It was transparent. The wide end of the bell was facing her. Within this shape were four lines of red that were sharp and well-defined far away but became fuzzy as they neared her. These were the hunters. All around her, but concentrated in the plane of the Rings, were slowly moving lines of all colors, each with an arrow at one end, each shifting perspective in a dazzling 3-D ballet.

None of it—the lines, the bells, the "hunters," even Saturn itself—none of it was any more real than the image in a picture tube. Some of it was even less real than that. The shifting lines, for instance, were vector representations of the large chunks of rock and ice within radar range of Equinox.

The bell was closer than it had been for days. That was bad news, because the space-time event it represented was the approach of the hunters and their possible locations projected from the time of the last fix. The fuzzy part was almost touching her. That meant they could be very close indeed, though it wasn't too likely. They were probably back in the stem where the projection looked almost solid, and almost certainly within the four lines that were their most probable location. But it was still too close.

"Since they know where we are, let's get a fix on *them*," Parameter decided, and as she thought it the bell disappeared, to be replaced by four red points that grew tails even as she watched.

"Too close. Way too close." Now they had two fixes on her: one of their own, and the one she had given them by bouncing a signal off them. From this, their Symbs could plot a course; therefore, it was time to alter it.

She couldn't afford to change course in the usual way, by bouncing off a rock. The hunters were close enough that they would detect the change in the rock's velocity and get a better idea of where she was. It was time for thrusters, though she could ill afford the wasted mass.

"Which way?" she asked.

"I suggest you move out of the plane. They won't expect that yet. They don't know you're in labor."

"That's pretty dangerous. There's nothing to hide in out there."

Equinox considered it. "If they get any closer, you'll have to do something at least that drastic, with less chance of success. But I only advise."

"Sure. All right, do it, my green pasture."

The world around her jerked, and all the colored lines started moving down around her, bending as their relative velocity changed. There was a gentle pressure at the small of her back.

"Keep an eye on them. I'm going back to the business of giving birth. How are they doing, by the way?"

"No sweat. One of the girls is in the tube right now—you can feel her—"

"You can tell me *that* three times . . ."

"—and she's a little puzzled by the pressure. But she's taking it well. She tells you not to worry, she'll be all right."

"Can I talk to her yet?"

"Not for another few hours. Be patient."

"Right. It shouldn't be long now."

And that was very true. She felt the wave of sensation as her uterus contracted again. She looked down at herself, absently expecting to see the first head coming out. But she could no longer see that far; her belly stuck out.

Nothing that Parameter saw was real; all was illusion. Her head was completely enclosed in the thick, opaque substance of Equinox, and all the sensory data she received was through the direct connection from Equinox's senses into her own brain. Much of this information was edited and embellished in ways that made it easier for Parameter to interpret.

So it was that when she looked down at herself she saw not the dark-green surface of Equinox, but her own brown skin. She had asked for that illusion long ago, when it had become a matter of some importance to her to believe she still had her own body. The illusion was flawless. She could see the fingerprints on her hand, the mole on her knee, the color of her nipples, the sentimental scar on her forearm, all illuminated by the soft diffusion of light from the Rings. But if she tried to touch herself, her hand would be stopped while still a good distance from what she saw as the surface of her body. Equinox was invisible to her, but she was certainly there.

She watched as the contraction caused her stomach to writhe and flow like putty. This was more like it. She remembered her other deliveries, before she married Equinox. One had been "natural" and it hadn't worked all that well. She didn't regret it, but it had been painful, not something she would want to repeat. The other had been under anesthetic, and no fun at all. She might as well not have bothered; there had been no pain, no pleasure, no *sensation*. It was like reading about it in the newspaper. But this one, her third birth, was different. It was intense, so intense she had difficulty concentrating on eluding the hunters. But there was no pain. All she felt was a series of waves of pleasure-pain that didn't hurt, and could be related to no other sensation humans had ever experienced.

One of the lines ahead seemed to point almost directly at her. It was a thick red line, meaning it was seventy percent ice and about a million kilograms in mass. The vector was short. It was moving slowly enough that rendezvous would be easy.

She took the opportunity and altered course slightly with the sure instinct she had developed. The line swung, foreshortened even more, then flashed brighter and began to pulse. This was the collision warning from Equinox's plotting sector.

When the rock was close enough to see as an object rather than a simulated projection, she rotated until her legs pointed at it. She soaked up the shock of the landing, then began to scuttle over the surface in a manner quite astonishing, and with a speed not to be believed. She moved with the coordinated complexity of a spider, all four limbs grasping at the rock and ice.

To an observer, she was a comical sight. She looked like a barbell with arms and legs and a bulge at the top that just might be a head. There were no creases or sharp lines anywhere on the outer surface of Equinox; all was gentle curves, absolutely featureless except for short claws on the hands and feet. At the ends of her legs were grasping appendages more like oversized hands than feet. And her legs bent the wrong way. Her knees were hinged to bend away from each other.

But she swarmed over the rock with effortless ease, not even hampered by her pregnancy, though the labor "pains" were getting intense.

When she was where she wanted to be, she pushed off with both hands and peds, rising rapidly. She was now on a course about ninety degrees away from her pursuers. She hoped they would not be expecting this. Now she had to rely on the screening effect of the billions of tiny rocks and ice crystals around her. For the next few hours she would be vulnerable if they beamed in her direction, but she didn't think it likely they would. Their Symbs would be plotting a course for her almost opposite to the one she was actually taking. If she had continued that way they would certainly have caught her later when she was burdened with five infants. Now was the time for audacity.

Having done that, she put the matter out of her mind again, and none too soon. The first baby had arrived.

The head was just emerging as she pushed off the rock. She savored the delicious agony as the head forced its way through her body, struggling to reach the air. It would never reach it. There was no air out here, just another womb that Equinox had prepared, a womb the baby would live in for the rest of its life. No first breath for Parameter's children; no breath at all.

The babies were not full-term. Each had been growing only seven months and would not be able to survive without extensive care. But Equinox was the world's best incubator. She had counseled, and Parameter had agreed, that it would be best to birth them while they were still small and get them out where Equinox could keep a closer eye on them.

Parameter moved her strangely articulated legs, bringing the hand-like peds up to the baby. She pressed slowly and felt the peds sink in as Equinox absorbed the outer covering. Then she felt the head with her own nerve endings. She ran her long fingers over the wet ball. There was another contraction and the baby was out. She was holding it in her peds. She couldn't see much of it, and suddenly she wanted to.

"This is one of the girls, right?"

"Yes. And so are two, three, and five. Navy, Marine, and Coastguard, if you want to get more personal."

"Those were just tags," she laughed. "I didn't even like them."

"Until you think of something else, they'll do."

"*They* won't want them."

"Perhaps not. Anyway, I'm thinking of shifting the boy around to fifth position. There's a little tangling of the cords."

"Whatever you want. I'd like to see her. 'Army,' I mean."

"Do you want a picture, or should I move her?"

"Move her." She knew it was only a semantic quibble as to whether she would actually "see" her child. The projection Equinox could provide would look just as real, hanging in space. But she wanted the picture to coincide with the feel she was getting of the baby against her skin.

By undulating the inner surface of her body, Equinox was able to move the infant around the curve of Parameter's belly until she was visible. She was wet, but there was no blood; Equinox had already absorbed it all.

"I want to touch her with my hands," Parameter thought.

"Go ahead. But don't forget there's another coming in a few minutes."

"Hold it up. I want to enjoy this one first."

She put her hands on the invisible surface of Equinox and they sank in until she was holding the child. It stirred and opened its mouth, but no sound came. There seemed to be no trauma involved for the brand-new human being; she moved her arms and legs slowly but seemed content to lie still for the most part. Compared to most human children, she hadn't really been born at all. Parameter tried to interest her in a nipple, but she didn't want it. She was the prettiest thing Parameter had ever seen.

"Let's get the next one out," she said. "This is so extravagant I still can't believe it. Five!"

She drifted into a wonderful haze as the others arrived, each as pretty as the last. Soon she was covered with tiny bodies, each still tied to an umbilicus. The cords would be left in place until Equinox had finished her childbirth and had five semiautonomous baby Symbs to receive the children. Until then, the children were still a part of her. It was a feeling Parameter loved; she would never be closer to her children.

"Can you hear them yet?" Equinox asked.

"No, not yet."

"You'll have to wait a while longer for mind contact. I'm tuning out. Are you all right? I shouldn't be longer than about two hours."

"Don't worry about me. I'll be fine. In fact, I've never been happier." She stopped verbalizing and let a wave of intense love flood over her; love for her invisible mate. It was answered by such an outpouring of affection that Parameter was in tears. "I love you, earthmother," she said.

"And you, sunshine."

"I hope it'll be as good for you as it was for me."

"I wish I could share it with you. But back to business. I really think we've shaken the hunters. There's been no signal from them for an hour, and their projected path is well away from us. I think we'll be safe, at least for a few hours."

"I hope so. But don't worry about me. I'll get along while you're away. I'm not scared of the dark."

"I know. It won't be for long. See you later."

Parameter felt her mate slipping away. For a moment she *was* afraid, but not of the dark. She was afraid of the loneliness. Equinox would be unavailable to her for the time it took to give birth to her children, and that meant she would be cut off from the outside. That didn't matter, but the absence of Equinox from Parameter's mind was a little frightening. It recalled an unpleasant incident in her past.

But as the lights faded she realized she was not alone. Cut off from sight, sound, smell, and taste by the shutdown of Equinox's interpretative faculties, she still had touch, and that was enough.

She floated in total darkness and felt the sharp tingle as a mouth found a nipple and began to suck. Imperceptibly, she drifted into sleep.

She awoke to a vague feeling of discomfort. It was small and nagging, and impossible to ignore. She felt in her mind for Equinox, and couldn't find her. So she was still in the process of giving birth.

But the feeling persisted. She felt helpless in the dark, then she realized it wasn't totally dark. There was a faint pinkness, like looking into closed eyelids. She could not account for it. Then she knew what was wrong, and it was worse than she could have imagined. The babies were gone.

She felt over her body with increasing panic, but they were nowhere to be found. Before her panic overwhelmed her, she tried to think of what could have happened that would have separated them, and all she could come up with was the hunters. But why would they take the babies? Then she lost control; there was nothing she could do in the darkness without Equinox to create the universe for her.

She was drawn back to rationality by a thought so black she could hardly credit it. In torment, she opened her eyes.

She could see.

She was floating in the center of a room hollowed out of bare rock. There was another person in the room, or rather another symbiote; all she could see was the dark-green, curved form of the Symb.

"Equinox!" she yelled, and heard herself. In a dream, she looked down at her body and felt the bare reality of it. She touched herself; there was no resistance. She was alone. Half of her was gone.

Her mind was dissolving; She watched it go, and knew it to be preferable to facing life without Equinox. She said good-bye to the last shreds of reality, rolled her eyes up into her head, and swallowed her tongue.

The figure looked like a cartoon of a human drawn by a three-year-old, one who was confused about sex. The broad shoulders and bullish neck were ludicrously like the build of a weightlifter, and the narrowing waist and bulbous ass were a moron's idea of a well-built woman. He was green, and featureless except for an oval opening where his mouth should have been.

"Just why do you want to become a Ringer?" The sound issued from the hole in his "face."

Parameter sighed and leaned back in her chair. The operation at Titan was anything but efficient. She had spent three days talking to people who had been no help at all and finally found this man, who seemed to have the authority to give her a Symb. Her patience—never very long—was at an end.

"I should make a tape," she said. "You're the fourth bastard who's asked me that today."

"Nevertheless, I must have your answer. And why don't you keep the smart remarks to yourself? I don't need them. For two cents I'd walk out of here and forget about you."

"Why don't you? I don't think you can even get out of that chair, much less walk out of here. I never expected anything like this. I thought you Consers wanted new people, so why are you giving me such a runaround? I might get up and walk out myself. You people aren't the only Ringers."

He proved her wrong by rising from the chair. He was awkward but steady, and, even more interesting, there was something in his hand that could only be a gun. She was amazed. He was sitting in a bare room, and had been empty-handed. Suddenly there was this gun, out of nowhere.

"If you mean that you're thinking of going over to the Engineers, it's my duty to blow your brains out. You have ten seconds to explain yourself." There was no trace of anger. The gun never wavered.

She swallowed hard, keeping very still.

"Uh, no, that's not what I meant."

The gun dropped slightly.

"It was a foolish remark," she said, her ears burning with shame and anger. "I'm committed to the Conservationists."

The gun vanished into the Symb he was wearing. It could still be in his hand for all she could tell.

"Now you can answer my question."

Keeping her anger rigidly in check, she started her story. She was quite good at it by now, and had it condensed nicely. She recited it in a singsong tone that the interrogator didn't seem to notice.

"I am seventy-seven Earth years old, I was born on Mercury, the Helios Enclave, the child of an extremely wealthy energy magnate. I grew up in the rigid, confining atmosphere that has always existed in Mercury, and I hated it. When I turned twelve, my mother gave me twenty percent of her fortune and said she hoped I'd use it wisely. Luckily for me, I was an adult and beyond her reach, because I disappointed her badly.

"I bought passage on the first ship leaving the planet, which happened to be going to Mars. For the next sixty years I devoted myself to experiencing everything the human organism can experience and still survive.

"It would be tedious and overlong to tell you everything I did, but so you won't think I'm hiding something, I can give you a random sample.

"Drugs: I tried them all. Some only once. Others for years at a time. I had to have my personality rebuilt three times and lost a lot of memory in the process.

"Sex: with two, three, four partners; seven partners; thirty partners; three hundred partners. All-week orgies. Men, women, girls, boys. Infants. Elephants. Pythons. Corpses. I changed sex so many times I'm not sure if I grew up as a male or a female.

"I killed a man. I got away with it. I killed a woman and got away again. I got caught the third time and spent seven years in rehabilitation.

"I traveled. I went to the Belt, to Luna, to the moons of Saturn, Uranus, Neptune. I went to Pluto, and beyond with a holehunter.

"I tried surgery. I joined up with a pair-cult and was connected for a year to another woman as a Siamese twin. I tried out weird new organs and sex systems. I tried on extra limbs.

"A few years ago I joined a passivity cult. They believed all action was meaningless, and demonstrated it by having their arms and legs amputated and relying on the mercy of random strangers to feed them and keep them alive. I lay for months in the public square beneath Coprates. Sometimes I went hungry and thirsty. Sometimes I stewed in my own filth; then someone would clean me up, usually with a stern lecture to quit this way of life and go straight. I didn't care.

"But the second time a dog used me for a urinal, I gave it up. I asked someone to carry me to a doctor, and walked out a changed woman. I decided I had *done* everything and had better start looking for an elaborate and original suicide. I was so bored, so jaded, that *breathing* seemed like too much of a bother.

"Then I thought of two places I'd never been: the sun and the Rings. The sun is the fancy suicide I told you about. The only way to get to the Rings is in a Symb. I tend to sympathize with you people over the Engineers. So here I am."

She settled back in her chair. She was not optimistic about being allowed to join the Conservationist Church, and was already planning ways to get over to the Engineers. If there was ever an unprepossessing story, it was hers, and she knew it. These Consers were supposed to be dedicated people, and she knew she couldn't present a very convincing line. In point of fact, she didn't give any thought at all to the Grand Design of the Engineers. Why should she care if a band of religious fanatics were trying to paint one of Saturn's Rings?

"The next to the last statement was a lie," the man informed her.

"Right," she spat. "You self-righteous bastards. It's the custom in polite society to inform someone when they're undergoing a lie-detector test. Even ask their consent." She got up to go.

"Please sit down, Parameter." She hesitated, then did so.

"It's time some false impressions were cleared up. First, this is not 'polite society,' this is war. Religious war, which is the dirtiest kind. We do what we have to in the interest of security. The sole purpose of this interview was to determine if your story was true. We don't care what you have done, as long as you haven't been consorting with our enemy. Have you?"

"No."

"That is a true statement. Now for the other mistake. We are not self-righteous bastards. We're pragmatists. And we're not religious fanatics, not really, though we all come to believe deeply in what we're doing out here. And that brings us to the third mistake. The primary reasons we're out here have little to do with defeating the Engineers. We're all out here for our own personal reasons, too."

"And what are they?"

"They're personal. Each of us had a different reason for coming. You are out here to satisfy the last dregs of a jaded appetite; that's a common reason. You have some surprises coming up, but you'll stay. You'll have to. You won't be able to bear leaving. And you'll like it. You might even help us fight the Engineers."

She looked at him with suspicion.

"We don't care why you're out here. Your story doesn't impress me one way or the other. You probably expected condemnation or contempt. Don't flatter yourself. As long as you're not here to help paint Ring Beta red, we don't care."

"Then when do I get a Symb?"

"As soon as you can undergo a bit of surgery." For the first time he unbent a little. The corners of the slit that covered his mouth bent up in a silly attempt at a smile. "I must confess that I *was* interested by one thing you said. *How* do you have sex with an elephant?"

Parameter kept a perfectly straight face.

"You don't have sex *with* an elephant. The best you can do is have sex *at* an elephant."

The Symb was a soft-looking greenish lump in the center of the room. With the best will in the world, Parameter could not see that it resembled anything so much as a pile of green cow manure. It was smaller than she had expected, but that was because it had no occupant. She was about to remedy that.

She stumped over to it and looked down dubiously. She had no choice but to walk awkwardly; her legs were no longer built for walking. They had been surgically altered so that the best she could do was a grotesque bowlegged prancing, stepping high so her long fingers would clear the floor. She was now ideally suited for a weightless existence. In a gravitational field, she was clumsy beyond belief.

The man who had interviewed her, whom she now knew by the name of Bushwacker, was the only other occupant of the room. He handled himself better than she did, but only slightly. He was itching to get back to the Rings; this base duty galled him. Gravity was for poor flatfoots.

"Just touch it, that's all?" she said. Now that it had come to it, she was having second thoughts.

"That's right. The Symb will do the rest. It won't be easy. You'll have between six weeks and three months of sensory deprivation while the personality develops. You'd go crazy in two days, but you won't be alone. All you'll have to hang on to will be the mind of the Symb. And it'll be a baby, hard to get along with. You'll grow up together."

She took a deep breath, wondering why she was so reluctant. She had done things easily that were much more repulsive than this. Perhaps it was the dawning realization that this would be much more than a simple lark. It could last a long time.

"Here goes." She lifted her leg and touched one of her ped-fingers to the blob. It stuck. The Symb slowly began stirring.

The Symb was . . . warm? No, at first she thought so, but it would be more accurate to say it was no temperature at all. It was thirty-seven degrees: blood temperature. It oozed up her leg, spreading itself thinner as it came. In a short time it was inching up her neck.

"Inhale," Bushwacker advised. "It'll help a little."

She did so, just as the Symb moved over her chin. It moved over her mouth and nose, then her eyes.

There was a moment of near-panic when part of her brain told her she *must* take a breath, and she dutifully tried to. Nothing happened, and she wanted to scream. But it was all right. She didn't need to breathe. When she opened her mouth the Symb flowed down her throat and trachea. Soon her lungs were filled with the interface tissue whose function it was to put oxygen in her blood and remove carbon dioxide. It filled her nasal passages, slithered up the eustachian tube to her inner ear. At that point she lost her balance and fell to the floor. Or she thought she did; she could no longer be sure. She had felt no impact. A wave of dizziness swept over her; she wondered what a Symb would do about vomiting. But it didn't happen, and she suspected it never would.

It was a shock, even though she had expected it, when the Symb entered her anus and vagina. Not a *bad* shock. Rather a thrill, actually. It filled the spaces in her uterus, wound into the urethra to fill the bladder, then up the ureter to mingle with the kidneys. Meanwhile another tendril had filled the large and small intestine, consuming the nutrients it found there, and joined with the tendril coming from her mouth. When it was done, she was threaded like the eye of a serpentine needle, and was revealed to any that could see as a topological example of a torus.

The silence closed in. It was absolutely quiet for a period of time she was powerless to measure, but couldn't have been longer than five minutes.

The obvious place where the human brain is accessible without violating any solid membranes is alongside the eyeball and through the supraorbital foramen. But the Symb would not be able to get a very substantial tendril through in the tight confines of the eye. So the genetic engineers, elaborating on the basic design for oxygen breathers received over the Ophiuchi Hotline, had given the Symb the capability of forcing an entry through the top of the skull.

Parameter felt a twinge of pain as a two-centimeter hole was eaten in the top of her head. But it subsided as the Symb began to feel out the proper places to make connections. The Symb was still a mindless thing, but was guided infallibly by the carefully designed instinct built into it.

Suddenly she was surrounded by fear; childish, inconsolable fear that frightened her out of her wits but did not come from her mind. She fought it, but it only became more insistent. In the end, she abandoned herself to it and cried like a baby. She became an infant, sloughing off her seventy-odd years there in the impalpable darkness like they had never happened.

There was nothing; nothing but two very lost voices, crying in the void.

There had been a debate raging for centuries as to whether the Symbiotic Space-Environment Organisms were really a form of artificial intelligence. (Or alien intelligence, depending on your definition.) The people who lived in them were unanimously of the opinion that they were. But the other side—who were mostly psychologists—pointed out that the people who actually *lived* in them were in the worst possible place to judge. Whatever one's opinion on the subject, it was based on personal prejudice, because there could be no objective facts.

The Symbs were genetically tailored organisms that could provide a complete, self-contained environment for a single human being in space. They thrived on human waste products: urine, feces, heat, and carbon dioxide.

They contained several chlorophyll-like enzymes and could

accomplish photosynthesis utilizing the human's body heat, though at a low efficiency. For the rest of the energy needs of the pair, the Symb could use sunlight. They were very good at storing energy in chemical compounds that could be broken down later at need. Together with a human, a Symb made a self-contained heat engine. They were a closed ecology, neither host nor parasite: a symbiosis.

To the human being, the Symb was a green pasture, a running brook, a fruit tree, an ocean to swim in. To the Symb, the human was rich soil, sunshine, gentle rain, fertilizer, a pollinating bee. It was an ideal team. Without the other, each was at the mercy of elaborate mechanical aids to survive. Humans were adapted to an environment that no longer existed for their use in a natural state; wherever humans lived since the occupation of the Earth, they had to make their own environment. Now the Symbs were to provide that environment free of charge.

But it hadn't worked that way.

The Symbs were more complicated than they looked. Humans were used to taking from their surroundings, bending or breaking them until they fit human needs. The Symbs required more of humanity; they made it necessary to give.

When inside a Symb, a human was cut off entirely from the external universe. The human component of the symbiosis had to rely on the Symb's faculties. And the sensory data were received in an unusual way.

The Symb extended a connection directly into the human brain and fed data into it. In the process, it had to get tied up in the brain in such a way that it could be difficult to say where human left off and Symb began. The Symb reorgnized certain portions of the human brain, freeing its tremendous potential for computation and integration, and using those abilities to translate the sensory data into pictures, sounds, tastes, smells, and touches, going directly through the sensorium. In the process, a mind was generated.

The Symb had no brain of its own, it merely was able to utilize the human brain on a time-sharing basis, and utilize it better than its original owner had been able to. So it would seem impossible that it could have a mind of its own. But every Ringer in the system would swear it had. And that was the crux of the debate:

Was it actually an independent mind, parasitically using the human brain as its vehicle for sentient thought, or was it merely schizophrenia, induced by isolation and projection?

It was impossible to decide. Without a human inside it, there is nothing more helpless than a Symb. Without the human brain in combination with the genetic information and enzymatically coded procedures, the Symb can do no more than lie there inert like the green turd it so closely resembles. It has only rudimentary musculature, and doesn't even use that when alone. There is no good analogy for a Symb without a human; nothing else is so dependent on anything else.

Once combined with a human, the pair is transformed, becoming much more than the sum of its parts. The human is protected against the harshest environment imaginable. The livable range with a Symb extends from just outside the orbit of Earth (radiation limit) to the orbit of Neptune (sunlight limit). The pair feed each other, water each other, and respirate each other. The human brain is converted into a supercomputer. The Symb has radio and radar sender and receiver organs, in addition to sensors for radiation and the electromagnetic spectrum from one thousand to sixteen thousand angstroms. The system can gain mass by ingesting rock and ice and the Symb can retain the valuable minerals and water and discard the rest. About all the pair cannot do is change velocity without a chunk of rock to push against. But it is a small matter to carry a rocket thruster instead of the whole apparatus of a space suit. In the Rings, they didn't even do that. The Symb could manufacture enough gas for attitude control. For major velocity changes, the Ringers carried small bottles of compressed gas.

So why weren't all humans in space installed in Symbs?

The reason was that the Symbs needed more than most people were willing to give. It wasn't a simple matter of putting it on when you needed it and taking it off later. When you took off your Symb, the Symb ceased to exist.

It was probably the heaviest obligation a human ever had to face. Once mated with a Symb, you were mated for life. There had never been a closer relationship; the Symb lived *inside your mind*, was with you even when you slept, moving independently through your dreams. Compared with that, Siamese twins were utter strangers who pass in the night.

It was true that all the humans who had ever tried it swore they hadn't even been alive before they joined their Symb. It looked attractive in some ways, but for most people the imagined liabilities outweighed the gains. Few people are able to make a commitment they *know* will be permanent, not when permanent could mean five or six hundred years.

After an initial rush of popularity the Symb craze had died down. Now all the Symbs in the system were in the Rings, where they had made possible a nomadic existence never before known.

Ringers are loners by definition. Humans meet at long intervals, mate if they are of a mind to, and go their separate ways. Ringers seldom see the same person twice in a lifetime.

They are loners who are never alone.

"Are you there?"

?????

"I can sense you. We have to do something. I can't stand this darkness, can you? Listen: *Let there be light!*"

?????

"Oh, you're hopeless. Why don't you get lost?"

Sorrow. Deep and childish sorrow. Parameter was drawn into it, cursing herself and the infantile thing she was caught with. She tried for the thousandth time to thrash her legs, to let someone out there know she wanted *out*. But she had lost her legs. She could no longer tell if she was moving them.

From the depths of the Symb's sorrow, she drew herself up and tried to stand away from it. It was no use. With a mental sob, she was swallowed up again and was no longer able to distinguish herself from the infant alien.

Her chest was rising and falling. There was an unpleasant smell in her nostrils. She opened her eyes.

She was still in the same room, but now there was a respirator clamped to her face, forcing air in and out of her lungs. She rolled her eyes and saw the grotesque shape of the other person in the room with her. It floated, bandy legs drawn up, hands and peds clasped together.

A hole formed in the front of the blank face.

"Feeling any better?"

She screamed and screamed until she thankfully faded back into her dream world.

"You're getting it. Keep trying. No, that's the wrong direction; whatever you were doing just then, do the opposite."

It was tentative; Parameter hadn't the foggiest idea of what opposite was, because she hadn't the foggiest idea of what the little Symb was doing in the first place. But it was progress. There was light. Faint, wavering, tentative; but *light*.

The undefined luminance flickered like a candle, shimmered, blew out. But she felt good. Not half as good as the Symb felt; she was flooded by a proud feeling of accomplishment that was not her own. But, she reflected, what does it matter if it's my own or not? It was getting to where she no longer cared to haggle about whether it was she who felt something or the Symb. If they both had to experience it, what difference did it make?

"That was *good*. We're getting there. You and me, kid. We'll go places. We'll get out of this mess yet."

Go? Fear. Go? Sorrow. Go? Anger?

The emotions were coming labeled with words now, and they were extending in range.

"Anger? Anger, did you say? What's this? Of course, I want to get out of here, why do you think we're going through this? It ain't easy, kid. I don't remember anything so hard to get a grip on since I tried to control my alpha waves, years ago. Now wait a minute . . ." Fear, fear, fear. "Don't do that, kid, you scare me. Wait. I didn't mean it . . ." Fear, fear loneliness, fear, FEAR! "Stop! Stop, you're scaring me to death, you're . . ." Parameter was shivering, becoming a child again.

Black, endless fear. Parameter slipped away from her mind; fused with the other mind; chided herself; consoled herself; comforted herself; loved herself.

"Here, take some water, it'll make you feel better."

"Ggggwwway."

"What?"

"Goway. Gway. Goaway. GO. A. WAY!"

"You'll have to drink some water first. I won't go away until you do."

"Go 'way. Murder. Murder'r."

Parameter was at a loss.

"*Why*, why won't you do it? For me. Do it for Parameter."

Negation.

"You mean 'no.' Where do you get those fancy words?"

Your memory. No. Will not do it.

Parameter sighed, but she had acquired patience, infinite patience. And something else, something that was very like love. At least it was a profound admiration for this spunky kid. But she was still scared, because the Symb was beginning to win her over and it was only with increasing desperation that she hung onto her idea of getting the child to open the outside world so she could tell someone she wanted out.

And the desperation only made matters worse. She couldn't conceal it from the Symb, and the act of experiencing communicated it in all its raw, naked panic.

"Listen to me. We've got to get off this merry-go-round. How can we talk something over intelligently if I keep communicating my fear to you, which makes you scared, which scares me, which makes you panicky, which scares me more, which . . . now stop that!"

Not my fault. Love, love. You need me. You are incomplete without me. I need commitment before I'll cooperate.

"But I can't. Can't you see I have to be *me*? I can't be you. And it's you who's incomplete without me, not the way you said."

Wrong. Both incomplete without the other. It's too late for you. You are no longer you. You are me, I am you.

"I won't believe that. We've been here for centuries, for eons. If I haven't accepted you yet, I never will. I want to be free, in time to see the sun burn out."

Wrong. Here for two months. The sun is still burning.

"Aha! Tricked you, didn't I? You can see out, you're further along than you told me. Why did you trick me like that? Why didn't you tell me you knew what time it was? I've been aching to know that. Why didn't you tell me?"

You didn't ask.

"What kind of answer is that?"

An honest one.

Parameter simmered. She knew it was honest. She knew she was belaboring the child, who couldn't tell a lie any more than she could. But she clung to her anger with the sinking feeling that it was all she had left of herself.

You hurt me. You are angry. I've done nothing to you. Why do you hate me? Why? ????? I love you. I'm afraid you'll leave me.

"I . . . I love you. I love you, godhelpme, I really do. But that's not me. No! It's something else. I don't know what yet, but I'll hang on. Hang on to it. Hang on to it."

Where are you?

Parameter?

"I'm here. Go away."

"Go away."

"You have to eat something. Please, try this. It's good for you. Really it is. Try it."

"Eat!" She turned in the air with sudden cramps of hunger and revulsion. She retched up stale air and thin fluid. "Get away from me. Don't touch me. Equinox! Equinox!"

The figure touched her with its hand. The hand was hard and cold.

"Your breasts," he said. "They've been oozing milk. I was wondering . . ."

"Gone. All gone."

Parameter.

"What is it? Are you ready to try again with that picture?"

No. No need. You can go.

"Huh?"

You can go. I can't keep you. You think you are self-sufficient; maybe you're right. You can go.

Parameter was confused.

"Why? Why so sudden?"

I've been looking into some of the concepts in your memory. Freedom. Self-determination. Independence. You are free to go.

"You know what I think, what I *really* think about those concepts, too. Unproven at best. Fantasies at worst."

You are cynical. I recognize that they may indeed be real, so you should be free. I am detaining you against your will. This is contrary to most ethical codes, including the ones you accept more than any others. You are free to go.

It was an awkward moment. It hurt more than she would have thought possible. And she was unsure of whose hurt she was feeling. Not that it mattered.

What was she saying? Here was what might be her one and only chance, and she was acknowledging what the kid had said all along, that they were already fused. And the kid had heard it, like she heard everything.

Yes, I heard it. It doesn't matter. I can hear your doubts about many things. I can feel your uncertainty. It will be with you always.

"Yes. I guess it will. But you. I can't feel much from you. Not that I can distinguish."

You feel my death.

"No, no. It isn't that bad. They'll give you another human. You'll get along. Sure you will."

Perhaps. Despair. Disbelief.

Parameter kicked herself in the mental butt, told herself that if she didn't get out now, she never would.

"Okay. Let me out."

Fade. A gradual withdrawal that was painful and slow as the tendril began to disengage. And Parameter felt her mind being drawn in two.

It would always be like that. It would never get any better.

"Wait, kid. Wait!"

The withdrawal continued.

"Listen to me. Really! No kidding, I really want to discuss this with you. Don't go."

It's for the best. You'll get along.

"No! No more than you will. I'll die."

No you won't. It's like you said; if you don't get out now, you never will. You'll...all right...bye...

"No! You don't understand. I don't want to go anymore. I'm afraid. Don't leave me like this. You can't leave me."

Hesitation.

"Listen to me. Listen. Feel me. Love. Love. Commitment, pure and honest commitment-forever-and-ever-till-death-us-do-part. Feel me."

"I feel you. We are one."

She had eaten, only to bring it back up. But her jailer was persistent. He was not going to let her die.

"Would it be any better if you got inside with me?"

"No. I can't. I'm half gone. It would be no good. Where is Equinox?"

"I told you I don't know. And I don't know where your children are. But you won't believe me."

"That's right. I don't believe you. Murderer."

She listened groggily as he explained how she came to be in this room with him. She didn't believe him, not for a minute.

He said he had found her by following a radio beacon signaling from a point outside the plane of the Rings. He had found a pseudosymb there; a simplified Symb created by budding a normal one without first going through the conjugation process. A pseudo can only do what any other plant can do: that is, ingest carbon dioxide and give out oxygen from its inner surface. It cannot contract into contact with a human body. It remains in the spherical configuration. A human can stay alive in a pseudosymb, but will soon die of thirst.

Parameter had been inside the pseudo, bruised and bleeding from the top of her head and from her genitals. But she had been alive. Even more remarkable, she had lived the five days it had taken to get her to the Conser emergency station. The Consers didn't maintain many of the stations. The ones they had were widely separated.

"You were robbed by Engineers," he said. "There's no other explanation. How long have you been in the Rings?"

After the third repeat of the question, Parameter muttered, "Five years."

"I thought so. A new one. That's why you don't believe me. You don't know much about Engineers, do you? You can't understand why they would take your Symb and leave you alive, with a beacon to guide help to you. It doesn't make sense, right?"

"I . . . no, I don't know. I can't understand. They should have killed me. What they did was more cruel."

No emotion could be read on the man's "face," but he was optimistic for the first time that she might pull through. At least she was talking, if fitfully.

"You should have learned more. I've been fighting for a century, and I still don't know all I'd like to know. They robbed you for your children, don't you see? To raise them as Engineers. That's what the real battle is about: population. The side that can produce the most offspring is the one that gains the advantage."

"I don't want to talk."

"I understand. Will you just listen?"

He took her lack of response to mean she would.

"You've just been drifting through your life. It's easy to do out here; we all just drift from time to time. When you think about the Engineers at all, it's just a question of evading them. That isn't too hard. Considering the cubic kilometers out here, the hunted always has the advantage over the hunter. There are so many places to hide; so many ways to dodge."

"But you've drifted into a rough neighborhood. The Engineers have concentrated a lot of people in this sector. Maybe you've noticed the high percentage of red rocks. They hunt in teams, which is not something we Consers have ever done. We're too loose a group to get together much, and we all know our real fight doesn't begin for another thousand years.

"We are the loosest army in the history of humanity. We're volunteers on both sides, and on our side, we don't require that individuals do anything at *all* to combat the Engineers. So you don't know anything about them, beyond the fact that they've vowed to paint Ring Beta red within twenty-five thousand years."

He at last got a rise out of her.

"I know a little more than that. I know they are followers of

Ringpainter the Great. I know he lived almost two hundred years ago. I know he founded the Church of Cosmic Engineering."

"You read all that in a book. Do you know that Ringpainter is still alive? Do you know how they plan to paint the Ring? Do you know what they do to Consers they catch?"

He was selective in his interpretations. This time he took her silence to mean she didn't know.

"He is alive. Only he's a she now. Her 'Population Edict' of fifty years ago decreed that each Engineer shall spend ninety percent of her time as a female, and bear three children every year. If they really do that, we haven't got a chance. The Rings would be solid Engineers in a few centuries."

She was slightly interested for the first time in weeks.

"I didn't know it was such a long-term project."

"The longest ever undertaken by humans. At the present rate of coloring, it would take three million years to paint the entire Ring. But the rate is accelerating."

He waited, trying to draw her out again, but she lapsed back into listlessness. He went on.

"The one aspect of their religion you don't seem to know about is their ban on killing. They won't take a human or Symb life."

That got her attention.

"Equinox! Where . . ." she started shaking again.

"She's almost certainly alive."

"How could they keep her alive?"

"You're forgetting your children. Five of them."

The last thing anyone said to Parameter for two years was, "Take this, you might want to use it. Just press it to a red rock and forget about it. It lasts forever."

She took the object, a thin tube with a yellow bulb on each end. It was a Bacteriophage Applicator, filled with the tailored DNA that attacked and broke down the deposits of red dust left by the Engineers' Ringvirus. Touching the end of it to a coated rock would begin a chain reaction that would end only when all the surface of the rock was restored to its original color.

Parameter absently touched it to her side, where it sank without a trace in the tough integument of Equinox's outer hide. Then she shoved out the airlock and into fairyland.

"I never saw anything like this, Equinox," she said.

"No, you certainly haven't." The Symb had only Parameter's experiences to draw on.

"Where should we go? What's that line around the sky? Which way is it to the Ring?"

Affectionate laughter. "Silly planteater. We're *in* the Ring. That's why it stretches all around us. All except over in that direction. The sun is behind that part of the Ring, so the particles are illuminated primarily from the other side. You can see it faintly, by reflected light."

"Where did you learn all that?"

"From your head. The facts are there, and the deductive powers. You just never thought about it."

"I'm going to start thinking a lot more. This is almost frightening. I repeat: Where do we go from here?"

"Anywhere at all, as long as it's away from this awful place. I don't think I want to come back to the Ringmarket for about a decade."

"Now, now," Parameter chided her. "Surely we'll have to go back before that. Aren't you feeling the least bit poetic?"

The Ringmarket was the clearinghouse for the wildly variant and irresistibly beautiful art that was the byproduct of living a solitary life in the Rings. Art brokers, musicmongers, poetry sellers, editors, moodmusic vendors . . . all the people who made a living by standing between the artist and the audience and raking off a profit as works of art passed through their hands; they all gathered at the Ringmarket bazaar and bought exquisite works for the equivalent of pretty-colored beads. The Ringers had no need of money. All exchanges were straight barter: a fresh gas bottle for a symphony that would crash through the mind with unique rhythms and harmonies. A handful of the mineral pellets the Ringers needed every decade to supply trace elements that were rare in the Rings could buy a painting that would bring millions back in civilization. It was a speculative business. No one could know *which* of the thousands of works would catch the public taste at high tide and run away with it. All the buyers knew was that for unknown reasons the art of the Rings had consistently captured the highest prices and the wildest reviews. It was different. It was from a whole new viewpoint.

"I can't feel poetic back there. Besides, didn't you know that when we start to create, it will be music?"

"I didn't know that. How do you know?"

"Because there's a song in my heart. Off-key. Let's get out of here."

They left the metallic sphere of the market and soon it was only a blue vector line, pointed away from them.

They spent two years just getting used to their environment. The wonder never wore off. When they met others, they avoided them. Neither was ready for companionship; they had all they needed.

She was sinking, and glad of it. Every day without Equinox was torture. She had come to hate her jailer, even if his story was true. He was keeping her alive, which was the cruelest thing he could do. But even her hatred was a weak and fitful thing.

She stared into the imaginary distance and seldom noticed his comings and goings.

Then one day there were two of them. She noted it dispassionately, watched as they embraced each other and began to flow. So the other person was a female; they were going to mate. She turned away and didn't see, as the two Symbs merged in their conjugation process and slowly expanded into a featureless green sphere within which the humans would couple silently and then part, probably forever.

But something nagged at her, and she looked back. A bulge was forming on the side of the sphere that was facing her. It grew outward and began to form another, smaller sphere. A pink line formed the boundary between the two globes.

She looked away again, unable to retain an interest as the Symbs gave birth. But something was still nagging.

"Parameter."

The man (or was it the woman?) was floating beside her, holding the baby Symb.

She froze. Her eyes filled with horror.

"You're out of your mind."

"Maybe. I can't force it on you. But it's here. I'm going now, and you'll never see me again. You can live or die, whichever you choose. I've done all I can."

It was a warm day in the Upper Half. But then it was always a warm day, though some were warmer than others.

Ringography is an easy subject to learn. There are the Rings: Alpha, Beta, and the thin Gamma. The divisions are called Cassini and Encke, each having been created by the gravitational tug-of-war between Saturn and the larger moons for possession of the particles that make up the Rings. Beyond that, there is only the Upper Half and the Lower Half, above and below the plane, and Inspace and Outspace. The Ringers never visited Inspace because it included the intense Van Allen-type radiation belts that circle Saturn. Outspace was far from the traveled parts of the Rings, but was a nice place to visit because the Rings were all in one part of the sky from that vantage point. An odd experience for children, accustomed from birth to see the sky cut in half by the Rings.

Parameter was in the Upper Half to feed on the sunlight that was so much more powerful there than in the Rings. Equinox was in her extended configuration. The pair looked like a gauzy parabolic dish, two hundred meters across. The dish was transparent, with veins that made it look like a spider web. The illusion was heightened by the small figure spread-eagled in the center of it, like a fly. The fly was Parameter.

It was delicious to float there. She looked directly at the sun, which was bright even this far away and would have burned her eyes quickly if she had been really looking at it. But she saw only a projection. Equinox's visual senses were not nearly as delicate as human eyes.

The front of her body was bathed in radiance. It was highly sensual, but in a new way. It was the mindless joy of a flower unfolding to the sun that Parameter experienced, not the hotter animal passions she was used to. Energy coursed through her body and out into the light-gathering sheets that Equinox had extended. Her mind was disconnected more completely than she would have believed possible. Her thoughts came hours apart, and were concerned with sluggish, vegetable pleasures. She saw herself as naked, exposed to the light and the wind, floating in the center of a silver circle of life. She could feel the wind on her body in this airless place and wondered vacantly how Equinox could be so utterly convincing in the webs of illusion she spun.

There was a sudden gust.

"Parameter. Wake up, my darling."

"Hmmm?"

"There's a storm coming up. We've got to furl the sails and head into port."

Parameter felt other gusts as she swam through the warm waters back to alertness.

"How far are we from the Ring?"

"We're all right. We can be there in ten minutes if I tack for a bit and then use a few seconds of thrust."

In her extended configuration, Equinox was a moderately efficient solar sail. By controlling the angle she presented to the incoming sunlight she could slowly alter velocity. All Parameter had to do was push off above or below the Rings in a shallow arc. Equinox could bring them back into the Rings in a few days, using solar pressure. But the storm was a danger they had always to keep in mind.

It was the solar wind that Equinox felt, a cloud of particles thrust out from the sun by storms beneath the surface. Her radiation sensors had detected the first speed-of-light gusts of it, and the dangerous stuff would not be far behind.

Radiation was the chief danger of life in the Rings. The outer surface of a Symb was proof against much of the radiation the symbiotic pair would encounter in space. What got through was not enough to worry about, certainly never enough to cause sickness. But stray high-energy particles could cause mutations of the egg and sperm cells of the humans.

The intensity of the wind was increasing as they furled their sails and applied the gas thrusters.

"Did we get moving in time?" Parameter asked.

"There's a good margin. But we can't avoid getting a little hard stuff. Don't worry about it."

"What about children? If I want to have some later, couldn't that be a problem?"

"Naturally. But you'll never give birth to a mutation. I'll be able to see any deviations in the first few weeks and abort it and not even have to tell you."

"But you would tell me, wouldn't you?"

"If you want me to. But it isn't important. No more than the daily control I exert over any of your other bodily processes."

"If you say so."

"I say so. Don't worry, I said. You just handle the motor control and leave the busy work to me. Things don't seem quite real to me unless they're on the molecular level."

Parameter trusted Equinox utterly. So much so that when the really hard wind began buffeting them, she didn't worry for a second. She spread her arms to it, embraced it. It was strange that the "wind" didn't blow her around like a leaf. She would have liked that. All she really missed was her hair streaming around her shoulders. She no longer had any hair at all. It got in the way of the seal between the two of them.

As soon as she thought it, long black hair whipped out behind her, curling into her face and tickling her eyes. She could see it and feel it against her skin, but she couldn't touch it. That didn't surprise her, because it wasn't there.

"Thank you," she laughed. And then she laughed even harder as she looked down at herself. She was covered with hair; long, flowing hair that grew as she watched it.

They reentered the Ring, preceded by a twisting, imaginary train of hair a kilometer long.

Three days later she was still staring at the floating ball.

On the fifth day her hand twitched toward it.

"No. No. Equinox. Where are you?"

The Symb was in its dormant state. Only an infant Symb could exist without a human to feed and water it; once it had become attached to a human, it would die very quickly without one. But in dormancy, they could live for weeks at a low energy level. It only needed the touch of her hand to be triggered into action.

The hunger was eating its way through her body; she ignored it completely. It had become a fact of life, something she clutched to her to forget about the *real* hunger that was in her brain. She would never be forced to accept the Symb from hunger. It didn't even enter the question.

On the ninth day her hand began moving. She watched it, crying for Equinox to stop the movement, to give her strength.

She touched it.

"I think it's time we tried out the new uterus."

"I think you're right."

"If that thing out there is a male, we'll do it."

Equinox had in her complex of capabilities the knack of producing a nodule within her body that could take a cloned cell and nurture it until it grew into a complete organ; any organ she wished. She had done that with one of Parameter's cells. She removed it, cloned it, and let it grow into a new uterus. Parameter's old one had run out of eggs long ago and was useless for procreation, but the new one was brimming with life.

She had operated on her mate, taking out the old one and putting in the new. It had been painless and quick; Parameter had not even felt it.

Now they were ready to have a seed planted in it.

"Male," came the voice of the other figure. Before, Parameter would have answered by saying, "Solitude," and he would have gone on his way.

Now she said, "Female."

"Wilderness," he introduced himself.

"Parameter."

The mating ritual over, they fell silent as they drifted closer. She had computed it well, if a little fast. They hit and clung together with all their limbs. Slowly the Symbs melted into each other.

A sensation of pleasure came over Parameter.

"What is it?"

"What do you think? It's heaven. Did you think that because we're sexless, we wouldn't get any pleasure out of conjugation?"

"I guess I hadn't thought about it. It's . . . different. Not bad at all. But nothing like an orgasm."

"Stick around. We're just getting started."

There was a moment of insecurity as Equinox withdrew her connections, leaving only the one into her brain. She shuddered as an unfamiliar feeling passed over her, then realized she was holding her breath. She had to start respirating again. Her chest crackled as she brought long-unused muscles into play, but once the reflex was started she was able to forget about it and let her hindbrain handle the chore.

The inner surface started to phosphoresce, and she made out

a shadowy figure floating in front of her. The light got brighter until it reached the level of bright moonlight. She could see him now.

"Hello," she said. He seemed surprised she wanted to talk, but grinned at her.

"Hello. You must be new."

"How did you know?"

"It shows. You want to talk. You probably expect me to go through an elaborate ritual." And with that he reached for her and pulled her toward him.

"Hold on there," she said. "I'd like to know you a little better first."

He sighed, but let her go. "I'm sorry. You don't know yet. All right, what would you like to know about me?"

She looked him over. He was small, slightly smaller than her. He was completely hairless, as was she. There didn't seem to be any way to guess his age; all the proper clues were missing. Growing out of the top of his head was a snaky umbilicus.

She discovered there was really little to ask him, but having made a point of it, she threw in a token question.

"How old are you?"

"Old enough. Fourteen."

"All right, let's do it your way." She touched him and shifted in space to accommodate his entry.

To her pleasant surprise, it lasted longer than the thirty seconds she had expected. He was an accomplished lover; he seemed to know all the right moves. She was warming deliciously when she heard him in her head.

"*Now* you know," he said, and her head was filled with his laughter.

Everything before that, good as it was, had been just a warm-up.

Parameter and the baby Symb howled with pain.

"I didn't want you," she cried, hurling waves of rejection at the child and at herself. "All I want is Equinox."

That went on for an endless time. The stars burnt out around them. The galaxy turned like a whirligig. The universe contracted;

exploded; contracted again. Exploded. Contracted and gave it up as a waste of time. Time ended as all events came to an end.

The two of them floated, howling at each other.

Wilderness drifted away against the swirling background of stars. He didn't look back, and neither did Parameter. They knew each other too well to need good-byes. They might never meet again, but that didn't matter either, because each carried all they needed of the other.

"In a life full of cheap thrills, I never had anything like that."

Equinox seemed absorbed. She quietly acknowledged that it had, indeed, been superduper, but there was something else. There was a new knowledge.

"I'd like to try something," she said.

"Shoot."

Parameter's body was suddenly caressed by a thousand tiny, wet tongues. They searched out every cranny, all at the same time. They were hot, at least a thousand billion degrees, but they didn't burn; they soothed.

"Where were you keeping *that*?" Parameter quavered when it stopped. "And why did you stop?"

"I just learned it. I was watching while I was experiencing. I picked up a few tricks."

"You've got *more*?"

"Sure. I didn't want to start out with the intense ones until I saw how you liked that one. I thought it was very nice. You shuddered beautifully; the delta waves were fascinating."

Parameter broke up with laughter. "Don't give me that clinical stuff. You liked it so much you scared yourself."

"That comes as close as you can come to describing my re-action. But I was serious about having things I think we'll like even better. I can combine sensations in a novel way. Did you appreciate the subtle way the 'heat' blended into the sensation of feathers with an electric current through them?"

"It sounds hideous when you say it in words. But that was what it was, all right. Electric feathers. But pain had nothing to do with it."

Equinox considered it. "I'm not sure about that. I was deep

into the pain-sensation center of you. But I was tickling it in a new way, the same way Wilderness tickled you. There is something I'm discovering. It has to do with the reality of pain. *All* you experience is more a function of your brain than of your nerve endings. Pain is no exception. What I do is connect the two centers—pain and pleasure—and route them through other sensorium pathways, resulting in..."

"Equinox."

?????

"Make love to me."

She was in the center of the sun, every atom of her body fusing in heat so hot it was icy. She swam to the surface, taking her time through the plastic waves of ionized gas, where she grew until she could hold the whole sputtering ball in her hand and rub it around her body. It flicked and fumed and smoked, gigantic prominences responding to her will, wreathing her in fire and smoke that bit and tickled. Flares snaked into her, reaming nerves with needle-sharp pins of gas that were soft as a kiss. She was swallowed whole by something pink that had no name, and slid down the slippery innards to splash in a pool of sweet-smelling sulfur.

It melted her; she melted it. Equinox was there; she picked her up and hurled her and herself in a wave of water, a gigantic wave that was gigatons of pent-up energy, rearing itself into a towering breaker a thousand kilometers high. She crashed on a beach of rubbery skin, which became a forest of snakes that squeezed her until the top of her head blew off and tiny flowers showered around her, all of them Equinox.

She was drawn back together from the far corners of the solar system and put into a form that called itself "Parameter" but would answer to anything at all. Then she was rising on a rocket that thrust deep into her vagina, into recesses that weren't even there but felt like mirrors that showed her own face. She was a fusion warhead of sensation; primed to blow. Sparks whipped around her, and each was a kiss of electric feathers. She was reaching orbital velocity; solar escape velocity; the speed of light. She turned herself inside out and contained the universe. The speed of light was a crawl slower than any snail; she transcended it.

There was an explosion; an implosion. She drew away from

herself and fell into herself, and the fragments of her body drifted down to the beach, where she and Equinox gathered them and put them in a pile of quivering parts, each smaller than an atom.

It was a long job. They took their time.

"Next time," Parameter suggested, "try to work in some elephants."

Someone had invented a clock. It ticked.

Parameter woke up.

"Did you do that?"

No answer.

"Shut the damn thing off."

The ticking stopped. She rolled over and went back to sleep. Around her, a trillion years passed.

It was no good; she couldn't sleep.

"Are you there?"

Yes.

"What do you think we ought to do?"

Despair. We've lost Equinox.

"You never knew her."

Part of her will always be with you. Enough to hurt you. We will always hurt.

"I want to live again."

Live with hurt?

"If there's no other way. Come on. Let's start. Try to make a light. Come on, you can do it. I can't tell you how; you have to do that yourself. I love you. Blend with me, wash me clean, wipe out the memory."

Impossible. We cannot alter ourselves. I want Equinox.

"Damn you, you never knew her."

Know her as good as you. Better. In a way, I *am* Equinox. But in another way, I can never be.

"Don't talk in riddles. Merge with me."

Cannot. You do not love me yet.

"You want to sleep on it another few thousand years?"

Yes. You are much nicer when you are asleep.

"Is that an insult?"

No. You have loved me in your sleep. You have talked to me, you have taught me, given me love and guidance, grown me up to an adult. But you still think I'm Equinox. I'm not. I am me.

"Who is that?"

No name. I will have a name when you start really talking to me.

"Go to sleep. You confuse me."

Love. Affection. Rockabye, rockabye, rockabye.

"You have a name yet?"

"Yes. My name is Solstice."

Parameter cried, loud and long, and washed herself clean in her own tears.

It took them four years to work their way around to Ringmarket. They traded a song, one that had taken three years to produce, a sweet-sad dirge that somehow rang with hope, orchestrated for three lutes and synthesizer; traded it and a promise of four more over the next century to a tinpan alleycat for an elephant gun. Then they went out on a trail that was four years cold to stalk the memory of those long-ago pachyderm days.

In the way that an earlier generation of humans had known the shape of a hill, the placement of trees and flowers on it, the smell and feel of it; and another generation could remember at a glance what a street corner looked like; or still another the details of a stretch of corridor beneath the surface of the moon; in that same way, Parameter knew rocks. She would know the rock she had pushed off from on that final day just before Equinox was taken from her, the rock she now knew to have been an Engineer way-station. She knew where it had been going on that day, and how fast, and for how long. She knew where it would be now, and that was where she and Solstice were headed. The neighborhood would be different, but she could find that rock.

They found it, in only three years of search. She knew it instantly, knew every crevice and pit on the side she had landed on. The door was on the other side. They picked a likely rock a few kilometers away and settled down for a long wait.

Seventy-six times Saturn turned below them while they used the telescopic sight of the gun to survey the traffic at the station.

By the end of that time, they knew the routine of the place better than the residents did. When the time came for action they had worked over each detail until it was almost a reflex.

A figure came out of the rock and started off in the proper direction. Parameter squinted down the barrel of the gun and drew a bead. The range was extreme, but she had no doubt of a hit. The reason for her confidence was the long red imaginary line that she saw growing from the end of the barrel. It represented the distance the bullet would travel in one-thousandth of a second. The figure she was shooting at also had a line extending in front of it, not nearly so long. All she had to do was bring the ends of the two lines together and squeeze the trigger.

It went as planned. The gun was firing stunbullets, tiny harmonic generators that would knock out the pair for six hours. The outer hide of a Symb was proof against the kinetic energy contained in most projectiles, natural or artificial. She didn't dare use a beam stunner because the Engineers in the station would detect it.

They set out in pursuit of the unconscious pair. There was no hurry; the longer it took to rendezvous, the farther they would be from danger.

It took five hours to reach them. Once in contact, Solstice took over. She had assured Parameter that it would be possible to fuse with an unconscious Symb, and she was right. Soon Parameter was floating in the dark cavity with the Engineer, a female. She put the barrel of the gun under the other's chin and waited.

"I don't know if I can do it, Solstice," she said.

"It won't be something you'll ever be proud of, but you know the reasons as well as I. Just keep thinking of Equinox."

"I wonder if that's a good idea? I'd rather do something for her that I *would* be proud of."

"Want to back out? We can still get away. But if she wakes up and sees us, it could get awkward if we let her live."

"I know. I have to do it. I just don't like it."

The Engineer was stirring. Parameter tightened her grip on the rifle.

She opened her eyes, looked around, and seemed to be listening. Solstice was keeping the other Symb from calling for help.

"I won't give you any trouble," the woman said. "But is it asking too much to allow me a few minutes for my death ritual?"

"You can have that and more if you're a fast talker. I don't want to kill you, but I confess I think I'll have to. I want to tell you some things, and to do it, I'll need your cooperation. If you don't cooperate, I can take what I need from you anyway. What I'm hoping is that there'll be some way you can show me that will make your death unnecessary. Will you open your mind to me?"

A light came into the woman's eyes, then was veiled. Parameter was instantly suspicious.

"Don't be nervous," the Engineer said, "I'll do as you ask. It was just something of a surprise." She relaxed, and Parameter eased herself into the arms of Solstice, who took over as go-between.

They had a lot staked on the outcome of this mutual revelation.

It came in a rush, the impalpable weight of the religious fervor and dedication. And above it all, the Great Cause, the project that would go on long after everyone now alive was dead. The audacity of it! The vision of Humanity the mover, the controller, the artist; the Engineer. The universe would acknowledge the sway of Humanity when it gazed at the wonder that was being wrought in the Rings of Saturn.

Ringpainter the Great was a utopian on a grand scale. He had been bitterly disappointed in the manner in which humanity had invaded the solar system. He thought in terms of terraforming and of shifting planets in their courses. What he saw was burrows in rock.

So he preached, and spoke of Dyson spheres and space arks, of turning stars on and off at will, of remodeling galaxies. To him and his followers, the universe was an immensely complex toy that they could do beautiful things with. They wanted to unscrew a black hole and see what made it tick. They wanted to unshift the red shift. They believed in continuous creation, because the big bang implied an end to all their efforts.

Parameter and Solstice reeled under the force of it; the conviction that this admittedly symbolic act could get humanity moving in the direction Ringpainter wanted. He had an idea that there were beings out there keeping score, and they could be impressed by the Grand Gesture. When they saw what a pretty thing Ring Beta had become, they would step in and give the forces of Ring-painter a hand.

The woman they had captured, whose name they learned was Rosy-Red-Ring 3351, was convinced of the truth of these ideas. She had devoted her life to the furtherance of the Design. But they saw her faith waver as she beheld what they had to show her. She cringed away from the shrunken, hardened, protectively encased memory of the days after the theft of Equinox. They held it up and made her look at it, peeling away the layers of forgetfulness they had protected themselves with and thrusting it at her.

At last they let her go. She crouched, quivering, in the air.

"You've seen what we've been."

"Yes." She was sobbing.

"And you know what we have to do to find Equinox. You saw that in my mind. What I want to know is, can this cup pass from us? Do you know another way? Tell me quick."

"I didn't *know*," she cried. "It's what we do to all the Consers we capture. We can't kill them. It's against the Law. So we separate them, keep the Symb, leave the human to be found. We know most of them are never found, but it's the best we can do. But I didn't know it was so bad. I never thought of it. I almost think—"

"No need to think. You're right. It *would* be more merciful to kill the human. I don't know about the Symb. I'll have to talk to Equinox about that. At first I wanted to kill all the Engineers in the Rings, with a lot of care put into the project so they didn't die too quick. I can't do that any more. I'm not a Conser. I never was. I'm not anything but a seeker, looking for my friend. I don't care if you paint the Ring; go ahead. But I have to find Equinox, and I have to find my children. You have to answer my question now. Can you think of a way I can let you live and still do what I have to do?"

"No. There's no other way."

Parameter sighed. "All right. Get on with your ritual."

"I'm not sure if I want to any more."

"You'd probably better. Your faith has been shaken, but you might be right about the scorekeepers. If you are, I'd hate to be the cause of you going out the wrong way." She was already putting her distance between herself and this woman she would kill. She was becoming an object, something she was going to do something unpleasant to; not a person with a right to live.

Rosy-Red-Ring 3351 gradually calmed as she went through the motions of her auto-extreme unction. By the time she had finished she was as composed as she had been at the start of her ordeal.

"I've experienced the fullness of it," she said quietly. "The Engineers do not claim to know everything. We were wrong about our policy of separating symbiotic pairs. My only regret is that I can't tell anyone about our mistake." She looked doubtfully at Parameter, but knew it was useless. "I forgive you. I love you, my killer. Do the deed." She presented her white neck and closed her eyes.

"Umm," Parameter said. She had not heard her victim's last words; she had cut herself off and could see only the neck. She let Solstice guide her hands. They found the pressure points as if by instinct, pressed hard, and it was just like Solstice had said it would be. The woman was unconscious in seconds. Now she must be kept alive for a few minutes while Solstice did what she had to do.

"Got it," came Solstice's shaken thought.

"Was it hard?" Parameter had kept away from it.

"Let's don't talk about it. I'll show it to you in about a decade and we can cry for a year. But I have it."

So the other Symb was already dead, and Solstice had been with it as it died. Parameter's job would not be nearly so hard.

She put her thumbs on the woman's neck again, bent her ear to the chest. She pressed, harder this time. Soon the heartbeat fluttered, raced briefly. There was a convulsion, then she was dead.

"Let's get out of here."

What they had acquired was the Symb-Engineer frequency organ. It was the one way the inhabitants of the Rings had of telling friend from foe. The radio organs of the Symbs were tuned from birth to send on a specific frequency, and the Engineers used one band exclusively. The Consers employed another, because they had a stake in identifying friends and foes, too. But Parameter no longer identified with either side, and now had the physical resources to back up her lack of conviction. She could send on either band now, according to the needs of the moment, and so could move freely from one society to the other. If caught, she would be seen as a spy by either side, but she didn't think of herself as one.

It had been necessary to kill the Engineer pair because the organ could not be removed without causing the death of the Symb. The organ could be cloned, and that was the escape Parameter had offered the other two. But it had been refused. So now Solstice had two voices; her own, and the one from the other organ which she had already implanted in herself.

In addition to the double voice, they had picked up information about the life of the Engineers without which it would be impossible to function without immediate exposure. They knew the customs and beliefs of the Engineers and could fit in with them as long as they didn't go into sexual rapport. That could get sticky, but they had a dodge. The most reliable way to avoid intercourse was to be pregnant, and that was what they set out to do.

It didn't seem too important, but his name was Appoggiatura. They had encountered him during the third week after the murder. It was a risk—a small one, but a risk all the same. He had been easy about it. He learned all about Parameter's deeds and plans during their intercourse and remained unperturbed. Fanatic dedication was rare among Consers; the only real fanatic Parameter had met was Bushwhacker, who had offered to shoot her at the hint of treason. Parameter and Solstice were aware that what they were doing was treason to the Conser cause. Appoggiatura didn't seem to care, or if he did, he thought it was justified after what they had been through.

"But have you thought about what you'll do if you find Equinox? I don't know what you think, but it sounds like a thorny problem to me."

"It's thorny, all right," Solstice agreed. "To me, especially. Don't talk to me about problems until you've gone through the insecurity I've felt when I think about that day."

"It's *my* insecurity, too," Parameter said. "We don't know.

But we do know we have to find her. And the children, though that isn't so strong. I only saw them for a few minutes, and they'll be seven years old now. I can't expect much there."

"I wouldn't expect much from Equinox, either," he said. "I know something about what happens to a Symb when it's separated from a human. Something dies; I don't know what. But it has to start over again from the beginning. She'll be a part of one of your children now, whichever one of them she took over when she was separated from you. You won't know her, and she won't know you."

"Still, we have to do this. I want to leave you now."

For six months they drifted, allowing Parameter's body to swell to the point that it would be obvious she was pregnant and not available for sex. During that time they thought.

Countless times they decided they were being foolish; that to complete their search would be to finish their life's mission and be faced with what to do with the next thousand years. But they could not just go through the motions. Perhaps one person could do that, but it wouldn't work with two. There was always that alter ego telling you by her very presence that you were living a lie.

And there was Rosy-Red-Ring 3351. If they quit, her murder would have been for no purpose. That would have been too much to bear. They had her in their memory, always cherishing her, always ashamed of what they had done. And the Symb, whose name Solstice had not yet been able to mention. One day Parameter would have to go through that killing again, but closer. Solstice was, if anything, even more determined than Parameter to verify the necessity of that terrible act.

So they started back to the Engineer-infested sector where so long ago Equinox had been made a prisoner of war.

There was a nervous moment the first time they used the stolen transmitter organ, but it went off smoothly. After that, they were able to move freely in Engineer society. It was a strange world, steeped in ritual that would have instantly confounded a novice. But they had received an instant course in religion and fell back on the memories of Rosy-Red-Ring that were burned into their minds.

They took the name Earth-Revenger 9954f, a common name attached to a random number with the "f" added as a mark of status. Only Engineers who had borne a hundred children were supposed to add the letter to their names. Theoretically, births were supposed to be recorded at Ringpainter Temple, clear across the Ring from them, where what records it was possible to keep in Ring society were stored. But there was no danger once they had verified that their stolen transmitter would fool the Engineers. Even in Engineer society, where social contact was more important than among Consers, the chance of meeting the same person twice was small. The chance of Parameter and Solstice meeting the real Earth-Revenger 9954f was not even worth thinking about.

The place they stayed around was the very rock she had pushed off from on the day of her capture, the rock from which Rosy-Red-Ring had left on her final day. It was a communications center, a social hall, a gossip rendezvous; the means by which the Engineers were able to keep their cohesiveness against the formidable odds of empty space.

She took over the job of station manager, a largely informal, voluntary post that meant you stayed in the station and loosely coordinated the activities there. These consisted of posting in written form information that was too important to entrust to word of mouth, and generally trying to pump each incoming Engineer for that type of information. As such, it was ideally suited for what she wanted to do.

There was the problem of her pregnancy. Pregnant women needed a lot of sunshine and rock and ice, and generally didn't take the job. She faced a lot of questions about it, but got away with her story about just plain liking the job so much she didn't want to give it up.

But the problem of getting enough sunlight was real. The location of the station was deep enough inside the Rings by now that the incident sunlight was low. She should have gone above the plane to where the light wasn't scattered off so many rocks, but she couldn't.

She compromised by spending all her free time outside the station with Solstice in her extended configuration.

The prime topic of conversation was the failure of the Pop Edict, and it was this that led her to information about Equinox.

Under the Edict, each Engineer was to undergo a sex change and spend nine years as a female for every year as a male. Three children were to be borne each of those years. The figures told a different story.

It was the first resistance to an Edict; unorganized, but still disturbing. There was much debate about it, and much solemn rededication. Everyone vowed to bear as many children as she could, but Parameter wondered how sincere it was. Her own sampling of Engineers revealed that females did outnumber males, but only by three to one, not nine to one.

There were several causes discussed for it. One, and the most obvious, was simple preference. Statistically, 90 percent of all people had a preferred sex, and of those, it was evenly divided as to which sex was the preferred one. For the target percentages to be in effect, 35 percent of the Engineers would have to be living as the sex they did not prefer. The actual figures indicated that not many of them were doing so. They were remaining defiantly male.

Then there was the logistical problem. To gain enough useful mass to produce one baby, a Symb-human pair had to ingest almost a thousand kilograms of rock and ice. Only a tiny fraction of it was the chemicals needed to produce a baby. Then, to convert the mass to useful form, energy was required. The pair had to spend long hours in the sunlight. After all that, there was little time for painting the Ring, and that was what most Engineers saw as their prime mission, not becoming baby factories.

It was said that Ringpainter was in meditation, and had been for the past ten years, trying to find a way out of the dilemma. She saw her Grand Gesture being slowed down to the point where it was actually in jeopardy. If, in the far future, the Engineer birthrate didn't outstrip the Conser birthrate, it would mean trouble. The time of the great Conser effort was yet to come. As things now stood, a Conser might not even see a painted rock in three or four days; they were too far apart. But as the number of painted rocks grew, the rate of recoloring would also grow. Then the Engineers would have to depend on the sheer rate of repainting to overpower the negative effect of the Consers. If their populations were nearly equal, it would be a stalemate, and only the Consers could win a stalemate. To accomplish the Grand Design,

90 percent of the rock in Ring Beta must be painted. To reach this figure, the Engineers must outnumber the Consers by ten to one, otherwise the number of painted rocks would stabilize below the target figure. It was a crisis of the first magnitude, though no one alive would see the outcome.

In discussing this with one of the Engineers, a woman named Glorious-Red-Ring 43f, the break came. She was one of the early followers of Ringpainter, had been in the Ring for two hundred years. She had birthed 389 children, and acknowledged it was below her quota. She was living proof that the goals of Ringpainter were unrealistic, but she had unshakable faith that it was the right policy. She blamed herself that she had not had six hundred children, and had dedicated herself to meeting her quota within the next century. To do that, she must bear five hundred children. Parameter thought she was pathetic. She was pregnant with septuplets.

"I see these young ones coming in here with twins in their wombs and wonder how they can call themselves Engineers," she complained. "Only last month I saw one with a single child on the way. One! Can you imagine? How many do you have there?"

"Three. Maybe it should have been more." Parameter tried to sound guilty about it.

"That's all right. Three is the right number. I won't ask if you had three *last* year.

"And the number of males I see makes me weep. I make it 7.43 to 2.57, female to male." She lapsed into a brooding silence.

"If that wasn't bad enough," Parameter prompted, "I understand the Conser birthrate has equalled ours."

"Has it?" She was concerned at this bit of news, and would have been relieved to learn it was totally spurious. Parameter used that line frequently to lead someone into a discussion of Conser women in general and one Conser in particular who had been captured around here several years ago while birthing quints.

"But it shouldn't surprise me," the Engineer said. "So many of the Consers we've taken lately have been pregnant with three, four, even five."

This was more like it. Parameter considered remarks that might draw the woman out.

"I recall, almost ten years ago . . . or was it five? I get confused. There was this Conser some of our people took. Five children she had just borne."

Parameter was so surprised she almost let the opportunity slip by.

"Five?" she managed to croak. It was enough.

"That's right. How long has it been since you saw one of ours give birth to five? And those anarchists don't even have a Pop Edict to tell them to do it. She was doing it for fun."

"Were you there when it happened? When they captured the woman?"

"I heard about it later. They had the pups around here for a few days. Didn't know what to do with them. No one had heard about the crèche."

"Crèche?"

"You, too. The newsmongering around here has fallen down. It should have been posted and circulated."

"I'll surely see that it's done if you'll tell me about it."

"There's a crèche for POW children about fifty thousand kilometers forward from here. That's where we're supposed to take captured Conser children for indoctrination."

They digested that, didn't like the taste of it.

"The indoctrination's pretty successful, is it?"

"Great Red Ring, I hope so. Haven't been there myself. But we need everything we can get these days."

"Just where is this crèche? I should post the orbital elements around here."

The triplets were a failure. During the tenth month, on the way to the crèche, Solstice notified Parameter that it was hopeless; they hadn't gotten enough energy and raw materials during their stay at the way-station. It was no longer possible to hold their development back, and it was too late to amass the necessary minerals to do the job.

Solstice aborted them and reabsorbed the dead bodies. With the extra energy from the abortion, they were able to make good time to the crèche. It only took two years.

The crèche was deserted; an empty shell. News traveled slowly in the Ring. Inquiring around, Parameter discovered that it had not been operating for fifteen years. So her children had never arrived, though they had set out.

This was the time for despair, but they were beyond despair. Somewhere on the way to the crèche they had stopped believing it was possible to do what they were trying to do. So it wasn't a blow to find the crèche deserted. Still, it was hard to accept that their search ended here; they had been on the trail for nine years.

But the figures were unimpeachable. The volume of Ring Beta was seventy billion cubic kilometers, and any one of them could hide a thousand children.

They hung around the crèche for a few weeks, questioning Engineers, trying to find an angle that would enable them to defeat the statistics. Without a known destination for their children, there was no way out; they could be anywhere, and that was so vast it didn't bear thinking about.

In the end they left, and didn't know where they were bound.

Three days later they encountered another Conser, a male, and mated with him. He was sympathetic to their plight, but agreed with them that there was no chance of finding their children. Solstice carefully saw to it that Parameter was not fertilized. They had had enough of pregnancy for the next century or so.

And after they left the Conser, they found themselves falling asleep. Only they knew it wasn't sleep.

Before she even opened her eyes, Parameter reached frantically for the top of her head.

"Solstice . . ."

"I'm here. Don't make any sudden moves. We've been captured. I don't know by whom, but he's armed."

She opened her eyes. She was in a conjugation sphere and the tendril from Solstice was still firmly planted in her head. There was another person with her, a small person. He waved his gun at her and she nodded.

"Don't be alarmed," he said. "If you can answer a few questions you'll probably come out of this alive."

"You can set your mind at ease. I won't cause any trouble."

She realized he was a child, about eleven years old. But he seemed to know about stunners.

"We've been watching you for about a week," he said. "You talked to Engineers, so we naturally assumed you were one. But just now you spoke to a Conser, and on the Conser frequency. I want an explanation."

"I was originally a Conser. Recently I killed an Engineer and stole her transmitter organ." She knew she couldn't think of a convincing lie quickly enough to be safe from his stunner. She wasn't sure there *was* a convincing lie to cover her situation.

"Which side do you identify with now?"

"Neither side. I want to be independent if anyone will allow that."

He looked thoughtful. "That may be easier than you know. Why did you kill the Engineer?"

"I had to do it so I could move in Engineer society, so I could hunt for my children and the Symb who was taken from me several years ago. I have been—"

"What's your name?"

"Parameter, and Solstice."

"Right. I've got a message for you, Parameter. It's from your children. They're all right, and looking for you around here. We should be able to find them in a few days' search."

The children recognized the awkwardness of the situation. As they joined the group conjugation, emerging from the walls of the slowly enlarging sphere, they limited themselves to a brief kiss, then withdrew into a tangle of small bodies.

Parameter and Solstice were so jittery they could hardly think. The five children they could get to know, but Equinox? What about her?

They got the distinct feeling that the children recognized Parameter, then realized it was possible. Equinox had been talking to them while still in the womb, urging their minds to develop with pictures and sounds. Some of the pictures would have been of Parameter.

Ring children are not like other human children. They are born already knowing most of what they need to survive in the Rings. Then they are able to join with an infant Symb and help guide its development into an adult in a few weeks. From there, the Symb takes over for three years, teaching them and leading them to the places they need to go to grow up strong and healthy. For all practical purposes they are mature at three years. They must be; they cannot count on being with their mother more than the few weeks it takes them to acquire an adult Symb. From that time, they are on their own. Infant physical shortcomings are made up by the guidance and control of the Symb.

Parameter looked at these strange children, these youngsters whose backyard was billions of cubic kilometers wide and whose toys were stars and comets. What did she know of them? They might as well be another species. But that shouldn't matter; so was Solstice.

Solstice was almost hysterical. She was gripped in fear that in some way she couldn't understand she was going to lose Parameter. She was in danger of losing her mind. One part of her loved Equinox as hopelessly as Parameter did; another part knew there was room for only one Symb for any one human. What if it came to a choice? How would they face it?

"Equinox?"

There was a soundless scream from Solstice. "Equinox?" ?????

"Is that you, Equinox?"

The answer was very faint, very far away. They could not hear it.

"It's me. Parameter."

"And Solstice. You don't know me—"

I know you. You are me. I used to be you. I remember both of you. Interesting.

But the voice didn't sound interested. It was cool.

"I don't understand." No one was sure who said it.

But you do. I am gone. There is a new me. There is a new you. It is over.

"We love you."

Yes. Of course you do. But there is no me left to love.

"We're confused."

You will get over it.

The children floated together: quietly, respectfully; waiting for their mother to come to grips with her new reality. At last she stirred.

"Maybe we'll understand it some day," Parameter said.

One of the girls spoke.

"Equinox is no more, Mother," she said. "And yet she's still with us. She made a choice when she knew we were going to be captured. She reabsorbed her children and fissioned into five parts. None of us got all of her, but we all got enough."

Parameter shook her head and tried to make sense out of it. The child who had brought her here had not been willing to tell her anything, preferring to wait until her children could be with her.

"I don't understand how you came to find me."

"All it took was patience. We never reached the crèche; we were liberated on the way here by Alphans. They killed all the Engineers who were guarding us and adopted us themselves."

"What's an Alphan?"

"Alphans are the Ringers who live in Ring Alpha, who are neither Conser nor Engineer. They are renegades from both sides who have opted out of the conflict. They took care of us, and helped us when we said we wanted to find you. We knew where we had been going, and knew it was only a matter of time until you showed up here, if you were still alive. So we waited. And you got here in only nine years. You're very resourceful."

"Perhaps." She was looking at her children's legs. They were oddly deformed. And what were those blunt instruments at the ends of them? How odd.

"Feet, Mother," the child said. "There are surgeons in Alpha, but we could never afford to go there until we had found you. Now we'll go. We hope you'll go with us."

"Huh? Ah, I guess I should. That's across the Cassini Division, isn't it? And there's no war there? No killing?"

"That's right. We don't care if they paint Ring Beta with stripes and polka dots. They're freaks: Conser and Engineers. We are the true Ringers."

"Solstice?"

"Why not?"

"We'll go with you. Say, what are your names?"

"Army," said one of the girls.
"Navy," said another.
"Marine."
"Airforce."
"And Elephant," said the boy.

Manikins

"YOU'RE SURE SHE'S NOT dangerous?"

"Not at all. Not to you, anyway."

Evelyn closed the sliding window in the door and made an effort to control the misgivings that tugged at her. It was a little late to discover in herself a queasiness about crazy people.

She looked around and discovered with relief that it wasn't the patients she feared. It was the fortress atmosphere of the Bedford Institution. The place was a nightmare of barred windows, padded rooms, canvas sheets and straightjackets and hypodermics and burly attendants. It was a prison. With all the precautions it was only natural that she should feel nervous about the people it was built to contain.

She peeked into the room again. The woman inside was so small, so quiet and composed to be the cause of all this fuss.

Doctor Burroughs closed the thick file he had been scanning. *Barbara Endicott. Age: 28. Height: 5' 3". Weight: 101. Diagnosis: Paranoid Schizophrenic. Remarks: Subject is to be considered dangerous. Remanded for observation from criminal court, Commonwealth of Massachusetts, murder. Intense hostility to men.* There was more, much more. Evelyn had read some of it.

"She's got a massively defended psychosis. As usual, granting the illogical assumptions, the delusional system is carefully worked out and internally consistent."

"I know," Evelyn said.

"Do you? Yes, I suppose you do, from books and films." He

closed the file and handed it to her. "You'll find it's a little different actually talking to one of them. They're sure of the things they say in a way that no sane person is ever likely to be. We all live with our little doubts, you know. They don't. They've seen the truth, and nothing will convince them otherwise. It takes a strong grip on reality to deal with them. You're likely to be a bit shaken when you're through with her."

Evelyn wished he'd finish and open the door. She had no worries about her sense of reality. Did he really worry that the woman would unsettle her with the kind of rubbish that was down in that file?

"We've had her on electroshock treatments for the last week," he said. He shrugged, helplessly. "I know what your teachers have said about that. It wasn't my decision. There's just no way to reach these people. When we run out of reason and persuasion, we try the shocks. It's not doing her any good. Her psychosis is as defended as it ever was." He rocked back on his heels, frowning.

"I guess you might as well go on in. You're perfectly safe. Her hostility is directed only at men." He gestured to the white-suited attendant, who looked like an NFL lineman, and the man turned a key in the lock. He opened the door, standing back to let her pass.

Barbara Endicott sat in a chair by the window. The sunlight streamed through and the bars made a cross-hatched pattern over her face. She turned, but did not get up.

"Hello, I'm...I'm Evelyn Winters." The woman had turned away as soon as she started talking. Evelyn's confidence, feeble enough in this forbidding place, threatened to leave her entirely.

"I'd like to talk to you, if you don't mind. I'm not a doctor, Barbara."

The woman turned back and looked at her.

"Then what are you doing in that white coat?"

Evelyn looked down at the lab smock. She felt silly in the damn thing.

"They told me I had to wear it."

"Who is 'they?'" Barbara asked, with the hint of a chuckle. "You sound paranoid, my dear."

Evelyn relaxed a little. "Now that should have been *my* question. 'They' are the staff of this...place." *Damn it, relax!* The woman seemed friendly enough now that she saw Evelyn wasn't a doctor. "I guess they want to know if I'm a patient."

"Right. They'd give you one of these blue outfits if you were."

"I'm a student. They said I could interview you."

"Shoot." Then she smiled, and it was such a friendly, sane smile that Evelyn smiled back and extended her hand. But Barbara was shaking her head.

"That's a man thing," she said, indicating the hand. "'See? I have no weapons. I'm not going to kill you.' We don't need that, Evelyn. We're women."

"Oh, of course." She awkwardly stuffed the hand into the pocket of the lab coat, clenched. "May I sit down?"

"Sure. There's just the bed, but it's hard enough to sit on."

Evelyn sat on the edge of the bed, the file and notebook in her lap. She poised there, and found that her weight was still on the balls of her feet, ready to leap away. The bleakness of the room assaulted her. She saw flaking gray paint, yellow window glass set in a well behind a mesh screen, gun-metal bolts securing it to the wall. The floor was concrete, damp and unfriendly. The room echoed faintly. The only furniture was the chair and the bed with gray sheets and blanket.

Barbara Endicott was small, dark-haired, with the smooth perfection of features that reminded Evelyn of an oriental. She looked pale, probably from two months in the cell. Under it, she had robust health. She sat in a checkerboard of sunlight, soaking up what rays passed through the glass. She wore a blue bathrobe with nothing underneath, belted at the waist, and cloth slippers.

"So I'm your assignment for the day. Did you pick me, or someone else?"

"They told me you'd only speak to women."

"That's true, but you didn't answer my question, did you? I'm sorry. I didn't mean to make you nervous, really. I won't be like that again. I'm acting like a crazy woman."

"What do you mean?"

"Being bold, aggressive. Saying whatever I want to. That's how all the crazy people around here act. I'm not crazy, of course." Her eyes were twinkling.

"I can't tell if you're putting me on," Evelyn admitted, and suddenly felt much closer to the woman. It was an easy trap to fall into, thinking of deranged people as mentally defective, lacking in reasoning powers. There was nothing wrong with Barbara Endicott in that direction. She could be subtle.

"Of *course* I'm crazy," she said. "Would they have me locked up here if I wasn't?" She grinned, and Evelyn relaxed. Her back loosened up; the bedspring creaked as she settled on them.

"All right. Do you want to talk about it?"

"I'm not sure if you want to hear. You know I killed a man, don't you?"

"Did you? I know the hearing thought you did, but they found you incapable of standing trial."

"I killed him, all right. I had to find out."

"Find out what?"

"If he could still walk with his head cut off."

And there it was; she was an alien again. Evelyn suppressed a shudder. The woman had said it in such a reasonable tone of voice, without any obvious try for shock value. And indeed, it had not affected her as strongly as it might have a few minutes ago. She was revolted, but not scared.

"And what made you think he might be able to?"

"That's not the important question," she chided. "Maybe it's not important to you, but it is to me. I wouldn't have done a thing like that unless it was important to know."

"To know . . . oh. Well, *did* he?"

"He sure did. For two or three minutes, he blundered around that room. I saw it, and I knew I was right."

"Will you tell me what led you to think he could?"

Barbara looked her over.

"And why should I? Look at you. You're a woman, but you've swallowed all the lies. You're working for them."

"What do you mean?"

"You've painted yourself up. You've scraped the hair off your legs and covered them with nylon, and you're walking inefficiently with a skirt to hobble your legs and heels designed to make you stumble if you run from them when they try to rape you. You're here doing their work for them. Why should I tell you? You wouldn't believe me."

Evelyn was not alarmed by this turn in the conversation. There was no hostility in what Barbara was saying. If anything, there was pity. Barbara would not harm her, simply because she was a woman. Now that she understood that, she could go on with more assurance.

"That may be true. But don't you owe it to me, as a woman, to tell me about this threat if it's really so important?"

Barbara slapped her knees in delight.

"You got me, doc. You're right. But that was sure tricky, turning my own delusions against me."

Evelyn wrote in her notebook: *Can be glib when discussing her delusional-complex. She is assured enough of her rightness to make jokes about it.*

"What are you writing?"

"Huh? Oh . . ." *Be honest, she'll know if you lie. Be straight with her and match her irreverence.* ". . . just notes on your condition. I have to make a diagnosis to my instructor. He wants to know what kind of crazy you are."

"That's easy. I'm paranoid schizophrenic. You don't need a degree to see that."

"No, I guess not. All right, tell me about it."

"Basically, what I believe is that the Earth was invaded by some kind of parasite at some point back in pre-history. Probably in cave-dwelling days. It's hard to tell for sure, since history is such a pack of lies. They rewrite it all the time, you know."

Again, Evelyn didn't know if she was being played with, and the thought amused her. This was a complex, tricky woman. She'd have to stay on her toes. That speech had been such an obvious paranoid construction, and Barbara was well aware of it.

"I'll play your game. Who is 'they?'"

"'They' is the all-purpose paranoid pronoun. Any group that is involved in a conspiracy, conscious or not, to 'get' you. I know that's crazy, but there are such groups."

"Are there?"

"Sure. I didn't say they had to be holding meetings to plot ways to bedevil you. They don't. You can admit the existence of groups whose interests are not your own, can't you?"

"Certainly."

"The more important thing is it doesn't matter if they're really an explicit conspiracy, or just have the same effect because that's the way they function. It doesn't have to be personal, either. Each year, the IRS conspires to rob you of money that you earned, don't they? They're in a plot with the President and Congress to steal your money and give it to other people, but they don't know you by name. They steal from everybody. That's the kind of thing I'm talking about."

Justifies her fear of external, inimical forces by pointing to real antagonistic groups.

"Yes, I can see that. But we all know the IRS is out there. You're talking about a secret that only you see. Why should I believe you?"

Her face got more serious. Perhaps she was realizing the strengths of her opponent. Her opponent always had the stronger arguments, it was the nature of things. *Why are you right and everyone else wrong?*

"That's the tough part. You can offer me reams of 'proof' that I'm wrong, and I can't show you anything. If you'd been there when I'd killed that fellow, you'd know. But I can't do it again." She drew a deep breath, and seemed to settle in for a long debate.

"Let's get back to these parasites," Evelyn said. "They're men? Is that what you're saying?"

"No, no." She laughed, without humor. "There's no such thing as a man, the way you're thinking about it. Only women who've been taken over at birth by these, these . . ." she groped in the air for a word hideous enough to express her distaste. She couldn't find it. "Things. Organisms. I said they invaded the Earth, but I'm not sure. They might be from here. There's no way to know, they've taken over too completely."

Leaves flexibility in her rationale. Yes, that would fit with what the books said. It would be hard to stump her, to ask her a question she couldn't answer in terms of her delusion. She admitted not knowing everything about the subject, and she was free to reject whole categories of argument as having been tampered with, like history.

"So how is it . . . no, wait. Maybe you'd better tell me more about these parasites. Where do they hide? How is it that no one but you is aware of them?"

She nodded. She now seemed totally serious. She could not joke about this subject when they got this specific.

"They're not strictly parasites. They're sort of symbiotic. They don't kill their hosts, not quickly. They even help the host in the short run, making them stronger and larger and more capable of domination. But in the long run, they sap the strength of the host. They make her more susceptible to disease, weaken her heart. As to what they look like, you've seen them. They're blind, helpless, immobile worms. They attach themselves to a woman's urinary tract, filling and covering the vagina and extending nerves into the ovaries and uterus. They inject hormones into her body and cause her to grow up with deformities, like facial hair, enlarged muscles, reduced thinking capacity, and wildly defective emotions. The host becomes aggressive and murderous. Her breasts never develop. She is permanently sterile."

Evelyn scribbled in her notebook to cover her emotions. She wanted to laugh; she felt like crying. Who could figure the human mind? She shuddered to think of the pressures that must have driven this outwardly normal woman to such a bizarre way of looking at the universe. Father? Lover? Was she raped? Barbara had been unhelpful in talking about these things, maintaining that they were no one's business but her own. Besides, they had no bearing on what she saw as the facts of the case.

"I hardly know where to begin," Evelyn said.

"Yes, I know. It's not the sort of thing they'd allow you to seriously consider, is it? It's too alien to what you've been led to believe. I'm sorry. I hope I can help you."

Damn! she wrote, then scratched it out. *Puts questioners on the defensive. Shows sympathy with their inability to see things as she sees them.*

"Call it the new biology," Barbara said, getting up and slowly walking back and forth in the confined space. Her loose slippers slipped off her heels with each step. "I began to suspect it several years ago. The world just didn't make *sense* any other way. You've got to begin to doubt what you've been told. You've got to trust the evidence of your intellect. You've got to allow yourself to look through your woman's eyes as a *woman* would, not as an imperfect man would. They've trained you to believe in their values, their system. What you begin to realize is that they are imperfect women, not the other way around. *They can't reproduce themselves,* shouldn't that tell you something? 'Males' live on our bodies as parasites, they use our fertility to perpetuate their species." She turned to Evelyn, and her eyes were burning. "Can you try to look at it that way? Just try? Don't try to be a man; redefine! You don't know what you are. All your life you've struggled to be a man. They've defined the role you should play. And you're not made for it. You don't have that parasite eating at your brain. Can you accept that?"

"I can, for the sake of argument."

"That's good enough."

Evelyn was treading cautiously. "Uh, just what do I have to do to . . . 'see things as a woman?' I feel like a woman right now."

"*Feel!* That's it, just feel. You know what 'woman's intuition' is? It's the human way to think. They've laughed at it to the point where we automatically distrust it. They *had* to; they've lost the capacity to see a truth intuitively. I can see you don't like that phrase. You wouldn't. It's been laughed at so much that an 'enlightened woman' like yourself doesn't believe it exists. That's what they want you to think. All right, don't use the word 'intuition.' Use something else. What I'm talking about is the innate capacity of a human being to feel the truth of a matter. We all know we have it, but we've been trained to distrust it. And it's gotten screwed up. Haven't you ever felt you're right for no reason you could name except that you knew you were *right*?"

"Yes, I guess I have. Most people do." *Rejects logical argument as being part of her oppression.* She decided to test that.

"What I've been . . . trained to do, is to apply the rules of logic to analyze a question. Right? And you say it's no good, despite thousands of years of human experience?"

"That's right. It's not human experience, though. It's a trick. It's a game, a very complicated game."

"What about science? Biology, in particular."

"Science is the biggest game of all. Have you ever thought about it? Do you seriously feel that the big questions of the universe, the important truths that should be easily in our grasp, will be solved by scientists haggling over how many neutrinos can dance on the head of a pin? It's a tail-eating snake, relevant only to itself. But once you accept the basic ground rules, you're trapped. You think that counting and sorting and numbering will teach you things. You have to reject it all and see the world with new eyes. You'll be astounded at what is there, ready for you to pick up."

"Genetics?"

"Hogwash. The whole structure of genetics has been put there to explain an untenable position: that there are two sexes, neither of them worthwhile alone, but together they're able to reproduce. It doesn't hold up when you think about it. Genes and chromosomes, half from each parent: no, no, *no*! Tell me, have you ever seen a gene?"

"I've seen pictures."

"Hah!" That seemed enough for the moment. She paced the floor, overwhelmed by the scope of it. She turned again and faced Evelyn.

"I know, I know. I've thought about it enough. There's this . . . this basic set of assumptions we all live by. We can't get along without accepting almost all of it, right? I mean, I could tell you that I don't believe in . . . Tokyo, for instance, that Tokyo doesn't exist simply because I haven't been there to see it for myself. The news films I've seen were all clever hoaxes, right? Travelogues, books, Japanese; they're all in a conspiracy to make me think there's such a place as Tokyo."

"You could make a case for it, I guess."

"Sure I could. We all exist, *all* of us, in our own heads, looking out through the eyeballs. Society isn't possible unless we can believe in second-hand reports of certain things. So we've all conspired together to accept what other people tell us unless we can think of a reason why we're being lied to. Society can be seen as a conspiracy of unquestioning acceptance of unprovable things. We all work together at it, we all define a set of things as needing no proof."

She started to say more, but shut her mouth. She seemed to be considering if she should go on. She looked speculatively at Evelyn.

Evelyn shifted on her cot. Outside, the sun was setting in a haze of red and yellow. Where had the day gone? What time had she come into this room, anyway? She was unsure. Her stomach grumbled at her, but she wasn't too uncomfortable. She was fascinated. She felt a sort of lassitude, a weakness that made her want to lie down on the bed.

"Where was I? Oh, the untested assumptions. Okay. If we can't accept anything that's told us, we can't function in society. You can get away with not accepting a lot. You can believe the world is flat, or that there are no such things as photons or black holes or genes. Or that Christ didn't rise from the grave. You can go a long way from the majority opinion. But if you evolve an entirely new world picture, you start to get in trouble."

"What's most dangerous of all," Evelyn pointed out, "is starting to live by these new assumptions."

"Yes, yes. I should have been more careful, shouldn't I? I could have kept this discovery to myself. Or I could have gone on wondering. I was *sure*, you see, but in my foolishness I had to have proof. I had to see if a man could live with his head cut off, against what all the medical books had told me. I had to know if it was the brain that controlled him, or if it was that parasite."

Evelyn wondered what to ask as Barbara quieted for a moment. She knew it wasn't necessary to ask anything. The woman was off now; she would not wind down for hours. But she felt she ought to try and guide her.

"I was wondering," she finally ventured, "why you didn't need a second case. A . . . a check from the other side. Why didn't you kill a woman, too, to see if . . ." The hair stood up on the back of her neck. Of all the things she should have kept her mouth shut about, and to a homicidal paranoid! She was painfully aware of her throat. She controlled her hand, which wanted to go to her neck in feeble protection. *She has no weapons, but she could be very strong . . .*

But Barbara didn't pick up the thought. She didn't appear to notice Evelyn's discomfort.

"Foolish!" she exploded. "I was foolish. Of *course* I should have taken it on faith. I felt I was right; I *knew* I was right. But the old scientific orientation finally drove me to the experiment. *Experiment*." She spat the word out. She paused again, calming down, and seemed to think back.

"Kill a woman?" She shook her head and gave Evelyn a wry smile. "Dear, that would be murder. I'm not a killer. These 'men' are already dead from my viewpoint; killing them is a mercy, and a defensive act. Anyhow, after I'd done the first experiment I realized I had really proved nothing. I had only disproved the assumption that a man cannot live with his head cut off. That left a whole range of possibilities, you see? Maybe the brain is not in the head. Maybe the brain isn't *good* for anything. How do you know what's inside you? Have you ever seen your brain? How do you know that you're not really a wired-up midget, two inches tall, sitting in a control room in your head? Doesn't it feel like that sometimes?"

"Ah . . ." Barbara had hit on a common nerve. Not the midget, which was only a fanciful way of putting it, but the concept of living in one's head with eye-sockets as windows on the universe.

"Right. But you reject the gut feelings. I listen to them."

The light in the room was rapidly failing. Evelyn looked at the bare bulb in the ceiling, wondering when it would come on. She was getting sleepy, so tired. But she wanted to hear more. She leaned back farther on the cot and let her legs and arms relax.

"Maybe you should . . ." she yawned, wider and wider, unable to control it. "Excuse me. Maybe you should tell me more about the parasites."

"Ah. All right." She went back to her chair and sat in it. Evelyn could barely see her in the shadows. She heard a faint creaking, as of wooden slats on a rocking chair. But the chair wasn't a rocker. It wasn't even made of wood. Nevertheless, Barbara's shadow was moving slowly and rhythmically, and the creaking went on.

"The parasites, I've already told you what they do. Let me tell you what I've managed to deduce about their life-cycle."

Evelyn grinned in the dark. *Life-cycle. Of course they'd have one.* She leaned on one elbow and rested her head on the wall behind her. It would be interesting.

"They reproduce asexually, like everything else. They grow by budding, since the new ones are so much smaller than the mature ones. Then doctors implant them into women's wombs when they know they're pregnant, and they grow up with the embryo."

"Wait a minute," Evelyn sat up a little straighter. "Why don't they implant them all children? Why are girls allowed to . . . oh, I see."

"Yes. They need us. They can't reproduce by themselves. They need the warmth of the womb to grow in, and we have the wombs.

So they've systematically oppressed the women they've allowed to remain uninfested so they'll have a docile, ready supply of breeders. They've convinced us that we can't have children until we've been impregnated, which is the biggest lie of all."

"It is?"

"Yes. Take a look."

Evelyn peered through the gloom and saw Barbara, standing in profile. She was illuminated by a sort of flickering candlelight. Evelyn did not wonder about it, but was bothered by a strange feeling. It was rather like wondering why she was not curious.

But before even that ephemeral feeling could concern her, Barbara loosened the cloth belt on her wrap and let it fall open. There was a gentle swell in her belly, unmistakably an early pregnancy. Her hand traced out the curve.

"See? I'm pregnant. I'm about four or five months along. I can't say for sure, you see, because I haven't had intercourse for over five years."

Hysterical pregnancy, Evelyn thought, and groped for her notebook. Why couldn't she find it? Her hand touched it in the dark, then the pencil. She tried to write, but the pencil broke. Did it break, she wondered, or was it bending?

She heard the creaking of the floorboards again, and knew Barbara had sat down in her rocker. She looked sleepily for the source of light, but could not find it.

"What about other mammals?" Evelyn asked, with another yawn.

"Uh-huh. The same. I don't know if it's only one sort of parasite which is adaptable to any species of mammal, or if there's one breed for each. But there are no males. Nowhere. Only females, and infested females."

"Birds?"

"I don't know yet," she said, simply. "I suspect that the whole concept of the sexes is part of the game. It's such an unlikely thing. Why should we need two? One is enough."

Leaves flexibility, she wrote. But no, she hadn't written, had she? The notebook was lost again. She burrowed down into the pile of blankets or furs on the cot, feeling warm and secure. She heard a sliding sound.

There in the peephole, ghostly in the candlelight, was a man's face. It was the attendant, looking in on them. She gasped, and started to sit up as the light got brighter around her. There was the sound of a key grating in a lock.

Barbara was kneeling at the side of the bed. Her robe was still open, and her belly was huge. She took Evelyn's hands and held them tight.

"The biggest giveaway of all is childbirth," she whispered. The light wavered for a moment and the metallic scraping and jiggling of the doorknob lost pitch, growled and guttered like a turntable losing speed. Barbara took Evelyn's head in her arms and pulled her down to her breasts. Evelyn closed her eyes and felt the taut skin and the movement of something inside the woman. It got darker.

"Pain. Why should giving birth involve pain? Why should we so often *die* reproducing ourselves? It doesn't feel right. I won't say it's illogical; it doesn't feel right. My intuition tells me that it isn't so. It's not the way it was meant to be. Do you want to know why we die in childbirth?"

"Yes Barbara, tell me that." She closed her eyes and nuzzled easily into the warmth.

"It's the poison they inject into us." She gently rubbed Evelyn's hair as she spoke. "The white stuff, the waste product. They tell us it's the stuff that makes us pregnant, but that's a lie. It warps us, even those of us they do not inhabit. It pollutes the womb, causes us to grow too large for the birth canal. When it comes time for us to be born, girl and half-girl, we must come through a passage that has been savaged by this poison. The result is pain, and sometimes death."

"Ummm." It was very quiet in the room. Outside, the crickets were starting to chirp. She opened her eyes once more, looked for the door and the man. She couldn't find them. She saw a candle sitting on a wooden table. Was that a fireplace in the other room?

"But it doesn't have to be that way. It doesn't. Virgin birth is quite painless. I know. I'll know again very soon. Do you remember now, Eve? Do you remember?"

"What? I . . ." She sat up a little, still holding to the comforting warmth of the other woman. Where was the cell? Where was the concrete floor and barred window? She felt her heart beating faster and began to struggle, but Barbara was strong. She held her tight to her belly.

"Listen, Eve. Listen, it's happening."

Eve put her hand on the swollen belly and felt it move. Barbara shifted slightly, reached down and cradled something wet and warm, something that moved in her hand. She brought it up to the light. Virgin birth. A little girl, tiny, only a pound or two, who didn't cry but looked around her in curiosity.

"Can I hold her?" she sniffed, and then the tears flowed over the little human. There were other people crowding around, but she couldn't see them. She didn't care. She was home.

"Are you feeling any better now?" Barbara asked. "Can you remember what happened?"

"Only a little," Eve whispered. "I was ... I remember it now. I thought I was ... it was awful. Oh, Barbara, it was terrible. I thought ..."

"I know. But you're back. There's no need to be ashamed. It still happens to all of us. We go crazy. We're programmed to go crazy, all of us in the infected generation. But not our children. You relax and hold the baby, darling. You'll forget it. It was a bad dream."

"But it was so *real*!"

"It was what you used to be. Now you're back with your friends, and we're winning the struggle. We have to win; we've got the wombs. There's more of our children every day."

Our children. Her own, and Barbara's and ... and Karen's, yes, Karen. She looked up and saw her old friend, smiling down at her. And Clara, and there was June, and Laura. And over there with her children was Sacha. And ... who was that? It's ...

"Hello, Mother. Do you feel better now?"

"Much better, dear. I'm all right. Barbara helped me through it. I hope it won't happen again." She sniffed and wiped her eyes. She sat up, still cradling the tiny baby. "What are you naming her, Barb?"

Barbara grinned, and for the last time Eve could see the ghostly outline of that cell, the blue robe, Doctor Burroughs. It faded out forever.

"Let's call her Evelyn."

Beatnik Bayou

THE PREGNANT WOMAN HAD been following us for over an hour when Cathay did the unspeakable thing.

At first it had been fun. Me and Denver didn't know what it was about, just that she had some sort of beef with Cathay. She and Cathay had gone off together and talked. The woman started yelling, and it was not too long before Cathay was yelling, too. Finally Cathay said something I couldn't hear and came back to join the class. That was me, Denver, Trigger, and Cathay, the last two being the teachers, me and Denver being the students. I know, you're not supposed to be able to tell which is which, but believe me, you usually know.

That's when the chase started. This woman wouldn't take no for an answer, and she followed us wherever we went. She was about as awkward an animal as you could imagine, and I certainly wasn't feeling sorry for her after the way she had talked to Cathay, who is my friend. Every time she slipped and landed on her behind, we all had a good laugh.

For a while. After an hour, she started to seem a little frightening. I had never seen anyone so determined.

The reason she kept slipping was that she was chasing us through Beatnik Bayou, which is Trigger's home. Trigger herself describes it as "twelve acres of mud, mosquitoes, and moonshine." Some of her visitors had been less poetic but more colorful. I don't know what an acre is, but the bayou is fairly large. Trigger makes the moonshine in a copper and aluminum still in the middle

146

of a canebrake. The mosquitoes don't bite, but they buzz a lot. The mud is just plain old mississippi mud, suitable for beating your feet. Most people see the place and hate it instantly, but it suits me fine.

Pretty soon the woman was covered in mud. She had three things working against her. One was her ankle-length maternity gown, which covered all of her except for face, feet, and bulging belly and breasts. She kept stepping on the long skirt and going down. After a while, I winced every time she did that.

Another handicap was her tummy, which made her walk with her weight back on her heels. That's not the best way to go through mud, and every so often she sat down real hard, proving it.

Her third problem was the Birthgirdle pelvic bone, which must have just been installed. It was one of those which sets the legs far apart and is hinged in the middle so when the baby comes it opens out and gives more room. She needed it, because she was tall and thin, the sort of build that might have died in childbirth back when such things were a problem. But it made her waddle like a duck.

"Quack, quack," Denver said, with an attempt at a smile. We both looked back at the woman, still following, still waddling. She went down, and struggled to her feet. Denver wasn't smiling when she met my eyes. She muttered something.

"What's that?" I said.

"She's unnerving," Denver repeated. "I wonder what the hell she wants?"

"Something pretty powerful."

Cathay and Trigger were a few paces ahead of us, and I saw Trigger glance back. She spoke to Cathay. I don't think I was supposed to hear it, but I did. I've got good ears.

"This is starting to upset the kids."

"I know," he said, wiping his brow with the back of his hand. All four of us watched her as she toiled her way up the far side of the last rise. Only her head and shoulders were visible.

"Damn. I thought she'd give up pretty soon." He groaned, but then his face became expressionless. "There's no help for it. We'll have to have a confrontation."

"I thought you already did," Trigger said, lifting an eyebrow.

"Yeah. Well, it wasn't enough, apparently. Come on, people.

This is part of your lives, too." He meant me and Denver, and when he said that we knew this was supposed to be a "learning experience." Cathay can turn the strangest things into learning experiences. He started back toward the shallow stream we had just waded across, and the three of us followed him.

If I sounded hard on Cathay, I really shouldn't have been. Actually, he was one damn fine teacher. He was able to take those old saws about learning by doing, seeing is believing, one-on-one instruction, integration of life experiences—all the conventional wisdom of the educational establishment—and make it work better than any teacher I'd ever seen. I knew he was a counterfeit child. I had known that since I first met him, when I was seven, but it hadn't started to matter until lately. And that was just the natural cynicism of my age-group, as Trigger kept pointing out in that smug way of hers.

Okay, so he was really forty-eight years old. Physically he was just my age, which was almost thirteen: a short, slightly chubby kid with curly blond hair and an androgenous face, just starting to grow a little fuzz around his balls. When he turned to face that huge, threatening woman and stood facing her calmly, I was moved.

I was also fascinated. Mentally, I settled back on my haunches to watch and wait and observe. I was sure I'd be learning something about "life" real soon now. Class was in session.

When she saw us coming back, the woman hesitated. She picked her footing carefully as she came down the slight rise to stand at the edge of the water, then waited for a moment to see if Cathay was going to join her. He wasn't. She made an awful face, lifted her skirt up around her waist, and waded in.

The water lapped around her thighs. She nearly fell over when she tried to dodge some dangling Spanish moss. Her lace dress was festooned with twigs and leaves and smeared with mud.

"Why don't you turn around?" Trigger yelled, standing beside me and Denver and shaking her fist. "It's not going to do you any good."

"I'll be the judge of that," she yelled back. Her voice was harsh and ugly and what had probably been a sweet face was now set in a scowl. An alligator was swimming up to look her over. She swung at it with her fist, nearly losing her balance. "Get out

of here, you slimy lizard!" she screamed. The reptile recalled
urgent business on the other side of the swamp, and hurried out
of her way.

She clambered ashore and stood ankle-deep in ooze, breathing
hard. She was a mess, and beneath her anger I could now see fear.
Her lips trembled for a moment. I wished she would sit down;
just looking at her exhausted me.

"You've got to help me," she said, simply.

"Believe me, if I could, I would," Cathay said.

"Then tell me somebody who can."

"I told you, if the Educational Exchange can't help you, I
certainly can't. Those few people I know who are available for
a contract are listed on the exchange."

"But none of them are available any sooner than three years."

"I know. It's the shortage."

"Then help me," she said, miserably. "Help me."

Cathay slowly rubbed his eyes with a thumb and forefinger,
then squared his shoulders and put his hands on his hips.

"I'll go over it once more. Somebody gave you my name and
said I was available for a primary stage teaching contract. I—"

"He did! He said you'd—"

"I never heard of this person," Cathay said, raising his voice.
"Judging from what you're putting me through, he gave you my
name from the Teacher's Association listings just to get you off
his back. I guess I could do something like that, but frankly, I
don't think I have the right to subject another teacher to the sort
of abuse you've heaped on me." He paused, and for once she
didn't say anything.

"Right," he said, finally. "I'm truly sorry that the man you
contracted with for your child's education went to Pluto instead.
From what you told me, what he did was legal, which is not to
say ethical." He grimaced at the thought of a teacher who would
run out on an ethical obligation. "All I can say is you should have
had the contract analyzed, you should have had a standby contract
drawn up *three years ago* . . . oh, hell. What's the use? That doesn't
do you any good. You have my sympathy, I hope you believe
that."

"Then help me," she whispered, and the last word turned into a sob. She began to cry quietly. Her shoulders shook and tears leaked from her eyes, but she never looked away from Cathay.

"There's nothing I can do."

"You have to."

"Once more. I have obligations of my own. In another month, when I've fulfilled my contract with Argus' mother," he gestured toward me, "I'll be regressing to seven again. Don't you understand? I've already got an intermediate contract. The child will be seven in a few months. I contracted for her education four years ago. There's no way I can back out of that, legally or morally."

Her face was twisting again, filling with hate.

"Why not?" she rasped. "Why the hell not? He ran out on *my* contract. Why the hell should I be the only one to suffer? Why me, huh? Listen to me, you shitsucking little son of a blowout. You're all I've got left. After you, there's nothing but the public educator. Or trying to raise him all by myself, all alone, with no guidance. You want to be responsible for that? What the hell kind of start in life does that give him?"

She went on like that for a good ten minutes, getting more illogical and abusive with every sentence. I'd vacillated between a sort of queasy sympathy for her—she *was* in a hell of a mess, even though she had no one to blame but herself—and outright hostility. Just then she scared me. I couldn't look into those tortured eyes without cringing. My gaze wandered down to her fat belly, and the glass eye of the wombscope set into her navel. I didn't need to look into it to know she was due, and overdue. She'd been having the labor postponed while she tried to line up a teacher. Not that it made much sense; the kid's education didn't start until his sixth month. But it was a measure of her desperation, and of her illogical thinking under stress.

Cathay stood there and took it until she broke into tears again. I saw her differently this time, maybe a little more like Cathay was seeing her. I was sorry for her, but the tears failed to move me. I saw that she could devour us all if we didn't harden ourselves to her. When it came right down to it, she was the one who had to pay for her carelessness. She was trying her best to get someone else to shoulder the blame, but Cathay wasn't going to do it.

"I didn't want to do this," Cathay said. He looked back at us. "Trigger?"

Trigger stepped forward and folded her arms across her chest.

"Okay," she said. "Listen, I didn't get your name, and I don't really want to know it. But whoever you are, you're on my property, in my house. I'm ordering you to leave here, and I further enjoin you never to come back."

"I won't go," she said, stubbornly, looking down at her feet. "I'm not leaving till he promises to help me."

"My next step is to call the police," Trigger reminded her.

"I'm not leaving."

Trigger looked at Cathay and shrugged helplessly. I think they were both realizing that this particular life experience was getting a little too raw.

Cathay thought it over for a moment, eye to eye with the pregnant woman. Then he reached down and scooped up a handful of mud. He looked at it, hefting it experimentally, then threw it at her. It struck her on the left shoulder with a wet plop, and began to ooze down.

"Go," he said. "Get out of here."

"I'm not leaving," she said.

He threw another handful. It hit her face, and she gasped and sputtered.

"Go," he said, reaching for more mud. This time he hit her on the leg, but by now Trigger had joined him, and the woman was being pelted.

Before I quite knew what was happening, I was scooping mud from the ground and throwing it. Denver was, too. I was breathing hard, and I wasn't sure why.

When she finally turned and fled from us, I noticed that my jaw muscles were tight as steel. It took me a long time to relax them, and when I did, my front teeth were sore.

There are two structures on Beatnik Bayou. One is an old, rotting bait shop and lunch counter called the Sugar Shack, complete with a rusty gas pump out front, a battered Grapette machine on the porch, and a sign advertising Rainbow Bread on the screen door. There's a gray Dodge pickup sitting on concrete blocks to one side of the building, near a pile of rusted auto parts overgrown with weeds. The truck has no wheels. Beside it is a Toyota sedan with no windows or engine. A dirt road runs in front of the shack, going down to the dock. In the other direction the road curves around a cypress tree laden with moss—

—and runs into the wall. A bit of a jolt. But though twelve acres is large for a privately owned disneyland, it's not big enough to sustain the illusion of really being there. "There," in this case, is supposed to be Louisiana in 1951, old style. Trigger is fascinated by the twentieth century, which she defines as 1903 to 1987.

But most of the time it works. You can seldom see the walls because trees are in the way. Anyhow, I soak up the atmosphere of the place not so much with my eyes but with my nose and ears and skin. Like the smell of rotting wood, the sound of a frog hitting the water or the hum of the compressor in the soft drink machine, the silver wiggle of a dozen minnows as I scoop them from the metal tanks in back of the shack, the feel of sun-heated wood as I sit on the pier fishing for alligator gar.

It takes a lot of power to operate the "sun," so we get a lot of foggy days, and long nights. That helps the illusion, too. I would challenge anyone to go for a walk in the bayou night with the crickets chirping and the bullfrogs booming and not think they were back on Old Earth. Except for the Lunar gravity, of course.

Trigger inherited money. Even with that and a teacher's salary, the bayou is an expensive place to maintain. It used to be a more conventional environment, but she discovered early that the swamp took less upkeep, and she likes the sleazy atmosphere, anyway. She put in the bait shop, bought the automotive mockups from artists, and got it listed with the Lunar Tourist Bureau as an authentic period reconstruction. They'd die if they knew the truth about the Toyota, but I certainly won't tell them.

The only other structure is definitely not from Louisiana of any year. It's a teepee sitting on a slight rise, just out of sight of the Sugar Shack. Cheyenne, I think. We spend most of our time there when we're on the bayou.

That's where we went after the episode with the pregnant woman. The floor is hard-packed clay and there's a fire always burning in the center. There's lots of pillows scattered around, and two big waterbeds.

We tried to talk about the incident. I think Denver was more upset than the rest of us, but from the tense way Cathay sat while Trigger massaged his back I knew he was bothered, too. His voice was troubled.

I admitted I had been scared, but there was more to it than that, and I was far from ready to talk about it. Trigger and Cathay sensed it, and let it go for the time being. Trigger got the pipe and stuffed it with dexeplant leaves.

It's a long-stemmed pipe. She got it lit, then leaned back with the stem in her teeth and the bowl held between her toes. She exhaled sweet, honey-colored smoke. As the day ended outside, she passed the pipe around. It tasted good, and calmed me wonderfully. It made it easy to fall asleep.

But I didn't sleep. Not quite. Maybe I was too far into puberty for the drug in the plant to act as a tranquilizer anymore. Or maybe I was too emotionally stimulated. Denver fell asleep quickly enough.

Cathay and Trigger didn't. They made love on the other side of the teepee, did it in such a slow, dreamy way that I knew the drug was affecting them. Though Cathay is in his forties and Trigger is over a hundred, both have the bodies of thirteen-year-olds, and the metabolism that goes with the territory.

They didn't actually finish making love; they sort of tapered off, like we used to do before orgasms became a factor. I found that made me happy, lying on my side and watching them through slitted eyes.

They talked for a while. The harder I strained to hear them, the sleepier I got. Somewhere in there I lost the battle to stay awake.

I became aware of a warm body close to me. It was still dark, the only light coming from the embers of the fire.

"Sorry, Argus," Cathay said. "I didn't mean to wake you."

"It's okay. Put your arms around me?" He did, and I squirmed until my back fit snugly against him. For a long time I just enjoyed it. I didn't think about anything, unless it was his warm breath on my neck, or his penis slowly hardening against my back. If you can call that thinking.

How many nights had we slept like this in the last seven years?

Too many to count. We knew each other every way possible. A year ago he had been female, and before that both of us had been. Now we were both male, and that was nice, too. One part of me thought it didn't really matter which sex we were, but another part was wondering what it would be like to be female and know Cathay as a male. We hadn't tried that yet.

The thought of it made me shiver with anticipation. It had been too long since I'd had a vagina. I wanted Cathay between my legs, like Trigger had had him a short while before.

"I love you," I mumbled.

He kissed my ear. "I love you, too, silly. But how *much* do you love me?"

"What do you mean?"

I felt him shift around to prop his head up on one hand. His fingers unwound a tight curl in my hair.

"I mean, will you still love me when I'm no taller than your knee?"

I shook my head, suddenly feeling cold. "I don't want to talk about that."

"I know that very well," he said. "But I can't let you forget it. It's not something that'll go away."

I turned onto my back and looked up at him. There was a faint smile on his face as he toyed with my lips and hair with his gentle fingertips, but his eyes were concerned. Cathay can't hide much from me anymore.

"It has to happen," he emphasized, showing no mercy. "For the reasons you heard me tell the woman. I'm committed to going back to age seven. There's another child waiting for me. She's a lot like you."

"Don't do it," I said, feeling miserable. I felt a tear in the corner of my eye, and Cathay brushed it away.

I was thankful that he didn't point out how unfair I was being. We both knew it; he accepted that, and went on as best he could.

"You remember our talk about sex? About two years ago, I think it was. Not too long after you first told me you love me."

"I remember. I remember it all."

He kissed me. "Still, I have to bring it up. Maybe it'll help. You know we agreed that it didn't matter what sex either of us was. Then I pointed out that you'd be growing up, while I'd become a child again. That we'd grow further apart sexually."

I nodded, knowing that if I spoke I'd start to sob.

"And we agreed that our love was deeper than that. That we didn't need sex to make it work. It *can* work."

This was true. Cathay was close to all his former students. They were adults now, and came to see him often. It was just to be close, to talk and hug. Lately sex had entered it again, but they all understood that would be over soon.

"I don't think I have that perspective," I said, carefully. "They know in a few years you'll mature again. I know it too, but it still feels like . . ."

"Like what?"

"Like you're abandoning me. I'm sorry, that's just how it feels."

He sighed, and pulled me close to him. He hugged me fiercely for a while, and it felt so good.

"Listen," he said, finally. "I guess there's no avoiding this. I could tell you that you'll get over it—you will—but it won't do any good. I had this same problem with every child I've taught."

"You did?" I hadn't known that, and it made me feel a little better.

"I did. I don't blame you for it. I feel it myself. I feel a pull to stay with you. But it wouldn't work, Argus. I love my work, or I wouldn't be doing it. There are hard times, like right now. But after a few months you'll feel better."

"Maybe I will." I was far from sure of it, but it seemed important to agree with him and get the conversation ended.

"In the meantime," he said, "we still have a few weeks together. I think we should make the most of them." And he did, his hands roaming over my body. He did all the work, letting me relax and try to get myself straightened out.

So I folded my arms under my head and reclined, trying to think of nothing but the warm circle of his mouth.

But eventually I began to feel I should be doing something for him, and knew what was wrong. He thought he was giving me what I wanted by making love to me in the way we had done since we grew older together. But there was another way, and I realized

I didn't so much want him to stay thirteen. What I really wanted was to go back with him, to be seven again.

I touched his head and he looked up, then we embraced again face to face. We began to move against each other as we had done since we first met, the mindless, innocent friction from a time when it had less to do with sex than with simply feeling good.

But the body is insistent, and can't be fooled. Soon our movements were frantic, and then a feeling of wetness between us told me as surely as entropy that we could never go back.

On my way home the signs of change were all around me.

You grow a little, let out the arms and legs of your pressure suit until you finally have to get a new one. People stop thinking of you as a cute little kid and start talking about you being a fine young person. Always with that smile, like it's a joke that you're not supposed to get.

People treat you differently as you grow up. At first you hardly interact at all with adults, except your own mother and the mothers of your friends. You live in a kid's world, and adults are hardly even obstacles because they get out of your way when you run down the corridors. You go all sorts of places for free; people want you around to make them happy because there are so few kids and just about everybody would like to have more than just the one. You hardly even notice the people smiling at you all the time.

But it's not like that at all when you're thirteen. Now there was the hesitation, just a fraction of a second before they gave me a child's privileges. Not that I blamed anybody. I was nearly as tall as a lot of the adults I met.

But now I had begun to notice the adults, to watch them. Especially when they didn't know they were being watched. I saw that a lot of them spent a lot of time frowning. Occasionally, I would see real pain on a face. Then he or she would look at me, and smile. I could see that wouldn't be happening forever. Sooner or later I'd cross some invisible line, and the pain would stay in those faces, and I'd have to try to understand it. I'd be an adult, and I wasn't sure I wanted to be.

It was because of this new preoccupation with faces that I noticed the woman sitting across from me on the Archimedes train. I planned to be a writer, so I tended to see everything in terms of stories and characters. I watched her and tried to make a story about her.

She was attractive: physically mid-twenties, straight black hair and brownish skin, round face without elaborate surgery or startling features except her dark brown eyes. She wore a simple thigh-length robe of thin white material that flowed like water when she moved. She had one elbow on the back of her seat, absently chewing a knuckle as she looked out the window.

There didn't seem to be a story in her face. She was in an unguarded moment, but I saw no pain, no big concerns or fears. It's possible I just missed it. I was new at the game and I didn't know much about what was important to adults. But I kept trying.

Then she turned to look at me, and she didn't smile.

I mean, she smiled, but it didn't say isn't-he-cute. It was the sort of smile that made me wish I'd worn some clothes. Since I'd learned what erections are for, I no longer wished to have them in public places.

I crossed my legs. She moved to sit beside me. She held up her palm and I touched it. She was facing me with one leg drawn up under her and her arm resting on the seat behind me.

"I'm Trilby," she said.

"Hi. I'm Argus." I found myself trying to lower my voice.

"I was sitting over there watching you watch me."

"You were?"

"In the glass," she explained.

"Oh." I looked, and sure enough, from where she had been sitting she could appear to be looking at the landscape while actually studying my reflection. "I didn't mean to be rude."

She laughed and put her hand on my shoulder, then moved it. "What about me?" she said. "I was being sneaky about it; you weren't. Anyhow, don't fret. I don't mind." I shifted again, and she glanced down. "And don't worry about that, either. It happens."

I still felt nervous but she was able to put me at ease. We talked for the rest of the ride, and I have no memory of what we talked about. The range of subjects must have been quite narrow, as I'm sure she never made reference to my age, my schooling, her profession—or just why she had started a conversation with a thirteen-year-old on a public train.

None of that mattered. I was willing to talk about anything. If I wondered about her reasons, I assumed she actually was in her twenties, and not that far from her own childhood.

"Are you in a hurry?" she asked at one point, giving her head a little toss.

"Me? No. I'm on my way to see—" No, no, not your mother. "—a friend. She can wait. She expects me when I get there." That sounded better.

"Can I buy you a drink?" One eyebrow raised, a small motion with the hand. Her gestures were economical, but seemed to say more than her words. I mentally revised her age upward a few years. Maybe quite a few.

This was timed to the train arriving at Archimedes; we got up and I quickly accepted.

"Good. I know a nice place."

The bartender gave me that smile and was about to give me the customary free one on the house toward my legal limit of two. But Trilby changed all that.

"Two Irish whiskeys, please. On the rocks." She said it firmly, raising her voice a little, and a complex thing happened between her and the bartender. She gave him a look, his eyebrow twitched and he glanced at me, seemed to understand something. His whole attitude toward me changed.

I had the feeling something had gone over my head, but didn't have time to worry about it. I never had time to worry when Trilby was around. The drinks arrived, and we sipped them.

"I wonder why they still call it Irish?" she said.

We launched into a discussion of the Invaders, or Ireland, or Occupied Earth. I'm not sure. It was inconsequential, and the real conversation was going on eye to eye. Mostly it was her saying wordless things to me, and me nodding agreement with my tongue hanging out.

We ended up at the public baths down the corridor. Her nipples were shaped like pink valentine hearts. Other than that, her body was unremarkable, though wonderfully firm beneath the softness. She was so unlike Trigger and Denver and Cathay. So unlike me.

I catalogued the differences as I sat behind her in the big pool and massaged her soapy shoulders.

On the way to the tanning room she stopped beside one of the private alcoves and just stood there, waiting, looking at me. My legs walked me into the room and she followed me. My hands pressed against her back and my mouth opened when she kissed me. She lowered me to the soft floor and took me.

What was so different about it?

I pondered that during the long walk from the slide terminus to my home. Trilby and I had made love for the better part of an hour. It was nothing fancy, nothing I had not already tried with Trigger and Denver. I had thought she would have some fantastic new tricks to show me, but that had not been the case.

Yet she had not been like Trigger or Denver. Her body responded in a different way, moved in directions I was not used to. I did my best. When I left her, I knew she was happy, and yet felt she expected more.

I found that I was very interested in giving her more.

I was in love again.

With my hand on the doorplate, I suddenly knew that she had already forgotten me. It was silly to assume anything else. I had been a pleasant diversion, an interesting novelty.

I hadn't asked for her name, her address or call number. Why not? Maybe I already knew she would not care to hear from me again.

I hit the plate with the heel of my hand and brooded during the elevator ride to the surface.

My home is unusual. Of course, it belongs to Darcy, my mother. She was there now, putting the finishing touches on a diorama. She glanced up at me, smiled, and offered her cheek for a kiss.

"I'll be through in a moment," she said. "I want to finish this before the light fails."

We live in a large bubble on the surface. Part of it is partitioned into rooms without ceilings, but the bulk forms Darcy's studio. The bubble is transparent. It screens out the ultraviolet light so we don't get burned.

It's an uncommon way to live, but it suits us. From our vantage point at the south side of a small valley only three similar bubbles can be seen. It would be impossible for an outsider to guess that a city teemed just below the surface.

Growing up, I never gave a thought to agoraphobia, but it's common among Lunarians. I felt sorry for those not fortunate enough to grow up with a view.

Darcy likes it for the light. She's an artist, and particular about light. She works two weeks on and two off, resting during the night. I grew up to that schedule, leaving her alone while she put in marathon sessions with her airbrushes, coming home to spend two weeks with her when the sun didn't shine.

That had changed a bit when I reached my tenth birthday. We had lived alone before then, Darcy cutting her work schedule drastically until I was four, gradually picking it up as I attained more independence. She did it so she could devote all her time to me. Then one day she sat me down and told me two men were moving in. It was only later that I realized how Darcy had altered her lifestyle to raise me properly. She is a serial polyandrist, especially attracted to fierce-faced, uncompromising, maverick male artists whose work doesn't sell and who are usually a little hungry. She likes the hunger, and the determination they all have not to pander to public tastes. She usually keeps three or four of them around, feeding them and giving them a place to work. She demands little of them other than that they clean up after themselves.

I had to step around the latest of these household pets to get to the kitchen. He was sound asleep, snoring loudly, his hands stained yellow and red and green. I'd never seen him before.

Darcy came up behind me while I was making a snack, hugged me, then pulled up a chair and sat down. The sun would be out another half hour or so, but there wasn't time to start another painting.

"How have you been? You didn't call for three days."

"Didn't I? I'm sorry. We've been staying on the bayou."

She wrinkled her nose. Darcy had seen the bayou. Once.

"*That* place. I wish I knew why—"

"Darcy. Let's not get into that again. Okay?"

"Done." She spread her paint-stained hands and waved them

in a circle, as if erasing something, and that was it. Darcy is good
that way. "I've got a new roommate."

"I nearly stumbled over him."

She ran one hand through her hair and gave me a lopsided
grin. "He'll shape up. His name's Thogra."

"Thogra," I said, making a face. "Listen, if he's housebroken,
and stays out of my way, we'll—" But I couldn't go on. We were
both laughing and I was about to choke on a bite that went down
wrong. Darcy knows what I think of her choice in bedmates.

"What about . . . what's-his-name? The armpit man. The guy
who kept getting arrested for body odor."

She stuck her tongue out at me.

"You know he cleaned up months ago."

"Hah! It's those months *before* he discovered water that I remember. All my friends wondering where we were raising sheep,
the flowers losing petals when he walked by, the—'

"Abil didn't come back," Darcy said, quietly.

I stopped laughing. I'd known he'd been away a few weeks,
but that happens. I raised one eyebrow.

"Yeah. Well, you know he sold a few things. And he had some
offers. But I keep expecting him to at least stop by to pick up his
bedroll."

I didn't say anything. Darcy's loves follow a pattern that she
is quite aware of, but it's still tough when one breaks up. Her men
would often speak with contempt of the sort of commercial art
that kept me and Darcy eating and paying the oxygen bills. Then
one of three things would happen. They would get nowhere, and
leave as poor as they had arrived, contempt intact. A few made
it on their own terms, forcing the art world to accept their peculiar
visions. Often Darcy was able to stay on good terms with these;
she was on a drop-in-and-make-love basis with half the artists in
Luna.

But the most common departure was when the artist decided
he was tired of poverty. With just a slight lowering of standards
they were all quite capable of making a living. Then it became
intolerable to live with the woman they had ridiculed. Darcy
usually kicked them out quickly, with a minimum of pain. They
were no longer hungry, no longer fierce enough to suit her. But
it always hurt.

Darcy changed the subject.

"I made an appointment at the medico for your Change," she said. "You're to be there next Monday, in the morning."

A series of quick, vivid impressions raced through my mind. Trilby. Breasts tipped with hearts. The way it had felt when my penis entered her, and the warm exhaustion after the semen had left my body.

"I've changed my mind about that," I said, crossing my legs. "I'm not ready for another Change. Maybe in a few months."

She just sat there with her mouth open.

"Changed your *mind*? Last time I talked to you, you were all set to change your *sex*. In fact, you had to talk me into giving permission."

"I remember," I said, feeling uneasy about it. "I just changed my mind, that's all."

"But Argus. This just isn't fair. I sat up two nights convincing myself how nice it would be to have my daughter back again. It's been a long time. Don't you think you—"

"It's really not your decision, Mother."

She looked like she was going to get angry, then her eyes narrowed. "There must be a reason. You've met somebody. Right?"

But I didn't want to talk about that. I had told her the first time I made love, and about every new person I'd gone to bed with since. But I didn't want to share this with her.

So I told her about the incident earlier that day on the bayou. I told her about the pregnant woman, and about the thing Cathay had done.

Darcy frowned more and more. When I got to the part about the mud, there were ridges all over her forehead.

"I don't like that," she said.

"I don't really like it, either. But I didn't see what else we could do."

"I just don't think it was handled well. I think I should call Cathay and talk to him about it."

"I wish you wouldn't." I didn't say anything more, and she studied my face for a long, uncomfortable time. She and Cathay had differed before about how I should be raised.

"This shouldn't be ignored."

"Please, Darcy. He'll only be my teacher for another month. Let it go, okay?"

After a while she nodded, and looked away from me.

"You're growing more every day," she said, sadly. I didn't know why she said that, but was glad she was dropping the subject. To tell the truth, I didn't want to think about the woman anymore. But I was going to have to think about her, and very soon.

I had intended to spend the week at home, but Trigger called the next morning to say that Mardi Gras '56 was being presented again, and it was starting in a few hours. She'd made reservations for the four of us.

Trigger had seen the presentation before, but I hadn't, and neither had Denver. I told her I'd come, went in to tell Darcy, found her still asleep. She often slept for two days after a Lunar Day of working. I left her a note and hurried to catch the train.

It's called the Cultural Heritage Museum, and though they pay for it with their taxes, most Lunarians never go there. They find the exhibits disturbing. I understand that lately, however, with the rise of the Free Earth Party, it's become more popular with people searching for their roots.

Once they presented London Town 1903, and I got to see what Earth museums had been like by touring the replica British Museum. The CHM isn't like that at all. Only a very few art treasures, artifacts, and historical curiosities were brought to Luna in the days before the Invasion. As a result, all the tangible relics of Earth's past were destroyed.

On the other hand, the Lunar computer system had a capacity that was virtually limitless even then; *everything* was recorded and stored. Every book, painting, tax receipt, statistic, photograph, government report, corporate record, film, and tape existed in the memory banks. Just as the disneylands are populated with animals cloned from cells stored in the Genetic Library, the CHM is filled with cunning copies made from the old records of the way things were.

I met the others at the Sugar Shack, where Denver was trying to talk Trigger into taking Tuesday along with us. Tuesday is the hippopotamus that lives on the bayou, in cheerful defiance of any sense of authenticity. Denver had her on a chain and she stood placidly watching us, blinking her piggy little eyes.

Denver was tickled at the idea of going to Mardi Gras with a hippo named Tuesday, but Trigger pointed out that the museum officials would never let us into New Orleans with the beast. Denver finally conceded, and shooed her back into the swamp. The four of us went down the road and out of the bayou, boarded the central slidewalk, and soon arrived in the city center.

There are twenty-five theaters in the CHM. Usually about half of them are operating while the others are being prepared for a showing. Mardi Gras '56 is a ten-year-old show, and generally opens twice a year for a two week run. It's one of the more popular environments.

We went to the orientation room and listened to the lecture on how to behave, then were given our costumes. That's the part I like the least. Up until about the beginning of the twenty-first century, clothing was designed with two main purposes in mind: modesty, and torture. If it didn't hurt, it needed redesigning. It's no wonder they killed each other all the time. Anybody would, with high gravity and hard shoes mutilating their feet.

"We'll be beatniks," Trigger said, looking over the racks of period clothing. "They were more informal, and it's accurate enough to get by. There were beatniks in the French Quarter."

Informality was fine with us. The girls didn't need bras, and we could choose between leather sandals or canvas sneakers for our feet. I can't say I cared much for something called Levis, though. They were scratchy, and pinched my balls. But after visiting Victorian England—I had been female at the time, and what those people made girls wear would shock most Lunarians silly—anything was an improvement.

Entry to the holotorium was through the restrooms at the back of a nightclub that fronted on Bourbon Street. Boys to the left, girls to the right. I think they did that to impress you right away that you were going back into the past, when people did things in strange ways. There was a third restroom, actually, but it was only a false door with the word "colored" on it. It was impossible to sort *that* out anymore.

I like the music of 1956 New Orleans. There are many varieties, all sounding similar for modern ears with their simple rhythms and blends of wind, string, and percussion. The generic term is jazz, and the particular kind of jazz that afternoon in the tiny, smoke-filled basement was called dixieland. It's dominated by two instruments called a clarinet and a trumpet, each improvising a simple melody while the rest of the band makes as much racket as it can.

We had a brief difference of opinion. Cathay and Trigger wanted me and Denver to stay with them, presumably so they could use any opportunity to show off their superior knowledge—translation: "educate" us. After all, they were teachers. Denver didn't seem to mind, but I wanted to be alone.

I solved the problem by walking out onto the street, reasoning that they could follow me if they wished. They didn't, and I was free to explore on my own.

Going to a holotorium show isn't like the sensies, where you sit in a chair and the action comes to you. And it's not like a disneyland, where everything is real and you just poke around. You have to be careful not to ruin the illusion.

The majority of the set, most of the props, and all of the actors are holograms. Any real people you meet are costumed visitors, like yourself. What they did in the case of New Orleans was to lay out a grid of streets and surface them as they had actually been. Then they put up two-meter walls where the buildings would be, and concealed them behind holos of old buildings. A few of the doors in these buildings were real, and if you went in you would find the interiors authentic down to the last detail. Most just concealed empty blocks.

You don't go there to play childish tricks with holos, that's contrary to the whole spirit of the place. You find yourself being careful not to shatter the illusion. You don't talk to people unless you're sure they're real, and you don't touch things until you've studied them carefully. No holo can stand up to a close scrutiny, so you can separate the real from the illusion if you try.

The stage was a large one. They had reproduced the French Quarter—or Vieux Carre—from the Mississippi River to Rampart Street, and from Canal Street to a point about six blocks east. Standing on Canal and looking across, the city seemed to teem with life for many kilometers in the distance, though I knew there was a wall right down the yellow line in the middle.

New Orleans '56 begins at noon on Shrove Tuesday and carries on far into the night. We had arrived in late afternoon, with the sun starting to cast long shadows over the endless parades. I wanted to see the place before it got dark.

I went down Canal for a few blocks, looking into the "windows." There was an old flat movie theater with a marquee announcing *From Here to Eternity,* winner of something called an Oscar. I saw that it was a real place and thought about going in, but I'm afraid those old 2-D movies leave me flat, no matter how good Trigger says they are.

So instead I walked the streets, observing, thinking about writing a story set in old New Orleans.

That's why I hadn't wanted to stay and listen to the music with the others. Music is not something you can really put into a story, beyond a bare description of what it sounds like, who is playing it, and where it is being heard. In the same way, going to the flat movie would not have been very productive.

But the streets, the streets! There was something to study.

The pattern was the same as old London, but all the details had changed. The roads were filled with horseless carriages, great square metal boxes that must have been the most inefficient means of transport ever devised. Nothing was truly straight, nor very clean. To walk the streets was to risk broken toes or cuts on the soles of the feet. No wonder they wore thick shoes.

I knew what the red and green lights were for, and the lines painted on the road. But what about the rows of timing devices on each side of the street? What was the red metal object that a dog was urinating on? What did the honking of the car horns signify? Why were wires suspended overhead on wooden poles? I ignored the Mardi Gras festivities and spent a pleasant hour looking for the answers to these and many other questions.

What a challenge to write of this time, to make the story a slice of life, where these outlandish things seemed normal and reasonable. I visualized one of the inhabitants of New Orleans transplanted to Archimedes, and tried to picture her confusion.

Then I saw Trilby, and forgot about New Orleans.

She was behind the wheel of a 1955 Ford station wagon. I know this because when she motioned for me to join her, slid over on the seat, and let me drive, there was a gold plaque on the bulkhead just below the forward viewport.

"How do you run this thing?" I asked, flustered and trying not to show it. Something was wrong. Maybe I'd known it all along, and was only now admitting it.

"You press that pedal to go, and that one to stop. But mostly it controls itself." The car proved her right by accelerating into the stream of holographic traffic. I put my hands on the wheel, found that I could guide the car within limits. As long as I wasn't going to hit anything it let me be the boss.

"What brings you here?" I asked, trying for a light voice.

"I went by your home," she said. "Your mother told me where you were."

"I don't recall telling you where I live."

She shrugged, not seeming too happy. "It's not hard to find out."

"I...I mean, you didn't..." I wasn't sure if I wanted to say it, but decided I'd better go on. "We didn't meet by accident, did we?"

"No."

"And you're my new teacher."

She sighed. "That's an oversimplification. I *want* to be *one* of your new teachers. Cathay recommended me to your mother, and when I talked to her, she was interested. I was just going to get a look at you on the train, but when I saw you looking at me...well, I thought I'd give you something to remember me by."

"Thanks."

She looked away. "Darcy told me today that it might have been a mistake. I guess I judged you wrong."

"It's nice to hear that you can make a mistake."

"I guess I don't understand."

"I don't like to feel predictable. I don't like to be toyed with. Maybe it hurts my dignity. Maybe I get enough of that from Trigger and Cathay. All the lessons."

"I see it now," she sighed. "It's a common enough reaction, in bright children, they—"

"Don't say that."

"I'm sorry, but I must. There's no use hiding from you that my business is to know people, and especially children. That means the phases they go through, including the phase when they like to imagine they don't go through phases. I didn't recognize it in you, so I made a mistake."

I sighed. "What does it matter, anyway? Darcy likes you. That means you'll be my new teacher, doesn't it?"

"It does not. Not with me, anyway. I'm one of the first big choices you get to make with no adult interference."

"I don't get it."

"That's because you've never been interested enough to find out what's ahead of you in your education. At the risk of offending you again, I'll say it's a common response in people your age. You're only a month from graduating away from Cathay, ready to start more goal-oriented aspects of learning, and you haven't bothered to find what that will entail. Did you ever stop to think what's between you and becoming a writer?"

"I'm a writer, already," I said, getting angry for the first time. Before that, I'd been feeling hurt more than anything. "I can use the language, and I watch people. Maybe I don't have much experience yet, but I'll get it with or without you. I don't even *have* to have teachers at *all* anymore. At least I know that much."

"You're right, of course. But you've known your mother intended to pay for your advanced education. Didn't you ever wonder what it would be like?"

"Why should I? Did you ever think that I'm not interested because it just doesn't seem important? I mean, who's asked me what I felt about any of this up to now? What kind of stake do I have in it? Everyone seems to know what's best for me. Why should I be consulted?"

"Because you're nearly an adult now. My job, if you hire me, will be to ease the transition. When you've made it, you'll know, and you won't need me anymore. This isn't primary phase. Your teacher's job back then was to work with your mother to teach you the basic ways of getting along with people and society, and to cram your little head with all the skills a seven-year-old can learn. They taught you language, dexterity, reasoning, responsibility, hygiene, and not to go in an airlock without your suit. They took an ego-centered infant and turned him into a moral being. It's a tough job; so little, and you could have been a sociopath.

"Then they handed you to Cathay. You didn't mind. He showed up one day, just another playmate your own age. You were happy and trusting. He guided you very gently, letting your natural curiosity do most of the work. He discovered your creative abilities before you had any inkling of them, and he saw to it that you had interesting things to think about, to react to, to experience.

"But lately you've been a problem for him. Not your fault, nor his, but you no longer want anyone to guide you. You want to do it on your own. You have vague feelings of being manipulated."

"Which is not surprising," I put in. "I *am* being manipulated."

"That's true, so far as it goes. But what would you have Cathay do? Leave everything to chance?"

"That's beside the point. We're talking about my feelings now, and what I feel is you were dishonest with me. You made me feel like a fool. I thought what happened was . . . was spontaneous, you know? Like a fairy tale."

She gave me a funny smile. "What an odd way to put it. What I intended to do was allow you to live out a wet dream."

I guess the easy way she admitted that threw me off my stride. I should have told her there was no real difference. Both fairy tales and wet dreams were visions of impossibly convenient worlds, worlds where things go the way you want them to go. But I didn't say anything.

"I realize now that it was the wrong way to approach you. Frankly, I thought you'd enjoy it. Wait, let me change that. I thought you'd enjoy it even *after* you knew. I submit that you *did* enjoy it while it was happening."

I once again said nothing, because it was the simple truth. But it wasn't the point.

She waited, watching me as I steered the old car through traffic. Then she sighed, and looked out the viewport again.

"Well, it's up to you. As I said, things won't be planned for you anymore. You'll have to decide if you want me to be your teacher."

"Just what is it you teach?" I asked.

"Sex is part of it."

I started to say something, but was stopped by the novel idea that someone thought she could—or *needed* to—teach me about sex. I mean, what was there to learn?

I hardly noticed it when the car stopped on its own, was shaken out of my musings only when a man in blue stuck his head in the window beside me. There was a woman behind him, dressed the same way. I realized they were wearing 1956 police uniforms.

"Are you Argus-Darcy-Meric?" the man asked.

"Yeah. Who are you?"

"My name is Jordan. I'm sorry, but you'll have to come with me. A complaint has been filed against you. You are under arrest."

Arrest. To take into custody by legal authority. Or, to stop suddenly.

Being arrested contains both meanings, it seems to me. You're in custody, and your life comes to a temporary halt. Whatever you were doing is interrupted, and suddenly only one thing is important.

I wasn't too worried until I realized what that one thing must be. After all, everyone gets arrested. You can't avoid it in a society of laws. Filing a complaint against someone is the best way of keeping a situation from turning violent. I had been arrested three times before, been found guilty twice. Once I had filed a complaint myself, and had it sustained.

But this time promised to be different. I doubted I was being hauled in for some petty violation I had not even been aware of. No, this had to be the pregnant woman, and the mud. I had a while to think about that as I sat in the bare-walled holding cell, time to get really worried. We had physically attacked her, there was no doubt about that.

I was finally summoned to the examination chamber. It was larger than the ones I had been in before. Those occasions had involved just two people. This room had five wedge-shaped glass booths, each with a chair inside, arranged so that we faced each other in a circle. I was shown into the only empty one and I looked around at Denver, Cathay, Trigger . . . and the woman.

It's quiet in the booths. You are very much alone.

I saw Denver's mother come in and sit behind her daughter,

outside the booth. Turning around, I saw Darcy. To my surprise, Trilby was with her.

"Hello, Argus." The Central Computer's voice filled the tiny booth, mellow as usual but without the reassuring resonance.

"Hello, CC," I tried to keep it light, but of course the CC was not fooled.

"I'm sorry to see you in so much trouble."

"Is it real bad?"

"The charge certainly is, there's no sense denying that. I can't comment on the testimony, or on your chances. But you know you're facing a possible mandatory death penalty, with automatic reprieve."

I was aware of it. I also knew it was rarely enforced against someone my age. But what about Cathay and Trigger?

I've never cared for that term "reprieve." It somehow sounds like they aren't going to kill you, but they are. Very, very dead. The catch is that they then grow a clone from a cell of your body, force it quickly to maturity, and play your recorded memories back into it. So someone very like you will go on, but *you* will be dead. In my case, the last recording had been taken three years ago. I was facing the loss of almost a quarter of my life. If it was found necessary to kill me, the new Argus—*not* me, but someone with my memories and my name—would start over at age ten. He would be watched closely, be given special guidance to insure he didn't grow into the sociopath I had become.

The CC launched into the legally required explanation of what was going on: my rights, the procedures, the charges, the possible penalties, what would happen if a determination led the CC to believe the offense might be a capital one.

"Whew!" the CC breathed, lapsing back into the informal speech it knew I preferred. "Now that we have that out of the way, I can tell you that, from the preliminary reports, I think you're going to be okay."

"You're not just saying that?" I was sincerely frightened. The enormity of it had now had time to sink in.

"You know me better than that."

The testimony began. The complainant went first, and I learned her name was Tiona. The first round was free-form; we could say anything we wanted to, and she had some pretty nasty things to say about all four of us.

The CC went around the circle asking each of us what had happened. I thought Cathay told it most accurately, except for myself. During the course of the statements both Cathay and Trigger filed counter-complaints. The CC noted them. They would be tried simultaneously.

There was a short pause, then the CC spoke in its "official" voice.

"In the matters of Argus and Denver: testimony fails to establish premeditation, but neither deny the physical description of the incident, and a finding of Assault is returned. Mitigating factors of age and consequent inability to combat the mob aspect of the situation are entered, with the following result: the charge is reduced to Willful Deprivation of Dignity.

"In the case of Tiona versus Argus: guilty.

"In the case of Tiona versus Denver: guilty.

"Do either of you have anything to say before sentence is entered?"

I thought about it. "I'm sorry," I said. "It upset me quite a bit, what happened. I won't do it again."

"I'm not sorry," Denver said. "She asked for it. I'm sorry for her, but I'm not sorry for what I did."

"Comments are noted," the CC said. "You are each fined the sum of three hundred Marks, collection deferred until you reach employable age, sum to be taken at the rate of ten percent of your earnings until paid, half going to Tiona, half to the State. Final entry of sentence shall be delayed until a further determination of matters still before the court is made."

"You got off easy," the CC said, speaking only to me. "But stick around. Things could still change, and you might not have to pay the fine after all."

It was a bit of a wrench, getting a sentence, then sympathy from the same machine. I had to guard against feeling that the CC was on my side. It wasn't, not really. It's absolutely impartial, so far as I can tell. Yet it is so vast an intelligence that it makes a different personality for each citizen it deals with. The part that had just talked to me was really on my side, but was powerless to affect what the judgmental part of it did.

"I don't get it," I said. "What happens now?"

"Well, I've been rashomoned again. That means you all told your stories from your own viewpoints. We haven't reached deeply enough into the truth. Now I'm going to have to wire you all, and take another round."

As it spoke, I saw the probes come up behind everyone's chairs: little golden snakes with plugs on the end. I felt one behind me search through my hair until it found the terminal. It plugged in.

There are two levels to wired testimony. Darcy and Trilby and Denver's mother had to leave the room for the first part, when we all told our stories without our censors working. The transcript bears me out when I say I didn't tell any lies in the first round, unlike Tiona, who told a lot of them. But it doesn't sound like the same story, nevertheless. I told all sorts of things I never would have said without being wired: fears, selfish, formless desires, infantile motivations. It's embarrassing, and I'm glad I don't recall any of it. I'm even happier that only Tiona and I, as interested parties, can see my testimony. I only wish I was the only one.

The second phase is the disconnection of the subconscious. I told the story a third time, in terms as bloodless as the stage directions of a holovision script.

Then the terminals withdrew from us and I suffered a moment of disorientation. I knew where I was, where I had been, and yet I felt like I had been told about it rather than lived it. But that passed quickly. I stretched.

"Is everyone ready to go on?" the CC asked, politely. We all said that we were.

"Very well. In the matters of Tiona versus Argus and Denver: the guilty judgments remain in force in both cases, but both fines are rescinded in view of provocation, lessened liability due to immaturity, and lack of signs of continuing sociopathic behavior. In place of the fines, Denver and Argus are to report weekly for evaluation and education in moral principles until such time as a determination can be made, duration of such sessions to be no less than four weeks.

"In the matter of Tiona versus Trigger: Trigger is guilty of an Assault. Tempering this judgment is her motive, which was the recognition of Cathay's strategy in dealing with Tiona, and her belief that he was doing the right thing. This court notes that he was doing the *merciful* thing; right is another matter. There can be no doubt that a physical assault occurred. It cannot be condoned, no matter what the motive. For bad judgment, then, this court fines Trigger ten percent of her earnings for a period of ten years, all of it to be paid to the injured party, Tiona."

Tiona did not look smug. She must have known by then that things were not going her way. I was beginning to understand it, too.

"In the matter of Tiona versus Cathay," the CC went on, "Cathay is guilty of an Assault. His motive has been determined to be the avoidance of just such a situation as he now finds himself in, and the knowledge that Tiona would suffer greatly if he brought her to court. He attempted to bring the confrontation to an end with a minimum of pain for Tiona, never dreaming that she would show the bad judgment to bring the matter to court. She did, and now he finds himself convicted of assault. In view of his motives, mercy will temper this court's decision. He is ordered to pay the same fine as his colleague, Trigger.

"Now to the central matter, that of Trigger and Cathay versus Tiona." I saw her sink a little lower in her chair.

"You are found to be guilty by reason of insanity of the following charges: harrassment, trespassing, verbal assault, and four counts of infringement.

"Your offense was in attempting to make others shoulder the blame for your own misjudgments and misfortunes. The court is sympathetic to your plight, realizes that the fault for your situation was not entirely your own. This does not excuse your behavior, however.

"Cathay attempted to do you a favor, supposing that your aberrant state of mind would not last long enough for the filing of charges, that when you were alone and thought it over you would realize how badly you had wronged him and that a court would find in his favor.

"The State holds you responsible for the maintenance of your own mind, does not care what opinions you hold or what evaluations you make of reality so long as they do not infringe on the rights of other citizens. You are free to think Cathay responsible for your troubles, even if this opinion is irrational, but when you assault him with this opinion the State must take notice and make a judgment as to the worth of the opinion.

"This court is appointed to make that judgment of right and wrong, and finds no basis in fact for your contentions.

"This court finds you to be insane.

"Judgment is as follows:

"Subject to the approval of the wronged parties, you are given the choice of death with reprieve, or submission to a course of treatment to remove your sociopathic attitudes.

"Argus, do you demand her death?"

"Huh?" That was a big surprise to me, and not one that I liked. But the decision gave me no trouble.

"No, I don't demand anything. I thought I was out of this, and I feel just rotten about the whole thing. Would you really have killed her if I asked you to?"

"I can't answer that, because you didn't. It's not likely that I would have, mostly because of your age." It went on to ask the other four, and I suspect that Tiona would have been pushing up daisies if Cathay had wanted it that way, but he didn't. Neither did Trigger or Denver.

"Very well. How do you choose, Tiona?"

She answered in a very small voice that she would be grateful for the chance to go on living. Then she thanked each of us. It was excruciatingly painful for me; my empathy was working overtime, and I was trying to imagine what it would feel like to have society's appointed representative declare me insane.

The rest of it was clearing up details. Tiona was fined heavily, both in court costs and taxes, and in funds payable to Cathay and Trigger. Their fines were absorbed in her larger ones, with the result that she would be paying them for many years. Her child was in cold storage; the CC ruled that he should stay there until Tiona was declared sane, as she was now unfit to mother him. It occurred to me that if she had considered suspending his animation while she found a new primary teacher, we all could have avoided the trial.

Tiona hurried away when the doors came open behind us. Darcy hugged me while Trilby stayed in the background, then I went over to join the others, expecting a celebration.

But Trigger and Cathay were not elated. In fact, you would have thought they'd just lost the judgment. They congratulated me and Denver, then hurried away. I looked at Darcy, and she wasn't smiling, either.

"I don't get it," I confessed. "Why is everyone so glum?"

"They still have to face the Teacher's Association," Darcy said.

"I still don't get it. They won."

"It's not just a matter of winning or losing with the TA," Trilby said. "You forget, they were judged guilty of assault. To make it even worse, in fact as bad as it can be, you and Denver were there when it happened. They were the cause of you two joining in the assault. I'm afraid the TA will frown on that."

"But if the CC thought they shouldn't be punished, why should the TA think otherwise? Isn't the CC smarter than people?"

Trilby grimaced. "I wish I could answer that. I wish I was even sure how I feel about it."

She found me the next day, shortly after the Teacher's Association announced its decision. I didn't really want to be found, but the bayou is not so big that one can really hide there, so I hadn't tried. I was sitting on the grass on the highest hill in Beatnik Bayou, which was also the driest place.

She beached the canoe and came up the hill slowly, giving me plenty of time to warn her off if I really wanted to be alone. What the hell. I'd have to talk to her soon enough.

For a long time she just sat there. She rested her elbows on her knees and stared down at the quiet waters, just like I'd been doing all afternoon.

"How's he taking it?" I said, at last.

"I don't know. He's back there, if you want to talk to him. He'd probably like to talk to you."

"At least Trigger got off okay." As soon as I'd said it, it sounded hollow.

"Three years' probation isn't anything to laugh about. She'll have to close this place down for a while. Put it in mothballs."

"Mothballs." I saw Tuesday the hippo, wallowing in the deep mud across the water. Tuesday in suspended animation? I thought of Tiona's little baby, waiting in a bottle until his mother became sane again. I remembered the happy years slogging around in the bayou mud, and saw the waters frozen, icicles mixed with Spanish moss in the tree limbs. "I guess it'll cost quite a bit to start it up again in three years, won't it?" I had only hazy ideas of money. So far, it had never been important to me.

Trilby glanced at me, eyes narrowed. She shrugged.

"Most likely, Trigger will have to sell the place. There's a buyer who wants to expand it and turn it into a golf course."

"Golf course," I echoed, feeling numb. Manicured greens, pretty water hazards, sand traps, flags whipping in the breeze. Sterile. I suddenly felt like crying, but for some reason I didn't do it.

"You can't come back here, Argus. Nothing stays the same. Change is something you have to get used to."

"Cathay will, too." And just how much change should a person be expected to take? With a shock, I realized that now Cathay would be doing what I had wanted him to do. He'd be growing up with me, getting older instead of being regressed to grow up with another child. And it was suddenly just too much. It hadn't been my fault that this was happening to him, but having wished for it and having it come true made it feel like it was. The tears came, and they didn't stop for a long time.

Trilby left me alone, and I was grateful for that.

She was still there when I got myself under control. I didn't care one way or the other. I felt empty, with a burning in the back of my throat. Nobody had told me life was going to be like this.

"What . . . what about the child Cathay contracted to teach?" I asked, finally, feeling I should say something. "What happens to her?"

"The TA takes responsibility," Trilby said. "They'll find someone. For Trigger's child, too."

I looked at her. She was stretched out, both elbows behind her to prop her up. Her valentine nipples crinkled as I watched.

She glanced at me, smiled with one corner of her mouth. I felt a little better. She was awfully pretty.

"I guess he can . . . well, can't he still teach older kids?"

"I suppose he can," Trilby said, with a shrug. "I don't know if he'll want to. I know Cathay. He's not going to take this well."

"Is there anything I could do?"

"Not really. Talk to him. Show sympathy, but not too much. You'll have to figure it out. See if he wants to be with you."

It was too confusing. How was I supposed to know what he needed? He hadn't come to see me. But Trilby had.

So there was one uncomplicated thing in my life right then, one thing I could do where I wouldn't have to think. I rolled over and got on top of Trilby and started to kiss her. She responded with a lazy eroticism I found irresistible. She *did* know some tricks I'd never heard of.

"How was that?" I said, much later.

That smile again. I got the feeling that I constantly amused her, and somehow I didn't mind it. Maybe it was the fact that she made no bones about her being the adult and me being the child. That was the way it would be with us. I would have to grow up to her; she would not go back and imitate me.

"Are you looking for a grade?" she asked. "Like the twentieth century?" She got to her feet and stretched.

"All right. I'll be honest. You get an A for effort, but any thirteen-year-old would. You can't help it. In technique, maybe a low C. Not that I expected any more, for the same reason."

"So you want to teach me to do better? That's your job?"

"Only if you hire me. And sex is such a small part of it. Listen, Argus. I'm not going to be your mother. Darcy does that okay. I won't be your playmate, either, like Cathay was. I won't be teaching you moral lessons. You're getting tired of that, anyway."

It was true. Cathay had never really been my contemporary, though he tried his best to look it and act it. But the illusion had started to wear thin, and I guess it had to. I was no longer able to ignore the contradictions, I was too sophisticated and cynical for him to hide his lessons in everyday activities.

It bothered me in the same way the CC did. The CC could befriend me one minute and sentence me to death the next. I wanted more than that, and Trilby seemed to be offering it.

"I won't be teaching you science or skills, either," she was saying. "You'll have tutors for that, when you decide just what you want to do."

"Just what *is* it you do, then?"

"You know, I've never been able to find a good way of describing that. I won't be around all the time, like Cathay was. You'll come to me when you want to, maybe when you have a problem. I'll be sympathetic and do what I can, but mostly I'll just point out that you have to make all the hard choices. If you've been stupid I'll tell you so, but I won't be surprised or disappointed if you go on being stupid in the same way. You can use me as a role model if you want to, but I don't insist on it. But I promise I'll always tell you things straight, as I see them. I won't try to slip things in painlessly. It's time for pain. Think of Cathay as a professional child. I'm not putting him down. He turned you into a civilized being, and when he got you you were hardly that. It's because of him that you're capable of caring about his situation now, that you have loyalties to feel divided about. And he's good enough at it to know how you'll choose."

"Choose? What do you mean?"

"I can't tell you that." She spread her hands, and grinned. "See how helpful I can be?"

She was confusing me again. Why can't things be simpler?

"Then if Cathay's a professional child, you're a professional adult?"

"You could think of it like that. It's not really analogous."

"I guess I still don't know what Darcy would be paying you for."

"We'll make love a lot. How's that? Simple enough for you?" She brushed dirt from her back and frowned at the ground. "But not on dirt anymore. I don't care for dirt."

I looked around, too. The place *was* messy. Not pretty at all. I wondered how I could have liked it so much. Suddenly I wanted to get out, to go to a clean, dry place.

Come on," I said, getting up. "I want to try some of those things again."

"Does this mean I have a job?"

"Yeah. I guess it does."

Cathay was sitting on the porch of the Sugar Shack, a line of brown beer bottles perched along the edge. He smiled at us as we approached him. He was stinking drunk.

It's strange. We'd been drunk many times together, the four of us. It's great fun. But when only one person is drunk, it's a little disgusting. Not that I blamed him. But when you're drinking together all the jokes make sense. When you drink alone, you just make a sloppy nuisance of yourself.

Trilby and I sat on either side of him. He wanted to sing. He pressed bottles on both of us, and I sipped mine and tried to get into the spirit of it. But pretty soon he was crying, and I felt awful. And I admit that it wasn't entirely in sympathy. I felt helpless because there was so little I could do, and a bit resentful of some of the promises he had me make. I would have come to see him anyway. He didn't have to blubber on my shoulder and beg me not to abandon him.

So he cried on me, and on Trilby, then just sat between us looking glum. I tried to console him.

"Cathay, it's not the end of the world. Trilby says you'll still be able to teach older kids. My age and up. The TA just said you couldn't handle younger ones."

He mumbled something.

"It shouldn't be that different," I said, not knowing when to shut up.

"Maybe you're right," he said.

"Sure I am." I was unconsciously falling into that false heartiness people use to cheer up drunks. He heard it immediately.

"What the hell do you know about it? You think you . . . damn it, what do you know? You know what kind of person it takes to do my job? A little bit of a misfit, that's what. Somebody who doesn't want to grow up any more than you do. We're *both* cowards, Argus. You don't know it, but *I* do. *I* do. So what the hell am I going to do? Huh? Why don't you go away? You got what you wanted, didn't you?"

"Take it easy, Cathay," Trilby soothed, hugging him close to her. "Take it easy."

He was immediately contrite, and began to cry quietly. He said how sorry he was, over and over, and he was sincere. He said, he hadn't meant it, it just came out, it was cruel.

And so forth.

I was cold all over.

We put him to bed in the shack, then started down the road.

"We'll have to watch him the next few days," Trilby said. "He'll get over this, but it'll be rough."

"Right," I said.

I took a look at the shack before we went around the false bend in the road. For one moment I saw Beatnik Bayou as a perfect illusion, a window through time. Then we went around the tree and it all fell apart. It had never mattered before.

But it was such a sloppy place. I'd never realized how ugly the Sugar Shack was.

I never saw it again. Cathay came to live with us for a few months, tried his hand at art. Darcy told me privately that he was hopeless. He moved out, and I saw him frequently after that, always saying hello.

But he was depressing to be around, and he knew it. Besides, he admitted that I represented things he was trying to forget. So we never really talked much.

Sometimes I play golf in the old bayou. It's only two holes, but there's talk of expanding it.

They did a good job on the renovation.

Good-bye, Robinson Crusoe

IT WAS SUMMER, AND Piri was in his second childhood. First, second; who counted? His body was young. He had not felt more alive since his original childhood back in the spring, when the sun drew closer and the air began to melt.

He was spending his time at Rarotonga Reef, in the Pacifica disneyland. Pacifica was still under construction, but Rarotonga had been used by the ecologists as a testing ground for the more ambitious barrier-type reef they were building in the south, just off the "Australian" coast. As a result, it was more firmly established than the other biomes. It was open to visitors, but so far only Piri was there. The "sky" disconcerted everyone else.

Piri didn't mind it. He was equipped with a brand-new toy: a fully operational imagination, a selective sense of wonder that allowed him to blank out those parts of his surroundings that failed to fit with his current fantasy.

He awoke with the tropical sun blinking in his face through the palm fronds. He had built a rude shelter from flotsam and detritus on the beach. It was not to protect him from the elements. The disneyland management had the weather well in hand; he might as well have slept in the open. But castaways *always* build some sort of shelter.

He bounced up with the quick alertness that comes from being young and living close to the center of things, brushed sand from his naked body, and ran for the line of breakers at the bottom of the narrow strip of beach.

His gait was awkward. His feet were twice as long as they should have been, with flexible toes that were webbed into flippers. Dry sand showered around his legs as he ran. He was brown as coffee and cream, and hairless.

Piri dived flat to the water, sliced neatly under a wave, and paddled out to waist-height. He paused there. He held his nose and worked his arms up and down, blowing air through his mouth and swallowing at the same time. What looked like long, hairline scars between his lower ribs came open. Red-orange fringes became visible inside them, and gradually lowered. He was no longer an air-breather.

He dived again, mouth open, and this time he did not come up. His esophagus and trachea closed and a new valve came into operation. It would pass water in only one direction, so his diaphragm now functioned as a pump pulling water through his mouth and forcing it out through the gill-slits. The water flowing through this lower chest area caused his gills to engorge with blood, turning them purplish-red and forcing his lungs to collapse upward into his chest cavity. Bubbles of air trickled out his sides, then stopped. His transition was complete.

The water seemed to grow warmer around him. It had been pleasantly cool; now it seemed no temperature at all. It was the result of his body temperature lowering in response to hormones released by an artificial gland in his cranium. He could not afford to burn energy at the rate he had done in the air; the water was too efficient a coolant for that. All through his body arteries and capillaries were constricting as parts of him stabilized at a lower rate of function.

No naturally evolved mammal had ever made the switch from air to water breathing, and the project had taxed the resources of bio-engineering to its limits. But everything in Piri's body was a living part of him. It had taken two full days to install it all.

He knew nothing of the chemical complexities that kept him alive where he should have died quickly from heat loss or oxygen starvation. He knew only the joy of arrowing along the white sandy bottom. The water was clear, blue-green in the distance.

The bottom kept dropping away from him, until suddenly it reached for the waves. He angled up the wall of the reef until his head broke the surface, climbed up the knobs and ledges until he was standing in the sunlight. He took a deep breath and became an air-breather again.

The change cost him some discomfort. He waited until the dizziness and fit of coughing had passed, shivering a little as his body rapidly underwent a reversal to a warm-blooded economy.

It was time for breakfast.

He spent the morning foraging among the tidepools. There were dozens of plants and animals that he had learned to eat raw. He ate a great deal, storing up energy for the afternoon's expedition on the outer reef.

Piri avoided looking at the sky. He wasn't alarmed by it; it did not disconcert him as it did the others. But he had to preserve the illusion that he was actually on a tropical reef in the Pacific Ocean, a castaway, and not a vacationer in an environment bubble below the surface of Pluto.

Soon he became a fish again, and dived off the sea side of the reef.

The water around the reef was oxygen-rich from the constant wave action. Even here, though, he had to remain in motion to keep enough water flowing past his external gill fringes. But he could move more slowly as he wound his way down into the darker reaches of the sheer reef face. The reds and yellows of his world were swallowed by the blues and greens and purples. It was quiet. There were sounds to hear, but his ears were not adapted to them. He moved slowly through shafts of blue light, keeping up the bare minimum of water flow.

He hesitated at the ten-meter level. He had thought he was going to his Atlantis Grotto to check out his crab farm. Then he wondered if he ought to hunt up Ocho the Octopus instead. For a panicky moment he was afflicted with the bane of childhood: an inability to decide what to do with himself. Or maybe it was worse, he thought. Maybe it was a sign of growing up. The crab farm bored him, or at least it did today.

He waffled back and forth for several minutes, idly chasing the tiny red fish that flirted with the anemones. He never caught one. This was no good at all. Surely there was an adventure in this silent fairyland. He had to find one.

An adventure found him, instead. Piri saw something swimming out in the open water, almost at the limits of his vision. It was long and pale, an attenuated missile of raw death. His heart squeezed in panic, and he scuttled for a hollow in the reef.

Piri called him the Ghost. He had seen him many times in the open sea. He was eight meters of mouth, belly and tail: hunger personified. There were those who said the great white shark was the most ferocious carnivore that ever lived. Piri believed it.

It didn't matter that the Ghost was completely harmless to him. The Pacifica management did not like having its guests eaten alive. An adult could elect to go into the water with no protection, providing the necessary waivers were on file. Children had to be implanted with an equalizer. Piri had one, somewhere just below the skin of his left wrist. It was a sonic generator, set to emit a sound that would mean terror to any predator in the water.

The Ghost, like all the sharks, barracudas, morays, and other predators in Pacifica, was not like his cousins who swam the seas of Earth. He had been cloned from cells stored in the Biological Library on Luna. The library had been created two hundred years before as an insurance policy against the extinction of a species. Originally, only endangered species were filed, but for years before the Invasion the directors had been trying to get a sample of everything. Then the Invaders had come, and Lunarians were too busy surviving without help from Occupied Earth to worry about the library. But when the time came to build the disneylands, the library had been ready.

By then, biological engineering had advanced to the point where many modifications could be made in genetic structure. Mostly, the disneyland biologists had left nature alone. But they had changed the predators. In the Ghost, the change was a mutated organ attached to the brain that responded with a flood of fear when a supersonic note was sounded.

So why was the Ghost still out there? Piri blinked his nictating membranes, trying to clear his vision. It helped a little. The shape looked a bit different.

Instead of moving back and forth, the tail seemed to be going up and down, perhaps in a scissoring motion. Only one animal swims like that. He gulped down his fear and pushed away from the reef.

But he had waited too long. His fear of the Ghost went beyond simple danger, of which there was none. It was something more basic, an unreasoning reflex that prickled his neck when he saw that long white shape. He couldn't fight it, and didn't want to. But the fear had kept him against the reef, hidden, while the person swam out of reach. He thrashed to catch up, but soon lost track of the moving feet in the gloom.

He had seen gills trailing from the sides of the figure, muted down to a deep blue-black by the depths. He had the impression that it was a woman.

Tongatown was the only human habitation on the island. It housed a crew of maintenance people and their children, about fifty in all, in grass huts patterned after those of South Sea natives. A few of the buildings concealed elevators that went to the underground rooms that would house the tourists when the project was completed. The shacks would then go at a premium rate, and the beaches would be crowded.

Piri walked into the circle of firelight and greeted his friends. Nighttime was party time in Tongatown. With the day's work over, everybody gathered around the fire and roasted a vat-grown goat or lamb. But the real culinary treats were the fresh vegetable dishes. The ecologists were still working out the kinks in the systems, controlling blooms, planting more of failing species. They often produced huge excesses of edibles that would have cost a fortune on the outside. The workers took some of the excess for themselves. It was understood to be a fringe benefit of the job. It was hard enough to find people who could stand to stay under the Pacifica sky.

"Hi, Piri," said a girl. "You meet any pirates today?" It was Harra, who used to be one of Piri's best friends but had seemed increasingly remote over the last year. She was wearing a handmade grass skirt and a lot of flowers, tied into strings that looped around her body. She was fifteen now, and Piri was . . . but who cared? There were no seasons here, only days. Why keep track of time?

Piri didn't know what to say. The two of them had once played together out on the reef. It might be Lost Atlantis, or Submariner, or Reef Pirates; a new plot line and cast of heroes and villains every day. But her question had held such thinly veiled contempt.

Didn't she care about the Pirates anymore? What was the matter with her?

She relented when she saw Piri's helpless bewilderment.

"Here, come on and sit down. I saved you a rib." She held out a large chunk of mutton.

Piri took it and sat beside her. He was famished, having had nothing all day since his large breakfast.

"I thought I saw the Ghost today," he said, casually.

Harra shuddered. She wiped her hands on her thighs and looked at him closely.

"Thought? You thought you saw him?" Harra did not care for the Ghost. She had cowered with Piri more than once as they watched him prowl.

"Yep. But I don't think it was really him."

"Where was this?"

"On the sea-side, down about, oh, ten meters. I think it was a woman."

"I don't see how it could be. There's just you and—and Midge and Darvin with—did this woman have an air tank?"

"Nope. Gills. I saw that."

"But there's only you and four others here with gills. And I know where they all were today."

"You used to have gills," he said, with a hint of accusation.

She sighed. "Are we going through that again? I *told* you, I got tired of the flippers. I wanted to move around the *land* some more."

"I can move around the land," he said, darkly.

"All right, all right. You think I deserted you. Did you ever think that you sort of deserted *me*?"

Piri was puzzled by that, but Harra had stood up and walked quickly away. He could follow her, or he could finish his meal. She was right about the flippers. He was no great shakes at chasing anybody.

Piri never worried about anything for too long. He ate, and ate some more, long past the time when everyone else had joined together for the dancing and singing. He usually hung back, anyway. He could sing, but dancing was out of his league.

Just as he was leaning back in the sand, wondering if there

were any more corners he could fill up—perhaps another bowl of that shrimp teriyaki?—Harra was back. She sat beside him.

"I talked to my mother about what you said. She said a tourist showed up today. It looks like you were right. It was a woman, and she was amphibious."

Piri felt a vague unease. One tourist was certainly not an invasion, but she could be a harbinger. And amphibious. So far, no one had gone to that expense except for those who planned to live here for a long time. Was his tropical hideout in danger of being discovered?"

"What—what's she doing here?" He absently ate another spoonful of crab cocktail.

"She's looking for *you*," Harra laughed, and elbowed him in the ribs. Then she pounced on him, tickling his ribs until he was howling in helpless glee. He fought back, almost to the point of having the upper hand, but she was bigger and a little more determined. She got him pinned, showering flower petals on him as they struggled. One of the red flowers from her hair was in her eye, and she brushed it away, breathing hard.

"You want to go for a walk on the beach?" she asked.

Harra was fun, but the last few times he'd gone with her she had tried to kiss him. He wasn't ready for that. He was only a kid. He thought she probably had something like that in mind now.

"I'm too full," he said, and it was almost the literal truth. He had stuffed himself disgracefully, and only wanted to curl up in his shack and go to sleep.

Harra said nothing, just sat there getting her breathing under control. At last she nodded, a little jerkily, and got to her feet. Piri wished he could see her face to face. He knew something was wrong. She turned from him and walked away.

Robinson Crusoe was feeling depressed when he got back to his hut. The walk down the beach away from the laughter and singing had been a lonely one. Why had he rejected Harra's offer of companionship? Was it really so bad that she wanted to play new kinds of games?

But no, damn it. She wouldn't play his games, why should he play hers?

After a few minutes of sitting on the beach under the crescent moon, he got into character. Oh, the agony of being a lone castaway, far from the company of fellow creatures, with nothing but faith in God to sustain oneself. Tomorrow he would read from the scriptures, do some more exploring along the rocky north coast, tan some goat hides, maybe get in a little fishing.

With his plans for the morrow laid before him, Piri could go to sleep, wiping away a last tear for distant England.

The ghost woman came to him during the night. She knelt beside him in the sand. She brushed his sandy hair from his eyes and he stirred in his sleep. His feet thrashed.

He was churning through the abyssal deeps, heart hammering, blind to everything but internal terror. Behind him, jaws yawned, almost touching his toes. They closed with a snap.

He sat up woozily. He saw rows of serrated teeth in the line of breakers in front of him. And a tall, white shape in the moonlight dived into a curling breaker and was gone.

"Hello."

Piri sat up with a start. The worst thing about being a child living alone on an island—which, when he thought about it, was the sort of thing every child dreamed of—was not having a warm mother's breast to cry on when you had nightmares. It hadn't affected him much, but when it did, it was pretty bad.

He squinted up into the brightness. She was standing with her head blocking out the sun. He winced, and looked away, down to her feet. They were webbed, with long toes. He looked a little higher. She was nude, and quite beautiful.

"Who . . . ?"

"Are you awake now?" She squatted down beside him. Why had he expected sharp, triangular teeth? His dreams blurred and ran like watercolors in the rain, and he felt much better. She had a nice face. She was smiling at him.

He yawned, and sat up. He was groggy, stiff, and his eyes were coated with sand that didn't come from the beach. It had been an awful night.

"I think so."

"Good. How about some breakfast?" She stood, and went to a basket on the sand.

"I usually—" but his mouth watered when he saw the guavas, melons, kippered herring, and the long brown loaf of bread. She had butter, and some orange marmalade. "Well, maybe just a—" and he had bitten into a succulent slice of melon. But before he could finish it, he was seized by an even stronger urge. He got to his feet and scuttled around the palm tree with the waist-high dark stain and urinated against it.

"Don't tell anybody, huh?" he said, anxiously.

She looked up. "About the tree? Don't worry."

He sat back down and resumed eating the melon. "I could get in a lot of trouble. They gave me a thing and told me to use it."

"It's all right with me," she said, buttering a slice of bread and handing it to him. "Robinson Crusoe never had a portable EcoSan, right?"

"Right," he said, not showing his surprise. How did she know *that*?

Piri didn't know quite what to say. Here she was, sharing his morning, as much a fact of life as the beach or the water.

"What's your name?" It was as good a place to start as any.

"Leandra. You can call me Lee."

"I'm—"

"Piri. I heard about you from the people at the party last night. I hope you don't mind me barging in on you like this."

He shrugged, and tried to indicate all the food with the gesture. "Anytime," he said, and laughed. He felt good. It was nice to have someone friendly around after last night. He looked at her again, from a mellower viewpoint.

She was large; quite a bit taller than he was. Her physical age was around thirty, unusually old for a woman. He thought she might be closer to sixty or seventy, but he had nothing to base it on. Piri himself was in his nineties, and who could have known that? She had the slanting eyes that were caused by the addition of transparent eyelids beneath the natural ones. Her hair grew in a narrow band, cropped short, starting between her eyebrows and going over her head to the nape of her neck. Her ears were pinned efficiently against her head, giving her a lean, stream-lined look.

"What brings you to Pacifica?" Piri asked.

She reclined on the sand with her hands behind her head, looking very relaxed.

"Claustrophobia." She winked at him. "Not really. I wouldn't survive long in Pluto with *that*." Piri wasn't even sure what it was, but he smiled as if he knew. "Tired of the crowds. I heard that people couldn't enjoy themselves here, what with the sky, but I didn't have any trouble when I visited. So I bought flippers and gills and decided to spend a few weeks skin-diving by myself."

Piri looked at the sky. It was a staggering sight. He'd grown used to it, but knew that it helped not to look up more than he had to.

It was an incomplete illusion, all the more appalling because the half of the sky that had been painted was so very convincing. It looked like it really was the sheer blue of infinity, so when the eye slid over to the unpainted overhanging canopy of rock, scarred from blasting, painted with gigantic numbers that were barely visible from twenty kilometers below—one could almost imagine God looking down through the blue opening. It loomed, suspended by nothing, gigatons of rock hanging up there.

Visitors to Pacifica often complained of headaches, usually right on the crown of the head. They were cringing, waiting to get conked.

"Sometimes I wonder how *I* live with it," Piri said.

She laughed. "It's nothing for me. I was a space pilot once."

"Really?" This was catnip to Piri. There's nothing more romantic than a space pilot. He had to hear stories.

The morning hours dwindled as she captured his imagination with a series of tall tales he was sure were mostly fabrication. But who cared? Had he come to the South Seas to hear of the mundane? He felt he had met a kindred spirit, and gradually, fearful of being laughed at, he began to tell her stories of the Reef Pirates, first as wishful wouldn't-it-be-fun-if's, then more and more seriously as she listened intently. He forgot her age as he began to spin the best of the yarns he and Harra had concocted.

It was a tacit conspiracy between them to be serious about the stories, but that was the whole point. That was the only way it would work, as it had worked with Harra. Somehow, this adult woman was interested in playing the same games he was.

Lying in his bed that night, Piri felt better than he had for months, since before Harra had become so distant. Now that he had a companion, he realized that maintaining a satisfying fantasy world by yourself is hard work. Eventually you need someone to tell the stories to, and to share in the making of them.

They spent the day out on the reef. He showed her his crab farm, and introduced her to Ocho the Octopus, who was his usual shy self. Piri suspected the damn thing only loved him for the treats he brought.

She entered into his games easily and with no trace of adult condescension. He wondered why, and got up the courage to ask her. He was afraid he'd ruin the whole thing, but he had to know. It just wasn't normal.

They were perched on a coral outcropping above the high tide level, catching the last rays of the sun.

"I'm not sure," she said. "I guess you think I'm silly, huh?"

"No, not exactly that. It's just that most adults seem to, well, have more 'important' things on their minds." He put all the contempt he could into the word.

"Maybe I feel the same way you do about it. I'm here to have fun. I sort of feel like I've been reborn into a new element. It's *terrific* down there, you know that. I just didn't feel like I wanted to go into that world alone. I was out there yesterday . . ."

"I thought I saw you."

"Maybe you did. Anyway, I needed a companion, and I heard about you. It seemed like the polite thing to, well, not to ask you to be my guide, but sort of fit myself into your world. As it were." She frowned, as if she felt she had said too much. "Let's not push it, all right?"

"Oh, sure. It's none of my business."

"I like you, Piri."

"And I like you. I haven't had a friend for . . . too long."

That night at the luau, Lee disappeared. Piri looked for her briefly, but was not really worried. What she did with her nights was her business. He wanted her during the days.

As he was leaving for his home, Harra came up behind him and took his hand. She walked with him for a moment, then could no longer hold it in.

"A word to the wise, old pal," she said. "You'd better stay away from her. She's not going to do you any good."

"What are you talking about? You don't even know her."

"Maybe I do."

"Well, do you or don't you?"

She didn't say anything, then sighed deeply.

"Piri, if you do the smart thing you'll get on that raft of yours and sail to Bikini. Haven't you had any . . . feelings about her? Any premonitions or anything?"

"I don't know what you're talking about," he said, thinking of sharp teeth and white death.

"I think you do. You have to, but you won't face it. That's all I'm saying. It's not my business to meddle in your affairs."

"I'll say it's not. So why did you come out here and put this stuff in my ear?" He stopped, and something tickled at his mind from his past life, some earlier bit of knowledge, carefully suppressed. He was used to it. He knew he was not really a child, and that he had a long life and many experiences stretching out behind him. But he didn't think about it. He hated it when part of his old self started to intrude on him.

"I think you're jealous of her," he said, and knew it was his old, cynical self talking. "She's an adult, Harra. She's no threat to you. And, hell, I know what you've been hinting at these last months. I'm not ready for it, so leave me alone. I'm just a kid."

Her chin came up, and the moonlight flashed in her eyes.

"You idiot. Have you looked at yourself lately? You're not Peter Pan, you know. You're growing up. You're damn near a man."

"That's not true." There was panic in Piri's voice. "I'm only . . . well, I haven't exactly been counting, but I can't be more than nine, ten years—"

"Shit. You're as old as I am, and I've had breasts for two years. But I'm not out to cop you. I can cop with any of seven boys in the village younger than you are, but not you." She threw her hands up in exasperation and stepped back from him. Then, in a sudden fury, she hit him on the chest with the heel of her fist. He fell back, stunned at her violence.

"She *is* an adult," Harra whispered through her teeth. "That's what I came here to warn you against. *I'm* your friend, but you don't know it. Ah, what's the use? I'm fighting against that scared old man in your head, and he won't listen to me. Go ahead, go with her. But she's got some surprises for you."

"What? What surprises?" Piri was shaking, not wanting to listen to her. It was a relief when she spat at his feet, whirled, and ran down the beach.

"Find out for yourself," she yelled back over her shoulder. It sounded like she was crying.

That night, Piri dreamed of white teeth, inches behind him, snapping.

But morning brought Lee, and another fine breakfast in her bulging bag. After a lazy interlude drinking coconut milk, they went to the reef again. The pirates gave them a rough time of it, but they managed to come back alive in time for the nightly gathering.

Harra was there. She was dressed as he had never seen her, in the blue tunic and shorts of the reef maintenence crew. He knew she had taken a job with the disneyland and had been working days with her mother at Bikini, but had not seen her dressed up before. He had just begun to get used to the grass skirt. Not long ago, she had been always nude like him and the other children.

She looked older somehow, and bigger. Maybe it was just the uniform. She still looked like a girl next to Lee. Piri was confused by it, and his thoughts veered protectively away.

Harra did not avoid him, but she was remote in a more important way. It was like she had put on a mask, or possibly taken one off. She carried herself with a dignity that Piri thought was beyond her years.

Lee disappeared just before he was ready to leave. He walked home alone, half hoping Harra would show up so he could apologize for the way he'd talked to her the night before. But she didn't.

He felt the bow-shock of a pressure wave behind him, sensed by some mechanism he was unfamiliar with, like the lateral line of a fish, sensitive to slight changes in the water around him. He knew there was something behind him, closing the gap a little with every wild kick of his flippers.

It was dark. It was always dark when the thing chased him. It was not the wispy, insubstantial thing that darkness was when it settled on the night air, but the primal, eternal night of the depths. He tried to scream with his mouth full of water, but it was a dying gurgle before it passed his lips. The water around him was warm with his blood.

He turned to face it before it was upon him, and saw Harra's face corpse-pale and glowing sickly in the night. But no, it wasn't Harra, it was Lee, and her mouth was far down her body, rimmed with razors, a gaping crescent hole in her chest. He screamed again—

And sat up.

"What? Where are you?"

"I'm right here, it's going to be all right." She held his head as he brought his sobbing under control. She was whispering something but he couldn't understand it, and perhaps wasn't meant to. It was enough. He calmed down quickly, as he always did when he woke from nightmares. If they hung around to haunt him, he never would have stayed by himself for so long.

There was just the moonlit paleness of her breast before his eyes and the smell of skin and sea water. Her nipple was wet. Was it from his tears? No, his lips were tingling and the nipple was hard when it brushed against him. He realized what he had been doing in his sleep.

"You were calling for your mother," she whispered, as though she'd read his mind. "I've heard you shouldn't wake someone from a nightmare. It seemed to calm you down."

"Thanks," he said quietly. "Thanks for being here, I mean."

She took his cheek in her hand, turned his head slightly, and kissed him. It was not a motherly kiss, and he realized they were not playing the same game. She had changed the rules on him.

"Lee . . ."

"Hush. It's time you learned."

She eased him onto his back, and he was overpowered with *deja vu*. Her mouth worked downward on his body and it set off chains of associations from his past life. He was familiar with the sensation. It had happened to him often in his second childhood. Something would happen that had happened to him in much the same way before and he would remember a bit of it. He had been seduced by an older woman the first time he was young. She had taught him well, and he remembered it all but didn't want to remember. He was an experienced lover and a child at the same time.

"I'm not old enough," he protested, but she was holding in her hand the evidence that he was old enough, had been old enough for several years. *I'm fourteen years old,* he thought. How could he have kidded himself into thinking he was ten?

"You're a strong young man," she whispered in his ear. "And I'm going to be very disappointed if you keep saying that. You're not a child anymore, Piri. Face it."

"I . . . I guess I'm not."

"Do you know what to do?"

"I think so."

She reclined beside him, drew her legs up. Her body was huge and ghostly and full of limber strength. She would swallow him up, like a shark. The gill slits under her arms opened and shut quickly with her breathing, smelling of salt, iodine, and sweat.

He got on his hands and knees and moved over her.

He woke before she did. The sun was up: another warm, cloudless morning. There would be two thousand more before the first scheduled typhoon.

Piri was a giddy mixture of elation and sadness. It was sad, and he knew it already, that his days of frolicking on the reef were over. He would still go out there, but it would never be the same.

Fourteen years old! Where had the years gone? He was nearly an adult. He moved away from the thought until he found a more acceptable one. He was an adolescent, and a very fortunate one to have been initiated into the mysteries of sex by this strange woman.

He held her as she slept, spooned cozily back to front with his arms around her waist. She had already been playmate, mother, and lover to him. What else did she have in store?

But he didn't care. He was not worried about anything. He already scorned his yesterdays. He was not a boy, but a youth, and he remembered from his other youth what that meant and was excited by it. It was a time of sex, of internal exploration and the exploration of others. He would pursue these new frontiers with the same single-mindedness he had shown on the reef.

He moved against her, slowly, not disturbing her sleep. But she woke as he entered her and turned to give him a sleepy kiss.

They spent the morning involved in each other, until they were content to lie in the sun and soak up heat like glossy reptiles.

"I can hardly believe it," she said. "You've been here for...how long? With all these girls and women. And I know at least one of them was interested."

He didn't want to go into it. It was important to him that she not find out he was not really a child. He felt it would change things, and it was not fair. Not fair at all, because it *had* been the first time. In a way he could never have explained to her, last night had been not a rediscovery but an entirely new thing. He had been with many women and it wasn't as if he couldn't remember it. It was all there, and what's more, it showed up in his lovemaking. He had not been the bumbling teenager, had not needed to be told what to do.

But it was *new*. That old man inside had been a spectator and an invaluable coach, but his hardened viewpoint had not intruded to make last night just another bout. It had been a first time, and the first time is special.

When she persisted in her questions he silenced her in the only way he knew, with a kiss. He could see he had to rethink his relationship to her. She had not asked him questions as a playmate, or a mother. In the one role, she had been seemingly as self-centered as he, interested only in the needs of the moment and her personal needs above all. As a mother, she had offered only wordless comfort in a tight spot.

Now she was his lover. What did lovers do when they weren't making love?

They went for walks on the beach, and on the reef. They swam together, but it was different. They talked a lot.

She soon saw that he didn't want to talk about himself. Except for the odd question here and there that would momentarily confuse him, throw him back to stages of his life he didn't wish to remember, she left his past alone.

They stayed away from the village except to load up on supplies. It was mostly his unspoken wish that kept them away. He had made it clear to everyone in the village many years ago that he was not really a child. It had been necessary to convince them that he could take care of himself on his own, to keep them from being overprotective. They would not spill his secret knowingly, but neither would they lie for him.

So he grew increasingly nervous about his relationship with Lee, founded as it was on a lie. If not a lie, then at least a withholding of the facts. He saw that he must tell her soon, and dreaded it. Part of him was convinced that her attraction to him was based mostly on age difference.

Then she learned he had a raft, and wanted to go on a sailing trip to the edge of the world.

Piri did have a raft, though an old one. They dragged it from the bushes that had grown around it since his last trip and began putting it into shape. Piri was delighted. It was something to do, and it was hard work. They didn't have much time for talking.

It was a simple construction of logs lashed together with rope. Only an insane sailor would put the thing to sea in the Pacific Ocean, but it was safe enough for them. They knew what the weather would be, and the reports were absolutely reliable. And if it came apart, they could swim back.

All the ropes had rotted so badly that even gentle wave action would have quickly pulled it apart. They had to be replaced, a new mast erected, and a new sailcloth installed. Neither of them knew anything about sailing, but Piri knew that the winds blew toward the edge at night and away from it during the day. It was a simple matter of putting up the sail and letting the wind do the navigating.

He checked the schedule to be sure they got there at low tide. It was a moonless night, and he chuckled to himself when he thought of her reaction to the edge of the world. They would sneak up on it in the dark, and the impact would be all the more powerful at sunrise.

But he knew as soon as they were an hour out of Rarotonga that he had made a mistake. There was not much to do there in the night but talk.

"Piri, I've sensed that you don't want to talk about certain things."

"Who? Me?"

She laughed into the empty night. He could barely see her face. The stars were shining brightly, but there were only about a hundred of them installed so far, and all in one part of the sky.

"Yeah, you. You won't talk about yourself. It's like you grew here, sprang up from the ground like a palm tree. And you've got no mother in evidence. You're old enough to have divorced her, but you'd have a guardian somewhere. Someone would be looking after your moral upbringing. The only conclusion is that you don't need an education in moral principles. So you've got a co-pilot."

"Um." She had seen through him. Of course she would have. Why hadn't he realized it?

"So you're a clone. You've had your memories transplanted into a new body, grown from one of your own cells. How old are you? Do you mind my asking?"

"I guess not. Uh... what's the date?"

She told him.

"And the year?"

She laughed, but told him that, too.

"Damn. I missed my one-hundredth birthday. Well, so what? It's not important. Lee, does this change anything?"

"Of course not. Listen, I could tell the first time, that first night together. You had that puppy-dog eagerness, all right, but you knew how to handle yourself. Tell me: what's it like?"

"The second childhood, you mean?" He reclined on the gently rocking raft and looked at the little clot of stars. "It's pretty damn great. It's like living in a dream. What kid hasn't wanted to live alone on a tropic isle? I can, because there's an adult in me who'll keep me out of trouble. But for the last seven years I've been a kid. It's you that finally made me grow up a little, maybe sort of late, at that."

"I'm sorry. But it felt like the right time."

"It was. I was afraid of it at first. Listen, I *know* that I'm really a hundred years old, see? I know that all the memories are ready for me when I get to adulthood again. If I think about it, I can remember it all as plain as anything. But I haven't wanted to, and in a way, I still don't want to. The memories are suppressed when you opt for a second childhood instead of being transplanted into another full-grown body."

"I know."

"Do you? Oh, yeah. Intellectually. So did I, but I didn't understand what it meant. It's a nine- or ten-year holiday, not only from your work, but from yourself. When you get into your nineties, you might find that you need it."

She was quiet for a while, lying beside him without touching.

"What about the reintegration? Is that started?"

"I don't know. I've heard it's a little rough. I've been having dreams about something chasing me. That's probably my former self, right?"

"Could be. What did your older self do?"

He had to think for a moment, but there it was. He'd not thought of it for eight years.

"I was an economic strategist."

Before he knew it, he found himself launching into an explanation of offensive economic policy.

"Did you know that Pluto is in danger of being gutted by currency transfers from the Inner Planets? And you know why? The speed of light, that's why. Time lag. It's killing us. Since the time of the Invasion of Earth it's been humanity's idea—and a good one, I think—that we should stand together. Our whole cultural thrust in that time has been toward a total economic community. But it won't work at Pluto. Independence is in the cards."

She listened as he tried to explain things that only moments before he would have had trouble understanding himself. But it poured out of him like a breached dam, things like inflation multipliers, futures buying on the oxygen and hydrogen exchanges, phantom dollars and their manipulation by central banking interests, and the invisible drain.

"Invisible drain? What's that?"

"It's hard to explain, but it's tied up in the speed of light. It's an economic drain on Pluto that has nothing to do with real goods and services, or labor, or any of the other traditional forces. It has to do with the fact that any information we get from the Inner Planets is already at least nine hours old. In an economy with a stable currency—pegged to gold, for instance, like the classical economies on Earth—it wouldn't matter much, but it would still have an effect. Nine hours can make a difference in prices, in futures, in outlook on the markets. With a floating exchange medium, one where you need the hourly updates on your credit meter to know what your labor input will give you in terms of material output—your personal financial equation, in other words—and the inflation multiplier is something you simply *must* have if the equation is going to balance and you're not going to be wiped out, then time is really of the essence. We operate at a perpetual disadvantage on Pluto in relation to the Inner Planet money markets. For a long time it ran on the order of point three percent leakage due to outdated information. But the inflation multiplier has been accelerating over the years. Some of it's been absorbed by the fact that we've been moving closer to the I.P.; the time lag has been getting shorter as we move into summer. But it can't last. We'll reach the inner point of our orbit and the effects will really start to accelerate. Then it's war."

"War?" She seemed horrified, as well she might be.

"War, in the economic sense. It's a hostile act to renounce a trade agreement, even if it's bleeding you white. It hits every citizen of the Inner Planets in the pocketbook, and we can expect retaliation. We'd be introducing instability by pulling out of the Common Market."

"How bad will it be? Shooting?"

"Not likely. But devastating enough. A depression's no fun. And they'll be planning one for us."

"Isn't there any other course?"

"Someone suggested moving our entire government and all our corporate headquarters to the Inner Planets. It could happen, I guess. But who'd feel like it was ours? We'd be a colony, and that's a worse answer than independence, in the long run."

She was silent for a time, chewing it over. She nodded her head once; he could barely see the movement in the darkness.

"How long until the war?"

He shrugged. "I've been out of touch. I don't know how things have been going. But we can probably take it for another ten years or so. Then we'll have to get out. I'd stock up on real wealth if I were you. Canned goods, air, water, so forth. I don't think it'll get so bad that you'll need those things to stay alive by consuming them. But we may get to a semibarter situation where they'll be the only valuable things. Your credit meter'll laugh at you when you punch a purchase order, no matter how much work you've put into it."

The raft bumped. They had arrived at the edge of the world.

They moored the raft to one of the rocks on the wall that rose from the open ocean. They were five kilometers out of Rarotonga. They waited for some light as the sun began to rise, then started up the rock face.

It was rough: blasted out with explosives on this face of the dam. It went up at a thirty-degree angle for fifty meters, then was suddenly level and smooth as glass. The top of the dam at the edge of the world had been smoothed by cutting lasers into a vast table top, three hundred kilometers long and four kilometers wide. They left wet footprints on it as they began the long walk to the edge.

They soon lost any meaningful perspective on the thing. They lost sight of the sea-edge, and couldn't see the dropoff until they began to near it. By then, it was full light. Timed just right, they would reach the edge when the sun came up and they'd really have something to see.

A hundred meters from the edge when she could see over it a little, Lee began to unconsciously hang back. Piri didn't prod her. It was not something he could force someone to see. He'd reached this point with others, and had to turn back. Already, the fear of falling was building up. But she came on, to stand beside him at the very lip of the canyon.

Pacifica was being built and filled in three sections. Two were complete, but the third was still being hollowed out and was not yet filled with water except in the deepest trenches. The water was kept out of this section by the dam they were standing on. When it was completed, when all the underwater trenches and mountain ranges and guyots and slopes had been built to specifications, the bottom would be covered with sludge and ooze and the whole wedge-shaped section flooded. The water came from liquid hydrogen and oxygen on the surface, combined with the limitless electricity of fusion powerplants.

"We're doing what the Dutch did on Old Earth, but in reverse,"

Piri pointed out, but he got no reaction from Lee. She was staring, spellbound, down the sheer face of the dam to the apparently bottomless trench below. It was shrouded in mist, but seemed to fall off forever.

"It's eight kilometers deep," Piri told her. "It's not going to be a regular trench when it's finished. It's there to be filled up with the remains of this dam after the place has been flooded." He looked at her face, and didn't bother with more statistics. He let her experience it in her own way.

The only comparable vista on a human-inhabited planet was the Great Rift Valley on Mars. Neither of them had seen it, but it suffered in comparison to this because not all of it could be seen at once. Here, one could see from one side to the other, and from sea level to a distance equivalent to the deepest oceanic trenches on Earth. It simply fell away beneath them and went straight down to nothing. There was a rainbow beneath their feet. Off to the left was a huge waterfall that arced away from the wall in a solid stream. Tons of overflow water went through the wall, to twist, fragment, vaporize and blow away long before it reached the bottom of the trench.

Straight ahead of them and about ten kilometers away was the mountain that would become the Okinawa biome when the pit was filled. Only the tiny, blackened tip of the mountain would show above the water.

Lee stayed and looked at it as long as she could. It became easier the longer one stood there, and yet something about it drove her away. The scale was too big, there was no room for humans in that shattered world. Long before noon, they turned and started the long walk back to the raft.

She was silent as they boarded, and set sail for the return trip. The winds were blowing fitfully, barely billowing the sail. It would be another hour before they blew very strongly. They were still in sight of the dam wall.

They sat on the raft, not looking at each other.

"Piri, thanks for bringing me here."

"You're welcome. You don't have to talk about it."

"All right. But there's something else I have to talk about. I . . . I don't know where to begin, really."

Piri stirred uneasily. The earlier discussion about economics had disturbed him. It was part of his past life, a part that he had not been ready to return to. He was full of confusion. Thoughts that had no place out here in the concrete world of wind and water were roiling through his brain. Someone was calling to him, someone he knew but didn't want to see right then.

"Yeah? What is it you want to talk about?"

"It's about—" she stopped, seemed to think it over. "Never mind. It's not time yet." She moved close and touched him. But he was not interested. He made it known in a few minutes, and she moved to the other side of the raft.

He lay back, essentially alone with his troubled thoughts. The wind gusted, then settled down. He saw a flying fish leap, almost passing over the raft. There was a piece of the sky falling through the air. It twisted and turned like a feather, a tiny speck of sky that was blue on one side and brown on the other. He could see the hole in the sky where it had been knocked loose.

It must be two or three kilometers away. No, wait, that wasn't right. The top of the sky was twenty kilometers up, and it looked like it was falling from the center. How far away were they from the center of Pacifica? A hundred kilometers?

A piece of the sky?

He got to his feet, nearly capsizing the raft.

"What's the matter?"

It was *big*. It looked large even from this far away. It was the dreamy tumbling motion that had deceived him.

"The sky is . . ." he choked on it, and almost laughed. But this was no time to feel silly about it. "The sky is falling, Lee." How long? He watched it, his mind full of numbers. Terminal velocity from that high up, assuming it was heavy enough to punch right through the atmosphere . . . over six hundred meters per second. Time to fall, seventy seconds. Thirty of those must already have gone by.

Lee was shading her eyes as she followed his gaze. She still thought it was a joke. The chunk of sky began to glow red as the atmosphere got thicker.

"Hey, it really is falling," she said. "Look at that."

"It's big. Maybe one or two kilometers across. It's going to make quite a splash, I'll bet."

They watched it descend. Soon it disappeared over the horizon, picking up speed. They waited, but the show seemed to be over. Why was he still uneasy?

"How many tons in a two-kilometer chunk of rock, I wonder?" Lee mused. She didn't look too happy, either. But they sat back down on the raft, still looking in the direction where the thing had sunk into the sea.

Then they were surrounded by flying fish, and the water looked crazy. The fish were panicked. As soon as they hit they leaped from the water again. Piri felt rather than saw something pass beneath them. And then, very gradually, a roar built up, a deep bass rumble that soon threatened to turn his bones to powder. It picked him up and shook him, and left him limp on his knees. He was stunned, unable to think clearly. His eyes were still fixed on the horizon, and he saw a white fan rising in the distance in silent majesty. It was the spray from the impact, and it was still going up.

"Look up there," Lee said, when she got her voice back. She seemed as confused as he. He looked where she pointed and saw a twisted line crawling across the blue sky. At first he thought it was the end of his life, because it appeared that the whole over-hanging dome was fractured and about to fall in on them. But then he saw it was one of the tracks that the sun ran on, pulled free by the rock that had fallen, twisted into a snake of tortured metal.

"The dam!" he yelled. "The dam! We're too close to the dam!"

"What?"

"The bottom rises this close to the dam. The water here isn't that deep. There'll be a wave coming, Lee, a big wave. It'll pile up here."

"Piri, the shadows are moving."

"Huh?"

Surprise was piling on surprise too fast for him to cope with it. But she was right. The shadows were moving. But *why?*

Then he saw it. The sun was setting, but not by following the tracks that led to the concealed opening in the west. It was falling through the air, having been shaken loose by the rock.

Lee had figured it out, too.

"What is that thing?" she asked. "I mean, how big is it?"

"Not too big, I heard. Big enough, but not nearly the size of that chunk that fell. It's some kind of fusion generator. I don't know what'll happen when it hits the water."

They were paralyzed. They knew there was something they should do, but too many things were happening. There was not time to think it out.

"Dive!" Lee yelled. "Dive into the water!"

"What?"

"We have to dive and swim away from the dam, and down as far as we can go. The wave will pass over us, won't it?"

"I don't know."

"It's all we can do."

So they dived. Piri felt his gills come into action, then he was swimming down at an angle toward the dark-shrouded bottom. Lee was off to his left, swimming as hard as she could. And with no sunset, no warning, it got black as pitch. The sun had hit the water.

He had no idea how long he had been swimming when he suddenly felt himself pulled upward. Floating in the water, weightless, he was not well equipped to feel accelerations. But he did feel it, like a rapidly rising elevator. It was accompanied by pressure waves that threatened to burst his eardrums. He kicked and clawed his way downward, not even knowing if he was headed in the right direction. Then he was falling again.

He kept swimming, all alone in the dark. Another wave passed, lifted him, let him down again. A few minutes later, another one, seeming to come from the other direction. He was hopelessly confused. He suddenly felt he was swimming the wrong way. He stopped, not knowing what to do. Was he pointed in the right direction? He had no way to tell.

He stopped paddling and tried to orient himself. It was useless. He felt surges, and was sure he was being tumbled and buffeted.

Then his skin was tingling with the sensation of a million bubbles crawling over him. It gave him a handle on the situation. The bubbles would be going up, wouldn't they? And they were traveling over his body from belly to back. So down was that way.

But he didn't have time to make use of the information. He hit something hard with his hip, wrenched his back as his body tried to tumble over in the foam and water, then was sliding along a smooth surface. It felt like he was going very fast, and he knew where he was and where he was heading and there was nothing he could do about it. The tail of the wave had lifted him clear of the rocky slope of the dam and deposited him on the flat surface. It was now spending itself, sweeping him along to the edge of the world. He turned around, feeling the sliding surface beneath him with his hands, and tried to dig in. It was a nightmare; nothing he did had any effect. Then his head broke free into the air.

He was still sliding, but the huge hump of the wave had dissipated itself and was collapsing quietly into froth and puddles. It drained away with amazing speed. He was left there, alone, cheek pressed lovingly to the cold rock. The darkness was total.

He wasn't about to move. For all he knew, there was an eight-kilometer drop just behind his toes.

Maybe there would be another wave. If so, this one would crash down on him instead of lifting him like a cork in a tempest. It should kill him instantly. He refused to worry about that. All he cared about now was not slipping any further.

The stars had vanished. Power failure? Now they blinked on. He raised his head a little, in time to see a soft, diffused glow in the east. The moon was rising, and it was doing it at breakneck speed. He saw it rotate from a thin crescent configuration to bright fullness in under a minute. Someone was still in charge, and had decided to throw some light on the scene.

He stood, though his knees were weak. Tall fountains of spray far away to his right indicated where the sea was battering at the dam. He was about in the middle of the tabletop, far from either edge. The ocean was whipped up as if by thirty hurricanes, but he was safe from it at this distance unless there were another tsunami yet to come.

The moonlight turned the surface into a silver mirror, littered with flopping fish. He saw another figure get to her feet, and ran in that direction.

The helicopter located them by infrared detector. They had no way of telling how long it had been. The moon was hanging motionless in the center of the sky.

They got into the cabin, shivering.

The helicopter pilot was happy to have found them, but grieved over other lives lost. She said the toll stood at three dead, fifteen missing and presumed dead. Most of these had been working on the reefs. All the land surface of Pacifica had been scoured, but the loss of life had been minimal. Most had had time to get to an elevator and go below or to a helicopter and rise above the devastation.

From what they had been able to find out, heat expansion of the crust had moved farther down into the interior of the planet than had been expected. It was summer on the surface, something it was easy to forget down here. The engineers had been sure that the inner surface of the sky had been stabilized years ago, but a new fault had been opened by the slight temperature rise. She pointed up to where ships were hovering like fireflies next to the sky, playing searchlights on the site of the damage. No one knew yet if Pacifica would have to be abandoned for another twenty years while it stabilized.

She set them down on Rarotonga. The place was a mess. The wave had climbed the bottom rise and crested at the reef, and a churning hell of foam and debris had swept over the island. Little was left standing except the concrete blocks that housed the elevators, scoured of their decorative camouflage.

Piri saw a familiar figure coming toward him through the wreckage that had been a picturesque village. She broke into a run, and nearly bowled him over, laughing and kissing him.

"We were sure you were dead," Harra said, drawing back from him as if to check for cuts and bruises.

"It was a fluke I guess," he said, still incredulous that he had survived. It had seemed bad enough out there in the open ocean; the extent of the disaster was much more evident on the island. He was badly shaken to see it.

"Lee suggested that we try to dive under the wave. That's what saved us. It just lifted us up, then the last one swept us over the top of the dam and drained away. It dropped us like leaves."

"Well, not quite so tenderly in my case," Lee pointed out. "It gave me quite a jolt. I think I might have sprained my wrist."

A medic was available. While her wrist was being bandaged, she kept looking at Piri. He didn't like the look.

"There's something I'd intended to talk to you about on the

raft, or soon after we got home. There's no point in your staying here any longer anyway, and I don't know where you'd go."

"No!" Harra burst out. "Not yet. Don't tell him anything yet. It's not fair. Stay away from him." She was protecting Piri with her body, from no assault that was apparent to him.

"I just wanted to—"

"No, no. Don't listen to her, Piri. Come with me." She pleaded with the other woman. "Just give me a few hours alone with him, there's some things I never got around to telling him."

Lee looked undecided, and Piri felt mounting rage and frustration. He had known things were going on around him. It was mostly his own fault that he had ignored them, but now he had to know. He pulled his hand free from Harra and faced Lee.

"Tell me."

She looked down at her feet, then back to his eyes.

"I'm not what I seem, Piri. I've been leading you along, trying to make this easier for you. But you still fight me. I don't think there's any way it's going to be easy."

"No!" Harra shouted again.

"What are you?"

"I'm a psychiatrist. I specialize in retrieving people like you, people who are in a mental vacation mode, what you call 'second childhood.' You're aware of all this, on another level, but the child in you has fought it at every stage. The result has been nightmares—probably with me as the focus, whether you admitted it or not."

She grasped both his wrists, one of them awkwardly because of her injury.

"Now listen to me." She spoke in an intense whisper, trying to get it all out before the panic she saw in his face broke free and sent him running. "You came here for a vacation. You were going to stay ten years, growing up and taking it easy. That's all over. The situation that prevailed when you left is now out of date. Things have moved faster than you believed possible. You had expected a ten-year period after your return to get things in order for the coming battles. That time has evaporated. The Common Market of the Inner Planets has fired the first shot. They've instituted a new system of accounting and it's locked into their computers and running. It's aimed right at Pluto, and it's been working for a month now. We cannot continue as an economic partner to the C.M.I.P., because from now on every time we sell or buy or move money the inflationary multiplier is automatically juggled against us. It's all perfectly legal by all existing treaties, and it's necessary to their economy. But it ignores our time-lag disadvantage. We have to consider it as a hostile act, no matter what the intent. You have to come back and direct the war, Mister Finance Minister."

The words shattered what calm Piri had left. He wrenched free of her hands and turned wildly to look all around him. Then he sprinted down the beach. He tripped once over his splay feet, got up without ever slowing, and disappeared.

Harra and Lee stood silently and watched him go.

"You didn't have to be so rough with him," Harra said, but knew it wasn't so. She just hated to see him so confused.

"It's best done quickly when they resist. And he's all right. He'll have a fight with himself, but there's no real doubt of the outcome."

"So the Piri I know will be dead soon?"

Lee put her arm around the younger woman.

"Not at all. It's a reintegration, without a winner or a loser. You'll see." She looked at the tear-streaked face.

"Don't worry. You'll like the older Piri. It won't take him any time at all to realize that he loves you."

He had never been to the reef at night. It was a place of furitve fish, always one step ahead of him as they darted back into their places of concealment. He wondered how long it would be before they ventured out in the long night to come. The sun might not rise for years.

They might never come out. Not realizing the changes in their environment, night fish and day fish would never adjust. Feeding cycles would be disrupted, critical temperatures would go awry, the endless moon and lack of sun would frustrate the internal mechanisms, bred over billions of years, and fish would die. It had to happen.

The ecologists would have quite a job on their hands.

But there was one denizen of the outer reef that would survive for a long time. He would eat anything that moved and quite a few things that didn't, at any time of the day or night. He had no fear, he had no internal clocks dictating to him, no inner pressures to confuse him except the one overriding urge to attack. He would last as long as there was anything alive to eat.

But in what passed for a brain in the white-bottomed torpedo that was the Ghost, a splinter of doubt had lodged. He had no recollection of similar doubts, though there had been some. He was not equipped to remember, only to hunt. So this new thing that swam beside him, and drove his cold brain as near as it could come to the emotion of anger, was a mystery. He tried again and again to attack it, then something would seize him with an emotion he had not felt since he was half a meter long, and fear would drive him away.

Piri swam along beside the faint outline of the shark. There was just enough moonlight for him to see the fish, hovering at the ill-defined limit of his sonic signal. Occasionally, the shape would shudder from head to tail, turn toward him, and grow larger. At these times Piri could see nothing but a gaping jaw. Then it would turn quickly, transfix him with that bottomless pit of an eye, and sweep away.

Piri wished he could laugh at the poor, stupid brute. How could he have feared such a mindless eating machine?

Good-bye, pinbrain. He turned and stroked lazily toward the shore. He knew the shark would turn and follow him, nosing into the interdicted sphere of his transponder, but the thought did not impress him. He was without fear. How could he be afraid, when he had already been swallowed into the belly of his nightmare? The teeth had closed around him, he had awakened, and remembered. And that was the end of his fear.

Good-bye, tropical paradise. You were fun while you lasted. Now I'm a grownup, and must go off to war.

He didn't relish it. It was a wrench to leave his childhood, though the time had surely been right. Now the responsibilities had descended on him, and he must shoulder them. He thought of Harra.

"Piri," he told himself, "as a-teenager, you were just too dumb to live."

Knowing it was the last time, he felt the coolness of the water flowing over his gills. They had served him well, but had no place

in his work. There was no place for a fish, and no place for
Robinson Crusoe.

Good-bye, gills.

He kicked harder for the shore and came to stand, dripping
wet, on the beach. Harra and Lee were there, waiting for him.

Lollipop and the Tar Baby

"ZZZZELLO. ZZZ. HELLO. HELLO." Someone was speaking to Xanthia from the end of a ten-kilometer metal pipe, shouting to be heard across a roomful of gongs and cymbals being knocked over by angry giant bees. She had never heard such interference.

"Hello?" she repeated. "What are you doing on my wavelength?"

"Hello." The interference was still there, but the voice was slightly more distinct. "Wavelength. Searching, searching wavelength . . . get best reception with . . . Hello? Listening?"

"Yes, I'm listening. You're talking over . . . My radio isn't even . . ." She banged the radio panel with her palm in the ancient ritual humans employ when their creations are being balky. "My goddamn *radio* isn't even on. Did you know that?" It was a relief to feel anger boiling up inside her. Anything was preferable to feeling lost and silly.

"Not necessary."

"What do you mean, not—who *are* you?"

"Who. Having . . . *I'm*, pronoun, yes, I'm having difficulty. Bear with. Me? Yes, pronoun. Bear with me. I'm not who. What. *What* am I?"

"All right. *What* are you?"

"Spacetime phenomenon. I'm gravity and causality-sink. Black hole."

Xanthia did not need black holes explained to her. She had

213

spent her entire eighteen years hunting them, along with her clone-sister, Zoetrope. But she was not used to having them talk to her.

"Assuming for the moment that you really are a black hole," she said, beginning to wonder if this might be some elaborate trick played on her by Zoe, "just taking that as a tentative hypothesis—how are you able to talk to me?"

There was a sound like an attitude thruster going off, a rumbling pop. It was repeated.

"I manipulate spacetime framework . . . no, please hold line . . . *the* line. I manipulate the spacetime framework with controlled gravity waves projected in narrow . . . a narrow cone. I direct at the speaker in your radio. You hear. Me."

"What was that again?" It sounded like a lot of crap to her.

"I elaborate. I will elaborate. I cut through space itself, through—hold the line, hold the line, reference." There was a sound like a tape reeling rapidly through playback heads. "This is the BBC," said a voice that was recognizably human, but blurred by static. The tape whirred again, "gust the third, in the year of our Lord nineteen fifty-seven. Today in—" Once again the tape hunted.

"chelson-Morley experiment disproved the existence of the ether, by ingeniously arranging a rotating prism—" Then the metallic voice was back.

"Ether. I cut through space itself, through a—hold the line." This time the process was shorter. She heard a fragment of what sounded like a video adventure serial. "Through a spacewarp made through the ductile etheric continuum—"

"Hold on there. That's not what you said before."

"I was elaborating."

"Go on. Wait, what were you doing? With that tape business?"

The voice paused, and when the answer came the line had cleared up quite a bit. But the voice still didn't sound human. Computer?

"I am not used to speech. No need for it. But I have learned your language by listening to radio transmissions. I speak to you through use of indeterminate statistical concatenations. Gravity waves and probability, which is not the same thing in a causality singularity, enables a nonrational event to take place."

"Zoe, this is really you, isn't it?"

Xanthia was only eighteen Earth-years old, on her first long orbit into the space beyond Pluto, the huge cometary zone where space is truly flat. Her whole life had been devoted to learning how to find and capture black holes, but one didn't come across them very often. Xanthia had been born a year after the beginning of the voyage and had another year to go before the end of it. In her whole life she had seen and talked to only one other human being, and that was Zoe, who was one hundred and thirty-five years old and her identical twin.

Their home was the *Shirley Temple,* a fifteen-thousand-tonne fusion-drive ship registered out of Lowell, Pluto. Zoe owned *Shirley* free and clear; on her first trip, many years ago, she had found a scale-five hole and had become instantly rich. Most hole hunters were not so lucky.

Zoe was also unusual in that she seemed to thrive on solitude. Most hunters who made a strike settled down to live in comfort, buy a large company or put the money into safe investments and live off the interest. They were unwilling or unable to face another twenty years alone. Zoe had gone out again, and a third time after the second trip had proved fruitless. She had found a hole on her third trip, and was now almost through her fifth.

But for some reason she had never adequately explained to Xanthia, she had wanted a companion this time. And what better company than herself? With the medical facilities aboard *Shirley* she had grown a copy of herself and raised the little girl as her daughter.

Xanthia squirmed around in the control cabin of *The Good Ship Lollipop,* stuck her head through the hatch leading to the aft exercise room, and found nothing. What she had expected, she didn't know. Now she crouched in midair with a screwdriver, attacking the service panels that protected the radio assembly.

"What are you doing by yourself?" the voice asked.

"Why don't *you* tell *me,* Zoe?" she said, lifting the panel off and tossing it angrily to one side. She peered into the gloomy interior, wrinkling her nose at the smell of oil and paraffin. She shone her pencil-beam into the space, flicking it from one component to the next, all as familiar to her as neighborhood corridors would be to a planet-born child. There was nothing out of place, nothing that shouldn't be there. Most of it was sealed into plastic blocks to prevent moisture or dust from getting to critical circuits. There were no signs of tampering.

"I am failing to communicate. I am not your mother, I am a gravity and causality—"

"She's not my mother," Xanthia snapped.

"My records show that she would dispute you."

Xanthia didn't like the way the voice said that. But she was admitting to herself that there was no way Zoe could have set this up. That left her with the alternative: she really was talking to a black hole.

"She's not my mother," Xanthia repeated. "And if you've been listening in, you *know* why I'm out here in a lifeboat. So why do you ask?"

"I wish to help you. I have heard tension building between the two of you these last years. You are growing up."

Xanthia settled back in the control chair. Her head did not feel so good.

Hole hunting was a delicate economic balance, a tightrope walked between the needs of survival and the limitations of mass. The initial investment was tremendous and the return was undependable, so the potential hole hunter had to have a line to a source of speculative credit or be independently wealthy.

No consortium or corporation had been able to turn a profit at the business by going at it in a big way. The government of Pluto maintained a monopoly on the use of one-way robot probes, but they had found over the years that when a probe succeeded in finding a hole, a race usually developed to see who would reach it and claim it first. Ships sent after such holes had a way of disappearing in the resulting fights, far from law and order.

The demand for holes was so great that an economic niche remained which was filled by the solitary prospector, backed by people with tax write-offs to gain. Prospectors had a ninety percent bankruptcy rate. But as with gold and oil in earlier days, the potential profits were huge, so there was never a lack of speculators.

Hole hunters would depart Pluto and accelerate to the limits of engine power, then coast for ten to fifteen years, keeping an eye on the mass detector. Sometimes they would be half a light-year from Sol before they had to decelerate and turn around. Less mass equalled more range, so the solitary hunter was the rule.

Teaming of ships had been tried, but teams that discovered a hole seldom came back together. One of them tended to have an accident. Hole hunters were a greedy lot, self-centered and self-sufficient.

Equipment had to be reliable. Replacement parts were costly in terms of mass, so the hole hunter had to make an agonizing choice with each item. Would it be better to leave it behind and chance a possibly fatal failure, or take it along, decreasing the range, and maybe miss the glory hole that is sure to be lurking just one more AU away? Hole hunters learned to be handy at repairing, jury-rigging, and bashing, because in twenty years even fail-safe triplicates can be on their last legs.

Zoe had sweated over her faulty mass detector before she admitted it was beyond her skills. Her primary detector had failed ten years into the voyage, and the second one had begun to act up six years later. She tried to put together one functioning detector with parts cannibalized from both. She nursed it along for a year with the equivalents of bobby pins and bubblegum. It was hopeless.

But *Shirley Temple* was a palace among prospecting ships. Having found two holes in her career, Zoe had her own money. She had stocked spare parts, beefed up the drive, even included that incredible luxury, a lifeboat.

The lifeboat was sheer extravagance, except for one thing. It had a mass detector as part of its astrogational equipment. She had bought it mainly for that reason, since it had only an eighteen-month range and would be useless except at the beginning and end of the trip, when they were close to Pluto. It made extensive use of plug-in components, sealed in plastic to prevent tampering or accidents caused by inexperienced passengers. The mass detector on board did not have the range or accuracy of the one on *Shirley*. It could be removed or replaced, but not recalibrated.

They had begun a series of three-month loops out from the mother ship. Xanthia had flown most of them earlier, when Zoe did not trust her to run *Shirley*. Later they had alternated.

"And that's what I'm doing out here by myself," Xanthia said.

"I have to get out beyond ten million kilometers from *Shirley* so its mass doesn't affect the detector. My instrument is calibrated to ignore only the mass of this ship, not *Shirley*. I stay out here for three months, which is a reasonably safe time for the life systems on *Lollipop*, and time to get pretty lonely. Then back for refueling and supplying."

"The *Lollipop*?"

Xanthia blushed. "Well, I named this lifeboat that, after I started spending so much time on it. We have a tape of Shirley Temple in the library, and she sang this song, see—"

"Yes, I've heard it. I've been listening to radio for a very long time. So you no longer believe this is a trick by your mother?"

"She's *not* . . ." Then she realized she had referred to Zoe in the third person again.

"I don't know what to think," she said, miserably. "Why are you doing this?"

"I sense that you are still confused. You'd like some proof that I am what I say I am. Since you'll think of it in a minute, I might as well ask you this question. Why do you suppose I haven't yet registered on your mass detector?"

Xanthia jerked in her seat, then was brought up short by the straps. It was true, there was not the slightest wiggle on the dials of the detector.

"All right, why haven't you?" She felt a sinking sensation. She was sure the punchline came now, after she'd shot off her mouth about *Lollipop*—her secret from Zoe—and made such a point of the fact that Zoe was not her mother. It was her own private rebellion, one that she had not had the nerve to face Zoe with. Now she's going to reveal herself and tell me how she did it, and I'll feel like a fool, she thought.

"It's simple," the voice said. "You weren't in range of me yet. But now you are. Take a look."

The needles were dancing, giving the reading of a scale-seven hole. A scale seven would mass about a tenth as much as the asteroid Ceres.

"Mommy, what *is* a black hole?"

The little girl was seven years old. One day she would call herself Xanthia, but she had not yet felt the need for a name and her mother had not seen fit to give her one. Zoe reasoned that you needed two of something before you needed names. There was only one other person on *Shirley*. There was no possible confusion. When the girl thought about it at all, she assumed her name must be Hey, or Darling.

She was a small child, as Zoe had been. She was recapitulating the growth Zoe had already been through a hundred years ago. Though she didn't know it, she was pretty: dark eyes with an oriental fold, dark skin, and kinky blonde hair. She was a genetic mix of Chinese and Negro, with dabs of other races thrown in for seasoning.

"I've tried to explain that before," Zoe said. "You don't have the math for it yet. I'll get you started on spacetime equations, then in about a year you'll be able to understand."

"But I want to know now." Black holes were a problem for the child. From her earliest memories the two of them had done nothing but hunt them, yet they never found one. She'd been doing a lot of reading—there was little else to do—and was wondering if they might inhabit the same category where she had tentatively placed Santa Claus and leprechauns.

"If *I* try again, will you go to sleep?"

"I promise."

So Zoe launched into her story about the Big Bang, the time in the long-ago when little black holes could be formed.

"As far as we can tell, all the little black holes like the ones we hunt were made in that time. Nowadays other holes can be formed by the collapse of very large stars. When the fires burn low and the pressures that are trying to blow the star apart begin to fade, gravity takes over and starts to pull the star in on itself." Zoe waved her hands in the air, forming cups to show bending space, flailing out to indicate pressures of fusion. These explanations were almost as difficult for her as stories of sex had been for earlier generations. The truth was that she was no relativist and didn't really grasp the slightly incredible premises behind black-hole theory. She suspected that no one could really visualize one, and if you can't do that, where are you? But she was practical enough not to worry about it.

"And what's gravity? I forgot." The child was rubbing her eyes to stay awake. She struggled to understand but already knew she would miss the point yet another time.

"Gravity is the thing that holds the universe together. The glue, or the rivets. It pulls everything toward everything else, and it takes energy to fight it and overcome it. It feels like when we boost the ship, remember I pointed that out to you?"

"Like when everything wants to move in the same direction?"

"That's right. So we have to be careful, because we don't think about it much. We have to worry about where things are because when we boost, everything will head for the stern. People on planets have to worry about that all the time. They have to put something strong between themselves and the center of the planet, or they'll go down."

"Down." The girl mused over that word, one that had been giving her trouble as long as she could remember, and thought she might finally have understood it. She had seen pictures of places where down was always the same direction, and they were strange to the eye. They were full of tables to put things on, chairs to sit in, and funny containers with no tops. Five of the six walls of rooms on planets could hardly be used at all. One, the "floor," was called on to take all the use.

"So they use their legs to fight gravity with?" She was yawning now.

"Yes. You've seen pictures of the people with the funny legs. They're not so funny when you're in gravity. Those flat things on the ends are called feet. If they had peds like us, they wouldn't be able to walk so good. They always have to have one foot touching the floor, or they'd fall toward the surface of the planet."

Zoe tightened the strap that held the child to her bunk, and fastened the velcro patch on the blanket to the side of the sheet, tucking her in. Kids needed a warm, snug place to sleep. Zoe preferred to float free in her own bedroom, tucked into a fetal position and drifting.

"G'night, Mommy."

"Good night. You get some sleep, and don't worry about black holes."

But the child dreamed of them, as she often did. They kept tugging at her, and she would wake breathing hard and convinced that she was going to fall into the wall in front of her.

"You don't mean it? I'm rich!"

Xanthia looked away from the screen. It was no good pointing out that Zoe had always spoken of the trip as a partnership. She owned *Shirley* and *Lollipop*.

"Well, you too, of course. Don't think you won't be getting a real big share of the money. I'm going to set you up so well that you'll be able to buy a ship of your own, and raise little copies of yourself if you want to."

Xanthia was not sure that was her idea of heaven, but said nothing.

"Zoe, there's a problem, and I . . . well, I was—" But she was interrupted again by Zoe, who would not hear Xanthia's comment for another thirty seconds.

"The first data is coming over the telemetry channel right now, and I'm feeding it into the computer. Hold on a second while I turn the ship. I'm going to start decelerating in about one minute, based on these figures. You get the refined data to me as soon as you have it."

There was a brief silence.

"What problem?"

"It's talking to me, Zoe. The hole is talking to me."

This time the silence was longer than the minute it took the radio signal to make the round trip between ships. Xanthia furtively thumbed the contrast knob, turning her sister-mother down until the screen was blank. She could look at the camera and Zoe wouldn't know the difference.

Damn, damn, she thinks I've flipped. But I *had* to tell her.

"I'm not sure what you mean."

"Just what I *said*. I don't understand it, either. But it's been talking to me for the last hour, and it says the *damnedest* things."

There was another silence.

"All right. When you get there, don't do anything, repeat, *anything*, until I arrive. Do you understand?"

"Zoe, I'm not crazy. I'm *not*."

Then why am I crying?

"Of course you're not, baby, there's an explanation for this and I'll find out what it is as soon as I get there. You just hang on. My first rough estimate puts me alongside you about three hours after you're stationary relative to the hole."

Shirley and *Lollipop*, traveling parallel courses, would both be veering from their straight-line trajectories to reach the hole. But Xanthia was closer to it; Zoe would have to move at a more oblique angle and would be using more fuel. Xanthia thought four hours was more like it.

"I'm signing off," Zoe said. "I'll call you back as soon as I'm in the groove."

Xanthia hit the off button on the radio and furiously unbuckled her seatbelt. Damn Zoe, damn her, damn her, *damn her*. Just sit tight, she says. I'll be there to explain the unexplainable. It'll be all right.

She knew she should start her deceleration, but there was something she must do first.

She twisted easily in the air, grabbing at braces with all four hands, and dived through the hatch to the only other living space in *Lollipop:* the exercise area. It was cluttered with equipment that she had neglected to fold into the walls, but she didn't mind; she liked close places. She squirmed through the maze like a fish gliding through coral, until she reached the wall she was looking for. It had been taped over with discarded manual pages, the only paper she could find on *Lollipop*. She started ripping at the paper, wiping tears from her cheeks with one ped as she worked. Beneath the paper was a mirror.

How to test for sanity? Xanthia had not considered the question; the thing to do had simply presented itself and she had done it. Now she confronted the mirror and searched for . . . what? Wild eyes? Froth on the lips?

What she saw was her mother.

Xanthia's life had been a process of growing slowly into the mold Zoe represented. She had known her pug nose would eventually turn down. She had known what baby fat would melt away. Her breasts had grown just into the small cones she knew from her mother's body and no farther.

She hated looking in mirrors.

Xanthia and Zoe were small women. Their most striking feature was the frizzy dandelion of yellow hair, lighter than their bodies. When the time had come for naming, the young clone had almost opted for Dandelion until she came upon the word *xanthic* in a dictionary. The radio call-letters for *Lollipop* happened to be

X-A-N, and the word was too good to resist. She knew, too, that Orientals were thought of as having yellow skin, though she could not see why.

Why had she come here, of all places? She strained toward the mirror, fighting her repulsion, searching her face for signs of insanity. The narrow eyes were a little puffy, and as deep and expressionless as ever. She put her hands to the glass, startled in the silence to hear the multiple clicks as the long nails just missed touching the ones on the other side. She was always forgetting to trim them.

Sometimes, in mirrors, she knew she was not seeing herself. She could twitch her mouth, and the image would not move. She could smile, and the image would frown. It had been happening for two years, as her body put the finishing touches on its eighteen-year process of duplicating Zoe. She had not spoken of it, because it scared her.

"And this is where I come to see if I'm sane," she said aloud, noting that the lips in the mirror did not move. "Is she going to start talking to me now?" She waved her arms wildly, and so did Zoe in the mirror. At least it wasn't that bad yet; it was only the details that failed to match: the small movements, and especially the facial expressions. Zoe was inspecting her dispassionately and did not seem to like what she saw. That small curl at the edge of the mouth, the almost brutal narrowing of the eyes...

Xanthia clapped her hands over her face, then peeked out through the fingers. Zoe was peeking out, too. Xanthia began rounding up the drifting scraps of paper and walling her twin in again with new bits of tape.

The beast with two backs and legs at each end writhed, came apart, and resolved into Xanthia and Zoe, drifting, breathing hard. They caromed off the walls like monkeys, giving up their energy, gradually getting breath back under control. Golden, wet hair and sweaty skin brushed against each other again and again as they came to rest.

Now the twins floated in the middle of the darkened bedroom. Zoe was already asleep, tumbling slowly with that total looseness possible only in free fall. Her leg rubbed against Xanthia's belly and her relative motion stopped. The leg was moist. The room was close, thick with the smell of passion. The recirculators whined quietly as they labored to clear the air.

Pushing one finger gently against Zoe's ankle, Xanthia turned her until they were face to face. Frizzy blonde hair tickled her nose, and she felt warm breath on her mouth.

Why can't it always be like this?

"You're not my mother," she whispered. Zoe had no reaction to this heresy. "You're *not*."

Only in the last year had Zoe admitted the relationship was much closer. Xanthia was now fifteen.

And what was different? Something, there had to be something beyond the mere knowledge that they were not mother and child. There was a new quality in their relationship, growing as they came to the end of the voyage. Xanthia would look into those eyes where she had seen love and now see only blankness, coldness.

"Oriental inscrutability?" she asked herself, half-seriously. She knew she was hopelessly unsophisticated. She had spent her life in a society of two. The only other person she knew had her own face. But she had thought she knew Zoe. Now she felt less confident with every glance into Zoe's face and every kilometer passed on the way to Pluto.

Pluto.

Her thoughts turned gratefully away from immediate problems and toward that unimaginable place. She would be there in only four more years. The cultural adjustments she would have to make were staggering. Thinking about that, she felt a sensation in her chest that she guessed was her heart leaping in anticipation. That's what happened to characters in tapes when they got excited, anyway. Their hearts were forever leaping, thudding, aching, or skipping beats.

She pushed away from Zoe and drifted slowly to the viewport. Her old friends were all out there, the only friends she had ever known, the stars. She greeted them all one by one, reciting childhood mnemonic riddles and rhymes like bedtime prayers.

It was a funny thought that the view from her window would terrify many of those strangers she was going to meet on Pluto. She'd read that many tunnel-raised people could not stand open spaces. What it was that scared them, she could not understand.

The things that scared her were crowds, gravity, males, and mirrors.

"Oh, damn. Damn! I'm going to be just *hopeless*. Poor little idiot girl from the sticks, visiting the big city." She brooded for a time on all the thousands of things she had never done, from swimming in the gigantic underground disneylands to seducing a boy.

"To *being* a boy." It had been the source of their first big argument. When Xanthia had reached adolescence, the time when children want to begin experimenting, she had learned from Zoe that *Shirley Temple* did not carry the medical equipment for sex changes. She was doomed to spend her critical formative years as a sexual deviate, a unisex.

"It'll stunt me forever," she had protested. She had been reading a lot of pop psychology at the time.

"Nonsense," Zoe had responded, hard-pressed to explain why she had not stocked a viro-genetic imprinter and the companion Y-alyzer. Which, as Xanthia pointed out, *any* self-respecting home surgery kit should have.

"The human race got along for millions of years without sex changing," Zoe had said. "Even after the Invasion. We were a highly technological race for hundreds of years before changing. Billions of people lived and died in the same sex."

"Yeah, and look what they were like."

Now, for another of what seemed like an endless series of nights, sleep was eluding her. There was the worry of Pluto, and the worry of Zoe and her strange behavior, and no way to explain anything in her small universe which had become unbearably complicated in the last years.

I wonder what it would be like with a man?

Three hours ago Xanthia had brought *Lollipop* to a careful rendezvous with the point in space her instruments indicated contained a black hole. She had long since understood that even if she ever found one she would never see it, but she could not restrain herself from squinting into the starfield for some evidence. It was silly; though the hole massed ten to the fifteenth tonnes (the original estimate had been off one order of magnitude) it was still only a fraction of a millimeter in diameter. She was staying a good safe hundred kilometers from it. Still, you ought to be able to sense something like that, you ought to be able to *feel* it.

It was no use. This hunk of space looked exactly like any other.

"There is a point I would like explained," the hole said. "What will be done with me after you have captured me?"

The question surprised her. She still had not got around to thinking of the voice as anything but some annoying aberration like her face in the mirror. How was she supposed to deal with it? Could she admit to herself that it existed, that it might even have feelings?

"I guess we'll just mark you, in the computer, that is. You're too big for us to haul back to Pluto. So we'll hang around you for a week or so, refining your trajectory until we know precisely where you're going to be, then we'll leave you. We'll make some maneuvers on the way in so no one could retrace our path and find out where you are, because they'll know we found a big one when we get back."

"How will they know that?"

"Because we'll be renting . . . well, *Zoe* will be chartering one of those big monster tugs, and she'll come out here and put a charge on you and tow you . . . say, how do you feel about this?'

"Are you concerned with the answer?"

The more Xanthia thought about it, the less she liked it. If she really was not hallucinating this experience, then she was contemplating the capture and imprisonment of a sentient being. An innocent sentient being who had been wandering around the edge of the system, suddenly to find him or herself . . .

"Do you have a sex?"

"No."

"All right, I guess I've been kind of short with you. It's just because you *did* startle me, and I *didn't* expect it, and it was all a little alarming."

The hole said nothing.

"You're a strange sort of person, or whatever," she said.

Again there was a silence.

"Why don't you tell me more about yourself? What's it like being a black hole, and all that?" She still couldn't fight down the ridiculous feeling those words gave her.

"I live much as you do, from day to day. I travel from star to star, taking about ten million years for the trip. Upon arrival, I plunge through the core of the star. I do this as often as is necessary, then I depart by a slingshot maneuver through the heart of a massive planet. The Tunguska Meteorite, which hit Siberia in 1908, was a black hole gaining momentum on its way to Jupiter, where it could get the added push needed for solar escape velocity."

One thing was bothering Xanthia. "What do you mean, 'as often as is necessary'?"

"Usually five or six thousand passes is sufficient."

"No, no. What I meant is *why* is it necessary? What do you get out of it?"

"Mass," the hole said. "I need to replenish my mass. The Relativity Laws state that nothing can escape from a black hole, but the Quantum Laws, specifically the Heisenberg Uncertainty Principle, state that below a certain radius the position of a particle cannot be determined. I lose mass constantly through tunneling. It is not all wasted, as I am able to control the direction and form of the escaping mass, and to use the energy that results to perform functions that your present-day physics says are impossible."

"Such as?" Xanthia didn't know why, but she was getting nervous.

"I can exchange inertia for gravity, and create energy in a variety of ways."

"So you can move yourself."

"Slowly."

"And you eat..."

"Anything."

Xanthia felt a sudden panic, but she didn't know what was wrong. She glanced down at her instruments and felt her hair prickle from her wrists and ankles to the nape of her neck.

The hole was ten kilometers closer than it had been.

"How could you *do* that to me?" Xanthia raged. "I trusted you, and that's how you repaid me, by trying to sneak up on me and... and—"

"It was not intentional. I speak to you by means of controlled gravity waves. To speak to you at all, it is necessary to generate an attractive force between us. You were never in any danger."

"I don't believe that," Xanthia said angrily. "I think you're doubletalking me. I don't think gravity works like that, and I don't think you really tried very hard to tell me how you talk to me, back when we first started." It occurred to her now, also, that the hole was speaking much more fluently than in the beginning. Either it was a very fast learner, or that had been intentional.

The hole paused. "This is true," it said.

She pressed her advantage. "Then why did you do it?"

"It was a reflex, like blinking in a bright light, or drawing one's hand back from a fire. When I sense matter, I am attracted to it."

"The proper cliché would be 'like a moth to a flame.' But you're not a moth, and I'm not a flame. I don't believe you. I think you could have stopped yourself if you wanted to."

Again the hole hesitated. "You are correct."

"So you were trying to . . . ?"

"I was trying to eat you."

"Just like *that?* Eat someone you've been having a conversation with?"

"Matter is matter," the hole said, and Xanthia thought she detected a defensive note in its voice.

"What do you think of what I said we're going to do with you? You were going to tell me, but we got off on that story about where you came from."

"As I understand it, you propose to return for me. I will be towed to near Pluto's orbit, sold, and eventually come to rest in the heart of an orbital power station, where your species will feed matter into my gravity well, extracting power cheaply from the gravitational collapse."

"Yeah, that's pretty much it."

"It sounds ideal. My life is struggle. Failing to find matter to consume would mean loss of mass until I am smaller than an atomic nucleus. The loss rate would increase exponentially, and my universe would disappear. I do not know what would happen beyond that point. I have never wished to find out."

How much could she trust this thing? Could it move very rapidly? She toyed with the idea of backing off still further. The two of them were now motionless relative to each other, but they were both moving slowly away from the location she had given Zoe.

It didn't make sense to think it could move in on her fast. If it could, why hadn't it? Then it could eat her and wait for Zoe to arrive—Zoe, who was helpless to detect the hole with her broken mass detector.

She should relay the new vectors to Zoe. She tried to calculate where her twin would arrive, but was distracted by the hole speaking.

"I would like to speak to you now of what I initially contacted you for. Listening to Pluto radio, I have become aware of certain facts that you should know, if, as I suspect, you are not already aware of them. Do you know of Clone Control Regulations?"

"No, what are they?" Again, she was afraid without knowing why.

The genetic statutes, according to the hole, were the soul of simplicity. For three hundred years, people had been living just about forever. It had become necessary to limit the population. Even if everyone had only one child—the Birthright—population would still grow. For a while, clones had been a loophole. No more. Now, only one person had the right to any one set of genes. If two possessed them, one was excess, and was summarily executed.

"Zoe has prior property rights to her genetic code," the hole concluded. "This is backed up by a long series of court decisions."

"So I'm—"

"Excess."

Zoe met her at the airlock as Xanthia completed the docking maneuver. She was smiling, and Xanthia felt the way she always did when Zoe smiled these days: like a puppy being scratched behind the ears. They kissed, then Zoe held her at arm's length.

"Let me look at you. Can it only be three months? You've *grown,* my baby."

Xanthia blushed. "I'm not a baby anymore, Mother." But she was happy. Very happy.

"No. I should say not." She touched one of Xanthia's breasts, then turned her around slowly. "I should say not. Putting on a little weight in the hips, aren't we?"

"And the bosom. One inch while I was gone. I'm almost there." And it was true. At sixteen, the young clone was almost a woman.

"Almost there," Zoe repeated, and glanced away from her twin. But she hugged her again, and they kissed, and began to laugh as the tension was released.

They made love, not once and then to bed, but many times, feasting on each other. One of them remarked—Xanthia could not remember who because it seemed so accurate that either of them might have said it—that the only good thing about these three-month separations was the homecoming.

"You did very well," Zoe said, floating in the darkness and sweet exhausted atmosphere of their bedroom many hours later. "You handled the lifeboat like it was part of your body. I watched the docking. I *wanted* to see you make a mistake, I think, so I'd know I still have something on you." Her teeth showed in the starlight, rows of lights below the sparkles of her eyes and the great dim blossom of her hair.

"Ah, it wasn't that hard," Xanthia said, delighted, knowing full well that it *was* that hard.

"Well, I'm going to let you handle it again the next swing. From now on, you can think of the lifeboat as *your* ship. You're the skipper."

It didn't seem like the time to tell her that she already thought of it that way. Nor that she had christened the ship.

Zoe laughed quietly. Xanthia looked at her.

"I remember the day I first boarded my own ship," she said. "It was a big day for me. My own ship."

"This is the way to live," Xanthia agreed. "Who needs all those people? Just the two of us. And they say hole hunters are crazy. I . . . wanted to . . ." The words stuck in her throat, but Xanthia knew this was the time to get them out, if there ever would be a time. "I don't want to stay too long at Pluto, Mother. I'd like to get right back out here with you." There, she'd said it.

Zoe said nothing for a long time.

"We can talk about that later."

"I love you, Mother," Xanthia said, a little too loudly.

"I love you, too, baby," Zoe mumbled. "Let's get some sleep, okay?"

She tried to sleep, but it wouldn't happen. What was *wrong?*

Leaving the darkened room behind her, she drifted through the ship, looking for something she had lost, or was losing, she wasn't sure which. What had happened, after all? Certainly nothing she could put her finger on. She loved her mother, but all she knew was that she was choking on tears.

In the water closet, wrapped in the shower bag with warm water misting around her, she glanced in the mirror.

"Why? Why would she do a thing like that?"

"Loneliness. And insanity. They appear to go together. This is her solution. You are not the first clone she has made."

She had thought herself beyond shock, but the clarity that simple declarative sentence brought to her mind was explosive. Zoe had always needed the companionship Xanthia provided. She needed a child for diversion in the long, dragging years of a voyage; she needed someone to talk to. *Why couldn't she have brought a dog?* She saw herself now as a shipboard pet, and felt sick. The local leash laws would necessitate the destruction of the animal before landing. Regrettable, but there it was. Zoe had spent the last year working up the courage to do it.

How many little Xanthias? They might even have chosen that very name; they would have been that much like her. Three, four? She wept for her forgotten sisters. Unless . . .

"How do I know you're telling me the truth about this? How could she have kept it from me? I've seen tapes of Pluto. I never saw any mention of this."

"She edited those before you were born. She has been careful. Consider her position: there can be only one of you, but the law does not say which it has to be. With her death, you become legal. If you had known that, what would life have been like in *Shirley Temple?*"

"I don't believe you. You've got something in mind, I'm sure of it."

"Ask her when she gets here. But be careful. Think it out, all the way through."

She had thought it out. She had ignored the last three calls from Zoe while she thought. All the options must be considered, all the possibilities planned for. It was an impossible task; she knew she was far too emotional to think clearly, and there wasn't time to get herself under control.

But she had done what she could. Now *The Good Ship Lollipop*, outwardly unchanged, was a ship of war.

Zoe came backing in, riding the fusion torch and headed for a point dead in space relative to Xanthia. The fusion drive was too dangerous for *Shirley* to complete the rendezvous; the rest of the maneuver would be up to *Lollipop*.

Xanthia watched through the telescope as the drive went off. She could see *Shirley* clearly on her screen, though the ship was fifty kilometers away.

Her screen lit up again, and there was Zoe. Xanthia turned her own camera on.

"There you are," Zoe said. "Why wouldn't you talk to me?"

"I didn't think the time was ripe."

"Would you like to tell me how come this nonsense about talking black holes? What's gotten into you?"

"Never mind about that. There never was a hole, anyway. I just needed to talk to you about something you forgot to erase from the tape library in the *Lol-* . . . in the lifeboat. You were pretty thorough with the tapes in *Shirley*, but you forgot to take the same care here. I guess you didn't think I'd ever be using it. Tell me, what are Clone Control Regulations?"

The face on the screen was immobile. Or was it a mirror, and was she smiling? Was it herself, or Zoe she watched? Frantically, Xanthia thumbed a switch to put her telescope image on the screen, wiping out the face. Would Zoe try to talk her way out of it? If she did, Xanthia was determined to do nothing at all. There was no way she could check out any lie Zoe might tell her, nothing she could confront Zoe with except a fantastic story from a talking black hole.

Please say something. Take the responsibility out of my hands. She was willing to die, tricked by Zoe's fast talk, rather than accept the hole's word against Zoe's.

But Zoe was acting, not talking, and the response was exactly what the hole had predicted. The attitude control jets were firing, *Shirley Temple* was pitching and yawing slowly, the nozzles at the stern hunting for a speck in the telescope screen. When the engines were aimed, they would surely be fired, and Xanthia and the whole ship would be vaporized.

But she was ready. Her hands had been poised over the thrust controls. *Lollipop* had a respectable acceleration, and every gee of it slammed her into the couch as she scooted away from the danger spot.

Shirley's fusion engines fired, and began a deadly hunt Xanthia could see the thin, incredibly hot stream playing around her as Zoe made finer adjustments in her orientation. She could only evade it for a short time, but that was all she needed.

Then the light went out. She saw her screen flare up as the telescope circuit became overloaded with an immense burst of energy. And it was over. Her radar screen showed nothing at all.

"As I predicted," the hole said.

"Why don't you shut up?" Xanthia sat very still, and trembled.

"I shall, very soon. I did not expect to be thanked. But what you did, you did for yourself."

"And you, too, you . . . you *ghoul!* Damn you, damn you to hell." She was shouting through her tears. "Don't think you've fooled me, not completely, anyway. I know what you did, and I know how you did it."

"Do you?" The voice was unutterably cool and distant. She could see that now the hole was out of danger, it was rapidly losing interest in her.

"Yes, I do. Don't tell me it was coincidence that when you changed direction it was just enough to be near Zoe when she got here. You had this planned from the start."

"From much further back than you know," the hole said. "I tried to get you both, but it was impossible. The best I could do was take advantage of the situation as it was."

"Shut up, shut up."

The hole's voice was changing from the hollow, neutral tones to something that might have issued from a tank of liquid helium. She would never have mistaken it for human.

"What I did, I did for my own benefit. But I saved your life. She was going to try to kill you. I maneuvered her into such a position that, when she tried to turn her fusion drive on you, she was heading into a black hole she was powerless to detect."

"You *used* me."

"You used me. You were going to imprison me in a power station."

"But you said you wouldn't *mind!* You said it would be the perfect place."

"Do you believe that eating is all there is to life? There is more to do in the wide universe than you can even suspect. I am slow. It is easy to catch a hole if your mass detector is functioning: Zoe did it three times. But I am beyond your reach now."

"What do you mean? What are you going to do? What am *I* going to do?" That question hurt so much that Xanthia almost didn't hear the hole's reply.

"I am on my way out. I converted *Shirley* into energy; I absorbed very little mass from her. I beamed the energy very tightly, and am now on my way out of your system. You will not see me again. You have two options. You can go back to Pluto and tell everyone what happened out here. It would be necessary for scientists to rewrite natural laws if they believed you. It has been done before, but usually with more persuasive evidence. There will be questions asked concerning the fact that no black hole has ever evaded capture, spoken, or changed velocity in the past. You can explain that when a hole has a chance to defend itself, the hole hunter does not survive to tell the story."

"I will. I *will* tell them what happened!" Xanthia was eaten by a horrible doubt. Was it possible there had been a solution to her problem that did not involve Zoe's death? Just how badly had the hole tricked her?

"There is a second possibility," the hole went on, relentlessly. "Just what *are* you doing out here in a lifeboat?"

"What am I...I told you, we had..." Xanthia stopped. She felt herself choking.

"It would be easy to see you as crazy. You discovered something in *Lollipop*'s library that led you to know you must kill Zoe. This knowledge was too much for you. In defense, you invented me to trick you into doing what you had to do. Look in the mirror and tell me if you think your story will be believed. Look closely, and be honest with yourself."

She heard the voice laugh for the first time, from down in the bottom of its hole, like a voice from a well. It was an extremely unpleasant sound.

Maybe Zoe had died a month ago, strangled or poisoned or slashed with a knife. Xanthia had been sitting in her lifeboat, catatonic, all that time, and had constructed this episode to justify the murder. It *had* been self-defense, which was certainly a good excuse, and a very convenient one.

But she knew. She was sure, as sure as she had ever been of anything, that the hole was out there, that everything had happened as she had seen it happen. She saw the flash again in her mind, the awful flash that had turned Zoe into radiation. But she also knew that the other explanation would haunt her for the rest of her life.

"I advise you to forget it. Go to Pluto, tell everyone that your ship blew up and you escaped and you are Zoe. Take her place in the world, and never, *never* speak of talking black holes."

The voice faded from her radio. It did not speak again.

After days of numb despair and more tears and recriminations than she cared to remember, Xanthia did as the hole had predicted. But life on Pluto did not agree with her. There were too many people, and none of them looked very much like her. She stayed long enough to withdraw Zoe's money from the bank and buy a ship, which she named *Shirley Temple*. It was massive, with power to blast to the stars if necessary. She had left something out there, and she meant to search for it until she found it again.

Picnic on Nearside

THIS IS THE STORY of how I went to the Nearside and found old Lester and maybe grew up a little. And about time, too, as Carnival would say.

Carnival is my mother. We don't get along well most of the time, and I think it's because I'm twelve and she's ninety-six. She says it makes no difference, and she waited so long to have her child because she wanted to be sure she was ready for it. And I answer back that at her age she's too far away from childhood to remember what it's like. And she replies that her memory is perfect all the way back to her birth. And I retort...

We argue a lot.

I'm a good debater, but Carnival's a special problem. She's an Emotionalist; so anytime I try to bring facts into the argument she waves it away with a statement like, "Facts only get in the way of my preconceived notions." I tell her that's irrational, and she says I'm perfectly right, and she meant it to be. Most of the time we can't even agree on premises to base a disagreement on. You'd think that would be the death of debate, but if you did, you don't know Carnival and me.

The major topic of debate around our warren for seven or eight lunations had been the Change I wanted to get. The battle lines had been drawn, and we had been at it every day. She thought a Change would harm my mind at my age. *Every*body was getting one.

We were all sitting at the breakfast table. There was me and

Carnival, and Chord, the man Carnival has lived with for several years, and Adagio, Chord's daughter. Adagio is seven.

There had been a big battle the night before between me and Carnival. It had ended up (more or less) with me promising to divorce her as soon as I was of age. I don't remember what the counterthreat was. I had been pretty upset.

I was sitting there eating fitfully and licking my wounds. The argument had been inconclusive, philosophically, but from the pragmatic standpoint she had won, no question about it. The hard fact was that I couldn't get a Change until she affixed her personality index to the bottom of a sheet of input, and she said she'd put her brain in cold storage before she'd allow that. She would, too.

"I think I'm ready to have a Change," Carnival said to us.

"That's not fair!" I yelled. "You said that just to spite me. You just want to rub it in that I'm nothing and you're anything you want to be."

"We'll have no more of that," she said, sharply. "We've exhausted this subject, and I will not change my mind. You're too young for a Change."

"Blowout," I said. "I'll be an adult soon; it's only a year away. Do you really think I'll be all that different in a year?"

"I don't care to predict that. I hope you'll mature. But if, as you say, it's only a year, why are you in such a hurry?"

"And I wish you wouldn't use language like that," Chord said.

Carnival gave him a sour look. She has a hard line about outside interference when she's trying to cope with me. She doesn't want anyone butting in. But she wouldn't say anything in front of me and Adagio.

"I think you should let Fox get his Change," Adagio said, and grinned at me. Adagio is a good kid, as younger foster-siblings go. I could always count on her to back me up, and I returned the favor when I could.

"You keep out of this," Chord advised her, then to Carnival, "Maybe we should leave the table until you and Fox get this settled."

"You'd have to stay away for a year," Carnival said. "Stick around. The discussion is over. If Fox thinks different, he can go to his room."

That was my cue, and I got up and ran from the table. I felt silly doing it, but the tears were real. It's just that there's a part of me that stays cool enough to try and get the best of any situation.

Carnival came to see me a little later, but I did my best to make her feel unwelcome. I can be good at that, at least with her. She left when it became obvious she couldn't make anything any better. She was hurt, and when the door closed, I felt really miserable, mad at her and at myself, too. I was finding it hard to love her as much as I had a few years before, and feeling ashamed because I couldn't.

I worried over that for a while and decided I should apologize. I left my room and was ready to go cry in her arms, but it didn't happen that way. Maybe if it had, things would have been different and Halo and I would never have gone to Nearside.

Carnival and Chord were getting ready to go out. They said they'd be gone most of the lune. They were dressing up for it, and what bothered me and made me change my plans was that they were dressing in the family room instead of in their own private rooms where I thought they should.

She had taken off her feet and replaced them with peds, which struck me as foolish, since peds only make sense in free-fall. But Carnival wears them every chance she gets, prancing around like a high-stepping horse because they are so unsuited to walking. I think people look silly with hands on the ends of their legs. And naturally she had left her feet lying on the floor.

Carnival glanced at her watch and said something about how they would be late for the shuttle. As they left, she glanced over her shoulder.

"Fox, would you do me a favor and put those feet away, Please? Thanks." Then she was gone.

An hour later, in the depths of my depression, the door rang. It was a woman I had never seen before. She was nude.

You know how sometimes you can look at someone you know who's just had a Change and recognize them instantly, even though they might be twenty centimeters shorter or taller and mass fifty kilos more or less and look nothing at all like the person you knew? Maybe you don't, because not everyone has this talent, but I have it very strong. Carnival says it's an evolutionary change in the race, a response to the need to recognize other individuals who can change their appearance at will. That may be true; she can't do it at all.

I think it's something to do with the way a person wears a body: any body, of either sex. Little mannerisms like blinking, mouth movements, stance, fingers; maybe even the total kinesthetic gestalt the doctors talk about. This was like that. I could see behind the pretty female face and the different height and weight and recognize someone I knew. It was Halo, my best friend, who had been a male the last time I saw him, three lunes ago. She had a big foolish grin on her face.

"Hi, Fox," she said, in a voice that was an octave higher and yet was unmistakably Halo's. "Guess who?"

"Queen Victoria, right?" I tried to sound bored. "Come on in, Halo."

Her face fell. She came in, looking confused.

"What do you think?" she said, turning slowly to give me a look from all sides. All of them were good because—as if I needed anything else—her mother had let her get the full treatment: fully developed breasts, all the mature curves—the works. She had been denied only the adult height. She was even a few centimeters shorter than she had been.

"It's fine," I said.

"Listen, Fox, if you'd rather I left . . ."

"Oh, I'm sorry, Halo," I said, giving up on my hatred. "You look great. Fabulous. Really you do. I'm just having a hard time being happy for you. Carnival is never going to give in."

She was instantly sympathetic. She took my hand, startling me badly.

"I was so happy I guess I was tactless," she said in a low voice. "Maybe I shouldn't have come over here yet."

She looked at me with big brown eyes (they had been blue, usually), and I started realizing what this was going to mean to me. I mean, Halo? A female? Halo, the guy I used to run the corridors with? The guy who helped me build that awful eight-legged cat that Carnival wouldn't let in the house and looked like a confused caterpillar? Who made love to the same girls I did and compared notes with me later when we were alone and helped me out when the gang tried to beat me up and cried with me and vowed to get even? Could we do any of that now? I didn't know. Most of my best friends were male, maybe because the sex thing tended to make matters too complicated with females, and I couldn't handle both things with the same person yet.

But Halo was having no such doubts. In fact, she was standing very close to me and practicing a wide-eyed innocent look that she knew did funny things to me. She knew it because I had told her so, back when she was a boy. Somehow that didn't seem fair.

"Ah, listen, Halo," I said hastily, backing away. She had been going for my pants! "Ah, I think I need some time to get used to this. How can I . . . ? You know what I'm talking about, don't you?" I don't think she did, and neither did I, really. All I knew was I was unaccountably mortified at what she was so anxious to try. And she was still coming at me.

"Say!" I said, desperately. "Say! I have an idea! Ah . . . I know. Let's take Carnival's jumper and go for a ride, okay? She said I could use it today." My mouth was leading its own life, out of control. Everything I said was extemporaneous, as much news to me as it was to her."

She stopped pursuing me. "Did she really?"

"Sure," I said, very assured. This was only a half lie, by my mother's lights. What had happened was I had meant to ask her for the jumper, and I was sure she would have said yes. I was logically certain she would have. I had just forgotten to ask, that's all. So it was almost as if permission had been granted, and I went on as if it had. The reasoning behind this is tricky, I admit, but as I said, Carnival would have understood.

"Well," Halo said, not really overjoyed at the idea, "where would we go?"

"How about to Old Archimedes?" Again, that was a big surprise to me. I had had no idea I wanted to go there.

Halo was really shocked. I jolted her right out of her new mannerisms. She reacted just like the old Halo would have, with a dopey face and open mouth. Then she tried on other reactions: covering her mouth with her hands and wilting a little. First-time Changers are like that; new women tend to mince around like something out of a gothic novel, and new men swagger and grunt like Marlon Brando in *A Streetcar Named Desire*. They get over it.

Halo got over it right in front of my eyes. She stared at me, scratching her head.

"Are you crazy? Old Archimedes is on the Nearside. They don't let anybody go over there."

"Don't they?" I asked, suddenly interested. "Do you know that for a fact? And if so, why not?"

"Well, I mean everybody knows . . ."

"Do they? Who is 'they' that won't let us go?"

"The Central Computer, I guess."

"Well, the only way to find out is to try it. Come on, let's go." I grabbed her arm. I could see she was confused, and I wanted it to remain that way until I could get my own thoughts together.

"I'd like a flight plan to Old Archimedes on the Nearside," I said, trying to sound as grownup and unworried as possible. We had packed a lunch and reached the field in ten minutes, due largely to my frantic prodding.

"That's a little imprecise, Fox," said the CC. "Old Archimedes is a big place. Would you like to try again?"

"Ah . . ." I drew a blank. Damn all computers and their literal-mindedness! What did I know about Old Archimedes? About as much as I knew about Old New York or Old Bombay.

"Give me a flight plan to the main landing field."

"That's better. The data are . . ." It reeled off the string of numbers. I fed them into the pilot and tried to relax.

"Here goes," I said to Halo. "This is Fox-Carnival-Joule, piloting private jumper AX1453, based at King City. I hereby file a flight plan to Old Archimedes' main landing field, described as follows . . ." I repeated the numbers the CC had given me. "Filed on the seventeenth lune of the fourth lunation of the year 214 of the Occupation of Earth. I request an initiation time."

"Granted. Time as follows: thirty seconds from mark. Mark."

I was stunned. "That's all there is to it?"

It chuckled. Damn maternalistic machine. "What did you expect, Fox? Marshals converging on your jumper?"

"I don't know. I guess I thought you wouldn't allow us to go to the Nearside."

"A popular misconception. You are a free citizen, although a minor, and able to go where you wish on the lunar surface. You are subject only to the laws of the state and the specific wishes of your parent as programmed into me. I . . . do you wish me to start the burn for you?"

"Mind your own business." I watched the tick and pressed the button when it reached zero. The acceleration was mild, but went on for a long time. Hell, Old Archimedes is at the antipodes.

"I have the responsibility to see that you do not endanger yourself through youthful ignorance or forgetfulness. I must also see that you obey the wishes of your mother. Other than that, you are on your own."

"You mean Carnival gave me permission to go to the Near-side?"

"I didn't say that. I have received no instruction from Carnival *not* to permit you to go to Nearside. There are no unusual dangers to your safety on Nearside. So I had no choice but to approve your flight plan." It paused, significantly. "It is my experience that few parents consider it necessary to instruct me to deny such permission. I infer that it's because so few people ever ask to go there. I also note that your parent is at the present moment unreachable; she has left instructions not to be disturbed. Fox," the CC said, accusingly, "it occurs to me that this is no accident. Did you have this planned?"

I *hadn't!* But if I'd known . . .

"No."

"I suppose you want a return flight plan?"

"Why? I'll ask you when I'm ready to come back."

"I'm afraid that won't be possible," it said, smugly. "In another five minutes you'll be out of range of my last receptor. I don't extend to the Nearside, you know. Haven't in decades. You're going out of contact, Fox. You'll be on your own. Think about it."

I did. For a queasy moment I wanted to turn back. Without the CC to monitor us, kids wouldn't be allowed on the surface for *years*.

Was I that confident? I know how hostile the surface is if it ever gets the drop on you. I thought I had all the mistakes trained out of me by now, but did I?

"How exciting," Halo gushed. She was off in the clouds again, completely over her shock at where we were going. She was bubble-headed like that for three lunes after her Change. Well, so was I, later, when I had my first.

"Hush, numbskull," I said, not unkindly. Nor was she insulted. She just grinned at me and gawked out the window as we approached the terminator.

I checked the supply of consumables; they were in perfect shape for a stay of a full lunation if need be, though I had larked off without a glance at the delta-vee.

"All right, smart-ass, give me the data for the return."

"Incomplete request," the CC drawled.

"Damn you, I want a flight plan Old Archimedes-King City, and no back talk."

"Noted. Assimilated." It gave me that data. Its voice was getting fainter.

"I don't suppose," it said, diffidently, "that you'd care to give me an indication of when you plan to return?"

Ha! I had it where it hurt. Carnival wouldn't be happy with the CC's explanation, I was sure of that.

"Tell her I've decided to start my own colony and I'll never come back."

"As you wish."

Old Archimedes was bigger than I had expected. I knew that even in its heyday it had not been as populated as King City is, but they built more above the surface in those days. King City is not much more than a landing field and a few domes. Old Archimedes was chock-a-block with structures, all clustered around the central landing field. Halo pointed out some interesting buildings to the south, and so I went over there and set down next to them.

She opened the door and threw out the tent, then jumped after it. I followed, taking the ladder since I seemed elected to carry the lunch. She took a quick look around and started unpacking the tent.

"We'll go exploring later," she said, breathlessly. "Right now let's get in the tent and eat. I'm hungry."

All right, all right, I said to myself. I've got to face it sooner or later. I didn't think she was really all that hungry—not for the picnic lunch, anyway. This was still going too fast for me. I had no idea what our relationship would be when we crawled out of that tent.

While she was setting it up, I took a more leisurely look around. Before long I was wishing we had gone to Tranquillity Base instead. It wouldn't have been as private, but there are no spooks at Tranquillity. Come to think of it, Tranquillity Base used to be on the Nearside, before they moved it.

About Old Archimedes:

I couldn't put my finger on what disturbed me about the place. Not the silence. The race has had to adjust to silence since we were forced off the Earth and took to growing up on the junk planets of the system. Not the lack of people. I was accustomed to long walks on the surface where I might not see anyone for hours. I don't know. Maybe it was the Earth hanging there a little above the horizon.

It was in crescent phase, and I wished uselessly for the old days when that dark portion would have been sprayed with points of light that were the cities of mankind. Now there was only the primitive night and the dolphins in the sea and the aliens—bogies cooked up to ruin the sleep of a child, but now I was not so sure. If humans still survive down there, we have no way of knowing it.

They say that's what drove people to the Farside: the constant reminder of what they had lost, always there in the sky. It must have been hard, especially to the Earthborn. Whatever the reason, no one had lived on the Nearside for almost a century. All the original settlements had dwindled as people migrated to the comforting empty sky of Farside.

I think that's what I felt, hanging over the old buildings like some invisible moss. It was the aura of fear and despair left by all the people who had buried their hopes here and moved away to the forgetfulness of Farside. There were ghosts here, all right: the shades of unfulfilled dreams and endless longing. And over it all a bottomless sadness.

I shook myself and came back to the present. Halo had the tent ready. It bulged up on the empty field, a clear bubble just a little higher than my head. She was already inside. I crawled through the sphincter, and she sealed it behind me.

Halo's tent is a good one. The floor is about three meters in diameter, plenty of room for six people if you don't mind an occasional kick. It had a stove, a stereo set, and a compact toilet. It recycled water, scavenged CO_2, controlled temperature, and could provide hydroponic oxygen for three lunations. And it all folded into a cube thirty centimeters on a side.

Halo had skinned out of her suit as soon as the door was sealed and was bustling about, setting up the kitchen. She took the lunch hamper from me and started to work.

I watched her with keen interest as she prepared the food. I wanted to get an insight into what she was feeling. It wasn't easy. Every fuse in her head seemed to have blown.

First-timers often overreact, seeking a new identity for themselves before it dawns on them there was nothing wrong with the old one. Since our society offers so little differentiation between the sex roles, they reach back to where the differences are so vivid and startling: novels, dramas, films, and tapes from the old days on Earth and the early years on the moon. They have the vague idea that since they have this new body and it lacks a penis or vagina, they should behave differently.

I recognized the character she had fallen into; I'm as interested in old culture as the next kid. She was Blondie and I was supposed to be Dagwood. The Bumsteads, you know. Typical domestic nineteenth-century couple. She had spread a red-and-white-checkered tablecloth and set two places with dishes, napkins, washbowls, and a tiny electric candelabra.

I had to smile at her, kneeling at the tiny stove, trying to put three pans on the same burner. She was trying so hard to please me with a role I was completely uninterested in. She was humming as she worked.

After the meal, I offered to clean up for her (well, *Dagwood* would have), but Blondie said no, that's all right, dear, I'll take care of everything. I lay flat on my back, holding my belly, and watched the Earth. Presently I felt a warm body cuddle up, half beside me and half on top of me, and press close from toenails to eyebrows. She had left Blondie over among the dirty dishes. The woman who breathed in my ear now was—Helen of Troy? Greta Garbo?—someone new, anyway. I wished fervently that Halo would come back. I was beginning to think Halo and I could screw like the very devil if this feverish creature that contained her would only give us a chance. Meantime, I had to be raped by Helen of Troy. I raised my head.

"What's it like, Halo?"

She slowed her foreplay slightly, but it never really stopped. She propped herself up on one elbow.

"I don't think I can describe it to you."

"Please try."

She dimpled. "I don't really know what it's *all* like," she said. "I'm still a virgin, you know."

I sat up. "You got *that, too?*"

"Sure, why not? But don't worry about it. I'm not afraid."

"What about making love?"

"Oh, Fox, Fox! Yes, yes. I . . ."

"No, no! Wait a minute." I squirmed beneath her, trying to hold her off a little longer. "What I meant was, wasn't there any problem in making the shift? I mean, do you have any aversion to having sex with boys now?" It was sure a stupid question, but she took it seriously.

"I haven't noticed any problem so far," she said, thoughtfully, as her hand reached down and fumbled, inexpertly trying to guide me in. I helped her get it right, and she poised, squatting on her toes. "I thought about that before the Change, but it sort of melted away. Now I don't feel any qualms at all. Ahhhhh!" She had thrust herself down, brutally hard, and we were off and running.

It was the most unsatisfactory sex act I ever had. It was not entirely the fault of either of us; external events were about to mess us up totally. But it wasn't very good even without that.

A first-time female Changer is liable to be in delirious oblivion through the entire first sex act, which may last all of sixty seconds. The fact that she is playing the game from the other court with a different set of rules and a new set of equipment does not handicap her. Rather, it provides a tremendous erotic stimulus.

That's what happened to Halo. I began to wonder if she'd wait for me. I never found out. I looked away from her face and got the shock of my life. There was someone standing outside the tent, watching us.

Halo felt the change in me and looked at my face, which must have been a sight, then looked over her shoulder. She fainted; out like a light.

Hell, I almost fainted myself. Would have, but when she did, it scared me even more, and I decided I couldn't indulge it. So I stayed awake to see what was going on.

It looked way too much like one of the ghosts my imagination had been walking through the abandoned city ever since we got there. The figure was short and dressed in a suit that might have been stolen from the museum at Kepler, except that it was more patches than suit. I could tell little about who might be in it, not even the sex. It was bulky, and the helmet was reflective.

I don't know how long I stared at it; long enough for the spook to walk around the tent three or four times. I reached for the bottle of white wine we had been drinking and took a long pull. I found out that's an old movie cliché; it didn't make anything any better. But it sure did things for Halo when I poured it in her face.

"Get in your suit," I said, as she sat up, sputtering. "I think that character wants to talk to us." He was waving at us and pointing to what might have been a radio on his suit.

We suited up and crawled through the sphincter. I kept saying hello as I ran through the channels on my suit. Nothing worked. Then he came over and touched helmets. He sounded far away.

"What're you doin' here?"

I had thought that would have been obvious.

"Sir, we just came over here for a picnic. Are we on your land or something? If so, I'm sorry, and . . ."

"No, no," he waved it off. "You can do as you please. I ain't your ma. As to owning, I guess I own this whole city, but you're welcome to do as you please with most of it. Do as you please, that's my philosophy. That's why I'm still here. They couldn't get old Lester to move out. I'm old Lester."

"I'm Fox, sir," I said.

"And I'm Halo." She heard us over my radio.

He turned and looked at her.

"Halo," he said, quietly. "A Halo for an angel. Nice name, miss." I was wishing I could see his face. He sounded like an adult, but he was sure a small one. Both of us were taller than he was, and we're not much above average for our age.

He coughed. "I, ah, I'm sorry I disturbed you folks...ah," he seemed embarrassed. "I just couldn't help myself. I haven't seen any people for a long time—oh, ten years, I guess—and I just had to get a closer look. And I, uh, I needed to ask you something."

"And what's that, sir?"

"You can knock off the 'sir.' I ain't your pa. I wanted to know if you folks had any medicine?"

"There's a first-aid kit in the jumper," I said. "Is there someone in need of help? I'd be glad to take them to a hospital in King City."

He was waving his arms frantically.

"No, no, no. I don't want doctors poking around. I just need a little medicine. Uh, say, could you take that first-aid kit out of the jumper and come to my warren for a bit? Maybe you got something in there I could use."

We agreed, and followed him across the field.

He led us into an unpressurized building at the edge of the field. We threaded our way through dark corridors.

We came to a big cargo lock, stepped inside, and he cycled it. Then we went through the inner door and into his warren.

It was quite a place, more like a jungle than a home. It was as big as the Civic Auditorium at King City and overgrown with trees, vines, flowers, and bushes. It looked like it had been tended at one time, but allowed to go wild. There were a bed and a few chairs in one corner, and several tall stacks of books. And heaps of junk; barrels of leak sealant, empty O_2 cylinders, salvaged instruments, buggy tires.

Halo and I had our helmets off and were half out of our suits when we got our first look at him. He was incredible! I'm afraid I gasped, purely from reflex; Halo just stared. Then we politely tried to pretend there was nothing unusual.

He looked like he made a habit of going out without his suit. His face was grooved and pitted like a plowed field after an artillery barrage. His skin looked as tough as leather. His eyes were sunk into deep pits.

"Well, let me see it," he said, sticking out a thin hand. His knuckles were swollen and knobby.

I handed him the first-aid kit, and he fumbled with the catches, then got it open. He sat in a chair and carefully read the label on each item. He mumbled while he read.

Halo wandered among the plants, but I was more curious about old Lester than about his home. I watched him handle the contents of the kit with stiff, clumsy fingers. All his movements seemed stiff. I couldn't imagine what might be wrong with him and wondered why he hadn't sought medical help long ago, before whatever was afflicting him could go this far.

At last he put everything back in the kit but two tubes of cream. He sighed and looked at us.

"How old are you?" he asked, suspiciously.

"I'm twenty," I said. I don't know why. I'm not a liar, usually, unless I have a good reason. I was just beginning to get a funny feeling about old Lester, and I followed my instincts.

"Me, too," Halo volunteered.

He seemed satisfied, which surprised me. I was realizing he had been out of touch for a long time. Just how long I didn't know yet.

"There ain't much here that'll be of use to me, but I'd like to buy these here items, if you're willin' to sell. Says here they're for 'topical anesthesia,' and I could use some of that in the mornings. How much?"

I told him he could have them for nothing, but he insisted; so I told him to set his own price and reached for my credit meter in my suit pouch. He was holding out some rectangular slips of paper. They were units of paper currency, issued by the old Lunar Free State in the year 76 O.E. They had not been used in over a century. They were worth a fortune to a collector.

"Lester," I said, slowly, "these are worth more than you probably realize. I could sell them in King City for..."

He cackled. "Good man. I know what them bills is worth. I'm decrepit, but I ain't senile. They're worth thousands to one what wants 'em, but they're worthless to me. Except for one thing. They're a damn good test for findin' an honest man. They let me know if somebody'd take advantage of a sick, senile ol' hermit like me. Pardon me, son, but I had you pegged for a liar when you come in here. I was wrong. So you keep the bills. Otherwise, I'd a took 'em back."

He threw something on the floor in front of us, something he'd had in his hand and I hadn't even seen. It was a gun. I had never seen one.

Halo picked it up, gingerly, but I didn't want to touch it. This old Lester character seemed a lot less funny to me now. We were quiet.

"Now I've gone and scared you," he said. "I guess I've forgot all my manners. And I've forgot how you folks live on the other side." He picked up the gun and opened it. The charge chamber was empty. "But you wouldn't of knowed it, would you? Anyways, I'm not a killer. I just pick my friends real careful. Can I make up the fright I've caused you by inviting you to dinner? I haven't had any guests for ten years."

We told him we'd just eaten, and he asked if we could stay and just talk for a while. He seemed awfully eager. We said okay.

"You want some clothes? I don't expect you figured on visiting when you come here."

"Whatever your custom is," Halo said, diplomatically.

"I got no customs," he said, with a toothless grin. "If you don't feel funny naked, it ain't no business of mine. Do as you please, I say." It was a stock phrase with him.

So we lay on the grass, and he got some very strong, clear liquor and poured us all drinks.

"Moonshine," he laughed. "The genuine article. I make it myself. Best liquor on the Nearside."

We talked, and we drank.

Before I got too drunk to remember anything, a few interesting facts emerged about old Lester. For one thing, he really was old. He said he was two hundred and fifty-seven, and he was Earthborn. He had come to the moon when he was twenty-eight, several years before the Invasion.

I know several people in that age range, though none quite that old. Carnival's great-grandmother is two twenty-one, but she's moonborn, and doesn't remember the Invasion. There's virtually nothing left of the flesh she was born with. She's transferred her memories to a new brain twice.

I was prepared to believe that old Lester had gone a long time without medical care, but I couldn't accept what he told us at first. He said that, barring one new heart eighty years ago, he was unreconstructed since his birth! I'm young and naive—I freely admit it now—but I couldn't swallow that. But I believed it eventually, and I believe it now.

He had a million stories to tell, all of them at least eighty years old because that's how long he had been a hermit. He had stories of Earth, and of the early years on the moon. He told us about the hard years after the Invasion. Everyone who lived through that has a story to tell. I drew a blank before the evening was over, and the only thing I remember clearly is the three of us standing in a circle, arms around each other, singing a song old Lester had taught us. We swayed against each other and bumped foreheads and broke up laughing. I remember his hand resting on my shoulder. It was hard as rock.

The next day Halo became Florence Nightingale and nursed old Lester back to life. She was as firm as any nurse, getting him out of his clothes over his feeble protests, then giving him a massage. In the soberness of the morning I wondered how she could bring herself to touch his wrinkled old body, but as I watched, I slowly understood. He was beautiful.

The best thing to compare old Lester to is the surface. There is nothing older, or more abused, than the surface of the moon. But I have always loved it. It's the most beautiful place in the system, including Saturn's Rings. Old Lester was like that. I imagined he *was* the moon. He had become part of it.

Though I came to accept his age, I could still see that he was in terrible shape. The drinking had taken a lot out of him, but he wouldn't be kept down. The first thing he wanted in the morning was another drink. I brought him one, then I cooked a big breakfast: eggs and sausage and bread and orange juice, all from his garden. Then we were off and drinking again.

I didn't even have time to worry about what Carnival and Halo's mother might be thinking by now. Old Lester had plainly adopted us. He said he'd be our father, which struck me as a funny thing to say since who the hell ever knows who their father is? But he began behaving in the manner I would call maternal, and he evidently thought of it as *pa*ternal.

We did a lot of things that day. He taught us about gardening. He showed me how to cross-fertilize the egg plants and how to tell when they were ripe without breaking the shells to see. He told us the secrets of how to grow breadfruit trees so they'd yield loaves of dark-brown, hard, whole wheat or the strangely different rye variety by grafting branches. I had never had rye before. And we learned to dig for potatoes and steakroots. We learned how to harvest honey and cheese and tomatoes. We stripped bacon from the surface of the porktree trunks.

And we'd drink his moonshine while we worked, and laugh a lot, and he'd throw in more of his stories between the garden lore.

Old Lester was not the fool he seemed at first. His speech pattern was largely affected, something he did to amuse himself over the years. He could speak as correctly as anyone when he wanted to. He had read much and remembered it all. He was a first-rate engineer and botanist, but his education and skills had to be qualified by this fact: everything he knew was eighty years out of date. It didn't matter much: the old methods worked well enough.

In social matters it was a different story.

He didn't know much about Changing, except that he didn't like it. It was Changing that finally decided him to separate himself from society. He said he had been having his doubts about joining the migration to Farside, and the sex-change issue had been the final factor. He shocked us more than he knew when he revealed that he had never been a woman. I thought his lack of curiosity must be monumental, but I was wrong. It turned out that he had some queer notions about the morality of the whole process, ideas he had gotten from some weirdly aberrant religion in his childhood. I had heard of the cult, as you can hardly avoid it if you know any history. It had said little about ethics, being more interested in arbitrary regulations.

Old Lester still believed in it, though. His home was littered with primitive icons. There was a central symbol he cherished above the others: a simple wooden fetish in the shape of a plus sign with a long stem. He wore one around his neck, and others sprouted like weeds.

I came to realize that this religion was at the bottom of the puzzling inconsistencies I began to notice about him. His "do as you please" may have been sincere, but he did not entirely live by it. It became clear that, though he thought people should have freedom of choice, he condemned them if the choice they made was not his own.

My spur-of-the-moment decision to lie about my age had been borne out, though I'm not sure the truth wouldn't have been better. It might have kept us out of the further lies we told or implied, and I always prefer honesty to deception. But I still don't know if old Lester could have been our friend without the lies.

He knew something of life on Farside and made it clear he disapproved of most of it. And he had deluded himself (with our help) that we weren't like that. In particular, he thought people should not have sex until they reached a "decent age." He never defined that, but Halo and I, at "twenty," were safely past it.

It was a puzzling notion. Even Carnival, who is a bit old-fashioned, would have been shocked. Granted, we speed up puberty now—I have been sexually potent since I was seven—but he felt that even *after* puberty people should abstain. I couldn't make any sense out of it. I mean, what would you *do?*

Then there was a word he used, "incest," that I had to look up when I got home to be sure I'd understood him. I had. He was against it. I guess it had a basis back in the dawn of time, when procreation and genetics were so tied up with sex, but how could it matter now? The only place Carnival and I get along at all is in bed; without that, we would have very little in common.

It went on and on, the list of regulations. Luckily, it didn't sour me on old Lester. All I disliked was the lies we had trapped ourselves into. I'm willing to let people have all sorts of screwball notions as long as they don't force them on me, like Carnival was doing about the Change. That I found myself expressing agreement with old Lester's ideas was my own fault, not his. I think.

The days went by, marred by only one thing. I had not broken any laws, but I knew I was being searched for. And I knew I was treating Carnival badly. I tried to figure out just how badly, and what I should do about it, but kept getting fogged up by the moonshine and good times.

Carnival had come to the Nearside. Halo and I had watched them from the shadows when old Lester's radar had picked them up coming in. There had been six or seven figures in the distance. They had entered the jumper and made a search. They had cast around at the edge of the field for our tracks, found them, and followed them to where they disappeared on concrete. I would have liked to have listened in, but didn't dare because they were sure to have detection apparatus for that.

And they left. They left the jumper, which was nice of them, since they could have taken it and rendered us helpless to wait for their return.

I thought about it, and talked it over with Halo. Several times we were ready to give up and go back. After all, we hadn't really set out to run away from home. We had only been defying authority, and it had never entered my head that we would stay as long as we had. But now that we were here we found it hard to go back. The trip to Nearside had acquired an inertia of its own, and we didn't have the strength to stop it.

In the end we went to the other extreme. We decided to stay on Nearside forever. I think we were giddy with the sense of power a decision like that made us feel. So we covered up our doubts with backslapping encouragement, a lot of giggling, and inflated notions of what we and old Lester would do at Archimedes.

We wrote a note—which proved we still felt responsible to *someone*—and taped it to the ladder of the jumper; then Halo went in and turned on the outside lights and pointed them straight up. We retired to a hiding place and waited.

Sure enough, another ship returned in two hours. They had been watching from close orbit and landed on the next pass when they noticed the change. One person got out of the ship and read the note. It was a crazy note, saying not to worry, we were all right. It went on to say we intended to stay, and some more things I'd rather not remember. It also said she should take the jumper. I was regretting that even as she read it. We must have been crazy.

I could see her slump even from so far away. She looked all around her, then began signaling in semaphore language.

"Do what you have to," she signaled. "I don't understand you, but I love you. I'm leaving the jumper in case you change your mind."

Well. I gulped, and was halfway up on my way out to her when, to my great surprise, Halo pulled me down. I had thought she was only going along with me to avoid having to point out how wrong I was. This hadn't been her idea; she had not been in her right mind when I hustled her over here. But she had settled down from all that lunes ago and was now as level-headed as ever. And was more taken with our adventure than I was.

"Dope!" she hissed, touching helmets. "I thought you'd do something like that. Think it through. Do you want to give up so easy? We haven't even tried this yet."

Her face wasn't as certain as her words, but I was in no shape to argue her out of it. Then Carnival was gone, and I felt better. It was true that we had an out if it turned sour. Pretty soon we were intrepid pioneers, and I didn't think of Carnival or the Farside until things *did* start to go sour.

For a long time, almost a lunation, we were happy. We worked hard every day with old Lester. I learned that in his kind of life the work was never done; there was always an air duct to repair, flowers to pollinate, machinery to regulate. It was primitive, and I could usually see ways to improve the methods but never thought of suggesting them. It wouldn't have fit with our crazy pioneer ideas. Things *had* to be hard to feel right.

We built a grass lean-to like one we had seen in a movie and moved in. It was across the chamber from old Lester, which was silly, but it meant we could visit each other. And I learned an interesting thing about sin.

Old Lester would watch us make love in our raggedy shack, a grin across his leathery face. Then one day he implied that lovemaking should be a private act. It was a sin to do it in front of others, and a sin to watch. But he still watched.

So I asked Halo about it.

"He needs a little sin, Fox."

"Huh?"

"I know it isn't logical, but you must have seen by now that his religion is mixed up."

"That's for sure. But I still don't get it."

"Well, I don't either, but I try to respect. He thinks drinking is sinful, and until we came along it was the only sin he could practice. Now he can do the sin of lust, too. I think he needs to be forgiven for things, and he can't be forgiven until he does them."

"That's the craziest thing I ever heard. But even crazier, if lust is a sin to him, why doesn't he go all the way and make love with you? I've been dead sure he wants to, but as far as I know, he's never done it. Has he?"

She looked at me pityingly. "You don't know, do you?"

"You mean he has?"

"No. I don't mean that. We haven't. And not because I haven't tried. And not because he doesn't want to. He looks, looks, looks; he never takes his eyes off me. And it isn't because he thinks it's a sin. He *knows* it's a sin, but he'd do it if he could."

"I still don't understand, then."

"What do you mean? I just told you. He *can't*. He's too old. His equipment won't function anymore."

"That's *terrible!*" I was almost sick. I knew there was a word for his condition, but I had to look it up a long time afterward. The word is crippled. It means some part of your body doesn't work right. Old Lester had been sexually crippled for over a century.

I seriously considered going home then. I was not at all sure he was the kind of person I wanted to be around. The lies were getting more galling every day, and now this.

But things got much worse, and still I stayed.

He was ill. I don't mean the way we think of ill; some petty malfunction to be cleared up by a ten-minute visit to the bioengineers. He was wearing out.

It was partly our fault. Even that first morning he was not very quick out of bed. Each lune—after a long night of drinking and general hell-raising—he was a little slower to get up. It got to where Halo was spending an hour each morning just massaging him into shape to stand erect. I thought at first he was just cannily malingering because he liked the massage and Halo's intimacy when she worked him over. That was not the case. When he did get up, he hobbled, bent over from pains in his belly. He would forget things. He would stumble, fall, and get up very slowly.

"I'm dying," he said one night. I gasped; Halo blinked rapidly. I tried to cover my embarrassment by pretending he hadn't said it.

"I know it's a bad word now, and I'm sorry if I offended you. But I ain't lived this long without being able to look it in the eye.

"I'm dying, all right, and I'll be dead pretty soon. I didn't think it'd come so sudden. Everything seems to be quittin' on me."

We tried to convince him that he was wrong and, when that didn't work, to convince him that he should take a short hop to Farside and get straightened out. But we couldn't get through his superstition. He was awfully afraid of the engineers on Farside. We would try to show him that periodic repairs still left the mind—he called it the "soul"—unchanged, but he'd get philsophical.

The next day he didn't get up at all. Halo rubbed his old limbs until she was stiff. It was no good. His breathing became irregular, and his pulse was hard to find.

So we were faced with the toughest decision ever. Should we allow him to die, or carry him to the jumper and rush him to a repair shop? We sweated over it all lune. Neither course felt right, but I found myself arguing to take him back, and Halo said we shouldn't. He could not hear us except for brief periods when he'd rouse himself and try to sit up. Then he'd ask us questions or say things that seemed totally random. His brain must have been pretty well scrambled by then.

"You kids aren't really twenty, are you?" he said once.

"How did you know?"

He cackled, weakly.

"Old Lester ain't no dummy. You said that to cover up what I caught you doin' so's I wouldn't tell your folks. But I won't tell. That's your business. Just wanted you to know you didn't fool me, not for a minute." He lapsed into labored breathing.

We never did settle the argument, unless by default. What I wanted to do took some action, and in the end I didn't have it in me to get up and do it. I wasn't sure enough of myself. So we sat there on his bed, waiting for him to die and talking to him when he needed it. Halo held his hand.

I went through hell. I cursed him for a vacuum-skulled, mentally defective, prehistoric poop, and almost decided to help him out in his pea-brained search for death. Then I went the other way; loving him almost like he loved his crazy God. I imagined he was the mother that Carnival had never really been to me and that my world would have no purpose when he was dead. Both those reactions were crazy, of course; old Lester was just a person. He was a little crazy and a little saintly, and hardly a person you should either love or hate. It was Death that had me going in circles: the creepy black-robed skeletal figure old Lester had told us about, straight out of his superstition.

He opened one bleary eye after hours of no movement.

"Don't ever," he said. "You shouldn't ever. You, I mean. Halo. Don't ever get a Change. You always been a girl, you always should be. The Lord intended it that way."

Halo shot a quick glance at me. She was crying, and her eyes told me: *don't breathe a word. Let him believe it.* She needn't have worried.

Then he started coughing. Blood came from his lips, and as soon as I saw it, I passed out. I thought he would literally fall apart and rot into some awful green slime, slime that I could never wash off.

Halo wouldn't let me stay out. She slapped me until my ears were ringing, and when I was awake, we gave up. We couldn't make a meaningful decision in the face of *this*. We had to give it to someone else.

So twenty-five minutes later I was over the pole, just coming into range of the CC's outer transmitters.

"Well, the black sheep return," the CC began in a superior tone. "I must say you outlasted the usual Nearside stay, in fact . . ."

"Shut *up!*" I bawled. "You shut up and listen to me. I want to contact Carnival, and I want her *now,* crash priority, emergency status. Get on it!"

The CC was all business, dropping the *in loco parentis* program and operating with the astonishing speed it's capable of in an emergency. Carnival was on the line in three seconds.

"Fox," she said, "I don't want to start this off on a bad footing; so, first of all, I thank you for giving me a chance to settle this with you face-to-face. I've retained a family arbiter, and I'd like for us to present our separate cases to him on this Change you want, and I'll agree to abide by his decision. Is that fair for a beginning?" She sounded anxious. I knew there was anger beneath it—there always is—but she was sincere.

"We can talk about that later, Mom," I sobbed. "Right now you've got to get to the field, as quick as you can."

"Fox, is Halo with you? Is she all right?"

"She's all right."

"I'll be there in five minutes."

It was too late, of course. Old Lester had died shortly after I lifted off, and Halo had been there with a dead body for almost two hours.

She was calm about it. She held Carnival and me together while she explained what had to be done, and even got us to help her. We buried him, as he had wanted, on the surface, in a spot that would always be in the light of Old Earth.

Carnival never would tell me what she would have done if he had been alive when we got there. It was an ethical question, and both of us are usually very opinionated on ethical matters. But I suspect we agreed for once. The will of the individual must be respected, and if I face it again, I'll know what to do. I think.

I got my Change without family arbitration. Credit me with a little sense; if our case had ever come up before a family arbiter, I'm sure he would have recommended divorce. And that would have been tough, because difficult as Carnival is, I love her, and I need her for at least a few more years. I'm not as grownup as I thought I was.

It didn't really surprise me that Carnival was right about the Change, either. In another lunation I was male again, then female, male; back and forth for a year. There's no sense in that. I'm female now, and I think I'll stick with it for a few years and see what it's about. I was born female, you know, but only lasted two hours in that sex because Carnival wanted a boy.

And Halo's a male, which makes it perfect. We've found that we do better as opposites than we did as boyfriends. I'm thinking about having my child in a few years, with Halo as the father. Carnival says wait, but I think I'm right this time. I still believe most of our troubles come from her inability to remember the swiftly moving present a child lives in. Then Halo can have her child—I'd be flattered if she chose me to father it—and . . .

We're moving to Nearside. Halo and me, that is, and Carnival and Chord are thinking about it, and they'll go, I think. If only to shut up Adagio.

Why are we going? I've thought about it a long time. Not because of old Lester. I hate to speak unkindly of him, but he was inarguably a fool. A fool with dignity, and the strength of his convictions; a likable old fool, but a fool all the same. It would be silly to talk of "carrying on his dream" or some of the things I think Halo has in mind.

But, coincidentally, his dream and mine are pretty close, though for different reasons. He couldn't bear to see the Nearside abandoned out of fear, and he feared the new human society. So he became a hermit. I want to go there simply because the fear is gone for my generation, and it's a lot of beautiful real estate. And we won't be alone. We'll be the vanguard, but the days of clustering in the Farside warrens and ignoring Old Earth are over. The human race came from Earth, and it was ours until it was taken from us. To tell the truth, I've been wondering if the aliens are really as invincible as the old stories say.

It sure is a pretty planet. I wonder if we could go back?

WIZARD

John Varley

Isaac Asimov has compared John Varley to the young Robert Heinlein and George R. R. Anderson called him 'the wildest and most original science fiction mind of the decade'. Both comments are convincingly borne out by this compelling sequel to *TITAN* in which Varley continues the story of Gaea, the planet-sized wheelgod which is a world.

Gaea, now three million years old, is a supreme ruler whose body is failing and whose mind is swiftly deteriorating. Signs from every quarter of her living world hint at one devastating conclusion: Gaea is insane.

WIZARD is more than an adventure novel; it is a thoughtful examination of free will taken to its profound and frightening extremes. Speculative fiction of the first rank and a novel of extraordinary power.

Futura Publications/An Orbit Book
Fiction/Science Fiction
0 7088 8076 2

All Futura Books are available at your bookshop or newsagent, or can be ordered from the following address:
Futura Books, Cash Sales Department,
P.O. Box 11, Falmouth, Cornwall.

Please send cheque or postal order (no currency), and allow 55p for postage and packing for the first book plus 22p for the second book and 14p for each additional book ordered up to a maximum charge of £1.75 in U.K.

Customers in Eire and B.F.P.O. please allow 55p for the first book, 22p for the second book plus 14p per copy for the next 7 books, thereafter 8p per book.

Overseas customers please allow £1 for postage and packing for the first book and 25p per copy for each additional book.